Prais... ...bestselling au...or Stella Ca...

"Steamy, atmospheric and fast-paced, Cameron's
romantic suspense novel delivers on all fronts."
—*Publishers Weekly* on *Key West*

"Cameron is a master at skillfully
integrating sizzling sensual love scenes
into her fast-moving plots."
—*Booklist* on *Cold Day in July*

"If you haven't read Stella Cameron,
you haven't read romantic suspense."
—Elizabeth Lowell

"A wonderful, fast-paced, furious page-turner."
—*Philadelphia Inquirer* on *Tell Me Why*

"Stella Cameron is a master storyteller with the
ability to surprise us again and again."
—Susan Elizabeth Phillips on *Finding Ian*

"Stella Cameron is sensational!"
—Jayne Ann Krentz

"A heart-pounding finale...readers who like
Tami Hoag and Karen Robards will surely enjoy
this romantic suspense novel."
—*Booklist* on *Key West*

"Outstanding! I couldn't turn the pages fast enough.
I wish I had written this wonderful book."
—Fern Michaels on *Kiss Them Goodbye*

STELLA
CAMERON
Body of Evidence

MIRA

ISBN 0-7783-2278-5

BODY OF EVIDENCE

www.MIRABooks.com

Printed in U.S.A.

For Spike, Mango and Millie—
companions on the night watch.

1

Late on a purple-sky afternoon.

On a day like this one, Emma Lachance almost remembered why she used to think Pointe Judah was the only place she would ever want to call home.

The sun wasn't quite down yet, but frogs already set up a gruff ruckus, and night-scented blooms began to waft musky sweetness on humid air.

She ran hard, harder than she needed to. Anger and hurt could drive you like that, send you pounding over the treacherous, partly finished sidewalks and gravel streets of The Willows, an abandoned retirement development. Concentrating on not turning an ankle helped keep her focused on the anger.

Emma needed to be angry.

Emma had a husband to divorce.

"You're stupid. And you're getting fat. I'm going to run for governor, remember? I intend to win. You'd better make sure you don't embarrass me, so get hold of yourself," Orville had told her less than an hour earlier, right before he left for another "important" evening appointment, which she could expect to keep him out most of the night.

Orville Lachance, mayor of Pointe Judah, Arcadia Parish, Louisiana, wanted—no, expected—his wife to take whatever insults he threw at her in private and keep smiling her adoration on him in public. She had stopped trying to talk to him when he arrived home in the early hours to slide into bed as if he was being thoughtful by not waking her.

Emma didn't sleep much anymore—something to do with the enemy beside her.

He frightened her, a deep, sickening fear. From the first time he'd let her see him in a violent rage, Emma knew her husband could be a dangerous man. With every smashing blow to a television or pile of dishes, the hate in his face suggested he would much rather beat her. In the coming weeks she must proceed carefully, gather evidence against him without making him suspicious. The mayor who would be governor would not quietly allow a scandal to interfere with his ambitions.

Squinting into the setting sun, Emma took the next right, downhill, and slowed to a jog. Her cheeks flushed, and the light, burning white from pale concrete turned the way ahead into a blinding landscape of shifting colors. Dark glasses were useless.

An engine, running rough, approached from behind, and an ancient Cadillac sailed slowly past. Emma doubted it had any shocks left at all. The white car continued on, weaving slightly, and since she could barely see the heads of the couple up front she figured them to be older. Probably wandered in for a look, thinking the retirement community was up and running.

Whoever came up with the idea and the money to start this development had not done their homework. The closest place to go, Pointe Judah, was a small bayou town that looked the same today as it had when Emma had been growing up. Getting from here to a city with a major downtown or an airport took too long for people with time on their hands and families to visit.

For a few moments she jogged in place, hopped from one foot to the other, shaded her eyes with a hand. Creepers snaked from overgrown lots onto the sidewalk. She ran the route at least once a week, because other people didn't go there.

A ways ahead a blue Honey Bucket stood in the road. The portable latrine hadn't been there before, so maybe they were going to start building again. With vines crawling up their frames and patches of purple, orange and white bougainvillea thrusting through open roof timbers, shells of houses in various stages of construction looked like greenhouses turned inside out.

Another runner approached her, taking the incline with an easy, loping stride. A man. A big, powerful man. Emma could tell that but nothing more, and she hesitated in the act of starting off in his direction. If she turned abruptly and dashed back the way she'd come, he would think she was running away from him.

She would be.

Regardless of which way she went, he could catch her if he wanted to.

Emma carried on, her pulse ringing in her ears and her lungs barely expanding. She responded to the man's "Hello" with one of her own. She didn't look at him when they passed one another.

Could Orville have found out she'd come here? Had he guessed her plans to leave him and decided she should die at some crazy stranger's hands rather than cause the mayor any inconvenience?

Now there was a paranoid thought.

The woman Finn Duhon had just passed could be Emma Balou, but it was a long shot. The Emma Balou he remembered from high school, the brainy, shy girl who never noticed how much time he spent looking at her, had been tall like the woman runner, and honey blond. That was where most of the obvious similarities ended, leaving him with only a feeling to go on. He guessed Emma Balou, who had been thin in that not-yet-grown way, could have matured into the shapely runner.

He shouldn't look back, but he was only a human; in fact, he was really human. Finn turned and ran backward, grateful the sun had sunk lower. In a white tank top and shorts, the woman kept going. There surely was something familiar about her. She had obviously overcome any curiosity she had about him—probably because he hadn't interested her in the first place.

The woman tried to look back at him without breaking stride.

Finn stood still and felt more pleased than he should. Evidently he'd had some effect on her after all.

The lack of female company in his life showed. Time was when he hadn't been standoffish around women, or suspicious of their motives for being interested in him. There were good reasons for the change in him.

Emma stopped running. She turned slowly and stared up-hill. He'd stopped, too, and shaded his eyes to stare down on her. He walked slowly back toward her. The impulse to run away, shrieking, passed blessedly quickly. The man had stopped because he thought he knew her, just as she thought she knew him.

Walking this time, she retraced her steps until they stood a few yards apart. She took off her glasses, found the handkerchief she carried in a back pocket and wiped her face thoroughly. Then she rubbed the long bangs that hung wet around her eyes and down the sides of her face.

"Hey," he said. "Emma Balou, is that you?" He swiped a

forearm across his brow and ran his fingers through short black hair.

The only people who wouldn't know she was Mrs. Lachance would be people who no longer lived in town, people who had moved away before she married Orville twelve years earlier.

The stranger's grin couldn't be missed, a big, white smile in a tanned face. They drew closer, and her hand went to her mouth. "Finn Duhon? Well, I'll be…Finn Duhon, it *is* you? I thought you were still in the marines."

"Army. Not anymore," he said and now she could see that his eyes were just as sharply hazel as they ever had been. A good-looking boy had grown into an arresting man. More than that, really. In his face she saw the look of a man who had seen too much for too long. His body testified to hard physical training.

"You were in Special Ops? I think that's what they call it."

He nodded. "Yep, that's it. What's been goin' on with you?"

A gust of hot breeze caught the door of the Honey Bucket. It rattled and creaked.

With her hands on her hips, she bent slightly and looked at her well-worn running shoes. "Not a whole lot. I went to Tulane but decided not to stay on after my second year. I've got a shop at the old Oakdale Mansion. It's called Poke Around." She laughed. "Sandra, the woman who works with me, came up with that because we have a pretty eclectic stock. And folks do come in because they're not sure what to expect. The shop keeps me busy."

But it didn't keep her happy, Finn decided. Sadness, or tension, hung around her eyes and mouth. He saw a wedding ring. So why hadn't she said she was married?

He would like to tell her she was a beautiful woman but most likely she wouldn't understand his—usually—uncomplicated appreciation for lovely females.

"My mother left me her house," he said. "I decided to come back and see if this was somewhere I could settle down."

"Of course." She turned pink. "Mrs. Duhon passed recently. I wasn't thinkin'. I'm so sorry for your loss. She was a sweet lady."

"That she was. And smart." He remembered his mother's face. "I never met a more determined woman, even when her life must have felt ruined."

Emma nodded, and the trouble in her expression wasn't faked. "I remember," she said.

She was remembering the circumstances of his father's death—just months before his mother's—and Finn didn't intend to get into that now. "Thank you for askin'. How are your folks?"

"'Where are they?' would be a better question. I think they're real well, but they're off in one of those RVs, drivin' all over the country and Canada. Who would have thought the town doctor and his schoolteacher wife would fall in love with drivin' from one RV park to the next? My dad says there's nuthin' like the smell of bacon cookin' outside in the mornin'. The two of them like to sit in their lawn chairs and soak up the scenery."

"Sounds good to me." He meant each word.

Emma looked into the distance. "Aren't you going back into stocks…somethin' to do with stocks? I remember hearin' you shocked your folks when you left your business in New York to go in the service."

"I was a stock-trader coach." A successful one, only it had come too easy, been too lucrative, surrounded him with too many people who wanted what he had. "No, ma'am, I'm not goin' back to that, either. Sometimes you've just got to cut loose and find a new way. Could be I'm comin' close to findin' it, too."

Emma met his eyes directly, but he felt she'd moved away from their conversation. Her lips parted, and she frowned. He expected her to say something, but she shook her head instead.

"Are you happy, Emma?" He had no right to ask, but he wanted to know.

"Is anyone?" She gave an openly bitter laugh and pushed damp hair back. It had started to curl, and he recalled she'd had curls in high school, lots of curls. The ponytail she wore was as honey blond as he remembered from school. And if anything, her blue eyes were more vivid.

Why not jump in with both feet? "You just startin' your run, or would you like to get a drink or some coffee somewhere in town? You could catch me up on the local action and be doin' an old acquaintance a favor." It was up to her to say yes or no, or that she was married. "I expect you've got a car with you."

"No car. I like long runs."

The old Caddy that passed him on his way up slowly retraced its route.

"These folks must be lost," Finn said. The car crawled, going slower and slower as it approached. "I guess we must be the most interesting thing they've seen around here." He laughed.

Emma grabbed his arm and pulled him back. The car took a too-wide arc and came straight for them. Correcting just in time, the driver, who peered out through thick glasses, glanced his front fender off the Honey Bucket, setting it rocking. Then he speeded up, slowed down again, and gradually climbed the hill.

"That's dangerous," Emma said, watching the car. "I think I'd like to get some coffee and catch up. You and I weren't exactly part of any in-crowd, so we can look at things from the outside, in, if you know what I mean. But I can't be long."

"Good enough. I drove here. My truck's close."

The latrine, still swaying a little, snapped open.

The top of a woman's head burst into view, swung forward, revealing a naked back. Light-colored hair matted with something dark. The woman kept falling in slow motion, her shoulder caught against the inside of the latrine.

Emma choked down a scream and started forward.

Automatically, Finn said, "Get back, Emma. I'll see to this."

She didn't move a muscle or avert her eyes—or scream. She gulped air through her mouth and turned chalky white.

"Call 911," he told her. "Don't touch anythin'."

He closed in. The angle of the dying sun hit the inside of the fiberglass door and the woman's lard-white skin. The pitch-dark interior of the latrine didn't reveal the rest of what had to be a horror picture.

"I don't have a phone," Emma said in a too-breathy voice. She ignored his instructions and stood beside him. "We have to see what's happened."

"What you don't see, you don't have to remember. Please step back. Take my phone." He slid it from his waist and gave it to her.

"She may still be alive," Emma said. "I'll feel her pulse."

Streamers of something other than blood marred the pale skin. Full breasts, trickled over with the same dark substance, added to her utter helplessness, her vulnerability to any curious eye. "She doesn't have a pulse," he said, looking at other telltale signs on the exposed skin. The legs were tucked back. "We shouldn't risk disturbing any evidence."

"Why doesn't she just fall out of there?" Emma walked away from him, then made to go closer to the latrine. He held her wrist only a moment before the look she gave him warned him to let go.

She leaned to see inside, to see the rest of the body, and held herself there, still except for a silently moving mouth and tears that slid down her face. Emma kept her hands clasped behind her back and began to shake. She turned her back to Finn and threw up, too horrified to care what he thought.

Gasping, holding her handkerchief to her mouth, she said, "Denise," and dropped to her knees while pressing buttons on the phone. "Denise Steen is dead." She spoke into the receiver and gave their location. "I think she's been murdered."

Finn leaned over her. The woman's body straightened inch by inch from the grotesque pose in which it had been left. Her left hand had been clamped under her on the toilet seat. Her own weight on top had kept her from falling forward—until the latrine started rocking. Whatever had been drizzled over head and body also streamed down her legs. "Looks like chocolate syrup," he said.

"No," Emma whispered, when Finn stepped back to keep away from the gradually sliding body. "She's so decent. Who would do this to her?"

The dead woman jerked against her own hand, thudded to the floor and came to rest in a twisted sitting position just inside the door.

"It's so sick," Emma said, pointing to an obscenely red cocktail cherry in the corpse's navel.

2

Emma watched the clock.

Seated in Chief Billy Meche's office at the police station, she and Finn held mugs of coffee and talked in subdued bursts whenever one of them found something to say.

She thought about Denise Steen propped against the latrine door and flinched. A shudder jerked her forward in her chair.

"You okay?" Finn asked.

"Fine," she said. She didn't think she would ever get that ghoulish picture out of her mind. Denise had been very slim, no little rolls of fat anywhere, and the syrup had coated part of her back and shoulders, and the upper sides of her breasts, smoothly. Like a chocolate-dipped marshmallow snow-woman. She shook her head violently. "No, I'm not fine. She was my friend. I've never felt so awful, or so helpless. De-nise, of all people. Shoved into that thing. She was in there like that, with her body arranged so it wouldn't fall, *before* they poured the syrup," she said quietly.

"Uh-huh. Try not to think about that." Finn reached to pat her hand. "Gradually the flashes, vignettes, or whatever they call 'em, fade. It helps if you don't consciously try to bring them back."

Emma glanced at him. "You sound like a shrink."

"Not me," he said. What he sounded like was a man who

had been into those screeching, sweating places where terrible visions waited.

She touched the back of a hand to her lips. "Did you notice anything about the syrup?"

He gave her an appraising look and nodded. "It wasn't completely dried up?"

Emma bit her lip and said, "We just missed the killer."

Finn continued to stare at her. "Maybe we didn't miss him. Maybe he was still there, hiding, waiting for someone to come along and open that door. He couldn't have planned for her to knock it open the way she did."

Emma leaned forward and followed faded green mottling on the chipped floor tile. Air-conditioning blasted, but sweat trickled between her shoulder blades. "He may even have wanted to see the reaction when she was found. He enjoyed it. I just know he did."

"If you're right, he had guts to take a risk like that. Or he's so crazy he thinks he's invincible." Finn paused. "Emma, you've got to take a step back from it. It's early, you can't just forget, but if you concentrate on it, turn it and turn it in your mind and start into the 'what-ifs,' you're choosin' a hard road."

"You saw horrible things in war, didn't you?"

He didn't say anything, but his mouth tightened, and he looked away.

"Good coffee," she said. He wasn't the only one who wanted to change the subject. "Better than I would have expected here." She'd never been in the police station before.

"Not bad," Finn said. "But if they keep us here much longer, we're gonna need more than a mug of coffee."

All Emma could concentrate on was getting home before Orville.

"The officers called you Mrs. Lachance," Finn said. "Did

your husband go to school with us? I don't remember the name, but there were a lot of kids I never knew."

"No, Orville's not from around here." She didn't want to talk to him about Orville.

"What does he do?"

It was an ordinary, expected question, so why feel mad? "He's a developer. He's also the mayor."

Finn looked at the floor. He snapped his fingers. "Of course, Orville Lachance. My sister, Eileen, mentioned that was the mayor's name. And he's running for governor?"

She'd forgotten his sister. Eileen Moggeridge as she was now. "Orville plans to run," she said vaguely.

"Can I call your husband for you, Emma? He'd want to be here with you."

Horrified at the thought of Orville hearing the voice of a man he didn't know, asking him to take care of Emma, she wasn't sure exactly what to say. "No… That's kind of you, but he's at a meetin', and I'll be okay. I'm a bit shaky, but that's to be expected." She stumbled over her words.

He smiled, and his face relaxed a little. "Of course it is." The toe of one foot pumped up and down. "I don't want to scare you, but you should probably be more careful than you normally would. Lock the doors if your husband's out. Lock your car doors as soon as you're inside. Look around when you park your car or go back to it. I don't just mean tonight. You need to make a habit of double-checking everything. Always be aware of your surroundings."

"Thank you." She could scarcely breathe or swallow. He was right, but she hated hearing the truth.

"Don't worry," he said. "There'll be plenty of people keeping their eyes on you."

Emma nodded. He hadn't reassured her. "Did you notice the way we were questioned earlier. Separately? So they could compare our stories." She cleared her throat nervously. "Do they suspect one of us?" She didn't think he had been involved, but responses to direct questions could be interesting.

"No," he said, very serious now. "But you're right about the reason they interviewed us separately. That's just routine. We wouldn't be hangin' out together now if they thought one of us knew somethin' more than we've said. They will already have noted the things we talked to them about."

The door stood open, and voices rose and fell in the reception area. Apart from September Festival, nothing much happened in Pointe Judah at this time of year—not so far as ordinary people would notice—and it was common knowledge that a few folks made a practice of dropping by the police station for coffee while they read any new "wanted" posters on the crowded bulletin boards.

Emma swiveled in her chair. The noise she heard from the lobby tonight had to be made by a whole gaggle of citizens who would normally be at home at this hour.

The raised voices made her nervous, particularly the high ones of women who almost shrieked to get attention.

Emma checked the clock again. She prayed she could get home without Orville finding out what had happened and showing up in Billy's office with a head of steam on. He never lost his temper in public, but there could be a first time if he felt his reputation was threatened.

"Was Denise an old friend?" Finn asked.

"Three or four years. She moved here from Lafayette because she wanted to work for a paper where she'd be a big fish in a really small bowl. There's just her and Rusty and the people who put the paper out. Rusty owns the *News*. That means—meant—she got to do things she hadn't been able to elsewhere. At first she came for a year or so, but she stayed." Emma's throat tightened. "We're both members of a women's club. *Angela's Secrets of a Successful Life.* We just call it Secrets. It's a place—an established group—where a few women can unwind without feeling judged. We study advances in women's medicine, the latest ideas on diet and exercises—and just plain fun stuff. If we want to roll in seaweed for an hour, we've got the facilities to do that. Denise could make anyone laugh. She was great. And she was a good listener. If one of us just wanted to talk something through, one-on-one, we went to Denise."

Finn rolled his eyes, grimaced and said, "Sorry. Knee-jerk reaction."

"I forgive you. I think," she said. "You fit in with the rest of the men around here. They all think Secrets is 'that silly place for females.'" When Finn didn't comment, she said, "We've been here over two hours. I guess we could just go home if we wanted to." Emma turned the statement into a question and waited for Finn's response.

He crossed his arms and jiggled his very muscular legs. Emma found it hard not to look at them—and other parts of his anatomy. This was a *male* male, and she couldn't recall the last time she'd responded as she was doing right now, to Finn. All her time and energy had been taken up with her complex marriage, so much so that she might even have stopped feeling feminine and desirable at all. Now she was overreacting because she was unsure of herself and reaching out for the strength she felt in him, that was all.

"I don't think Billy would take a shine to our walkin' out," Finn said. "He wanted us to wait here."

He got up and prowled. Why didn't she remember him better from school? True, he'd graduated a year earlier than she had and taken off for some East Coast school—on a full scholarship, if she remembered correctly—but she should have found him hard to forget.

She guessed fifteen years could turn a teenager into this specimen who showed off the extension and contraction of every suntanned muscle when he walked. Emma looked at his back and drew a shaky breath.

In truth, Orville's protracted campaign to undermine her confidence had all but wiped out any interest she had in men. The old familiar burning started in her eyes. How sad to have loved a man so much, only to end up hating him.

She tented her fingers and tapped the ends together. "Couldn't we leave if we wanted to?" Orville would hear what had happened soon enough, but she could cut off any scary reaction by explaining the situation herself.

Emma hunched her shoulders. Orville would be so angry with her for what he would call drawing negative attention to herself.

Finn had not answered her question. Facing her, he sat on the edge of the chief's desk with his ankles crossed.

Emma couldn't decide where to look. "It's nasty here," she said, desperate for something to say—anything to say.

Finn chuckled. "You mean you don't like the pale brown walls and ceiling and the brown shutters over the windows? I expect having the windows so high is a precaution against some crazy emptying a gun in here from outside."

"Don't say that." Emma gripped her throat and shivered.

"I'm afraid it's true. Look, Emma, we happened on something horrible earlier, and it isn't going away very quickly. Can you try to get a little tougher, just to help yourself through this?"

"I'm not a wimp."

"Of course not. Earlier, when you said you'd have a drink with me, you said you couldn't be out long. What was that about? You've been out several hours."

"I have a routine." That much was true. "I go to the shop early, and I need plenty of sleep. Tomorrow we get the new espresso machine."

Why bore him with the little details of her life? She propped her face in a hand and closed her eyes.

When she opened them, her spine tingled. Without moving her head, she glanced at Finn through her fingers…and caught him giving her a thorough once-over. He shifted on the desk while he followed the lines of her legs. It wasn't a whole lot of shifting, only that kind of readjustment a man made when he was reacting to a woman.

Just what she needed. Absolutely wonderful. A man she found as sexy as hell getting turned on by simply looking at her, and right when she couldn't feel more off balance. Come to that, how could he be thinking lustful thoughts when they'd found Denise's body only a couple of hours ago?

His study took her in from her feet all the way up, and, mesmerized, she didn't look away in time when he met her eyes. His smile was slow, but purely unrepentant, showing dimples beside his mouth. He raised his eyebrows, and the look in his glittering hazel eyes said it all. Finn was more than casually interested in her. And it wasn't as if he hadn't learned she was married from the first moment the police arrived at the housing development and started calling her Mrs. Lachance. Then there was the ring on her finger.

His eyes didn't leave hers. Not even a flicker showed, as if he thought he had a right to nail her like that.

"Caught," Finn said, and laughed. He spoke slowly, and his voice was deep, a little hoarse. "You can't blame me for trying to reconcile Emma today with Emma fifteen years ago. How long have you been married?"

"Twelve years."

"Always to the mayor."

"Uh-huh. Only he wasn't mayor when we met." She was answering all the questions. "How about you? Are you married? Children?" He didn't wear a ring, but some men never did.

"No, on both counts. You married after you finished your second year at Tulane? You're so bright, Emma, that could be a shame. How did your folks feel about it?"

"They did everything they could to persuade me to stay in school." She looked at the chaos on top of Billy's metal desk. "But not every woman is cut out for a career. Not that kind of career. Bein' a homemaker is a good thing, and now I've got the shop to keep me really busy." Talking about this set her nerves on edge.

"What were you studying?"

"Marketing. In a small way, what I learned is useful for Poke Around."

"You have children?"

Her heart missed a beat. "No." And it was none of his business.

"Your Orville sounds like a successful man."

"Yes." She turned her head in Finn's direction and followed the expanse of a shoulder that could belong to a football player and a solid chest to match before glancing at his face again. "Orville's been established a long time. We met casually here in Pointe Judah when he was buyin' a piece of property. It's the golf course now. Then he came lookin' for me in New Orleans. He'd decided to make Pointe Judah his home. He wanted me to be close to my folks."

"I was going to mention you going back to school, but I suppose you're too busy being Mrs. Mayor to do that, and if your Orville wins, you'll be worked off your feet being Mrs. Governor." He didn't feel proud of sounding snide. "You must prefer older men." He tried to sound light.

"Orville is fifteen years my senior. Now you know everything there is to know about me."

No anger radiated from Emma, just resignation. If anything, she grew more listless. Her husband had good taste; she was a beautiful woman, and when she'd been twenty, La-chance must have salivated at the thought of picking her off the tree. "I'm really surprised the mayor's not here by now," he said, and knew he was digging to find out what kind of re-lationship the Lachances had. "I wouldn't think he'd want his wife hanging around the cop shop."

"May I borrow your phone?" Emma asked him.

He handed it over and avoided watching her place a call. She put in a long string of numbers, and he figured she was listening to messages, only she clicked off so fast there couldn't have been any. She let out a slow breath. Relief?

"My dad was police chief before Billy Meche," Finn said, making conversation.

"I remember that. Tom Duhon. He…had an accident. Sorry, I shouldn't talk about it. It's got to be hard to lose both your parents the way you have."

He grunted. Most people would never know how hard. "An accident" was one term for the way his father died. The wrong term.

He tried to rotate his left shoulder without being too obvi-ous. When he became tense, the scar sometimes pinched, contracted. Stretching from the middle of his back up and around the shoulder, the still-red, knotted welt wasn't a pretty sight. These days he wore T-shirts rather than tank tops—to avoid frightening small children.

Billy walked into the room and closed the door behind him. His gray-peppered red crew cut bristled; so did his mustache, and the color of his broad face almost matched his hair. "This is messy," he said. "You should see it out there." He inclined his head toward Reception. "We've got a houseful, and they all want to tell me what they've seen or heard or been told about Denise Steen. Tips to the right of us, tips to the left of us, and I doubt a one of them means diddly."

Finn caught a flash of an expression on Emma's face. She was scared of something. What was that all about?

"How can people know about it so soon?" she asked Billy. "That retirement development is three miles out of town, and I surely didn't see another soul—apart from Finn."

"You never could keep a secret here," Billy said.

"That's never goin' to change," Finn said.

"An officer went over to see Rusty Barnes at the paper, and he fell apart," Billy said. "I can't believe it. Rusty's too tough for that."

"He loved Denise," Emma said quietly. "He wanted to be more than her employer."

Billy looked at her sharply. "How did Denise feel about that?"

Emma made fists on her thighs. "Denise was independent. I don't think she was ready for the responsibility of a partner."

"Were they lovers?" Billy said.

Emma paused longer than she should have. "I wouldn't know about that. People's business is people's business."

Sure it was, Finn thought, but he had no doubt this Rusty Barnes and the victim had been real close, and Emma knew about it.

A very young officer knocked and came in when he was told to. He probably only needed to shave once a week, and this should have been the day. He looked meaningfully at Finn and Emma, and said, "Mrs. Forestier insists you'll want to read this, Chief."

"Would you like us to leave?" Emma asked.

"Stay put," was all she got from Billy.

"Lobelia Forestier," Billy muttered, taking the sheet of lined paper. "President of the chamber of commerce. Why do we need a chamber of commerce? You tell me that. What commerce? Outside the folks who stop in for an hour to visit the Oakdale development and shop, if we get twenty-five tourists a year it's a record. And they only come because they ran out of gas on the way to somewhere else. That Lobelia, she sits down there with her bird's-eye view over the square and holds court. Chamber of gossip, more like. It isn't even a paid position, on account of we don't have the money to pay her for doin' nothin'."

The officer cleared his throat and jabbed his head in the direction of the open door.

Billy, no more than five foot nine but built like a fireplug, shot to his feet. "Were you born in a field, Sampson?" he said to the other man. "Close the friggin' thing."

Sampson did as he was told, and Finn could tell the man would rather be on the other side of the door.

Back in his squeaky chair, popping little white mints into his mouth while he read, Billy's breathing grew louder. "I don't see any place where you could tote a rifle without it being seen," he said, looking at Finn's shorts and T-shirt. "Sharpshooter, huh? Maybe I knew that."

Finn chewed at a hangnail. "I used to be a sharpshooter— among other things I've given up."

"Well, you'll be pleased to know Mrs. Forestier and her cronies have solved the case for us. You shot Miz Steen through the open door of the latrine, then ran around the corner and met up with Miz Lachance here. That would be after you hid the rifle."

A glance at Emma's face almost undid Finn. Her lips were parted, her brows pushed down in a confused frown. "That door was closed," she said. "Until it was open. And if there'd been a shot, I'd have heard it. Those people need something to do."

"Miz Forestier has organized a party to search for the rifle," Billy said in a monotone. "They'll bring it here *at once* when they find it."

Emma snickered, and Finn grinned.

"Thank Mrs. Forestier for me," Billy told Sampson. "And tell her we've got an official crime site there, so she won't be able to get close. You might also mention there's a killer on the loose, and we don't know when or where he might pop up."

"She said she'd like a word before she leaves."

Billy rolled his eyes. "Tell her the commissioner's in here and wants my ass for not solving the case on my own. Deal with it."

Sampson scurried away, and Finn tried to remember what it felt like to be that young.

"We'll get the pair of you out the back way," Billy said. "I'll have an officer drive you home, Mrs. Lachance."

"I'll take her," Finn said, and knew at once that he should have been a bit slower with his offer.

"I'd advise you to watch your back, Finn. There could be someone with a grudge against you. Hard to tell at this point. And Mrs. Lachance—I'm not relaxed about your safety. I'll want to discuss that with Mayor Lachance."

Emma nodded, and Finn admired her composure.

"Denise Steen wasn't well liked in this town," Billy said, almost to himself. "She wrote a lot of stuff that made people mad."

"She *was* well liked," Emma said. She slid to the front of her chair. "Denise said and wrote what she believed. And she didn't suck up to people who think they're important around here. They're the ones who didn't like her, because they were afraid of her. Regular folks thought she was great."

"Unfortunately, she went after some of the slick bastards who didn't want their dirty laundry aired," Billy murmured. "Do you belong to that club?"

When Emma didn't immediately answer, Finn stared at her. He'd only been back in town a couple of days, and the place looked the same, but he already knew a lot had changed around here.

"What club?" Emma said, giving Billy an in-your-face look.

Billy's expression softened. "Calm down, Emma. You and I have known each other a long time, since way before you married our major mover and shaker. And you know what club I mean."

"Yes, I do, and you already know it. There's a little bunch of us, and we're real close. And I don't like the way you make Secrets sound like somethin' grubby. *That club?* We're just women supportin' women."

"And encouragin' some to defy their husbands and boy-friends, from what I hear," Billy said. "Assertiveness trainin'. Self-confidence. Learnin' you can be whatever you want to be—if you want it bad enough."

"That's right," Emma said. "We help each other, and learn that other people don't have the right to put us down and make us miserable." And now it was her turn to act on what she believed in.

"Denise was a member, wasn't she?" Billy asked.

Emma felt herself getting trapped, although there should be no need. "Denise didn't come often, but she did belong. She put some of our recipes and tips in one of the columns in the paper. And she published exercise routines that made us laugh—she did them with stick figures. She wrote about new makeup tips and affirmations. Instructions for mud baths with cayenne to make the skin glow. Slabs of cucumber over the eyes to make sure they stayed cool and the cayenne didn't get in and burn. Soaking your feet in hot milk. Learning to say 'no.' All stuff she thought other women could benefit from."

"That's the way I thought it went," Billy said. "Did it ever strike you that some men might not like their women getting ideas that changed them?"

Finn looked at Emma's lips.

"That was always a possibility, but we are all about liftin' each other up, nothing else. Nothing mean. Nothing intended to split couples up." Even though she'd learned enough to know she couldn't stay with Orville.

"A lot of men in town don't believe that, particularly the ones with wives who aren't as docile anymore," Billie said.

Emma got to her feet. "Then we're succeeding," she said, and Finn heard confrontation in her tone. "The only men who would feel like that are the insecure kind who want to keep women down—usually by any means they can. A confident man is glad when a woman is his equal."

Billy's bright brown eyes crinkled at the corners. "Hold your horses, Emma. I know it's all innocent fun, but I hope my Blanche doesn't decide to join."

Emma sat down again.

Finn chuckled, then snuffled to cover his amusement. He guessed Emma might consider him another chauvinist pig, and that wasn't true.

The noise outside the room rose higher. Someone said, "Yessir," loudly.

Finn watched Emma's eyes open wide, noticed the way she gripped the arms of her chair.

The door flew open, and a blond, brown-eyed man, too pretty for Finn's taste, strode into the room. He turned back, caught the edge of the door as if he would slam it, but controlled himself and shut it firmly instead. He still created enough of a breeze to start a pile of papers on Billy's desk sliding. At first they slid just a little, then created a waterfall to the floor.

"Emma," the man said, his face unnaturally expressionless. "What are you doin' here, drawin' all kinds of attention to yourself, darlin'? Can't I leave you alone for a little while without you gettin' into trouble?"

Before anyone else could speak, Emma said, "I was in the wrong place at the wrong time, Orville. These things happen."

Orville pushed back his straw-colored linen suit jacket and put his hands on his hips. He lowered his head and approached Emma. "What were you doin' in a deserted place like that old development? And findin' a *body?* How the hell did that happen?" The man held himself in such rigid control, Finn could feel the tension like something he might reach out and touch.

Finn's knuckles began to itch. The mayor had fifteen years on Emma, fourteen on Finn, and they showed. The once square jaw was turning a little slack, and deep lines flared from his eyes. There was a softness about Orville Lachance that suggested too much good living and not enough physical exercise.

"I asked you a question, darlin'," Lachance said to Emma, leaning down into her face.

Billy caught Finn's eye and shook his head slightly. Too bad. If Lachance put a hand on Emma, Finn would flatten the creep.

Before Lachance could do or say another thing, Emma all but hopped from her chair and took several steps backward. "It's a shock," she said to her husband. "I can't explain what a shock it was. Billy here had to ask questions, but I think he's about ready to let me go home."

"I don't recall the name of that place where the killin' happened," Orville said.

"The Willows," Emma said. "That retirement estate they started building—"

"I know what it is. What I don't know is why you were there, puttin' yourself in danger. You've got a gym at the house that cost me a fortune. Use it."

"I do. The fresh air is nice sometimes. You know I jog."

"Use the gym," Orville said. Lachance kept his voice soft, and anyone watching casually would think he was being solicitous of his younger wife. Finn sensed something else. Loathing? The notion seemed bizarre.

The man noticed Finn. "Who are you? What are you doing in here?"

"Finn Duhon," Billy said. "Tom Duhon was his dad. Finn's been away in the service."

Grinding his back teeth, Finn offered the man his hand and got a glancing squeeze.

Orville snapped his fingers. "Eileen Moggeridge is your sister. Married to that no-good Chuck. Probably a good thing he's gone on the oil rigs so much. From what I hear, the boy—Aaron if I remember right—looks like he's followin' in his daddy's footsteps. He'll be takin' up jail space in no time. He'd have had your daddy turnin' in his grave."

Finn squelched his temper. "You've got the names right, Lachance. The rest is hearsay."

"And inappropriate, Orville," Emma said, her face too bright.

Lachance shrugged. "Could be. Forgive me if I've offended you. Is it hearsay that the Rangers got too tough for you so you found a way to get out? You *were* an army ranger, right?"

Finn bit the inside of his cheek and tasted blood. Didn't this mouthy fool sense he could be beaten to a pulp and Finn wouldn't even break a sweat? "You've got to wean yourself off hearsay," Finn said. "It could get you into some really nasty trouble."

"I asked you why you're here," Orville said. "With my wife."

"I was talking to Emma when the body...we saw the body in a portable latrine. Your wife's been through a lot."

Muscles worked in Orville's jaws. He stood straight, and Finn took him to be around five-ten. "You were talking to Emma out at some deserted development? Am I hearin' things?"

"Please, Orville, let me explain all this when we're alone," Emma said, swallowing acid. "Can we use the back door, please, Billy?"

"I've got more questions to ask," Orville said, and to Billy, "You won't need to talk to my wife again."

"Yes," Billy said, "I'm sure I will."

Lachance turned a little red along his cheekbones. "Have you forgotten who I am?" He crossed his arms, and the anger faded from his manner. "Forgive me. When they came with a message and said it was about my wife, you can't imagine all the thoughts that went through my head. I'll hold a meetin' at city hall tomorrow mornin', Billy, just to reassure the folks.

"Now, who responded to the emergency call? I assume you or Duhon made one, Emma?"

Billy had already opened a door leading to an entryway on the other side of his office, and Emma walked through it. "I can answer any questions you've got, Orville. Thank you for taking care of me, Billy, Finn. I can come back in for more questioning any time. Come along, honey."

She left, and Orville followed her slowly, obviously reluctant to go now.

Finn and Billy didn't say anything for several minutes before Finn asked, "Is he likely to do her any harm?"

Billy scrubbed at his face and hair. "Damn, I wish I hadn't given up drinkin'. Where are my mints?" He found the tin on his desk.

"Billy?" Finn said.

"He's too smooth to do anything like that," Billy closed the tin and threw it back on the desk. "He was wound tight tonight, is all."

Finn wasn't convinced.

3

Orville's house. Emma always thought of it that way, because a prenuptial agreement had made it plain when they were married that she would get a significant allowance but nothing more unless she gave birth to Orville's child.

Emma's only pregnancy had ended in a miscarriage.

Orville paid the rent on the shop at Oakdale Mansion, too; she'd had to borrow the money to get started. He was listed as the owner of the business. Originally he'd said he would probably change things when they had been together a few years, but the subject had never been brought up again.

Emma's dad had done his best to make her see that such an agreement flagged Orville's lack of commitment to the marriage. Back then, though, she'd refused to listen to anyone who questioned his devotion to her.

The single-story Lachance house stood on a golf course owned by a small group of exceedingly wealthy men, of whom Orville was one. Emma watched the lights lining the driveway grow closer. Apart from running Poke Around, she hadn't worked since her years in college. If she operated the shop alone, she might just get by, but with her allowance gone, she probably couldn't make the rent *and* cover her living expenses. The idea of finding a way to support herself was daunting, but she could do it. She had promised to look after

Stella Cameron

her parents' house until they got back, and once she was alone, she planned to live there and find a job. When they returned, she hoped to move out again and go back to school.

Orville hadn't said a word by the time he drove his Mercedes into the garage, beside his yellow Corvette, his boat and Emma's Lexus SUV. She realized that during the trip from the police station, she'd been leaning away from her husband and holding her stomach so tight it hurt. He could come around and decide to be decent. While they'd been driving, the reality of what she had been through might have softened him.

"Hearin' the news must have shocked you," she said. She wanted out of this relationship with as little acrimony as possible. "I'm sorry about that. I feel nervous. It's not likely, but what if the murderer decides to get rid of me, too, or just to frighten me half to death to make sure I don't think too hard about anythin' I saw?"

"You've got a lot to answer for," Orville said. "The mayor's wife doesn't go runnin' in deserted areas, wearin' almost nothing, so she can meet up with some old boyfriend."

Emma gasped. "Orville, you sound crazy." Let him lose his temper. "I hardly remembered Finn. We never even dated. He left Pointe Judah a year before I did and went to school back East. It's too bad you felt you had to insult him. He's a decorated war hero and a successful businessman, too. If you keep on making stupid suggestions about him, you'll look like a fool. He could also be a bad enemy during the campaign, I should think. People around here think Finn is special."

Orville jerked sideways in his seat and raised a hand to hit her. He made a fist and lowered it slowly. He'd hit her before, but never where a bruise might show. Without a word, he slammed from the car.

For a second or two, Emma hesitated. Then she knew, absolutely for certain, that she would set a divorce action in motion as soon as she had a complete plan. Her husband treated her badly, and he frightened her. What reason did she have to stay? She'd loved him so much when they'd met, but he'd smothered all that.

She had already spoken to a lawyer over in Toussaint who had represented a member of Secrets. Emma liked him. Both of the lawyers in Pointe Judah were among Orville's golfing buddies.

"Listen to you," she said, getting out into the garage and walking past him on her way inside the house. "A friend of mine has been murdered. I had the rotten luck to find her body, and you're ranting at me about your reputation. You're screwed up—or worse."

"You don't respect me," Orville said. "Look at all I've given you, but you treat it like nothing. If you're not very careful, I'll have to reevaluate this marriage."

Please do that. Do it now. "If that's what you want, I'll have to understand. We could work something out so it didn't become public until after the election—if that's what you'd prefer." She was careful to sound deeply sad.

Amazement silenced him long enough for Emma to walk quickly through a terra-cotta-tiled hallway to the foyer and take the two steps up into the open, all-beige living room she hated—even if the designer, according to Orville, had been the best in New Orleans. Going directly to a wall of glass, which in daylight overlooked the golf course, she stared at the illuminated turquoise waters of the pool outside. Palmettos in stone pots cast shadows like fistfuls of long knives on the surface.

Orville's shoes hit the floor in quick succession. He was running toward her. She had no way to escape him. He grabbed the top of her arm hard enough to make her cry out. He swung her around, backed her away from the windows and shoved her against a wall. "That's the first and the last time you ever speak to me like that. I tell you to jump, you jump. You were a dropout, and I picked you up and gave you a dream life. I bought you and treated you like a queen. I own you."

"You insisted I drop out, but I don't want to argue with you," she said, aware that recessed shelves holding art glass stood beside her. "Push me again and you could have your precious glass all over the floor. Let me go, please—if you want to find a civilized way to work this out."

Shaking her again, he brought his face close to hers. "I could have made you look like an idiot in front of Meche and your friend. I held back to save your feelings. Now I wish I hadn't."

"You held back because you don't want anyone to know you abuse me," she said, bracing for his reaction.

He took his hand from her arm but cuffed her across the back of the head. *"Bitch,"* he said.

Emma would not let him see her cry or show how he humiliated her. "Do you want to talk about this?" she said. "Or would you rather leave the house until you've calmed down?"

"Leave my own house? Hah, you always were a dreamer, I—"

"Either we talk or one of us has to get out of here."

He opened his mouth, no doubt with another load of invective to spew at her, but he closed it again slowly and gave a slightly silly, one-sided smile. "You're not yourself."

"I'm as close to bein' myself as anyone would be after the experience I've had," Emma said. "All I can see in my mind is my friend dead and obscenely posed. You haven't even said you're sorry about what happened to her. And somethin' else—we're livin' in a town with a murderer on the loose, a deranged person. He could be anywhere. Don't you think you should already be out there makin' sure the folks stay calm? The news will be all over town by now."

"I don't need you to tell me how to do my job," Orville said and checked his watch. "Billy's the one I'll be talkin' to. Less said to get the town on edge, the better. If necessary, I'll say a few words in the mornin', like I told Billy I would. And nothin's gonna happen to *you*. Your problem is you only think about yourself."

As far as Emma was concerned, the talking was over for tonight.

"Denise Steen was a bitch," Orville said. He had regained his unruffled appearance. "I wouldn't have wanted her to die, but she asked for it. She got people all riled up—givin' women ideas that made trouble for their husbands and men in general."

Emma's head stung where he'd hit her, but she kept her hands away from it. She sat on the edge of a chair shaped like a manta ray. The lighted glass shelves and the brilliant pieces displayed there shone behind Orville in the otherwise dimly lit room. She felt him waiting for her to respond, to give him another opening to revile Denise.

"You're not to speak to that man Duhon again," he said.

Let him rant.

"Do you hear me?"

Now he could accuse her of ignoring him. So be it.

"Dammit, Emma, I had to break away from an important meetin' to come and rescue you."

"I didn't need to be rescued," she shot back at him. "Go back to your meetin'. It's nowhere near time for it to be over. Before you go, though, you should get it straight that Denise was just a member of Secrets, not the one who started it or kept it goin'. That's Angela. Denise was so busy she couldn't even get there very often."

"You're tryin' to work me up," he said, his voice rising. "I'm runnin' for governor. I'm startin' early because I've got a long way to go, a lot of useful contacts to make—and a lot of palms to grease. I have important things to do, and you're not goin' to get in my way. You are never goin' to hold me back. Do you understand?"

She was quiet again.

"I'll have to rethink lettin' you belong to that club. You spend too much time there." He snorted. "*Secrets.* Why not just hang out a flag that says, Man Haters Welcome Here?"

"Because it's not a club for man haters," she told him quietly. "Quite the reverse. Secrets of a Successful Life is the whole name. It's about women givin' support to other women. It's a gentle, safe place to spend a few hours." She'd told him all this before, but he never listened to her.

"Sure it is," he said. "But I'm pretty sure I don't want you goin' there. Time was when you never answered me back. You knew your place. That was before you had a bunch of disgruntled women puttin' ideas in your head. You aren't a businesswoman in some big city—*payin' her own bills*—you're a Southern wife of a prominent man, and I'm your only work. That was the agreement. And that shop isn't work. It's a playpen."

Emma got up. "I need to shower and change." Every word he spoke to her came loaded with a mean hate. When they'd met and he'd persuaded her to leave school, the talk had been all about love, home, a family. And she'd believed he meant what he said. "Excuse me, Orville." She turned to go.

"Don't you leave this room until I say so."

Her legs trembled inside. "I've been meanin' to ask you. I hear you're part of a group that calls itself Pat's Pack. I suppose you get together at Patrick Damalis's place. Would that be an all men's club?"

His expression darkened. "I don't know where you heard about that, but I intend to find out. A few guys get together to discuss business. Now keep your nose out of my affairs."

"Gladly. I reckon I can be out of here in a few hours." Now

her heart bumped. She shouldn't have mentioned Pat's Pack—someone else might get into trouble for talking to her about it. "I could probably leave tonight. After all, there's pretty much nothin' that belongs to me here."

"Includin' your car," Orville said, his nostrils flaring.

"The car is mine, remember? A birthday gift from your father." She'd opened a safety deposit box, and the papers for the Lexus were safely stowed there, together with a few other small treasures, including a stack of savings bonds her grandmother had left her.

He came closer, and Emma had a struggle not to fall back. "Where would you go? You don't have the money to leave town."

In that he was right, but she knew how to work hard. "I'll move into Mom and Dad's place for now. And I'll get a job." She glanced at the cream-colored grand piano Orville had bought just prior to their marriage because he loved to show off her musical talents. "Someone will be glad of a hardworking waitress. Maybe I could play a bit here and there, too. I used to when I was at school in New Orleans, and people liked it."

"You'd go out to that dump where you grew up? It's in the middle of nowhere."

"My parents' home is no dump. I love that house, and that's where I'll go."

He pushed his shoulders back and raised his head so he could look down at her. "You're afraid of bein' alone. Particularly at night."

Emma laughed; she couldn't help it. "Don't you think I've gotten over that by now? You leave me alone every night."

"Damn you," he ground out. "I'll make sure you can't get a job and embarrass me all over Pointe Judah…. It's that man, isn't it? Mr. War Hero and *businessman*. What kind of business would that be? Think he'll arrive on his white horse to turn your nights into hours of sweaty sex? You fool. He thinks you're rolling in it—that's why he wants you. Have you thought about that? You didn't tell him all you get is a very good allowance unless you have a child, did you? Or that you don't even get the allowance if we split up?"

She shook her head, hating him more with every second.

"'Course you didn't. I'll go after him, y'know. He's the one in the wrong, and I'll make him pay for it, then pay some more. He's gonna wish he never set foot back in this town."

"Listen to yourself," she said, helpless to steady her voice. "You're makin' things up. Threatenin' a man I never really knew when we were in high school. A man I saw for the first time in years and almost didn't recognize. Go ahead, make a fool of yourself. That should help your campaign."

Orville sat down and let his hands hang between his knees. "I've got to think."

"I'll leave you to do that, then."

"Don't go…please. Stay with me."

He looked up at her, and she couldn't tell if he was really calm or just hiding his anger. "Emma, I don't want a divorce—ever."

Because his image needed her. "You were the one who brought the subject up."

"I was angry, is all." He looked at her with the mournful eyes he could accomplish at a moment's notice. "Remember how it was when we met?"

"Oh, please. That's hardly even a memory."

"To you, maybe." His eyes glittered, and she thought he might actually be crying. "To me, you were a dream come true."

The perfect political wife in the making.

He held a hand out to her, and she looked at it.

"Please, darlin'," he said, beckoning her closer. "I don't know what comes over me sometimes. Just seems I say things I wouldn't if I thought them through."

Emma's soft heart had been a liability throughout this marriage. She went to his side, but she crossed her arms. She couldn't bear the idea of holding a hand he freely used to punish her.

Orville looked up at her with pleading in his eyes. "I've got a temper," he said. "But don't you know the reason I got so mad tonight was because I was thinkin' how I'd feel if it was you they found murdered out there?"

No, she didn't.

"It would break my heart to lose you—under any circumstances. This campaignin' is gettin' to me. I want the office because I know I can do good, but the wranglin' and the process is killin' me."

"Give it up, then," she said promptly. Emma doubted she could find too many people who would believe Orville Lachance wanted to be governor to do good for others.

A different light flared in his eyes, but he quickly smothered his fury. "It's my duty," he said. "Just as it's your duty to be at my side. Your duty because we're man and wife, and I wouldn't be whole without you. Stick with me, darlin'. I haven't been myself, I know it, but give me more time. And if you still want to, we'll see someone about gettin' help with havin' a baby."

She couldn't respond to him. For months he'd behaved as if she physically repulsed him. And she'd lost her baby ten years earlier.

"Emma, I'm givin' a party on the fourteenth. I know it's short notice, but I also know if anyone can pull it off perfectly, you can. Can't you see how much I need you? And you need me? You need someone strong in your life, and that's what I am."

"How big a party?"

"Not big—but important. Donors with deep pockets. Maybe thirty couples, so it would be nice right here. I can get the list to you in the mornin'.'" Yet again he looked at the time. "I want things lush. Impressive. We'll woo the big bucks right out of their bank accounts."

"Get me the list," she said, out of fight for the present.

"You won't forget to put your name on the invitations?"

She really had shaken his self-assurance, at least a little. "The invitations will be appropriate. I do need to know exactly what you have in mind, so e-mail me, please."

He was on his feet. "Thank you," he said. "I'm so grateful we know how to get through a little bump like this. I'll work hard to make sure we don't misunderstand each other again. We've got a long way to go in this race. Get yourself the sexiest dress on the planet."

Emma didn't look at him. He honestly thought he was persuasive. All that mattered were his political ambitions, and as long as she understood that, she wouldn't inconvenience him.

Scuffling sounded from the area of the front door. The knock that came would have gone unheard if she and Orville hadn't been so close.

"Let me deal with this," Orville said, frowning. "Stay back so you won't be seen—for your safety."

He went to the door, and Emma stayed exactly where she was.

Clustered together outside stood Angela, founder of Secrets of a Successful Life, Frances Brussard, Holly Chandall and Wendy Saunders. The last three were members of the group.

Emma couldn't believe Angela had left her home. She rarely, if ever, went out. Statuesque, with long white-blond curls and an exceedingly pale face webbed with severe burn scars on one side, she bowed her head and said, "Mayor Lachance, please forgive us for interrupting you, but we came to comfort Emma. And ourselves." Angela's vocal chords had been damaged during the fire, and her voice sometimes faded away if she was nervous. She pulled locks of blond hair farther over her scars. All four women wore the loose pink robes members of the club wore to be comfortable at meetings. The robes were kept at the club, and seeing them here like this meant the women were so upset they'd forgotten to change out of them.

For the first time that evening, Emma sobbed. She beckoned her friends into the house, and they crowded around her, joined arms and pressed close—and cried. She thought of Orville watching them, then didn't care.

"We know what happened," Angela said, her blue eyes puffy. "It's cruel fate that you were the one to find her."

"That's what I thought at first," Emma said. "But it was better for me to be there than just strangers."

Holly Chandall rushed out her words, as she always did. "Rusty thinks Denise must have been working on a story about someone who didn't want to see their name in the paper, so they killed her to stop her from writing the article." She had tied a pink and white scarf around her auburn hair, turban style. Her deep brown eyes were wide with anxiety.

"Sounds obvious but reasonable to me." Frances, with her bunches of black cornrow braids decorated with colored beads, had a level head but lousy taste in partners. "Wendy thinks we should go to the police and tell them what we think. Just in case they haven't thought of that angle."

"They've thought of that angle." Orville's voice intruded. "You've probably come to the same conclusion as the authorities. It's the only one that makes sense."

"Most likely you're right," Wendy said. "I don't know why I always think someone else might miss the obvious."

Emma caught Angela's eye, and understanding passed between them. They knew why Wendy doubted a lot of things.

"Ladies?" Orville cleared his throat. "I do thank you for coming to make sure Emma's all right. She isn't, of course, but she'll be okay, and your concern has helped her. Be careful to lock up when you get home. Get some sleep. Tomorrow we'll probably all face a lot more questions. Did y'all come together?"

Angela's expression lost any trace of softness. Her thin, high brows rose even closer to her hairline. She pulled at her hair again and nodded at Orville. "We came in my van, thank you." Her robe swirled around her. A deeper pink than the others, it was made from heavy silk rather than cotton. Her burns, caused by a kitchen fire many years before, extended to her hands, and she wore pink crocheted gloves without fingers. Her nails were long and painted.

Orville held the front door wide open. "Good. Now you be careful drivin' back. Give your dear mother my best wishes, please, Frances."

The women left with faint goodbyes, and Emma saw her husband for the patronizing chameleon he was.

"I guess they mean well," he said once the two of them were alone. "Why the ugly pink dresses?"

"We wear them at meetings." Emma hated explaining any of this to him. "We like them. They're comfortable, and they're a sign of our solidarity. And pink makes any woman look better." She smiled at him.

Orville paused before returning her smile with one that came loaded with what might be pity. "You don't need extra pink to make you pretty," he said.

With his chin held up as if he were listening for something, he stood where he was. What felt like minutes passed before he said, "You're the prettiest woman I've ever seen."

He had to know how forced he sounded, how awkward they were together. "Thank you," she said, looking away. "I guess I'll finally get that shower I keep talkin' about." And a chance to start grieving in peace for a dear friend.

"Good idea. Then you turn in, darlin'. I suppose I'll be answerin' some questions I won't like when I get back to the meetin'. They'll have been waitin' for me all this time. I'll try not to wake you when I get back."

4

In the bathroom of the master suite, Emma stripped and stepped under a pulsing stream of hot water. She let it beat down on the top of her head, turned, and hoped the jets would ease the knots in her back.

She washed her hair, winced when she touched the bump Orville had caused, and hurried to finish.

How dare he say she needed him because she was afraid to be alone at night? It was as if he'd stopped noticing her at all years ago, about when he'd started being a casual resident who passed through his home to get clean clothes and hand out orders. Tonight would be another night alone, and she wanted to spend it in the house where she'd been born.

Back in the red-and-white bedroom, Emma threw on a clean T-shirt with black sweats on top.

The phone rang, and she jumped. Her hands flew to her cheeks. "Settle down," she muttered, and picked up on the second ring. "Hello?" She listened to electric silence. *"Hello?"* she repeated.

"Damn you," she said and hung up. My, she was brilliant. That could have been the killer. If so, she'd just made sure she antagonized him.

Soon a canvas tote held all she needed for a night away. She wrote a note of explanation to Orville, said she would be back in the morning and ran downstairs to tape it to the front of the refrigerator. Since the first thing he did when he came in from the garage was get a beer from the kitchen, he was bound to find the note.

She gathered a few grocery essentials and put them in a bag.

Her hair would be a mess, because she didn't want to stop and dry it. But, as Orville had reminded her, she would be alone, so there was no one to impress.

The back of the Lexus was filled with boxes of merchandise for the store. She would need to get there fairly early in the morning. Sandra Viator worked with her and had a saleswoman's heart—she also had an eye for making the shop appealing and for drawing people in. People read the name, "Poke Around," in incongruously perfect script surrounded by beribboned country bouquets, fancy packages, cups of hot coffee and grinning alligators, and smiled. Sandra and Emma got a fair amount of traffic from people who were too curious not to go in.

Sandra was Emma's best friend; she was also married to Carl Viator, partner and close ally of Orville. The four of them socialized together, not so much now as they had, but Carl and Sandra had witnessed Orville's bad treatment of Emma often enough. Carl tried to look out for Emma without making Orville mad, and Emma could tell Sandra anything. Emma didn't want to think about life at Poke Around without Sandra.

It wouldn't happen, because she wouldn't have the business once she was divorced.

Emma hopped into the vehicle and jabbed the button to open the garage door. Her sweaty fingers fumbled the keys. The call had bothered her, but most of all she wanted to be in her childhood home, well locked in and comfortable in her old room.

The garage door didn't open.

She pressed the button harder. Not a thing.

Emma got out of the vehicle, went immediately to set the alarm inside the house, then locked the door to the garage. Since they rarely used the alarm, Orville would be in for a surprise unless he acted quickly. But he would just have to understand the precaution.

She hurried to the Corvette, where the keys were usually left in the ignition, and got in. The keys hung there. Emma plunked her finger on the opener button.

The garage door slid upward.

She closed it again.

Driving the Corvette was out of the question—Orville would go ballistic. She remembered the control panel she'd never had a reason to use, went to find it inside a metal door set flush with the garage wall, and peered at the switches. Throwing a switch to engage the vacation mode would keep a door shut. The one for the door behind Emma's car had been set to the vacation position, and pulling it back wasn't easy.

You had to want to keep a garage door closed—or get it open.

Obviously Orville had decided he would make sure she didn't go out. He never had given her any credit for intelligence.

The phone call. Emma shivered and jumped into her SUV. She locked the doors and sighed with relief when the garage door behind her swung open.

What if the call had been to find out if she was there, then an intruder had sneaked inside somehow and gone into the garage to make sure she couldn't get away quickly? He would have had time to get to her by now—unless he planned to follow her into the garage but had heard her put on the alarm and was waiting for her to leave so he could escape unseen. Or he could be "just" a burglar....

Emma wasn't sticking around to check for killers and thieves inside the house.

She put her foot to the floor and shot out into a hot, black night. Thrown back and forth by her own jerky foot on the brake and the gas, her already aching head throbbed. Only a few houses stood in this section of the golfing community— mostly because the lots were huge and the homes outrageously large. There were no streetlights. The residents provided their own illumination, and that left long dark stretches between properties.

Nothing moved, or nothing that Emma saw. At the rate of speed she traveled, everything became blurred.

A route through town would be safest.

Should she call Billy Meche? Not unless she thought a call, possibly a wrong number, and her own fearful imagination were worthy of a complaint to the law.

The clock on the dash showed midnight had just passed. Her breathing came in short, shallow bursts, and her heart beat so hard she heard it in her ears.

In ten minutes she reached the outskirts of town and slowed down to drive along Main Street. Here there was a lot more light, and she drove past businesses and offices she had known all her life.

Two police cars blocked off civilian vehicles parked outside Buzzard's Wet Bar. Several people were rolling around on the ground, while the cops leaned on their cars, waiting for a break in the action to take the brawlers in.

A neon pig flashed atop the butcher's shop. Dangling strands of white Christmas lights, missing more bulbs than the number alight, flashed in the single window of Kay's Handcrafts. By daylight, cobwebs could be seen in the corners of that window.

Emma reached the square and steered around the grassy

park in the center. Bars covered the grocery store window, and the establishment was dark inside. Sadie and Sam Moss believed in security. The Moss family had owned the store for several generations. The first proprietors had been Sadie and Sam, and those names were repeated across the windows and the door in gold lettering. The store kept the same name regardless of who was in charge. Coincidence had led a Moss boy— another Sam—to marry a girl named Sadie, back twenty-five or so years ago, and now the name fit the owners once more.

A car pulled to the curb just before the stop sign at the junction of Main and Rice Streets. Emma held her breath. Much farther up Rice, Patrick Damalis had his plush establishment in what resembled a Tudor mansion. The owner lived on the premises and advertised that he could accommodate any event. Patrons came from many miles for wedding receptions, banquets and business meetings. She imagined Pat's Pack met in a private room somewhere. Patrick's was the best restaurant in town, would be in most towns. It was incongruous in a place where grits, sausage, three poached eggs and a basket of hot, sweet *calas*—rice fritters dredged in powdered sugar—was considered as gourmet as a meal needed to be. You went to Ona's on the next block for that.

The car at the stop sign wasn't a Mercedes, and the driver wasn't Orville. The couple in the front seats lip-locked together, and the driver rose over his companion. Emma saw elbows and struggling bodies. He must have put the parking break on.

She drove as fast as she dared, with images whirling through her fevered brain. Orville doing whatever he did in the secretive men's club people avoided talking about. Denise as she'd been in life, confident and smiling—in death, a grotesque, defiled mannequin. Then she saw the shadows of Finn Duhon's thick lashes reflected in his eyes, and the way his mouth flipped up at the corners when he smiled—the dimples beside his mouth.

She fiddled with buttons until a Mario Frangoulis CD helped close out the mad rotation of imagined slides. Pointe Judah's small downtown, with its rows of houses stretching out behind the business area, didn't take long to leave behind. Nor did a trailer park on a piece of land that bordered Bayou Nespique to the west.

Emma's folks liked privacy. They'd bought north of town on a winding road where the few people who already lived there had built way back in the trees. Without the trees, negotiating the road in the dark might have been less dangerous. As it was, each turn came up before her headlights picked out a solid wall of trees ahead, indicating a sharp bend.

Just let me get there in one piece. She second-guessed every decision she made now.

At least Emma knew the twists and turns well. She held back on the gas when all she wanted to do was race ahead. The changes in elevation were small, and rose and fell slowly. She came to a T-junction and turned right without slowing down. The trusty Lexus didn't even begin to fishtail.

On a long, slow, downhill drop, Emma looked in the rearview mirror and came close to missing a left-hand jog. Headlights glared behind her.

Idiot, you're not the only one on this road.

She punched off the CD player. The distraction muddled her. She negotiated three more turns, and when the road straightened out, the lights were still there—and much closer.

When she accelerated, the other vehicle dropped back, but when she slowed, the lights grew closer.

If she turned off into the next driveway she came to, it would prove whether or not she was being followed.

Gravel kicked up by the front tires pinged on the under-carriage.

She could just drive on to the next town.

Or maybe she could make a dash for home and lock herself inside before he could get to her.

Emma floored the vehicle and shot forward. This stretch of road rose and fell more than most parts, but it was fairly straight.

Trees swung up in front of her when she didn't expect them. Emma attempted to ease the brake on, but it was too late and the trees too close. She stamped on the brakes, and this time the rear wheels of the Lexus did skate a little on the loose gravel. Just the smallest slide before she had it completely under control again.

She didn't have to look in the mirror. Headlights broke over her, blazed inside the vehicle. Emma screamed, managed to shut her mouth, but broke into a clammy sweat.

On the straight again, she wrapped her shaking hands around the wheel and prepared for another dash.

The dark-colored predator suddenly swung wide, into the oncoming lane, and traveled beside her. From the corner of her eye, Emma saw a light go on in the cab of the large pickup.

Reluctantly, she made herself look at the other driver.

Finn Duhon? She almost choked. He rolled down his passenger window and indicated for her to open her own.

Emma followed his directions, and she heard Finn's voice faintly as the wind ripped his words away. "Slow down. You'll kill yourself."

She took her foot off the gas, and they both lost speed.

"I was worried about you!" he yelled. "Your husband left you alone, and you shot out of there. I'll make sure you're safe where you're goin'."

"Get back on the right side of the road," she shouted, peering ahead. It was his fault she'd driven wildly.

"Okay," Finn said. "Your parents' house, right?"

"Yes."

"I'll go first. Maybe that way I can get you there alive."

He waved, and Emma waved back. Her heart had slowed a little but her head still ached, along with her eyes now.

Before long, Finn made a right turn into the driveway of the Balous' two-story house.

Emma followed, but slammed on the brakes once she was off the road.

What do I really know about this man?

5

The lady was married.

Finn knew he was on shaky ground, but it was up to him to keep things friendly and uncomplicated.

So why stake out Emma's house until Lachance drove off on his own, then call to make sure she was okay, then follow her all the way here?

Because dislike-at-first-sight covered his reaction to Lachance, and he didn't trust him to be as good to Emma as she deserved? Because Finn wished he had the right to get real close to Emma Lachance, so he was torturing himself? Because the Lachances didn't look like Mr. And Mrs. American Harmony, and there was nothing wrong with wanting to be around in case the couple quit making apple pies together?

Yes, those were honest reasons, but also, at Billy's office, dislike had been too weak to describe Finn's reaction to Lachance. The man had filed the ends off his nerves. Billy could be too used to Mr. Mayor to notice the man's complex reactions. But some folks responded to snakes the way Finn had to Orville.

Finn had parked directly in front of the Balous' wrap-around gallery and switched off the ignition. A double spotlight, with one bulb burned out, cast a circular beam. Once Emma was in the driveway, she stopped, and he hadn't taken his eyes off her vehicle since. Her high beams still shone, and when he concentrated, he heard the even hum of the engine.

And why shouldn't she pause at the idea of being alone with him in a deserted place? Damn, she didn't know him, and he'd followed her. Right now he would lay odds that he was being tried for murder in that Lexus—maybe even convicted.

He took a chance on getting an earful for waking Billy and dialed his number.

"Meche here."

"I need you, man," Finn said. "I've followed Emma Lachance up to her parents' place just to make sure she's safe—"

Billy interrupted him. "You what? Why would you do a thing like that?"

"Later," Finn said.

"Where's her husband?"

"I don't know. She's alone. I'm alone. This is plain old neighborly concern, is all." *Liar.*

Billy was quiet for an instant. "You're right, we'll talk more about this later."

"Emma knows I'm here now, but she's locked in her car with the engine runnin'. Wouldn't you think that could mean she's afraid of me and about to take off?"

"You know it does, jerk. You got the hots for her?"

Finn took the phone from his ear and looked at it; then he said, "I'd appreciate it if you'd tell the lady she can trust me. She probably intends to spend the night here, and I think I ought to check out the house before she does."

"Okay. You do that, then get the hell back to your own place. You don't want to tangle with that husband of hers."

"Yeah? I won't take the time now, but I'm goin' to hound you for more information on that topic. Remember my folks' house isn't so far from hers—my house now, I guess. If I was going the other direction, the Balou place would be on my way. Now, I'm going to find a way to get this phone to her."

"You didn't come from the other way," Billy growled. "And you passed your place going to hers."

Finn didn't debate the issue. Expecting Emma to flee, he opened his door and left it open while he walked into the blinding glare of her headlights. He held the cell phone out in his left hand and prayed she wouldn't think it was a gun. He also prayed she didn't get scared enough to floor the gas and kill him.

Carefully, he placed the phone to his ear again. "I'm walking straight into her headlights. I'm gonna leave the phone on the hood, then get back into my truck. With luck, she'll pick up the phone."

"Next time you get an urge to put your life on the line, call me. Got that?"

Finn grinned. "I did this time, didn't I? Hang on, here we go." He set the phone on the hood of the Lexus, pointed to it and then to the driver's window, waved, and returned to the truck.

"Back in the jungle again," he sang under his breath, aware of his shirt clinging to his skin and a hot, damp wind rustling in the pines around the house—and the unpredictable human behind him. Without warning, the scar on his back knotted and his muscles locked.

This was no jungle in El Salvador, and Emma Lachance was unlikely to attack him with a machete or a big spike meant for staking out an animal.

He slammed his door behind him, and almost instantly her headlights went out. Finn rolled down his window and heard footsteps crunching on gravel. She gave a little laugh and said things he couldn't hear. It shouldn't annoy him that while he got no trust, Billy Meche's words were golden.

He did hear her say, "Bye," before she arrived and thrust

the cell toward him. "Billy wants to say good-night," she said, and scrunched up her face as if embarrassed.

"Goodnight, Billy," Finn said. "Thanks for the help."

In a hoarse whisper Billy said, "One wrong move with Emma and you're history around here, Duhon."

"If you say so."

"Finn!"

"I was an Eagle Scout. Sleep. Tomorrow's goin' to be a busy day."

Billy hung up, and Finn put the phone in his pants pocket. "What's that puckered-up face for?" he asked Emma.

"I feel silly. I overreacted. If I'd seen what you drove earlier, I might have wondered if it was you in the truck in the first place."

He jumped out beside her and squashed the impulse to put an arm around her shoulders. "You got cold feet about me. Right?"

"Right."

"That makes you a smart woman. You don't know me. Why wouldn't you worry about my reasons for following you up here? I'm going to come clean about it. I decided to take a run by your place. Don't ask me why, but I feel kind of responsible for you. Probably something to do with sharing what we did."

She had turned her face up to his, but her eyes slid away.

"I don't know why I didn't keep on drivin', except your husband hadn't closed the garage door behind the Mercedes, and I wanted to make sure he wouldn't leave again."

Her eyes returned to his, and she frowned.

"When he did—" Finn grimaced "—I tried to go, but in the end I had to call, just to hear your voice so I knew you were okay. Sorry I hung up on you like a kid after Orville bolted out of there."

She didn't pick up on the comment about her husband. "Do you think someone wants to hurt me?" she asked.

He should have anticipated the question, but his mind went blank.

"Finn? You scared me to death. When I saw you in your truck, I couldn't figure out what you were up to, and I still can't. Billy says you've got some sort of second sense about trouble."

Billy gets a beer—hell, a six-pack. In an attempt to keep things light, he said, "Maybe. But nuthin' voodoo goin' on here, ma'am. I don't even know for sure why I followed when you left home."

She smiled, and the light came back into her eyes. "Oh, fess up, you've got special powers."

"That's got to be it." There could be something quite special about the physical powers he felt right now—other than the way they made his knees weak. "Are you intendin' to spend the night up here? If so, Billy agrees I should check out the house before I leave." Good, that sounded sensible and innocent.

"I've wasted enough of your time," she said. "I'll be stayin' here, but I'm very careful about making sure everything's locked up."

"When I set out to do something, I do it," Finn said. "That will include replacing the floodlight. Where's the key?"

She spun around and ran to the Lexus. With a purse strung over her shoulder and a bag in each hand, she returned and gave him a bundle of keys. "It's the one with the string tied to it."

The way he pushed doors open before entering each room gave Emma the feeling she was in an urban battle zone. She kept close behind him on the ground floor, then followed him upstairs.

He stopped suddenly, holding up a hand, and she bumped into him.

Finn turned and bent down to whisper in her ear. "You don't have to back me up. I can manage."

Her teeth chattered, but she whispered back, "I'm a coward," she said. "I don't want to stay by myself."

"And you were coming up here on your own? In the middle of the night?"

"Yes. This is home. I'd have been all right, but you've made me jumpy."

"That makes perfect sense. Why didn't I figure that out right off? I'm goin' to take out my gun, just in case I did hear somethin'."

Emma grabbed the back of his belt. "What? What did you hear?"

"Hush," he told her and carried on, this time with a gun in his left hand.

She didn't care if he thought her a sissy, or if she made a ridiculous picture; she kept a firm grip on his belt. He'd taken time to go home from the police station and change, she realized. Evidently his concern for her had taken a while to surface.

Brain fever. She'd heard of that and began to think she had it now. A normal woman didn't feel slighted because a stranger took his time before following her around.

"All clear," Finn said in a normal voice. He switched on lights. "I'll double check the locks and get out of your hair."

Her stomach felt wobbly. "You're goin' to have some coffee before you go out on that road again. Did you have dinner? You couldn't have."

"I'm just fine." He ran down the stairs ahead of her. "I'll fix that flood."

Before she could stop him, he went ahead of her and outside, only to return in a couple of minutes. "Bulbs needed screwing in, is all," he said.

"The least I can do is make sure you don't fall asleep at the wheel. I'm very touched by your concern." And she didn't expect to have a moment's peace once he left. "Thank you."

"Are you uneasy about being here alone, Emma?" He stood in the hall and looked at her. The black jumpsuit looked terrific on her, and her hair sprang about, wonderfully wild. "I hope you're confident, because I'm sure it's safe. I should probably have stayed out of it and you'd have been just dandy."

"I *am*," she said with some force. "I'll have to be."

"Meanin'?"

She shook her head, but blushed. "Meanin' I have a rule about the way I live my life. I don't give in to fear. Now, let's have coffee."

Finn put his gun away. He smiled at her while he cursed himself for winding her up. "Coffee sounds good." Emma wanted him around because she was scared, and that wasn't what he had in mind.

"C'mon, the kitchen is my favorite room in the house. The air-conditionin' keeps things comfortable, doesn't it?"

"Surely does." As they had walked through, the whole house had surprised him. Though furnished with antiques, there was nothing rustic about the place. Paintings on the walls hadn't been picked up in garage sales, and the furniture must be worth a chunk of change. Good rugs lay on gleaming oak floors. "Your folks have a beautiful home. I'm not sure I'd want to leave all this unattended."

"I come up here all the time," Emma said, walking into a kitchen that matched the rest of the house. A cherry table polished by long use stood in a window alcove. She drew down Austrian lace blinds and waved him to a chair. "Be comfortable. We could even do some of that catchin' up we talked about this afternoon."

He didn't miss her little frown as she must be remembering Denise Steen again. But he was relaxing with the idea of hanging around with her as long as he could. "You *do* have curly hair," he said, slapping his forehead. "That's what must have thrown me off track. You used to have curly hair, but it was straight today."

"I usually…you don't want dumb details about ironing hair. I make it straight, but I left in a hurry tonight and didn't take the time. It must be a mess."

"I like it. I used to stare at it in the cafeteria at school. Why would you take the curl out?" He raised his palms. "None of my business. I expect it's a style thing."

"Orville likes it smooth," she said, scooping coffee.

Ouch. "You didn't migrate far from Pointe Judah," he said. "Did you decide to quit school because you missed the place?"

"Not really. I dropped out to get married, and Orville was already building a house here."

"I should have stuck closer to home," he said. "I bought into the theory that you couldn't succeed unless you went to the best schools and the brightest cities."

"You don't think that anymore?" She moved about rapidly. The coffee was brewing, and she unpacked a few things from a grocery sack.

"I'm not sure. I guess I'll give the idea some time before I decide."

"Stayin' here seemed the thing for me."

"Does it still?" Every answer gave away a little more.

Emma glanced ahead as if seeing nothing. "I'm married…."

She almost said more but stopped herself. Talking to Finn was very easy, too easy. Emma opened a white box from

Sadie and Sam's, put the contents on a large platter and placed it on the table. Plates, coffee mugs, silverware and napkins followed.

Smiling slightly, Finn was counting the pastries. "Ten," he said, shaking his head. "Are you sure you've got enough to last you?"

"This was from before I decided runnin' would be a better way to deal with bein' angry. It's a reaction I have. I get upset, I buy food." She leaned on the table, supporting her weight on spread fingers. "I end up givin' a lot away, so don't go thinkin' I intended to sit up all night, watchin' TV and hoggin' all of those."

"Uh-uh," he said, holding a serious expression. "No, ma'am, I never would think that."

"Drink your coffee."

He cleared his throat. "You sure you can spare one of these belly broadeners?"

"From what I'm told, it's not my belly that broadens." Emma reddened and added, "Whatever I have is yours."

Finn blinked several times before settling his eyes on her face. He took too long to turn up the corners of his mouth, and when he did, she didn't fool herself she was seeing a genuine smile. The look probed and returned to her mouth. Her own breathing became shallow, and she deliberately took a deep breath. Then his attention went to her breasts as they rose.

He might feel responsible for her, as he said he did, but he was far from unaware of her as a woman.

Even thinking about this was wrong when she wasn't free.

"You have a sweet tooth," he said without looking at the platter again. "Cinnamon rolls, donuts with every evil fillin' known to man."

"It's comfort food," she told him. "Sometimes you just want somethin' because it sounds good. It sounds as if you'll feel better if you have it. At times like that the sensible…person, indulges and then doesn't waste time with guilt."

"You were goin' to say sensible *woman*." He gave a genuine grin. "Good recovery. But for what it's worth, I subscribe to that notion, and I bet a whole heap of other men do, too. I'd like to see my sister, Eileen, belong to something like Secrets. She doesn't have the ego of a fly some of the time. It would do her good to be with other women."

The same women had been together for a long time, but Emma didn't see why they shouldn't open their arms to someone new. "I'll mention Eileen. Maybe she can come and see if she likes it."

"Thank you," he said. "Emma, who said a shapely woman like you was broadenin' *anywhere?* Not that it would matter if you did."

How could a woman not feel real warm around Finn?

"I was just jokin'," she told him. It wasn't a terrible lie.

He reached for a cinnamon roll. "Ah-ah," Emma said. She tapped the back of his hand and he chuckled. "That's for after."

He didn't ask, "After what?" but crossed his arms and waited while she produced a frying pan and started working away, her cheeks growing pink.

She poured coffee for each of them and took her own mug back to the stove. Within minutes she slid a soft, floury bun onto his plate, then a second, and put one on her own. "Dig in," she said. "I'm starving, and you have to be, too."

"Salmon burgers with cheese?" he said, closing his eyes and savoring the fragrant thing. "My, you can cook for me anytime, *cher.*" You could call a puppy *cher,* or the woman who waited on you in a store, so there was no harm in him saying it to Emma. He opened his eyes, ready to take another bite, and saw how she looked at him. Aw, hell, he never called anyone *cher* anymore, and she knew it had meant he felt good—and familiar—just being with her.

The coffee took his breath away, and he finished the burgers too soon.

Emma looked impish. She took the plate away, placed another in front of him and put a huge cinnamon roll in the middle. She poured more coffee, put the dirty plates in the sink and returned to survey the sweet goodies on the platter while she held the tip of her tongue between her teeth.

He wanted to touch her.

She nibbled all around the outside of a doughnut covered with whipped cream and sprinkles, reminding him of the way some folks ate corn. Cream stuck to her top lip.

Finn ran his tongue along his teeth. He wanted to lick that cream off for her.

"What's that?" She took his right hand and flattened it on the table, then she took her bottom out of the chair so she could lean over and peer at the still-discolored scar at the very base of his wrist.

She looked up at him, her face close to his. Her fine skin shone slightly, and he noticed how delicate her brows were, how long her lashes. He didn't resist when she turned the hand over but wished he had when she covered her mouth. Her eyes filled with tears, and he was helpless to know what to do or say.

"It went all the way through," she said. "Someone drove a knife all the way through. Did they use it to hold you down?"

"You're perceptive," he told her. "Only it was a metal spike, not a knife. But I was real lucky. A good surgeon put it back together again, and it's as good as new."

"It's horrible," she whispered. "Who did it?"

"It's all over. Thanks for being concerned."

"Were you always left-handed?"

The lady didn't give up. "I am now. Ambidextrous once the wound really healed, so I guess I owe someone a thank-you."

"Finn, I need to apologize." She rested her fingers lightly on the inside of his scarred wrist. "I'm pretty isolated most of the time. I don't get into town much, and people don't talk as freely to the mayor's wife as they could. I'd known your father was shot to death. It just didn't come to mind at once."

"Don't worry about it." Thoughts of the way Tom Duhon had died never completely left Finn. "My mother and sister had it the worst. I was overseas."

"Your mother was dyin' and she didn't last long after your dad." Emma held his wrist, and the feathery touch of her fingertips caused his gut to tighten. "My folks were pretty shaken up about it. And it was bad for you, too. I can tell you've got deep feelings about your dad, about both your folks. And you aren't over it."

"I am," he lied. "Some tell me I'm an intense guy, so I probably always seem distant."

"No, you don't. But I understand if you don't want to talk about it."

"Thanks. Hold still." He leaned across the table and flipped the spot of cream carefully from her lip. "You really get into your goodies," he said, showing her the cream…before he sucked it off his finger.

If he knew how she felt about his finger on her mouth, that the sight of him sucking that finger sent her tummy flipping…he would probably laugh. Emma felt hot and figured she would be blushing about now.

He had no way of knowing what she felt. Certainly the idea of her swallowing her heart, or feeling like she had, would make no sense to him at all.

Apparently they had run out of things to say. Finn looked at his plate, and picked up crumbs and abandoned raisins to pop into his mouth. The kind of mouth that held her attention. If he had cream on his lips, and she wished he did, she could make a joke of flipping it off and putting it in her own mouth. She could. But she would be too shy to do it.

A raisin had fallen under the rim of Finn's plate.

Emma breathed in deeply through her mouth, and he glanced at her. She had made a sighing sound. Smiling, she hooked out the raisin. "You missed one," she said, offering it to him.

His smile stopped her from breathing at all. He rested his weight on his forearms and stretched forward until he could take the raisin between his teeth. And when she made herself look at his eyes, she might have laughed if she hadn't felt like an overwound clock. The devil looked back at Emma and beguiled goose bumps into popping out on her arms and legs, or did he scare them out?

Dangerous waters, Finn thought. Warm waters.

And he felt as much as saw Emma close down. She slid to the back of her chair. The smile was gone as if it had never existed, and pink blossomed along her cheekbones.

Time to quit being selfish and give her a graceful out, not that he would be forgetting how she'd reacted to him any time soon.

"Whoa," he said, showing his wristwatch as if she could see it. "This has been one strange day. It's after two. Time got away from me." He stood up. "I'd better check to see if I've got company tonight."

Well, *hell,* now why did that sound as if he was expecting a call girl?

Emma got up, too, and everything about her said she had a vision of women waiting in his bed. "Frosty" covered it.

"My nephew, Aaron, shows up at my place sometimes," he said in a hurry. "He's Eileen's boy. I've been home for less than two weeks, but for some reason he thinks I understand him better than anyone else does. I like the kid, he's a good boy, and he'll surprise anyone who thinks…" It was definitely time to get out of here before he totally sank himself.

"Orville says a lot of things he shouldn't," Emma said. "It's a habit he needs to break. As far as I know, he's never crossed paths with your Aaron, so any impressions he has are what you said they were in Billy's office, hearsay. But I apologize for the offence."

"You have nothing to apologize for. And I shouldn't get bent out of shape by a casual comment, anyway." He picked up his mug and plate, using the interval to search for a way out of the tension he'd caused.

"No, no," Emma said. She took the dishes out of his hands, stacked them with her own and put them on a counter near the sink. "You are my guest, and guests don't do dishes. I'm so grateful to you for carin' enough to come and check up on me."

Hoo Mama, and thank you Madam Luck for thawing out this sweet thing. "It would be hard not to care what happens to you, Emma. You are a good woman, and it shows." *Now get out of here.* "Good night to you. I'm goin' to leave my cell and home numbers. Call anytime if you need somethin', includin' an interested ear to listen." He gave her one of his new cards.

"Thank you," Emma said. "Wait a moment. I can't eat all of these, and I'll bet your nephew could help me out. Keep them cool." She put all but one of the pastries back into their box and handed it to Finn. "Maybe he'll share with his uncle." Her smile returned, and he relaxed a little.

Outside and walking back to his car, Finn ran over the good and the bad moments during his time with Emma. They hadn't done any catching up on the town. Also, they had almost steered clear of the murder, but he wasn't sure why.

He wanted to find out about the autopsy reports and figured Billy could be persuaded to get moderately loose-lipped. Even now, the search for clues was on out there. The location where the body had been found would be taped off, but the crime scene would also have been triangulated by now to cover a much larger area of potential interest. His father would have been up all night with a case like this one, crawling home at dawn, still making notes, thinking, pacing around the house.

He glanced over his shoulder and saw Emma leaning against the doorjamb. She was seeing him off. How long had it been since a woman had done that? He turned and walked backward, raised a hand, and chided himself for being all kinds of a fool.

A smart man avoided getting involved with a woman who was off-limits.

Finn reached the truck. Emma gave a last wave and went inside the house.

He got in quickly and drove away, repeatedly looking back at the Balou house until he couldn't see it anymore. Leaving her there alone made him uneasy, more than uneasy, but he had no right to hang around.

Half a mile down the road, he pulled over and switched off the engine. Would she use the numbers he'd left if she needed help? How could he know? But one woman had met a grue-some death in this town, and the killer was still out there. Emma and Finn had found the body and had to be on the radar scope of that maniac.

Finn felt no fear for himself; he was intimately acquainted with violence and had the skills to defend himself. But Emma would be no match for an attacker, and he didn't fool himself that Denise Steen's murderer was the only danger she faced. Maybe the thought of Orville Lachance as another threat to Emma gave Finn some sort of excuse for keeping tabs on her. Yeah, he would confess that to himself. Especially because from what he'd already witnessed of the man, and the snippets he'd heard from Billy, there had to be a lot he didn't know about the town's mayor.

Slowly, he turned the engine on again and made a U-turn. He found a spot where he could see the Balou house and parked. Billy had told the truth when he had said Finn had a second sense when it came to danger. It was working hard right now, and he would be only steps behind Emma Lachance until he could be certain she was okay. To hell with the kind of grief that was likely to send his way.

6

If this didn't beat everything. Here she was, shaken to her toes even if she had told Finn otherwise, and with a case on the man she'd been reacquainted with for less than twenty-four hours, not that she'd known him well when he left town as a teenager.

He'd flirted with her. More than flirted—he'd seriously come on to her. And he knew full well he shouldn't have. Anymore than she should have encouraged him….

Emma finished putting up the dishes in the kitchen and considered eating the lone pastry she'd kept for herself but fought off temptation. She smiled again over Finn's comment about her not broadening anywhere.

Scratching sounded at the back door, and she couldn't make herself ignore Teddy, the white curly-haired, part Devon Rex cat who split her time between the garden shed that had a cat door with her name on it and the house. Emma let her in, quickly slammed and locked the door again, and crossed her arms while she watched Teddy stalk to her food and water bowls. Incongruously light, high cries followed. The cat had a habit of opening her mouth until the top of her head all but disappeared, then shocking you with her pathetic mewling.

Emma scurried around, filling the dishes. Teddy rolled over for a belly scratch, then nipped her benefactor before daintily picking at her food.

Dragging her feet, Emma went upstairs, pausing each two or three steps to listen. Logic said the house was silent, yet myriad creaks, taps, snaps and faint buzzings shouted in her ears. Almost at the top, she waited with eyes closed and strained to identify any distinct noise that didn't belong.

The chorus stopped, and the lack of sound pressed in on her from all sides.

Her cotton T-shirt stuck to her skin as if she had sweated but turned cold again. Emma shivered. She knew the night was hot, but the air-conditioning should keep the inside temperature comfortable.

This cold came from her core, not the air around her.

Pushing ahead once more, Emma walked along the landing outside the bedrooms. The one she still thought of as her own faced the back of the house. She opened the door Finn had closed after checking for lurking maniacs.

Darn it, for as long as she remembered, joking to herself about things that frightened her had been automatic, a way to pretend she wasn't anxious.

Emma folded her arms tightly as she entered the bedroom. *Anxious?* What a laugh. If she didn't control herself, she could have hysterics. Or she might if she ever had and knew how.

She owned a gun, a tiny Beretta Bobcat. She'd learned how to use it but hadn't taken it with her. Maybe she would in future.

A single thud on the landing whipped her around. Flattened again a wall, she worked her way toward the door, ready to fling it closed.

Teddy trotted into the room and disappeared under the bed. Emma hung her head while the pounding at her temples subsided. She climbed onto her mattress, sat cross-legged and allowed her muscles to relax.

The house had been locked up tightly, and it was hours past

time for bed. A nightgown and robe hung in the closet—"just in case," her mom said when asked why it was always there. Emma collected what she needed and went into the bathroom. She didn't need another shower.

"That dump," Orville had called her parents' home. Doc and Miriam Balou would laugh at that, before Emma's dad got *really* mad. He never had warmed up to Orville.

Leaning over the sink in the lemon-colored bathroom she still loved, Emma brushed her teeth until she remembered she needed toothpaste. She patted her chin with a towel and remedied the problem. Her hair did stand out in curls, but she liked it. Finn had liked it, too. Time to go back to curly hair. She groaned at her own behavior and brushed again.

The overhead light in the bedroom went out.

Emma remained bent forward but stared at the bedroom reflection in her wall mirror. The room wasn't completely dark. It wouldn't be, as long as the bathroom light was on. The stairwell light, too.

She couldn't move. Big breaths through her mouth made her more light-headed and didn't slow the beat of her heart.

A figure walked into her line of sight.

Clutching the edge of the counter, Emma stood where she was, her eyes straining. Her right knee shook so badly it gave out, but she locked the leg, and then she couldn't move at all.

The man, average in height and not thin, wore a big white Stetson with a wide brim curled high at the sides, tipped way forward, to hide his face. He stopped at the foot of the bed and stared at her.

Emma didn't take her eyes off him. She thought about the things close at hand, searching for anything she might be able to use to defend herself. A toothbrush wouldn't cut it. Her scissors were in her toiletry case. Scissors with about one-inch blades—useless, even if she could get them and rush the man.

Some hope. At last he moved again, raised a hand and offered her a sharp salute with a white-gloved hand. He put the same hand inside his jean jacket, and she braced, expecting a bullet.

He shook his head and produced a fat, doubled-over manilla envelope.

The creep was behaving like a sad mime. And any moment he would be playing to an empty auditorium, because his audience of one had passed out.

Slowly, moving with great care, Emma turned and faced the bedroom and the man. He was all cowboy, from the crown of his hat to the tips of his alligator boots. If he didn't kill her, she would want to remember everything she could about him.

She couldn't see his face except for a pointed chin. And she thought his mouth moved as if he were chewing. Could be tobacco.

He held the palm of a leather-gloved hand toward her. The message was clear; she was to stay where she was.

As if she could go anywhere…

He would kill her; she was sure of it.

This was the man who had killed Denise. Had to be, didn't he? A scream rushed to Emma's throat.

"Relax." His croaking whisper shocked her. "I'm your friend. Nothing's gonna happen to you. I'll keep you safe. Stay away from the new man—he could be dangerous. I'll deal with him if I have to." He tossed the envelope on her bed. "Hide it. There's plenty to keep you warm in there. I'm goin' to help you get free of the mayor. Don't tell anyone I was here."

7

Her cell phone rang at four in the morning. It didn't wake Emma, because she hadn't attempted to sleep.

"Yes," she said into the mouthpiece. Spread before her in a half circle on the bed were banded wads of hundred-dollar bills. She hadn't counted them.

Orville said, "What the fuck are you tryin' to do to me, bitch?"

"That's it," Emma said. "That's all I'm taking from you." She punched off and trembled so badly her teeth chattered.

On top of a pile of money sat Teddy, her big, tufted ears twitching, and her eyes, one light blue, one green, fixed on Emma, unblinking.

She didn't know what to do, and Orville swearing at her on the phone was worse than no help. Time slipped away like water through her fingers. She had to act but didn't know what to do, what would be safest for everyone.

The phone rang, just as she'd expected. Orville again. Emma needed to be quiet while she decided what all this meant, and she almost didn't pick up. But she did. Her husband was a big reason why she hadn't just gone straight to Billy Meche when the man left. Billy would insist on notifying Orville, and she didn't want to give him an excuse to "protect" her. Translated, that would mean he would insist on keeping her even more locked down and probably having her every move watched.

"Emma? You there?"

"Yes."

"I thought we had an agreement. We stick together. Emma, you promised, but you ran off on me."

At least he'd stopped shouting and cursing. "I left you a note. You weren't home, and I felt like coming up here. You make your decisions. I make mine—I hope without hurting you or anyone else."

"Are you alone?"

Some might say she had no right to be indignant, but she was. "Teddy's with me," she said, unsure he would even remember the cat.

"Very funny." He remembered.

Would Orville be calm and sensible if she told him about the intruder?

"Look, Emma, you've had your little demonstration. You're not good at lookin' after yourself, and I'd like you to come home now."

"I'll be back later in the day, after I make a delivery to Poke Around. If your guest list is on my computer, I'll see to the invitations for the party then."

"Well, darlin', aren't you the cool one?" He forced a laugh. "The list will be there. I'll see you later.... Is that place locked?"

"It is."

"Just be careful, okay?"

I am so touched by your concern. "Later, Orville." She put the phone aside before he could ooze more phoney charm.

She had a possibly infatuated stalker on her tail. Someone had to be told, and it ought to be the police. As soon as it was light, she would tour the house and property for signs of a visitor. Where had he gotten inside?

If she asked Sandy Viator for advice, and to keep quiet, her friend would be in a bad position whichever way she went. If she didn't tell her husband and it came out later, Carl would feel betrayed. If Sandy told Carl, he would feel honor bound to go directly to his partner, and there Emma would be, with Orville madder than a wet hen in winter and making enough of a stir to fire up the whole town.

If she told Sandy, it would be forcing her to make the kind of choice that, at the very least, might end their friendship.

Finn wasn't biased. He could be dispassionate enough to advise her, and she trusted him because she knew his reputation—even if she didn't know him well herself.

She knelt on the mattress and took his card from the bottom of her sweatpants pocket. Quickly, before she could talk herself out of it because of the hour and a bunch of other reasons, Emma dialed his home number.

All she got was his answering machine. She rang off and tried his cell.

"Duhon." He'd picked up at once.

"I'm sorry." Emma panicked. "I dialed the wrong number."

She hung up and sat with her hands clamped between her knees. You couldn't call 911 when more than two hours had elapsed since an incident. Her skin prickled.

The phone rang, jarred her violently. She looked at the readout, expecting it to be Orville again. Instead it said "private," and she watched until the ringing stopped.

That call didn't have to be from the cowboy mime. Lots of people had blocked numbers.

"Oh!" Again the air-zinging ring. And again "private" on the readout. Hesitantly she picked up and said, "Yes?" very quietly.

"What's up, Emma?"

Of course it was Finn. He would have been able to identify her from the first so-called wrong number. "Something happened here, but I've decided it would be better if you weren't involved," she told him.

"I already am. Don't pussyfoot around. Spit it out."

"I'm okay. I shouldn't—"

"Don't waste my time with that stuff," Finn snapped. "Lay it on me."

"Someone broke in." There, now she'd told him. "But he's gone, and I'm not hurt. It's just that I haven't called the police, and it happened over two hours ago. You'll think I'm indecisive, but I'm not sure what to do next."

"Where are you?"

"Locked in my room with the cat."

"If you don't tell me to stay away, I'll be right there."

Emma squeezed her eyes tight shut. She had made something bad even worse. And the way she was going, it would only get messier.

"I'm a couple of minutes from you. Keep the bedroom locked and stay inside until I get there." He was gone, just like that.

"Come here, Teddy." She picked up the cat who, true to habit, didn't relax but assumed a long-suffering expression and a frown. Emma had never seen another cat who frowned. "I've done everythin' wrong, cat. Now I'm out of choices— unless Finn agrees I shouldn't go to Billy yet."

Two minutes seemed more like fifteen, but she heard an engine exactly three minutes after Finn had said he was on his way. He wouldn't be able to get in if she sat on her bed with the door locked.

She ran through the house and whipped open the front door, exactly in time to find him bending over to examine something in his hands.

He straightened and pushed her, none too gently, into the hall. "I told you not to leave your bedroom."

"How did you get here so fast?"

He ignored the question. "You should have stayed upstairs."

"I didn't think you'd appreciate being locked out when you got here."

"I wouldn't have been." He dropped something into his pocket.

It was Emma's turn to do some frowning. "You were going to pick the lock, weren't you? You're not supposed to do that."

"Yes, I was going to do that. Turn me in, if you think that's appropriate."

Emma felt silly. "Don't take any notice of me. I guess you could say I've been a bit sheltered. You probably did things like that before. Picked locks. In your work, I mean."

The faintest of hard-eyed smiles crossed his face. "I probably did. Are you fairly certain whoever got in got out and stayed out?"

She dropped her voice. "Fairly, but not completely."

"A man?"

"Yes. Dressed like a weird cowboy." She shuddered.

Finn didn't waste time asking her what that meant exactly. He considered an instant before turning on a light. "Do you know how he got in?"

She shook her head, no.

"Okay, before I do anythin' else I've got to find that out. I'll take you back to your room."

"No."

"Yes, ma'am. Just in case your cowboy's still around, you have to do what I tell you to do. I need to concentrate."

"I'm not goin' into that bedroom alone."

A woman could be downright unreasonable. Particularly if she was scared, and this one was. "Calm down. I'll see you up there and make sure you're okay."

"Not unless you give me a gun."

Patience. "Are you losin' it?" he asked, hoping to shame her into submission. "If so, we'd better get you medical help. If not, quit wastin' time."

"I'm ready when you are. You've got a gun, right?"

He couldn't be sure every word of this wasn't going directly to a lurking enemy's ears. "Don't say another word," he said into her ear. "Stay close, but not too close, and keep your eyes open. I don't want you in a hostage situation." And he couldn't keep arguing with her.

"You can rely on me," she said, in his ear this time.

He narrowed his eyes and prayed for another shot of that patience.

When he'd searched the house before he must have missed something. The idea annoyed him. His life had too often depended on covert searches, often in the dark, and often when the enemy could be scattered all over a building. The kind of mistake he'd made here could well have cost him, and others, their lives in the crude dwellings where El Salvadoran rebels went to ground and plotted their next moves.

This was no rebel stronghold. The rooms were open, with no odd doors or windows hidden by rags. He took his time, ran his fingers under ledges looking for a spring lock that might produce a secret entrance. What reason would there be for such a thing?

He felt Emma slipping along behind him and couldn't help grinning. His Ranger buddies would get a kick out of this effort. She patted his back, and he whipped around. Stepping backward, Emma's eyes got huge; he could see them even in the gloom.

"What?" he whispered in her ear. "Touching me like that could get you shot." He felt like a heel—but he could live with that.

The instant he turned from her, she tapped him again.

"Are you nuts?" He took her by the shoulders.

"You wouldn't shoot me. I only wanted to tell you I just remembered something. I may know what you're looking for and where it is."

Now she smiled at him, damn it. "You do?"

"Follow me."

"No, no, no." He grabbed her before she took another step. "Back behind me—where you belong. Tell me where to go."

He heard her snort before she whispered, "Kitchen."

"Here we go." Still cautious, still checking for hidden intruders, Finn went directly to the kitchen.

"Don't worry," Emma said and walked a wide circle around him. She opened the pantry door.

"I looked in there before."

"Not at this—if my dad didn't block it off. Mom didn't like it there, and she kept askin him to board it up. Dad said it was an oddity and he thought it should stay."

She went to one of the floor-to-ceiling shelving units, reached past cans of food and fiddled until he heard metal on metal. The block of shelves swung wide, away from the wall.

"He did get in here," she said. "Look."

"Well, hell," Finn said. "Why would anyone have an outside door behind their pantry shelves?"

Emma bristled at the idea of anyone questioning her parents' decisions. "It was there when my folks bought the house."

"But they obviously renovated the place. It didn't look the way it does now when they got it. I know it didn't because I saw it. Don't forget, my folks'—*my* place is about three lots from yours. Even if we weren't close, my dad and yours respected each other."

"They did. And for what it's worth, I was a very shy kid, and I don't remember you saying a word to me."

"I watched you plenty. Back to this door. Why didn't your father block it off? Or did he? Are you sure the guy came this way?"

Emma shook her head, apparently disgusted, and grabbed the bolt before he could stop her. "It's open, see? Mom and Dad would never leave it like that. There's another lock on the outside. That's why the door won't open. He locked the outside after him, but he must have found a way to jam it open ahead of time. Maybe he was hiding in here for ages."

"Please take your hands off that," Finn told her. "There could be useful prints."

Emma shot home the bolt and dropped her hands. She gave him a sideways glance that was purely guilty and said, "Well, I'd already touched it, and we couldn't leave it unlocked, could we?"

"Mmm," he said. "I'm all ears now. Tell me what went on here."

"It's going to sound way out. I'm even beginnin' to wonder if I imagined the whole thing."

"No, you aren't, you just wish you could."

She sighed. "You're right, but I'm still in a mess."

"Sit down and talk to me."

"I want to show you somethin' first. Upstairs."

They went in silence, and Emma led Finn into her bedroom. "That's Teddy. She makes the most of having me here."

"Is she a cat or a poodle?"

"Very funny. The curly hair goes with the breed, the breed she partly is. Look at the money on the bed."

He did as she asked. "So you've got money on your bed."

"It isn't mine. The man left it."

Finn raised one brow. She had turned on the bedside light, and it deepened the shadows on his face, including a beard in need of shaving. Emma looked away from him; it was safer that way.

"I was in there." She pointed to the bathroom. "Brushing my teeth. The overhead light went out in here, and a guy dressed in cowboy duds walked in. He just walked right in and stood at the bottom of the bed. Finn, I thought I would die on the spot."

"I'm sorry. It must have been awful."

He sounded sincerely concerned, and her eyes stung. Years of indifference from her husband meant that when a man offered her something different, something kind, sadness at what she'd missed overwhelmed her.

"I could see him, but not clearly. He wore a jeans jacket, and jeans and alligator boots. And a big Stetson, white, with the brim flattened up on the sides. And he had those white leather gloves with fringes."

Finn sat on the bottom of the bed and patted the mattress for her to join him.

She hesitated.

"I promise I won't ravish you," he said, and grinned. "Not that it might not be fun. We need to get some things straight. There's a reason why you didn't call the police, and I need to know it."

Emma sat gingerly on the very bottom of the bed. She watched as Finn lifted the corners of one wad of bills with his fingernails. "I think there's ten thousand here."

"No. A complete stranger wouldn't hand over that much money to me."

"Was there a message?" he asked. "He didn't walk in here, leave ten grand and leave without letting you know what was on his mind, did he?"

Misery engulfed her. The tiredness that had seemed so far away seeped back in. "He said he was my friend." She had to be careful.

"Did you recognize his voice?"

"No. Never heard it before."

"What else did he say?"

She shrugged, sorting through for what she could safely tell him. "He said he would look after me and he'd keep me safe. That's about it."

"What do you think about that?"

He questioned her like a machine, like a stranger. "I'm not sure, but I have my reasons for not wantin' what happened spread all over the place. That's why I didn't call Billy."

"You know you'll have to talk to him, though, right? Look at the timin' of all this. Denise was murdered yesterday afternoon, and a few hours later some whacko gets into this house…bringin' good-sized gifts. You're not tellin' me the whole story, are you?"

A curl fell over her face, and she worked it into the rest of her hair, then tried to flatten everything by passing her hands repeatedly over her head.

"Please leave it," Finn said. "And I'm not bein' bossy. You're a bundle of nerves, but there's no reason to spoil the way you look. Tell me the rest of what he said."

"He said not to tell anyone he was here."

"Figures."

"I think I'm okay now," she said, knowing all too well he wouldn't just go away because she tried to put him off.

"That's great," Finn said. "Now finish the story."

She put her face in her hands. "I can't."

"Why?"

"Other people could be in trouble."

"Who?"

"Finn, don't push me." It was her own fault. She'd called him, but she had tried to back out.

"I'm pushin'." The bed moved, and he settled closer to her. "I promise I'll steer you right—to the best of my ability."

"You're going to blow up when I ask you this. Tell me you won't go to Billy if I ask you not to."

"What makes you expect me to get mad?"

Orville always does. "I know I haven't handled this right, so I feel guilty, I guess."

He rested a hand on top of her head. "I'll do my best to make the right decision."

He'll go straight to Billy Meche.

"Come *on*, Emma." He passed his hand from the top of her head to frame her cheek. She wanted to close her eyes, stay right where she was and not answer more questions.

"He didn't make much sense. He told me to stay away from what he called *'the new man,'* and I'm pretty sure he meant you. I haven't met any other men. He said you could be dangerous." She swallowed twice. "And he said he'd deal with you if he had to." It sounded awful that she hadn't told him about the warning at once.

"A threat, and it sounded like a threat of bodily harm...or death?"

"Yes. And I should have told you as soon as he left. I guess I don't see how he could be any match for you, and I'm afraid of Orville.... It will be harder if Orville finds out I got into another scrape."

"What does that mean?"

Emma didn't intend to discuss her marriage. "Nothin' really."

"Did the guy say anything about Orville?"

"Kind of."

Miraculously, Finn let the topic drop. "We have to go to the police." He inclined his head to look at her closely. "You're worn out. We waited this long, we might as well wait a while longer. Try to get a couple of hours sleep, then we'll go in."

Orville could decide to come up here.

No. Orville had never gone out of his way for her, why would he start now? He would be fast asleep.

"Okay," she said. "But I can go into town on my own. You were so sweet to come and help me out—and make me see what I have to do." Not that she didn't expect to be tongue-lashed by Billy—and eventually by Orville.

"I'll be taking you downtown," Finn said.

"No, really. I… It's not a good idea."

"In case your husband sees me?"

He understood too much, and figuring her out hadn't taken nearly long enough. "Orville gets uptight about things like this. I don't need the extra grief."

"Doesn't sound like your husband's as supportive as he might be. Sorry."

If she didn't keep running off at the mouth, he wouldn't get ammunition to use against Orville. "It's okay. We're just fine."

"Good. I'll tell him I live down the road, so it was easy—"

"Please don't do that. Okay? You promise?"

He looked at her too sharply. "I promise I won't." Whatever he had to say to settle her down, he would say it. But he thought he had the picture. Mrs. Lachance's husband was no Santy Claus type. Finn doubted there was a whole lot of laughter in their home, and the lady was afraid of Orville.

"I'll stay in here, then. You can—"

"I'll be fine on a couch downstairs. I may close my eyes for a few."

Once he was back downstairs, he pulled his shirt over his head and stretched out on a couch in the living room, where he had a wall at his back and a perfect visual sweep of the area.

Another reason for not rushing to the cop shop was that those folks were already in over their heads with a murder investigation. They'd done a good job of securing the crime scene and following protocol, but he could see the inexperience of a couple of the younger officers. Billy would have his hands full making sure the case didn't get derailed.

Finn faced the back of the couch. Lying on his back didn't always feel so great anymore. He would rely on his excellent hearing for half an hour or so.

He was tired, and his eyelids slid shut. One lucky skill he had was being able to decide when he would wake up. He would take an hour.

For an exhausted woman, Emma had no luck switching her brain off and getting some rest. Teddy wrapped herself around her benefactor's head and licked her ear, then got bored and burrowed under the covers. She found Emma's middle and scratched it with her rough tongue.

Billy would definitely insist on talking to Orville, but still, Emma would try to buy some time before he did. That could be worked out.

She sat up.

More than one or two people had said the reason for Denise's murder might be something to do with her pointed articles. She wondered if the police would have searched Denise's place and maybe the paper already. Could be they hadn't had time.

She slipped from the bed and walked on bare feet to the landing and down the stairs. Blinking, she allowed her eyes to adjust to the darkness. Dawn still hadn't shown her pale, blurry fingers, and the house felt too still.

Emma made out Finn's silhouette sprawled on a couch and crept closer. When she was close enough, she peered at him. His back was to her, and one arm trailed to the floor. The other cradled his head. He'd taken off his shirt and she could make out his muscular back and arms quite well. She smiled at herself.

A spike through his wrist hadn't been all he'd suffered. Emma bent as close as she dared. From beneath his right shoulder blade, across his back, then swerving up and over his left shoulder, a knotted insult of a scar showed wide and dark even without more light. She closed her eyes and shook her head. A battle wound? She thought so. Visions of him being pinned down with the stake while someone tried to kill him with some sort of knife brought sweat to her upper lip and a deep sickness to her belly. She guessed this was why he wasn't going back into the service. Or at least a big part of the reason.

He moved so fast she didn't have a hope of getting out of his way. A hand shot out, twisted Emma around and landed her, facedown, on the rug. Her forehead, knees and other parts stung.

"Move, sucker, and you're history."

Tears squeezed from her eyes but she made no sound. He wouldn't hear her cry, but unfortunately, she didn't seem able to talk anyway.

"Don't...move. *Emma!* Oh, for cryin' out loud, you're going to turn me into a gibberin' idiot. What the hell are you doin', sneakin' up on me like that?"

He'd released her arm and jumped to his feet. He swept her up in a King Kong move, sat her on the couch and turned on a lamp at either end. "You're injured." He sounded amazed. "This stinks. You've got rug burns on your face."

"And my knees and elbows. And my shoulder feels dislocated—and probably is. My ankle's twisted, and my neck hurts."

He stood there, mute, his head to one side while he looked at her, moving his eyes from one place she'd mentioned to another—as if he could see anything through her clothes.

She wrapped her arms around her waist and held on. Thinking about him seeing through her clothes embarrassed her.

"You got your nose," he said.

Emma shook her head. "*You* got my nose." She sighed. "But what the hey, you didn't mean to. I suppose you're just hypervigilant from being a Ranger."

"That could well be it, *cher.*" He reached for his shirt.

What a shame to cover up a chest like that. The breadth of his powerful shoulders and heavily muscled arms would have been out of place with a skinny little body, but no problem there. Mmm, she wouldn't blame mere men for resenting the washboard abs and smooth, rippling pecs. Neither could she blame a mere woman for drooling at the sight of smooth, black, manly hair that disappeared behind his zipper.

You're a disgrace, she told herself. *You're married and no longer see other men as sexual objects.* What was Orville always saying when he leered after a sexy woman? "I may be on a diet, darlin', but that doesn't mean I can't look at the menu." Chuckle, chuckle, chuckle. He made her sick, and he was a phoney, too.

"You seem a long way away."

At the sound of Finn's voice, she started. "You have a terrible scar on your back. Did it happen—"

"I'm not comfortable talkin' about it. Just think of it as a war wound." He spread his arms. "And as you can see, the guy who wanted me dead did a lousy job. Now, I should get some ice. Any bleeding anywhere? What should I do first, reduce the shoulder dislocation or strap your ankle?"

"Everything feels better now. I was overreacting. If you ever see that murderous bastard who attacked you, give me a sign and I'll kick him for you."

Finn laughed.

"What's so funny? I mean it."

"Of course you do, but I think you need to remember your limitations sometimes. What brought you down here, anyway?"

She'd almost forgotten. "Do you think they'll have searched Denise's house yet?"

"Probably not. It'll be taped off. Probably there's an officer on duty. But a small force can't move as quickly as a big one."

"I know how to get to the back door, and I've got a key."

"Uh-uh. Absolutely not. If you want to get arrested, do somethin' easy. Rob a bank. If we got caught messin' with evidence inside Denise's place, we'd be for the high jump. They'd slam the cuffs on, and we'd be lookin' out from a jail cell."

"Would not," Emma said, giving him a down-turned smile. "You're overreacting now. Billy would tell us off, and it wouldn't be nice. But I don't want to talk about this, I want to do it. What if there's someone corrupt on the force and they steal the evidence we need? We've got to get over there."

He shoved his hands in his pockets. "Nope. Not goin' to happen."

"It is. With or without you. See you later." She marched to the hall, where he caught up with her. Emma dropped her head and looked up at him with evil in her eyes. "I don't advise you to try to stop me."

"You don't?"

"I don't."

With his hands on his hips, he studied his bare feet, then hers. "Okay, I won't, but I suggest we wear shoes. And make sure you've got your lawyer's number with you."

"How do you know about that?" She turned and stared into his eyes. "Who have you been talking to?"

"Huh? How do I know about what?"

Her mouth worked, and she turned distinctly red. "Nothin'. Let's go. We should take both cars, because I've got things to do afterward."

He didn't like that idea but wasn't in a position to argue. "Take it easy, okay?"

"You've got it. I'll go first. Denise's house is pretty close to Bayou Nespique. We'll approach from the Bayou side, through the trees. It's pretty deserted around there."

"After you," he said. "Do you have the money?"

"Oh, no." She hared upstairs and returned, stuffing the money back in its envelope. "There will be days when I wish I had a little of… We'd better hurry."

Days when she would wish she had some of that money? Sounded as if she expected to be financially strapped. Figuring she might be planning on getting rid of Orville and being left without money wasn't too big a jump. Sure seemed as if that was what she meant. And he was a wishful thinker….

She walked through the hall, making sure the money was safely packed away, and accidentally brushed against him.

Finn's standard reaction to Emma might have been irritatingly predictable if it hadn't felt so good. She deserved better than to be hit on by some horny guy who'd been alone too long. Not that he was hitting on her, just thinking about it, and the thought wouldn't be going any further.

Abruptly, she stopped beside him and gave the softest smile. "I'm glad I met you again, Finn Duhon. You're a decent man, and you're pretty extraordinary. Thank you for lookin' out for me." Bobbing to her toes, she rested her hands on his shoulders and reached up to peck his cheek, only she missed and caught his bottom lip instead.

"Oh dear." She hunched her shoulders. "I never did have good aim. Forgive me."

He raised a finger. "Shoes," he said, and strode back to push his feet into his sneakers. Emma's were upstairs so, yet again, she rushed up, then returned wearing running shoes with trailing laces. She paused to stoop and tie them.

"We should get to Denise's before it's light," she said. "I'm hoping the police aren't there yet."

He followed her outside and locked the door behind him.

"Afterwards, I'll talk to Billy," Emma said.

"Can we rethink going to Denise's?" Finn said.

"I told you, I'll go on my own. I understand that you don't want to come and risk getting more involved. You go home, and I'll call you later."

"No way." He groaned and got into his truck, watching Emma hop up into her Lexus and turn on the engine.

He stomped on the gas, and blinding red smoke billowed to fill the cab.

8

"Get out!" Emma shrieked, running toward the truck. "Finn!" She reached the driver's door and yanked it open.

Smoke poured out.

She tore at his arm. "Get out! It's going to blow up!"

"No, it's not." Finn jumped down and hurried her to fresh air. He caught her in a hug tight enough to wind her. "Thanks, though."

Emma kept hold on a handful of his shirt and watched the smoke gradually dissipate. "I thought you were goin' to die," she said in a voice that wobbled despite her best efforts.

"So you decided the smartest thing was to die with me?"

"No." She tilted her chin up to see his face. "I was goin' to get you out. Oh, so I sound stupid. I didn't think, okay? What caused that stuff?"

He rubbed her back. "A smoke bomb under the pedal. I'm drivin' in with you. They'll want to look the truck over. Best not mess with it anymore until they have."

"A smoke bomb," she repeated slowly. "Like a kid's firework?"

"Close, but not exactly. Someone made this one special." He released her. "I'll get a ride back up here with Billy."

That meant anyone who drove by and looked toward the

house would see Finn's truck. She would just have to deal with it.

In the Lexus, Emma drove without saying anything until Finn broke the silence. "You doin' all right?"

"I'm shaken up is all. I really thought you were going to get spread all over my folks' front yard."

"Nice picture," he said. "How do you think that went down? The smoke bomb under my gas pedal? How did it get there?"

"I sneaked out and put it there."

"Sure you did," Finn said. "Think harder."

She tilted her head. "It's obvious. The cowboy was still around, watchin' the house when you arrived. He left us a warnin'."

"Uh-huh. We're supposed to think the next time will be the real thing."

Emma felt overheated and chilled at the same time. Chilled inside. She rolled down her window. The air had not cooled down much overnight, but the wind pretended it was fresh, and, but for the dust particles, it might have been.

"He was still there," Emma said, almost to herself. "And I was plannin' to search the property and the outside of the house as soon as it was light enough. I knew I had to find out how that man got inside. That was before I got cold feet and called you. *Almost* called you."

Finn leaned forward and rubbed his forehead hard.

"What?" she said. "What's wrong?"

"You're scary. Emma, you don't think things all the way through. You're just one woman, and you're not superhuman. Please, from here out, would you call me the moment you even *think* about putting yourself in danger?"

She looked at his curly black hair, his long, strong fingers. The obvious answer came to her lips, but she held back, and she knew why. She didn't want to tell him that what happened to her shouldn't concern him, that they had no right to care about each other. Emma glanced at him repeatedly. He massaged his temples and appeared deep in thought.

Just thinking about the scar on his back sent a watery horror climbing her spine. As he sat there now, with his shirt stretched over his skin and his short sleeves riding up, the long ridge pressed against the cotton, and the very end of the welt showed below his sleeve. "It wasn't dealt with quickly enough," she blurted out.

"What?" He looked at her over his shoulder.

"I'm sorry. I know you don't like talkin' about it. The wound, it wasn't cleaned and sutured quickly enough."

"No, it wasn't. Maybe I'll tell you about it one day." He doubted it. Talking hadn't helped him get over the flashes of memory in the night, the sweating, the fight to get his breath. "You never really said why you decided to spend last night at your parents' place."

She didn't blame him for asking. "I like to do it sometimes. Teddy loves it when I come. She gets lonely without me. I make sure she always has what she needs."

"You could take her home and have her with you all the time."

"Orville doesn't get along with animals."

He just bet he didn't. Finn couldn't imagine Orville endearing himself to many animals or people. "Does your husband spend most nights away from home?" Now he was way out of line.

"He's busy." It would be a relief if she could put her foot down and really move. She was tempted to do it anyway, just to keep Finn's mind off her personal situation. "Orville goes to a lot of meetings, and, like he says, there just aren't enough hours in the day."

Finn laughed but didn't comment. If he had Emma in his

bed, that was where he would be every night. But that scenario wasn't likely.

"You're drivin' too fast," he said, suddenly seeing how they whipped past the trees.

Emma held her tongue, but she didn't slow down. She sensed time running out if they were going to beat the police to Denise's house.

Before entering the town, she took a right turn—on the other side of the trailer park—and set off in the direction of the bayou.

"This is goin' to be a mistake," Finn muttered. "I feel trouble in my bones. I tell you, Emma, I've got a really bad feelin'. Billy's goin' to shred us and throw away the bones."

"Ooh-ooh, I know how terrified you are of Billy. Quit tryin' to scare me off, because I'm fearless."

"Right."

She reached a narrow road above the bayou and made her way along yet another winding way. Trees and bushes brushed the sides of the SUV, and draping moss swished across the windshield like the brushes inside a car wash.

"Are you sure this is the way?" Finn said. "It's completely overgrown."

"People don't come this way usually. They take the road at the top, but this way we've got a better chance of runnin' for it if Billy's boys are already there."

"You think of everything." Running away with Billy's boys on his tail had always been one of Finn's ambitions.

Emma ducked her head to search for the back of Denise's house. She moved more slowly, peering through breaks in the thick tangle of undergrowth, until she caught a flash of pale siding and steered off the gravel and onto the wildly overgrown verge. Pulled under the umbrella of an oak, Emma switched off and pointed uphill. "There it is. We'll go up there carefully. The moment we see a cop, we run."

"Brilliant," Finn said, joining her at the edge of the property. "If we're really lucky, we get away. If we're not, we get shot."

"You are *so* negative."

He chuckled. "Let's go." And uphill they went, batting a path through grasses and vines that rose higher than their heads.

"Ouch." A thorn speared the palm of Emma's right hand.

Finn whipped around. "Keep it down, for God's sake."

She frowned at him and concentrated on removing the thorn. "You're hardened," she muttered.

"That's me. Looks like an interestin' house."

Emma looked up at the pale green house on its cinder block stilts, and her eyes filled with tears. "Denise loved it. It was everythin' she always wanted. Private, intimate, the kind of place you wanted to curl up in. She even had a pirogue she took on the bayou. She never locked the doors. She felt completely safe here."

She caught Finn's eye, and he stared at her. He didn't have to tell her he was thinking it might have been better if Denise *had* locked her doors.

"Doesn't look as if anyone's here," she told him. "It's okay to go in, because Denise said I could—anytime I wanted to."

"I don't think she died where we found her."

Emma had thought plenty about that. "Neither do I. She could have been killed here." Her abrupt shudder surprised her. "This isn't the time for weak knees, so give me a shake if I start foldin' up on you."

"I'll remember you told me to. Why don't you go first?"

Crouching, Emma carried on. No lights showed in the windows. She reached the steps to the gallery that surrounded the house and climbed them quietly. Denise had preferred the shades open, and Emma could see inside. It looked just as it had the last time she'd been there. Denise should be curled up in her favorite basket chair with her nose in a book.

"Come on." Emma opened a screen door and tried the door handle. It turned, and she walked inside with Finn at her heel. She whispered, "Denise worked in the room upstairs. She researched and wrote up there."

"If there's somethin' that might help us, it's not likely to be folded up in plain sight and marked 'clue.' Whatever we think we're doin', let's do it and split."

Emma didn't have to be told twice. She took the stairs that rose directly from the open downstairs, where the kitchen, living room and dining nook were in one area. The stairs were open, and quilts had been hung over a balcony at the top.

They didn't talk anymore.

At the door to Denise's studio, Emma stood still and recoiled a little.

Finn reached past her and pushed open the door.

Everything that had ever been on a shelf, in a drawer or cupboard, or on Denise's big table in the middle of the room had been scattered all over the area. Papers pulled from their folders fanned across the floor. Denise had also slept up here, and her bedding had been ripped off, the mattress hacked open and its innards pulled out in lumps—leaving the springs naked.

A vase lay smashed on the wooden floor, shards of glass mixed with wilting white daisies and baby's breath.

"Hoo Mama," Finn murmured. "The police didn't do this. It's not the way they operate."

"How's that?" Furious, Emma tried to push clumps of paper together and slide them back into folders. "How do the police operate?"

"Stop it." Finn took hold of her wrist and shook it till she dropped a wad of papers. "When are you gonna learn not to disturb evidence?"

"I've never been part of anythin' like this before." She

looked angry and as if she might cry, too. "This is my friend's home. She loved it here. Everythin' you see, she chose. Now look what they've done to it."

"You're upset."

"You bet your boots I'm upset. What a stupid thing to say. *Upset.* We've got to get whoever did that to Denise."

"He'll be caught," Finn said, but his confidence didn't match his bravado.

"You don't know that. I want to look around. She could have left some message, some sign."

"We aren't goin' to make progress here. We wouldn't have time before we got interrupted."

"That's right." Billy Meche, with another, much taller officer behind him, slapped open the door. His normally ruddy complexion shone a little purple, and his eyes looked like he'd never had a gentle thought. Both officers held guns. "You're already interrupted."

"She could have tried to contact us," Emma said, knowing very well that Billy didn't want any help from her, not at this moment. "Denise. That's why we came, because I wondered if there could be…a…clue…."

The second officer, Matt Boudreaux, who was considered Billy's second-in-command, stood behind his boss and gave Emma a faint, reassuring smile. Matt was the man most red-blooded women in town fantasized about.

"A clue?" Billy said softly. "You came looking for clues. And whose job would that be, hmm? *Yours?*"

His thunderous tone jolted Emma.

"It's a good idea to let the police look for those, Mrs. Lachance," Matt said in his deep voice. "Y'see, when folks decide to just look around on their own, they can end up destroyin' the most important evidence there was in the first place. I'm sure you understand."

Emma scowled at him. He was talking to her as if she were a kindergartner.

"Emma isn't a child," Finn said, very clearly. "We're all guilty of bad judgement sometimes."

"You, young Duhon, are a numbskull," Billy roared. "Is that your excuse, too? *Bad judgement?* Your father will be turnin' over in his grave with shame."

Matt continued to study Emma. His black eyes with their long, thick lashes smiled at her, and she felt uncomfortable. His shoulders strained at his starched shirt, and his dark pants fit his lean hips like another skin. And he was too darn good-looking, just like too many Cajun men were.

"Did you have a question for Mrs. Lachance, Boudreaux?"

Emma whipped her face around to stare at Finn, who was looking at Matt with no attempt to hide his dislike.

Matt gave Finn the warmest of boy-to-boy, we're-in-this-together glances. With a curl of horror in her stomach, Emma saw the way Finn flexed his hands. "I'm sure this will be sorted out soon enough," she said with a bright smile of her own. In different circumstances, Finn's proprietary attitude might be nice, but right now...

"How long have you two been here?" Billy said. He holstered his weapon. "You're in trouble, you know that? We're takin' you in."

"You're not takin' us in," Emma said. "We're comin' in. There's things we've got to tell you."

Billy adjusted his belt and wouldn't meet her eyes. He produced a tiny Swiss Army Knife, hooked the plastic toothpick from one end and stuck it between his teeth. "Still takin' you in," he said. "Gotta have standards around here."

"What are you chargin' us with?" Finn didn't sound worried.

"Never can find the damn mints when I need 'em," Billy said. He screwed up his eyes. "Tamperin' with evidence.

Maybe you'll even be persons of interest in the murder of Denise Steen."

Emma didn't stop to think. She went directly to Finn. "If they do that, I'm goin' to have a bigger problem than bein' in jail."

He didn't smile, but he said, "Hush. Don't you worry. Everyone's on edge, is all."

Footsteps clattered on the wooden stairs from the lower floor. Both Billy and Matt gestured for silence and moved softly aside.

"It's okay," a familiar voice called. "It's me, Rusty Barnes."

Billy closed his eyes and shook his head. He patted his pockets until he fingered something in the bottom seam of his shirt pocket and scraped out a mint with a fingernail. The mint went in his mouth, and he looked like a man saved from unspeakable things, only he immediately scrunched and swallowed the thing, then shot a furious glance in all directions.

Rusty, around six foot, lean, with dark red hair, couldn't have slept the night before. His green eyes seemed to melt into the circles underneath. He looked hellish. He was a man who wore life like a comfortable bathrobe, and Emma couldn't believe the change in him. When he caught her looking at him, he swallowed convulsively and made a pathetic attempt at a smile. Denise would have married him in time, when she was ready—Emma thought it could be important to find a time to tell him that.

He held the doorjamb and swayed slightly. "You don't know what you're talking about, Billy Meche. They just got here before you. Just after me. I was first. I heard them coming in the back, same as I did, and I hid in the coat closet." He surveyed the room. "Who did this?"

"You, possibly," Billy said, savagely chewing the toothpick.

"Please," Rusty said. "If I'd searched the room, you wouldn't know it."

Matt chuckled. "Years of practice, right, Rusty?"

"I didn't say that." Rusty sounded miffed. "But in my line of work, it happens now and then." He crouched and began gathering the fallen daisies.

"Best leave them," Matt said, and there was nothing sarcastic about him. "We'll have a squad in to go over this."

"Denise loved flowers," Rusty said quietly, carefully setting down the daisies.

9

Sandy Viator dropped two galvanized buckets filled with dried flowers to the cobbles and stared at Emma with her mouth open.

One of the buckets overturned, and Emma stooped to right it and rearrange the bulrushes inside. "Do you have to be such a drama queen?" she asked Sandy. "In case you're interested, I'm as tired as I look."

"Long night of hard sex?" Sandy said, making owlish eyes. "It's noon. You've got to change your evil ways before they kill you, girl."

"Very funny. Did the espresso machine get here?"

"Are you kiddin' me you care?" Sandy smoothed a calico apron over her wouldn't-dare-to-wrinkle lime-green sheath, turned on a four-inch matching green heel and walked into Poke Around with her customary slow, hip-swinging sashay.

Emma glared at a cloudless sky and followed. Her sweats might as well have been made of damp sponge. She saw the machine from the doorway. Red, built like a classic Cadillac, complete with silver bumpers, it sat beneath a forest of hanging sun catchers, hummingbird feeders and windchimes on an antique chest they had bought just for the purpose. Housed in what had once been the conservatory at sprawling Oakdale Mansion, copper and glass enclosed the shop. Sandy and

Emma had cleared an area of merchandise and set up five small ice-cream tables surrounded by matching chairs.

"Sandy?" Emma skidded to a stop. "Is the man comin' back? Oh, please say you didn't just sign for that thing and let him go on. We'll never figure it out on our own. He's supposed to give us a thorough lesson."

"Sit." Sandy winked and took her by the arm. "C'mon, sit, sit, sit." And she plunked Emma into a chair where she could smell the little bunch of lavender at the center of the table. "Watch," Sandy ordered. "Say nothin'."

She grabbed a big cup and manipulated knobs and skinny chrome faucets. Using a hot, wet cloth, she wiped down each part she used with a flourish. Coffee was measured and pressed and clamped and dripped, and milk steamed pale clouds toward the glass ceiling.

Sandy turned to Emma and said, "Plain, chocolate, almond, macadamia nut? Take your pick."

Without a clue, Emma said, "Almond," and a red cup, bubbling like a miniature witches' cauldron, with a chocolate bar balanced across the rim and an almond biscotti in the saucer, landed softly on the table in front of her. Sandy slid into a chair beside her to watch.

Emma barely rescued the chocolate before it bent in the heat and collapsed into the latte. She plopped the melting bar on top of her almond biscotti, spread the chocolate over the sweet biscuit with the back of her spoon, and dunked the whole thing rapidly into her coffee. She closed her mouth around the soft on the outside, crisp on the inside, morsel and shut her eyes.

"You like it?" Sandy asked anxiously. "We're gonna have to sell a lot of those suckers to make our money back."

Emma opened her eyes again. "No sweat."

"Really?"

"Haven't you tried one?"

"I wanted you to be first."

"Pull the bib of that apron up. Folks'll be askin if they can buy polka-dot bras like yours."

Sandy glanced down, wiggled and rearranged herself to cover the bra—but left plenty of voluptuous bosom on display. She winked. "Men forget to hold on to their wallets when there's somethin' to take their mind off 'em."

Emma and Sandy had been friends ever since the Viators showed up in Pointe Judah eight years earlier. The two women formed a pact. They'd married serious, seriously ambitious men with a tendency to forget the little woman. While they hatched their plots, sold their properties—often, it seemed, without actually physically owning them—Sandy and Emma kept each other from going nuts. At least during the day.

The coffee helped, but energy seeped out of Emma too fast. True to his word, Billy Meche had put Finn, Rusty and her through their paces, grilling them like they were total strangers—in those horrible interview rooms again, three of them this time. They would, Billy said, once and for all learn that messing with the law was no joking matter. A little more respect, that was all he asked for.

When he was good and ready he'd sent them packing, all but Finn, who he decided was a better bet to return with him to the Balou house than Emma herself. Suited her fine. She was in no hurry to go back up there right now.

"Look at me, Emma," Sandy said. "Just like I thought. You're a total mess. Somethin's happened. Tell me what, and don't try to get out of it, because I won't shut up until you do."

This was where the balancing act came in. Emma would trust Sandy with anything—except whatever she didn't want Orville to know. Not that Sandy would be likely to run to him with tales, but she might mention the wrong thing to Carl, which was the same as telling Orville.

Sandy got up, went to the door to lock it and turned over the sign to read Closed. Emma crossed her arms on the table and rested her head on top. She was about to be questioned—again.

She breathed in the luscious scents of candles, soaps, sachets, eye compresses and lotions, and let her muscles get heavy. Opening one eye a crack, she saw a stuffed pink pig in a glittering tulle tutu, grabbed it and snuggled up.

"Not good enough," Sandy said. Her voice laughed even when she was very serious. "Into the back room with you."

Emma's head popped up. "I've got all those china dolls in the Lexus. I'd better get 'em in. I stopped by and looked at the curly ponchos Mrs. Wallis is making. Fabulous, Sandy, absolutely fabulous. They're like cobwebs, and that lady is so honest she kept telling me how inexpensive they are to make."

"Cheap?" Sandy said.

Emma grimaced. "You know I hate that word."

Sandy smiled. "Yes, I know. That's why I say it. So, are we going to carry the ponchos?"

"We're starting off with ten to see how they go. I bet we need more before the end of the month. Odie's original bayou miniatures are going to be big for us, too. I thought we'd put some of them in the window. Well, will you look at that?" Emma pointed to a copper tree hung with crystal aardvarks— or what was left of them. "How would you know those would walk out the door like that? Order more."

"Already did. Have you quit avoidin' the current issue yet?"

Emma looked at her folded hands on the table. She drank more of the wonderful coffee but didn't meet Sandy's all-seeing light brown eyes,

"Don't do this to me," Sandy said. She lifted one of Emma's hands and pulled her from the table. "I'm gonna brighten you up, honey pie."

Emma didn't go willingly. At the back of the store, in what had once been a mudroom, was a boutique where the women kept an eclectic stock of clothing, funky shoes and purses, hats, craft jewelry—and the occasional good bauble that required the locked cabinet. The locked cabinet with a panel that slid out of the back if you knew how to do it.

Sandy trailed the racks, whipped out a pair of shiny, lilac-colored crop pants and a skimpy pink top sporting a single glittery-eyed lilac dragonfly, over the left breast. "Put these on." Emma landed behind the curtain in a tiny dressing room with the clothes popped in behind her. Pink and purple striped mules followed.

"Hurry up," Sandy said. "We'll be missin' business this way. Your hair looks fantastic. I didn't think Orville liked it curly."

Emma looked at it in a mirror and smiled. "I do." She took a brush from a drawer and worked until she cried, "ouch." The effort was worthwhile. The curls caught the light and shone. She and Sandy kept makeup bags in the bottom drawer of a little chest. Emma felt better when she had applied lipstick and mascara. Still, she looked tired, but there was a certain appealing softness to her. She almost laughed aloud. The outfit was one she would never have chosen, but she couldn't hurt Sandy's feelings.

"Ta-da," she said, posing. "Satisfied?"

"Uh-huh. You look like a delectable ice-cream cone."

Emma frowned. "All soft and drippy, with too much on top and skinny legs? I don't think I'll go there."

"Now. What's happened?" Sandy said. "Don't hold back, because I'll chivvy someone into telling me. If I do that, they'll turn it into some giant mystery, and all because you wouldn't tell me yourself."

There was no way out. Emma summed up her argument with Orville and made a brief mention about another meeting at Pat Damalis's, at which Sandy made a sour moue. Orville expected Carl at his side most of the time, and she said he'd been with the Pack, too. It was Sandy who first told Emma about Pat's Pack, which was why she'd worried after she let it slip to Orville that she knew about it.

Emma went on to explain spending the previous night at her folks' house, and how the cowboy had turned up, leaving out the bits about what the man had said and the money. Sandy found a ledge to sit on. Guiltily, Emma went on to say, "Things are nicely in hand, so I'm not worried. It would be easier on me if Orville didn't find out, though. You know how upset he gets about things like that."

"I don't recall anythin' like that happenin'—ever," Sandy said, then squeezed Emma's arm and added, "Don't you think Orville *ought* to know?"

"Things haven't been so easy between us." Sandy was the one person she confided in. "I don't want to risk makin' it worse."

"He won't hear anythin' from me," Sandy said, and her mouth turned down. She tried to be diplomatic, but she wasn't an Orville fan.

Emma also didn't mention Finn Duhon, although the longer she waited, the more suspicious Sandy would be when she *did* find out about him.

Emma paused and gave Sandy a quizzical look. "Billy Meche is so mad at me, he's spitting. I went to Denise's first thing this mornin' to see if she'd left anything that would help find her killer."

Sandy's mouth worked; then she burst into tears. She couldn't have known about Denise's death. Sometimes Emma forgot that Sandy was about as cut off as she was, although

Orville should have told Carl about it at the club. "I'm sorry to spring that on you," Emma said. She sat beside her, and put an arm around her shoulders. "I kind of assumed everyone in town knew by now." She explained what had happened, and got worried when beads of sweat popped out on Sandy's upper lip and her eyes fixed.

Emma sat there and gave her friend all the time she needed. Sandy's long, straight black hair hung past her shoulders, and she had the smooth, pale skin of the true brunette with Irish ancestry. A beautiful woman with rounded features, she turned heads everywhere. And it wasn't only her facial features that were rounded. Sandy occasionally joked that with breasts as big as hers, she never bothered to listen to airline instructions about flotation devices. The rest of her body was also round, but small, and perfect legs didn't hurt the picture.

"I can't believe it," Sandy said. "Denise? Of all people. That girl didn't have a mean bone in her body." She caught Emma's eye and smiled. "Well, maybe she had a sharp tongue when she felt like it, but she had a purely golden heart. How did you hear about it?"

This time there was no keeping Finn out of the story. Emma gave an unvarnished account, while Sandy drew her lips back from her teeth in horror. "They've got to get him. *Quick.*"

"They're on it."

"*You* found her. Oh, Emma, how awful." Sandy cried afresh and swept tears away with her knuckles.

Emma's throat felt clogged, but she didn't cry. "I still can't believe it," she said. Sometimes she thought the long struggle with Orville was blunting her emotions.

"I don't recall any Finn Duhon."

Here we go. Emma gave a brief history and made absolutely certain she sounded casual, but she felt Sandy watching her narrowly throughout. "Who could imagine meetin' someone you hadn't seen since high school like that? He's a nice guy, but he's probably here because things haven't worked out too well for him." She mentioned the Army Rangers and his career in stocks.

"Did you go to Denise's on your own this morning?" Sandy said. She'd dried her eyes but still sniffed.

"Finn and Rusty were there. Have you seen that Matt Boudreaux up close?"

Sandy rolled her eyes. "Honey girl, *every* woman in this town has seen Matt close up. The problem is, to hear any of them tell it, they haven't managed to see him quite close enough."

Satisfied with her temporary diversion, Emma returned to the front of the shop and turned over the sign on the door. Immediately a gaggle of enthusiastic ladies crowded in. A bunch of fat purchases later, they left, chirping about returning for coffee.

"Hope we get more busloads like that today," Emma said, and started ferrying in boxes from her Lexus.

A number of shops occupied the lower floor of Oakdale Mansion, along with several offices. The white antebellum building still belonged to the one remaining member of the Thompson family whose ancestors had built the place, and who was said to be ancient and a bachelor. The only remaining sign of the Thompsons' presence was the management office. Upstairs, the larger rooms were used for receptions and parties.

"Emma," Sandy said suddenly, dramatically. "What if that person in the house last night was the one who murdered poor Denise? Oh, my, *Emma,* he could have killed you, too." Sandy cried afresh.

"He didn't kill me," Emma said shortly. "Most likely because he didn't have anythin' to do with what happened to Denise. He said he'd look after me. This guy was just a whacko, I tell you."

"Like the guy who killed Denise wasn't?"

Sandy had a point. "I don't believe it was the same person," Emma said.

"I'm goin' to call Angela and see if we can all get together a day early," Sandy said, while Emma took creamy porcelain dolls from between layers of tissue paper and set up a display. "We all need each other. Are you free after work?"

A meeting of Secrets sounded wonderful, like a warm bath on a chilly day. "You bet I am. You have the best ideas. She'll know how to lead us so we don't collapse in puddles of tears every few minutes."

"Emma," Sandy said. "Do they have any idea how Denise was killed yet?"

She shook her head. "They said by later today or tomorrow." She shuddered. "I can't bear to think of them cuttin' her up."

"Don't." Sandy hugged herself.

Emma looked at her while she tried to make the abbreviated top she wore meet her lilac pants. "At Denise's this mornin', someone had already been there. They'd been lookin for a lead, just like we wanted to—and just like Rusty wanted to." If she wasn't careful, she would slip off the high, cork-soled mules.

"You mean the police had already been there?"

"No, someone else. We don't know who it was."

"Does anyone know what they're looking *for?*" Sandy said. "That would be a big help."

"I've got a hunch everyone thinks Denise was writin' an exposé someone didn't want published. That's likely to be what we're all searching for."

Sandy looked beyond the glass walls in all directions and rubbed her arms. "We mustn't be here late until this is over. It's too remote once the offices and some of the other shops close up." The mansion occupied part of a large, heavily treed acreage. "It won't be over till the murderer's caught."

"No." Emma wished she didn't have to think about it. She left Sandy to continue unloading and went to the store computer. Shortly she looked at Orville's guest list and printed out a copy. "Party, party," she said, holding up the list when Sandy came in again. "Big do at our place in just over two weeks."

"Well." Sandy smoothed the green dress once more. "I never got an invitation, that's for sure."

"Neither did anyone else. They'll go out today. Orville decided at the last minute, so I'll be scramblin'."

"The printers won't be able to do the invitations fast enough."

"Nope. But I can. I'm doin my own, and if Orville doesn't like it, well then…" She selected some of the special card stock they carried and set to work.

Why not use a nice script on the printer to address the envelopes? Emma did so and had the stack of invitations almost done in no time.

"You're not even going to write out the envelopes?" Sandy said. Then she gave an exaggerated shrug. "I may just follow your lead next time. It sure saves time."

Emma frowned at the last few names on the list: Mr. Finn Duhon and Guest? Orville didn't know Finn, but he already hated him. Now he'd invited the other man to the house. She was tempted not to send the invitation, but curiosity won out, and she decided the party could turn out to be a whole lot more interesting than she'd expected. Orville never did anything without a purpose, and she had no doubt he'd decided Finn had money that could be put to good use on the campaign.

Orville wanted Finn to show up with another woman. The whole point of inviting him was to make Emma miserable and put her in her place.

Too bad for Orville, because it could be time to give him back some of his own medicine. After all, she was duty bound to be a good, attentive hostess.

The shop bell rang, and she glanced up to see John Sims, who lived in a rambler on a lot in Mill Lane, out back of Lynnette's Nail Art in the town square. The house Angela rented and where Secrets met was built on the same parcel of land and abutted John's rambler on the other side. John had inherited the property from his grandparents and owned both houses.

"Afternoon, lovely ladies," John said. Since he traveled, selling pharmaceuticals, he spent little time in town, but he was a good neighbor to the women. "I should be in Lafayette by now. It's been one of those days. Did you hear about Denise?"

"Yes," Emma said.

Sandy looked away and fanned packages of cocktail napkins on a shelf in a wooden dresser.

"I didn't know where to come but here. Angela's not home. I thought of stoppin' by the station house, but it's a zoo there."

"Don't go there," Sandy told him. "Billy's in a rage about everythin', or so Emma says. She can tell you anythin' you want to know. She found Denise."

"You know as much as I do," Emma said, unwilling to go over every detail again. "I'm goin' to run into town and mail these invitations. I may be an hour. I need to go up to the house and talk to the pool guy. Orville's havin' fits because he says it's not being properly cleaned."

"You must be shaken up," John said. Of slightly above average height, he resembled a husky blond athlete, and Emma figured his healthy, masculine appearance probably helped him in sales. "Let me run you around to do your errands. You look beat, Emma."

"I know." She gave him a wry smile. "But I'm fine, and it's

good for me to be busy. Sandy, make John one of those fabulous coffee drinks. It'll knock your socks off," she said to him, and took the invitations and her purse with her when she left.

She put her things on the passenger seat and remembered the ponchos were still in the back. At least they hardly weighed anything. She lifted the hatch and pulled out the white box where Mrs. Wallis had lovingly placed her pretty knits.

Back at the shop, she opened to door and called out, "Here are the ponchos, Sandy. See you later."

"Sure thing," Sandy said.

Some idiot had parked their black van too close to the driver's side of the Lexus. The van passenger door was ajar, and she decided to get out of there before her paint job got ruined. Emma went swiftly to her own passenger side, slid in and over the console.

She put on the air-conditioning and turned the fan up high, switched on the engine and looked over her right shoulder to check behind.

A rush of warm air from outside slithered around her neck. Emma whipped back just in time to see a man's hand get a firm grip on the top of her door. Frantic, leaning away from the fingers, she tried to see who he was, but he was reaching from inside the van and the windows, tinted black, gave no hint.

Tendons stood out in the strong hand and wrist.

Emma opened her mouth to scream, then remembered the horn. Before she could lean on it, a slim manilla envelope shot into the car and hit her in the face.

10

"She's gone," John Sims said, watching Emma peel out of the parking lot. "Looks like she's in a hurry. Does she know anyone with a black van?"

"Not as far as I know." Sandy heard the unevenness in her own voice.

John clicked his tongue. "I'd swear she went after a black van. It pulled out, and she shot after it. I guess it's not our business. How're you feeling?" He put his sample case on the floor.

"Fine," she said, tensing more with every second that passed. "You?"

"Terrific, never better. How's Carl?"

"He's well, thank you." Her throat dried out.

"Still spending a lot of time at Damalis's?"

"Fair amount." She ordered her mind. John was getting too interested in Carl. So far she'd avoided the hints about an introduction to the Pack, but John wasn't giving up. She had not had the courage to ask how he knew about the group. Sandy smiled at him. "You were already living in Pointe Judah when Carl and I arrived. I know about you inheriting your grandparents' property but I never thought to ask you if you were born here."

"You think I was born?" His gray eyes never smiled, not even when the corners crinkled like they did now. "I kinda think I crawled out of a hole somewhere and I've been thriving ever since. Never did believe that crap about the benefits of mother's milk."

"Where did you grow up?"

"California…mostly. I settled here when I did because I like it. Everyone's got an agenda, but they're too sheltered to play games well."

Sandy didn't think she liked what he was suggesting, but she kept her mouth shut. "Will you have that coffee, John?"

"Ooh, I don't think so. I didn't come for coffee."

A sudden sharp twinge hit in the increasingly moist places between her legs. She forced a smile. "Hearin' about Denise puts you off, doesn't it? I didn't know till Emma told me." She hated him, but he excited her. How sick was that?

"Bigmouth ballbreaker," he said.

Shocked, she said, *"Emma?"*

"Emma's soft as dog shit. And just about as bright. I was talking about Denise. I used to watch the way she ran her boss around by the short hairs, and it made me want to puke."

Sandy didn't answer him.

"Your hands are shaking," he said. "You nervous? Afraid of me?"

"Nervous maybe, a nice nervous. But of course I'm not afraid of you." He terrified her and always had. She didn't understand him at all. He would never talk to Emma the way he did to her, and she couldn't do anything about it, because it all sounded innocuous when they were in front of other people. It was only when he got her alone that he turned crude and degrading.

Be honest, you can't do anything about it anyway. Two winters ago Carl had taken her skiing and she'd blown a knee. The knee got completely better, but she'd had too many pain killers hanging around afterward, and she fell in love with them. They suppressed her appetite, and made her feel powerful and excited. The lows that followed, the occasional hallucination, weren't too bad, and as long as she had a supply of the drugs, she could juggle the rotten times to get back to the highs. That was where John Sims came in.

John had been there one time when Sandy got desperate, and he knew enough to recognize her problem. The little envelopes of samples he'd given her had been golden. She had almost loved him for them. And he'd introduced her to other, more exotic drugs that allowed her to tailor her moods. Mostly she wanted to be up, up, up. But then John had let her know what he expected from her, and now they were a habit together.

"I've got a little windfall for you today, sweetheart," he said. She stood behind a glass counter, her heart fluttering with anticipation, and he said, "I'd like to see something in there first." He pointed down through the glass. "The pen shaped like a pink flamingo with feathers on its head. The big one."

"You're kidding." She laughed.

"Shut your mouth and open the case."

Sandy swallowed and leaned down to slide open one door and reach inside.

John leaned on the counter. "Not the small one, the big one. You know I like big things." He shot a hand inside her bra. She held still. He'd taught her that it was a bad idea to complain or try to move away.

His second hand joined the first and he squeezed her breasts together, pushing her bra aside. She felt a strap rip free. He pulled her nipples between fingers and thumbs until her breasts stood out, naked and huge, and she was all but naked to the waist. He pinched hard and laughed when she drew a sharp breath. "You're the best, Sandy. I never saw better tits than yours. Now, gimme my pen." He let her go, and she quickly pulled the front of her dress together, looking at the windows surrounding them.

"You know I like this as much as you do," she said. "But we should be careful in here. It's so open."

He looked up. "Well, I'll be. Would you look at that rain? I doubt if you'll get many customers while the skies are open."

She couldn't argue. Lightning shot across the sky, and thunder rumbled on and on.

"It won't last," Sandy said. "Good weather for sellin' coffee, though."

"If anyone wants to get soaked coming to get it." John lifted one side of his mouth. Apart from pointed incisors, he had straight, completely even teeth and liked to show them off. "Hey, I know what we'll do. We'll go in that back room of yours and have a party."

Her heart began a too-familiar, breath-stealing thump, thump, and she shook her head. "We can't do that, John. There could be customers at any moment."

He took a sticky note and wrote GONE TO BANK in block letters, then added, Back in 45. This he stuck on the outside of the door before he closed and locked it.

"Emma will be back," Sandy said, panicking.

He walked slowly toward her. "Guess I'll just have to take that present back with me."

She didn't tell him the truth, that when he brought her something it was never free but she had to have it anyway.

He picked up the pink, fluffy pen and ran the feathers over his lips. "Useful little thing. I'd kind of like to try it on something tender. Soft—responsive." From a pants pocket he took a handful of packets. He opened one and held it out for Sandy to see inside.

She swallowed.

"You're wasting time," he said. "You know you want this. But if I don't get what I want, it'll go away."

John spun her around and propelled her into the boutique, where there were plenty of lights but no windows.

She let out a shuddering breath.

"Excited?"

Sandy nodded. She *was* excited, despite the disgust she felt for him, and for herself when she was with him.

"Apron."

She took it off and put it on an upholstered chair without arms.

John walked around her. A glance at his pants brought blood pulsing into her face. He looked down and smiled, held himself and narrowed his eyes at her. "I need the most you've got to offer today. Take off the dress."

Imagining how the broken bra strap would look, she reluctantly undid the two buttons that closed the cross-over sheath at the waist. When she hesitated, he said, "Off—unless you don't want to be able to wear it again."

Sandy took the dress off and put it on top of the apron.

She held up the bra cup where the strap had snapped.

"Let it go. You look good just the way you are."

Like the bra, her yellow wisp of a thong was printed with green polka dots, and her garter belt matched. Ivory hose with deep lace tops barely cleared midthigh.

"You love sex," he said. "You think about sex every moment you're awake. You walk around knowing what you're wearing under your clothes and wanting to feel a man watching you. And his hands stripping you."

"Maybe I do." Sometimes she did.

"Walk for me." When she didn't move, his lip curled and he flapped a hand at her. "Strut. Go on. Get the tits up. Good. Now turn around slowly. Put your foot on the chair. The right leg, whore. I want to see your pussy from a different angle.

Oh, yeah, baby. Oh, yeah. Stand up again." When she did, he gave her bra one hard yank, and she was left with her panties, garter belt, stockings and shoes. "Walk some more. Keep 'em up. That's right. You know how, woman. Hands on your hips and shake your shoulders."

She did it. She did whatever he asked. All she did was put her body to work for her. What was so wrong with that? Everyone used their strongest talents to make their way.

John unzipped his pants and pulled out his penis. While he watched her, he stroked, but not hard enough to take anything away from what he intended to do to her.

"Stay where you are." He walked behind her. "Grasp your ankles."

She moaned a little. It would be good…and painful. But she did as he told her.

"Mmm-mmm, sweet ass." She heard him drop his pants, then felt his fluffy little pen slip into her slick folds. He flipped it back and forth and laughed. She panted, and he laughed again. "Know how lucky you are that I like to see you get off first?"

"Yes," she said, and she did. "You're a fantastic lover, John."

"You really think so?"

She sighed and said, "The best."

John replaced the pen with his fingers and worked her so close to a climax, she made high, moaning noises. He moved in front of her and caught first one, then the other of her swaying nipples with his teeth. He knelt between her feet with his tongue doing a much better job than the pen or his hands, then reached up and wiggled her nipples convulsively.

Sandy heard her own thin scream as she came, and caught at his shoulders when her knees wanted to buckle. Laughing, he jerked her upright, resumed his place behind her and grabbed the hair at the base of her neck. He pushed her head down over the back of the upholstered chair.

He went wild, pumping into her, forcing her high heels off the floor. She tossed her head and guided his hands back to her breasts. A minute, two, she didn't know how long they slapped together before she howled with pleasure and John bit into her shoulder. He poured into a condom. She felt the heat.

As he spun her around, squeezing her over and over again, John's face gradually calmed and his lips closed over his teeth, over the two sharp incisors that showed when he went into a kind of rictus with his release.

He had kept all of his clothes more or less on. Zipping his partially tumescent penis away, he pulled out the samples again and opened them. "Hold out your hands," he said.

Trembling, afraid he would change his mind, Sandy cupped her hands.

John Sims poured out a stream of pills in different sizes and colors, all of which she recognized like old friends. Sandy bent over them and giggled. She fell to her knees thanking him and giggling.

"Put them away," he snapped. "Is that your purse?"

She looked behind her and nodded, then went quickly to drop his payment for the use of her body into a big side pocket.

John raised her chin. "Heard anything about restarting construction at the Willows?"

She tried to pull away, but he held her too tightly. "Not much," she said.

"The owners are going under?"

"I don't know."

"Yes, you do. What I just gave you won't last so long…"

"They're goin' under."

"Thank you, babydoll. And lover boy and his friends intend to pick up the parcel for peanuts—or maybe pine nuts? And certain incentives?"

She couldn't answer him but looked directly into his eyes.

"I heard they might have another property interest. A big surprise. Know what it is?"

"No. I swear I don't." And she didn't.

"What I want, I want, and I want better connections in this town," he said. "Get me some invites. I hope we understand each other."

11

Emma let the black van go.

All the way up C Street from Oakdale Mansion, she'd stayed close behind it, a shiny new van with no license plate and rain bouncing off its waxed finish. At the junction with Circle, which more or less went all around the town, she watched him turn right and pulled her own vehicle to the side of the road.

What would she do if she caught up with him?

She didn't want to catch up with him.

Her cheek, just below her right eye, stung, and when she touched it a spot of blood came away on her finger. The envelope had ricocheted off her face and landed on the passenger floor mat. She leaned down, picked up the envelope and pried the flap open.

Emma only slid the contents halfway out. Immediately she jammed them back inside and tried to reseal the self-sticking flap.

She drove too fast to the center of town, her mind like a tangled cat's cradle. Pain, real pain, tightened her chest and gripped her head. Where could she go? Home? Where was home? She needed a place where no one would think to look for her, a place where she could be quiet and calm down...and make plans.

Easing back on her speed, she passed the corner of Rice Street and wondered if Orville even found excuses to go there and plot at Damalis's in the middle of the day. She was sure her dear, upright husband spent most of his waking hours plotting his way to real power.

Limbs on oaks lining the street slashed to and fro, and bundles of dry weeds jumped and rolled along the road. A rising wind buffeted the SUV.

Mill Alley came and went. She needed her friends, and she hoped Sandy wouldn't forget to make arrangements for tonight.

A sword of lightning shot into her sight and sliced straight to earth. The rain grew heavier, but she didn't hear thunder, probably because the engine drowned it out.

Ona's could make a good refuge. There was Ona's Out Front, where all the men and the breakfast crowd went, and Ona's Out Back, a small area with a corrugated, semitransparent plastic roof, old armchairs around an assortment of low tables, and enough plants to make a person wonder if Ona really wanted to serve in there or if it was just supposed to be her greenhouse. Emma had met friends there before and found it peaceful.

Steering down the alley beside the shop, Emma parked at the back and just sat there, her purse and the envelope on her lap. Ideas shot through her mind, each one sounding good until another came along.

She answered the ring of her cell phone. "Yes, Orville?"

"Did you get the invitations off?"

Her face felt stiff. "They're going in the mail shortly."

"This is goin' to be a test balloon, sweetheart. I'll talk, but I'll keep it short, and the response will be obvious. I expect it to be a success, a big success. I want you to help me polish what I'm sayin'. You were always good with that stuff, and that way I don't have to risk someone leakin' what I'm gonna talk about. My manager's working on press coverage."

"You settled on a manager?"

"Didn't I tell you? Carl's got all kinds of publicity experience, and he wants to do it. I decided to let him, and if he's not up to it when I get further along, I'll just have to make a change. There won't be any room for sentimental stuff in this game."

When has there ever been room for sentimentality when it comes to your plans, Orville? You'd better pray Carl remains the saint he's always been where you're concerned.

"Honey, I've already made some stabs at my speech. I've got a meetin' tonight, but d'you suppose you could put together some comments and suggest changes before you go to bed?"

What a surprise, Orville had a meeting tonight. She thought rapidly. "I'll be at Secrets this evenin', so I may not see you. I'll look at the speech in the next couple of days. And don't worry about the party. I've got Holly Chandall doing the food, and she's really good."

"Her husband isn't any more pleased with her hangin' around that Angela than I am with you."

"That's too bad," she said, and felt absolutely calm.

"Oh, sweetheart." He dropped his voice. "I owe you apologies for my lack of sympathy last night. I don't know what came over me, except I got scared for you. I was thinkin' you might like it if we had dinner with the Viators at Patrick's. It's been too long and I know you love it there."

She'd never liked the place or its ostentatious presentations. "We should do that," she told him. She didn't want a protracted war with him, she just wanted out, so the fewer opportunities she gave him to argue with her, the better. "Let's think about a date when we can do it. What on earth made you invite Finn Duhon to your party, Orville? You've already shown you don't like him."

"*Our* party. And I don't like or dislike him. You know me and how I am when it comes to you. I don't want any other men sniffin' around you, and I thought that's what he was doin'. I should have known better. I should have trusted you." He chuckled. "Anyway, I hear your Finn is a really successful businessman, like you said. His money's the same color as anyone else's. What did you think of my speech on the radio this mornin'?"

To tell him she hadn't heard it could bring on another tirade, and it wasn't worth the effort. "Very reassurin'," she said, crossing her fingers.

"That's what everyone says. Carl reckons I made good points and should have the town calmed down and believin' what happened to Denise was a random thing by some low-life passin' through town."

"I'm sure that's right."

"Can't get home tonight, sweets. I'm sorry you're goin' out, though. I miss knowin' you're there waitin' for me."

She wrinkled her nose. "I'm already committed. I learned how important commitments are from the best. You, Mayor Orville Lachance."

He chuckled. "That's right. Okay, I'll check in with you later. I do like a lot of showy flowers, hon. For the party. And people still seem impressed by a champagne fountain if the champagne's the best. I want an ice sculpture of the state building. Do and pay whatever you have to. Plenty of help, too—the kind who know what they're doin'. I thought it might be fun to invite people to stay late and go in the pool or the hot tub if they feel like it."

Finally he let her go, and she slipped the phone away. He used it like a lifeline—or maybe a noose.

There were plenty of cars angle-parked by the windows of Ona's Out Front, and the place looked crammed with customers. The area behind Ona's place was mostly deserted, and Emma figured it was a little early for the back to be crowded.

She took a chance and made her way in that direction, with her purse shielding her hair from the rain.

She'd been right. Not a single customer sat in one of the sagging, overstuffed chairs. Emma took one in a corner where she could see the whole room. A customer couldn't go from Out Front to Out Back without walking outside, because the only other way would be through the kitchen, and Ona wasn't the type to invite customers in there.

Emma didn't care if Ona never realized she was around. Maybe she would get lucky and hours would go by uninterrupted. Tears filled her eyes, and she blinked them back, angry and, yes, sorry for herself. She moved her fingertips over the envelope. *Dry the tears. You'll figure it out.*

A table loaded with orchids in colorful bloom shielded her view of the alley. Some of Ona's ivy plants and philodendron vines climbed sturdy stakes all the way to the corrugated ceiling, where fine creepers managed to cling and spread.

An ancient upright piano stood against the common wall with Out Front. A white crocheted runner and a row of lush violet plants decorated the top.

"Hello." A slim blond woman Emma hadn't seen before walked straight toward her from the kitchens.

"Hi," Emma said. "You're new in town, aren't you?"

"I've been here several weeks now. I'm Annie Duhon. In addition to traditional dishes, we have fresh sandwiches and salads. And there's pastries and hot tea, if you'd like. Or iced, of course. Lemonade, coffee."

Emma only vaguely heard what Annie said once she announced her name. Should she ask if this was a relative of Finn's?

Rubbing her forehead, she tried to think.

"Do you have a headache, ma'am? Oh, you cut your face. Looks like you nicked a little vein or somethin'."

"No. It's nothin'. Everythin' sounds so good, but I have to behave myself and choose just one thing."

"Well…" Annie gave a shy smile. "Just one to start with, maybe, then see how you feel?"

"I'll try some hot tea. It sounds good today. You bring me what you think I'd like, because I don't know one thing about it. And if you have a really yummy cookie, I'll take that, too."

Annie put silverware and a napkin on the table. She had smooth, shiny patches on her hands where they must have been burned. Emma glanced at her face again and realized Annie probably wasn't thirty yet.

Once she was alone, she listened to the rain on the plastic roof and thought about Finn. She had seen and felt his interest in her. At the moment she could be dangerous to be around, unavailable or otherwise.

If she would quit trying to fool herself, she would admit she thought about him a good deal of the time. She felt like he was the one person she would like to talk to right now. She'd brought the envelope in rather than risk leaving it in her vehicle. Each time she glanced at it, her stomach turned over.

One day she would be in a different position, free to make new friends without feeling guilty. A bitter smile pulled the corners of her mouth down. By then Finn Duhon would have decided what to do with his life, and even if he stayed here, he would have met more people, more women, perhaps one special woman who didn't have the kind of baggage Emma hauled around.

Annie returned with a wooden box carried proudly before her. Ona, a substantial woman with bleached white hair and a sweet, liberally made-up face, followed. "Emma," she said. "Welcome. I haven't seen you around here lately. I remember when you and your mama and daddy used to come in ev'ry

Sunday after services." On each occasion when they met, Ona mentioned this. Emma enjoyed the memory.

"You always did make the best breakfasts in town, Ona," Emma said.

Ona looked around, and when she was satisfied they couldn't be overheard, other than by Annie, she said, "Do you believe Denise was killed by someone just passin' through— like the mayor said?"

Did she? There was nothing to be gained by frightening anyone, and going against Orville's wisdom would not be a good idea. "It's likely," she said and frowned. She'd intended to give a resounding endorsement of Orville's theory.

"Denise was a character." Ona's glittery dark eyes filled with tears, surprising Emma, who had never seen the woman upset over anything. "I reckon she and Rusty Barnes would have tied the knot in time. She would always have had a mouth on her, but so what? A person gets sick of mealy-mouthed people who don't have an opinion of their own."

"She was my dear friend," Emma said.

"I know," Ona said. "And you had to be the one who found her. I'm real sorry."

Ona was soon on her way, and Annie, her face real serious, said, "This is a tea caddy," opening the top of the box. "See all the different kinds of tea bags? I can make you loose leaf, too, but I wanted you to see this. The green teas are really popular now. They've got a lot of antioxidants in them."

"Do you like green tea?" Emma asked.

"Oh, yes, it's lovely. There's a lot of kinds, mind you."

"I'll have the green tea you like best."

That earned her a purely sweet smile.

"I'm dying of curiosity. Are you related to Finn Duhon? We went to school together, and I know he's in Pointe Judah now."

Annie almost closed her fingers in the caddy. "Why, yes,

ma'am. Finn's my cousin. So's Eileen Moggeridge. She's a sweetheart—lets me live with her until I decide if I'm stayin'."

"Stayin'?"

Annie turned pink. "One day I want my own business. I've dreamed about that since I was a little girl, but things, well, they got in my way, if you know what I mean."

"I know," Emma said.

"For now I'm workin' for Ona. She's got a heart of gold, that woman. And I just started in with Holly Chandall. Do you know her? She caters big important parties, and I've had good trainin' as a cook. Her business has grown, and she needed someone, so she hired me."

The world began to feel awful small. "I've known Holly for years. I called her earlier, and she's caterin' a party for me in a couple of weeks."

"How many people?"

"Around sixty."

"She told me about one for the mayor, but—"

"That's the one," Emma said, not without reluctance.

Annie's lips parted. "You'll be the mayor's wife, then."

"Mmm. The mayor's house is nice for entertainin'. Will you be helpin' with that?"

"I'll be fixin' the desserts, ma'am. That's one of my specialties. And I'll be servin'."

"I'm Emma."

Annie looked uncertain, but said, "Emma, then. Thank you, ma'am. Holly and me will make your party the best. Holly's so clever."

"I know," Emma said. "And if she's hired you, you're clever, too. I don't suppose you know anything about ice sculpting?"

Annie showed no surprise. "What do you want?"

Mortified, Emma said, "The state senate building."

If Annie found that strange, she didn't show it. "I've got a friend I went to school with in Lafayette. He's in New Orleans, and he's better than anyone I ever saw. We can get the sculpture brought here in a refrigerated van. I don't know how much that would cost, though."

"Just arrange it Annie. I'm starting to think my lucky angel brought me in here today."

"I'll see to things," Annie said. She turned to leave but paused. "I know Finn was with you when you…well, you know, when you found the dead lady. He mentioned you and said how brave you were."

The ridiculous pleasure Annie's remark brought ought to embarrass her, Emma thought, but it didn't. "I wouldn't have been so brave if he hadn't been there."

Annie nodded. "He makes you feel safe, doesn't he? He's been through so much, but if he's feelin' bad, he never lets it show." She started to leave again, and again stopped. "When he jumps the way he does sometimes, you know he can't help it, don't you? Oh, it'd probably never happen around you, but just in case. It's because somethin' pretty bad happened to him when he was a Ranger. Leastwise, that's what Eileen and me think. He never talks about it. He won't stay at Eileen's, and we think it's because he doesn't sleep."

Emma couldn't imagine why Annie had chosen to reveal all this to her. "If he doesn't stay, how do you know he doesn't sleep?"

Annie turned red. "It's none of my business, is it? But I worry about him and want him to be happy. Aaron stays over at Finn's place now and then, and he said Finn walks around a lot at night. Oh, listen to me. Forget I said anythin'. But you are an old friend of his—you said you were—and he'd hate it if he heard me say as much, but I think he needs a good friend."

At last Annie returned to the kitchens, leaving Emma with even more to think about.

Then, as if she'd summoned him up, Finn walked through the back door. He headed straight for Emma, showing no surprise at finding her there. "I thought I'd see how my cousin's doin'," he said. "Saw your car out back and figured I'd hit pay dirt. Where've you been? Couldn't find you anywhere."

"Where did you try?" she asked nervously.

He smiled, and Emma smiled back. "I'm a circumspect man," he said, and she decided this wasn't an infatuation she was likely to get over soon.

"What did Billy say about your truck?" she asked.

"No useful prints after you and I had our mitts all over it—if there ever were any. Nothing but a battered tennis ball. They don't hold much hope of matching fibers from that."

She raised her eyebrows at that.

"That's what they used to make the smoke bomb. Silly kids' stuff, but it works if all you want is to shock someone."

"It shocked me," she said, and shook her head. "I was goin' to tear you out of that thing bodily. I think it's true you get superhuman strength when you're scared."

Finn didn't laugh, or smile; he stared down at her, the irresistible shadow from his lashes in his eyes. Rain had dampened his hair. She noticed every detail about him. He didn't look particularly tired.

He broke the silence. "With your permission, I'd like to replace the locks on your doors. Even if you don't intend to stay up there again, they should be attended to. Several of them are real old and wouldn't take much to force."

"You've got your own business to deal with. I'll get Len up there. He does a lot of locks. I think I'll have the windows gone over, too, and seal up that stupid door in the pantry."

"Okay. Sounds like a good idea. Let me do the door into

the pantry, though, okay? The wall needs reinforcin', and I'll feel better if I do it myself."

If she had a backbone, she would refuse. "That's kind of you. Thank you." After all, she couldn't be rude to him.

He stood there, glancing at her, then away again, and Emma couldn't think what to say next.

"I've got some news you'll want to know," he said. "Or you may not want to know it, but I'd rather you hear it from me today than on the street tomorrow."

Annie appeared with a tray and set it on the table. "Hi there, Finn. Saw you come in, so I brought an extra cup. I know you like green tea."

She put a teapot, a pot of boiling water, a small glass bowl filled with lemon slices, and a plate of cookies and cakes on the table. "You'll say you weren't goin' to stay, Finn, but Emma knows you and me are cousins, and I know you two went to school together, so I reckon it's only polite for you to keep the lady company. I'll just bet he was a terror in school," she said to Emma, smiling her shy smile. "Did all the girls run after him?"

Finn grimaced, but Emma kept a straight face and said, "Absolutely."

"I thought so. It's a good thing he's come back where he belongs. Maybe he'll find a new wife, and this one will want him for himself and not his money. It would be nice if he settled down here, where he's got some family."

When Annie finally stopped talking, she studied her cousin's face and looked horrified. Emma wasn't surprised that Finn wouldn't meet her eyes. Annie left, and when she got close to the kitchen, she broke into a trot.

Finn sat in a chair beside Emma's. With the seat so close to the ground, his knees stuck way up.

Emma poured two cups of pale green tea. "Annie was just

bein' friendly and kind," she said. "There was no need to look as if you'd swallowed an aardvark just because she mentioned somethin' a little personal."

He turned his head sharply in her direction. *"Aardvark?"*

She shrugged. "First thing that came into my head. I didn't realize you'd been married."

"I'm not generally inclined to spill my business."

A flare of annoyance sharpened Emma's tongue. "But it's okay to dig at mine?"

"I haven't *'dug'* at your business."

"What would you call it, then?" She gave him a cup and saucer, and he drained the cup immediately.

"Annie didn't mean any harm," Finn said. "She's gentle and shy. And she's had a bad deal. I hope her luck has changed."

"So do I," she said. "What's your problem, Finn? You're wound up tighter than a spring. You said you had news—is that what's upsetting you?"

"I don't have any problems. And I'm not upset. The news will wait till we're out of here."

"Whatever you say." She ate part of a pink-frosted shortbread cookie and made satisfied noises. "Annie's a good baker."

"Yes," he said. Two donuts disappeared in rapid succession. "Now—" he used his napkin "—I have to talk to you. You're going to have to trust me, be honest with me."

"The way you have with me?" she asked mildly.

"I haven't told you any lies. You've got troubles of your own. Why would I start unloadin' mine?"

"To make me feel less of a nuisance, maybe. And to let me know you understand at least part of what I'm goin' through because you've been there yourself." She paused. "Annie did mean you used to be married, didn't she?"

"Uh-huh."

"You're not anymore?"

"Nope."

He wouldn't volunteer details, and she wouldn't dig for them. "I'd better get over to Len's," she said. "I want to see how quickly he can get the job done at Mom and Dad's place."

"In a hurry now?"

"You sound so irritable. Yes, I'm in a hurry. I intend to live up there just as soon as I can."

"How's Orville going to take that?"

Emma looked at her purse on the floor and the envelope beneath it. She'd planned to sit here and take her time thinking over the contents. "That's not something I can discuss—not yet."

"Eventually?"

She put fallen cookie crumbs on her plate. "Could be."

"What happened to your face? You cut it on something. What? It hit pretty close to the eye, and it's bruisin'."

"The corner of an envelope," she said. Truth was so much easier. "It caught me there." She didn't know how much she could confide in Finn or anyone else. He felt like an old and trusted friend, but they'd only been reacquainted a short time.

"This isn't a good place to talk about private things," he told her.

"Why not? We're the only ones here."

"At the moment. We'll be interrupted. When do you plan to move to the Balou house?"

Tea dripped from the bottom of her cup onto the lilac crop pants that embarrassed her. She took a napkin, dipped it in the pot of water and rubbed at the tea.

"Hot water sets in stains," Finn said.

She threw the napkin on the table. "I'm getting rid of these—and this," she plucked at the sweater, "the moment I can get to my own clothes. These were just a stopgap."

He gave her a quizzical glance.

"I went straight from Billy's inquisition to the shop, and my sweats needed to be burned. Sandy picked these out for me."

"Including the shoes?"

She sighed. "Yes."

"Not your style. Not any of it."

"Thanks for making me feel better." Suddenly, she laughed. "Snip, snipe. Will you listen to us?"

He smiled faintly. "You look sexy in that stuff. Might as well admit it. But it's too obvious."

Emma felt very warm.

"You didn't say when you're movin'," he said.

"That's because I don't know. We'll have to see. I may split my time between Orville's house and Mom and Dad's."

"Why do you call it Orville's house?"

"Because it is."

"O-kay."

"Do you have children?"

"Unfortunately not," he said.

Emma's stomach turned over. Every one of her reactions was way off base.

He checked around to be sure they were completely alone. "My wife didn't do anythin' wrong. She married someone in finance, not an Army Ranger. She made it through the first tour. I knew the second one had to be my last, but she needs life around her. She's vibrant." Sliding even deeper in the chair, he looked like a human tarantula—an attractive one. "She met someone else. Just as well, because she wouldn't have understood it when I wouldn't go back to tradin' and coachin'."

"She's an idiot," Emma said, and slapped a hand over her mouth.

Finn fought down a laugh and looked at Emma. Her blush looked as if it might burn. "Thanks for that vote of confidence." He picked up an oatmeal cookie. "I do have some questions of my own in this town. About somethn' personal. Somethn' that's probably as much responsible for bringing me back here as anythin'. With what's come up with Denise, I feel my own interests have to wait, though. Most of all, you take precedence, as long as you need me."

She didn't know what to say.

"Hey," he said. "Don't look like that. You don't have to be uncomfortable because an old friend wants to make sure you're okay. You'd do the same if I needed help."

She could tell him she was fine and didn't need anyone's help, but it would be a lie. "You've got troubles of your own," she told him. "Can I help you?"

He held her hand and squeezed. "If you'll listen to me ramblin' from time to time, it would be a big help. I figure I'll be doing a lot of that, but not until we're sure Denise's killing wasn't the first of a string." When he looked into her eyes, she couldn't turn away.

She removed her hand, and he sighed. Emma punched his arm lightly. "Say the word, Finn, and I'll be there for you. You've been too good to me."

"Emma." He turned in his seat. "I've batted this around and changed my mind a dozen times, but if I don't say what I think and something happens, I'll never forgive myself."

The tone of his voice, what he said, turned her ice-cold.

"Don't look like that," he said. "I'm going to make sure you're okay."

He scared her. "You think I'm really at risk."

Finn frowned.

"Because of the cowboy," she said. "Finn, I think the guy's a joker. He hasn't done anything but play games, I don't think he ever will."

He stood up, put money on the table and grabbed Emma

by the elbow. "How can you pretend this is nothing? They don't have anyone in custody. Why can't the killer be the cowboy, as you call him?"

"I just don't think he is. I think there are two different men."

"Let's get outside." He walked with her outside and into the slanting rain. They ran to her SUV, and she got in. He stood with water beating on top of his head, streaming down his face. He refused to get in beside her. "I'm not going to varnish this, but I want you to answer me one more time. Do you believe you're safe, that you're not in any danger?"

Emma looked at her hands in her lap. As nonchalantly as she could, she put the envelope on the seat beside her with her purse on top. "Yes," she said honestly. "But I'm in a bigger mess than you know, and I won't involve you more than I have already."

"Emma! Look at me."

She shook her head.

"For God's sake, don't close me out."

"Look, I promise I'll let you know if I need help. We've got time to see if something else happens." She sounded crazy even to herself, but her life was turning crazy. "I've got to believe someone had a vendetta against Denise. It makes sense that she was a threat to someone."

"And the guy who sneaked into your house and left you ten grand? And hung around to prove how easy it was for him to be there whenever he wanted to?"

"Billy knows now. He'll take care of it." She wanted to be alone, to scream and scream. If she tried to contact her folks, they would tell her to come to them. But she was thirty-two, and they'd never wanted her to marry Orville. They thought she couldn't take care of herself and had made bad decisions.

Finn stuck his hands in the pockets of his jeans and raised his face to the sky. He swallowed rainwater that ran into his mouth. "And I'm just one more stranger," he said, sounding bitter. "For all you know, I'm the cowboy. Wouldn't have been hard for me to put the smoke bomb in my truck. Want to get Billy and his sidekicks to look around my place for a white Stetson?"

"It wasn't you." She sniffed, dragged air into a sore throat. "He wasn't as big as you, and even if he was, you would never do a thing like that. Finn…" She mustn't say things she would regret later.

"There's always the chance that I've got the biggest syringe you ever saw somewhere at my place. Could be under my bed. Billy would check for you."

"What are you sayin'? Why would you tell me that?"

"Because Denise died of a lethal injection. That's what I had to tell you. And she was raped."

12

"*Cher,* you know how I feel," Angela said. "If one of you believes we can help someone, that's good enough for me. I think you should bring Eileen Moggeridge with you next time, Emma. Are we all agreed?" She looked around the room.

"Yes, bring Eileen," the others murmured, crowding close to rub her back and shoulders, her arms, to stroke her hair. "Poor Emma."

Suky-Jo, who made the silk, satin and brocade sachets Emma and Sandy sold at Poke Around, took a sky-blue satin pillow from a paper bag. She gave it to Emma and said, "Rub your hands over it and the lavender smell will get more intense. Use it when you're anxious or just testy. Take a nap and put it over your eyes. I made it for you, and put a few extra bits and pieces in there." She winked a cheerful brown eye.

"Now," Angela said, "this is our poor dear Emma's night. We're all here to support her and bring her through her time of trouble."

Irritated, Emma turned to her benefactor. "You are a sweet lady, a tower of strength in hard times, but please don't talk as if I'm about to be thrown in jail for credit card fraud. I should think we all need some reassurance at a time like this. We've all lost Denise." She had intended to tell them how their friend died, but couldn't do it.

Holly Chandall's mouth made an elongated O. "Emma, if you needed money, you could have come to me. It's not so easy for me to get any out of Harold, but I'd have managed to do it from my business before the money went into the bank."

Emma peered at her, then smiled. "Holly, the credit card thing was only a joke."

"Oh." Holly cheered up immediately.

Even on an evening like this, when Emma had accepted that she hated her husband and was no longer sure who she could trust, Holly's innocence could still make her smile.

"Forgive me, Emma. I hardly know what to say for the best." Angela nodded and smiled gently. "But this is so like you. Always thinking of others first. Very well. Let's sign up, then, ladies. The book is by my chaise. If you don't have anything pressing and you can give someone else your time just for this gathering, that would be so sweet. Did you want to have new tips, too, Emma, or not? Probably not, dear."

"Absolutely we want tips, too," Emma said. "Let's do whatever makes us feel good and supported. You've taught us well, Angela. A one-way conversation is like clappin' with one hand, that's what you've said."

"You have, Angela," Holly Chandall said. "I've got a group butt-buster exercise you won't believe. But I'll wait my turn."

"Peace is power, then, my friends," Angela said, holding out her arms and letting the full sleeves of her pink silk tunic flow. Each of them, dressed in their comfortable pink tunics, joined hands. Tonight they were seven, with Angela and Emma, and every woman present was dear to Emma. Angela said, "Denise, we miss you. You're here with us, but we can't hold you, and that makes our hearts empty. Tonight we celebrate you." Her pale, ageless face, her deep blue eyes, grew still, and as Emma looked around the circle, she held her breath at the weight of sadness among them.

Angela had not always lived in Pointe Judah, but she'd been there when Emma came home from New Orleans to be married. She remembered her mother saying that Angela had moved there from Georgia in search of a quiet place where she could mend after losing her husband. She never mentioned her own grave losses but poured herself into helping others.

Slowly they released hands and went to put their names in the book. The room, used only for Secrets meetings, had been built onto the back of Angela's house. She rented John's second house and had poured a lot of money into the place, considering it wasn't hers. Each member had a chaise, and these circled a deeply sunken pool the size of a very large hot tub. They called this pink-tiled room, with its soaring ceiling, The Chamber, and didn't always go there. Often they met in a much smaller, cozier room inside the house, especially when the reason for being together was for simple sharing and exchanging ideas. Emma would have preferred to be there this evening.

"We'll start with you, Emma," Angela said when they were settled. "If there's time left over, we'll move to other things."

Emma found she only wanted to rest, to be quiet. Several formal stands of white lilies stood about, and the funereal scent brought her mood lower. Her friends didn't seem inclined to talk, either, and avoided her eyes whenever she glanced at one of them.

"I have to divorce Orville," Emma blurted out. "Now. Not *now* now, but soon, as soon as I can do it without makin' myself a target for the kind of viciousness he's capable of. I have a lawyer." She stopped speaking, her lips parted, her heart pounding. "He's the one Betty used. Over in Toussaint."

"Congratulations," Frances said, her beaded braids clicking together as she tossed her head. "I am so happy for you. I would never have pushed you, mind, but you know how I feel. That is not a good man, not good at all. I reckon the night he was born someone fed his mama bat droppings and messed him up somethin' awful. Why do you have to wait? Just go, girl."

"I have to make sure I protect myself," Emma said, feeling a little ashamed for sounding tentative. "My husband is an ambitious man. He's completely wrapped up in politics and becoming more important. I think he's got a chance to become state governor, and if he does, he'll be too busy and full of himself to hound me. On the other hand, an immediate divorce could hamper his expectations."

Holly snorted. "It sure could if it comes out he's a sneaky, vicious abuser."

"You'll have to be careful," Sandy said. She stood up, stripped off her tunic and sat unselfconsciously on the edge of the pool. There was nothing amusing about her big breasts or small waist, or the flare of her firm hips. "Would the jets make too much noise?" she said.

Angela flipped a switch, setting water the color of creme de menthe into almost silent motion.

"Wait, wait!" Lynnette, who loved her nail and hair salon—Frances was the star hairdresser there—had never met a product she didn't like at the beauty supply house. She rushed forward with a big white plastic tub, wrestled the top off, peeled back a foil safety seal and dug out a handful of orange goop. "This is going to make your flesh perk up and dance," she said. "It says it takes ten years off your age, pops out cellulite dimples and makes those nipples take another look at the sky—and I'm tellin' you, girlfriends, my nipples been lookin' at my belly for years."

The first club members had met at Lynnette's salon when Angela had ventured forth to buy hair spray.

Smothered titters went through the members. Angela knelt

beside Suky-Jo and helped smooth the miracle mud over Sandy. Once finished, she held up her hands and said, "Next? Emma?"

"Not yet." She noted Denise's demise had slipped into the background quite quickly at the prospect of perky nipples, which was fine. She just loved being there with all of them. And she would not think about the disaster her life had become until she had to.

Suky-Jo whipped off her voluminous tunic and sat with an expression of bliss on her face while Sandy and Angela ministered to her ample figure.

"I think we should talk about Emma's divorce," Holly said. She never had learned to be subtle. "Threaten him, Emma. Tell him you'll put up billboards with pictures of him in his shorts with his tummy hangin' over."

"I should never have mentioned that," Emma said, and meant it fervently. She couldn't completely forget that Sandy might have divided loyalties and it was too late to take back what had been said. "What I have to figure out is how to get started without Orville knowin'."

"Why?" Frances said. "Why are you tryin' to make things easier for that no good…mmm-mmm, I gotta watch my mouth."

"I don't want to make it easier for him." Emma watched for Sandy's reaction. "For once, I'm thinkin' about myself. As soon as he finds out, he'll have his lawyer buddies goin' to town on me. I'll get dragged in for lectures on how it's my duty to make my marriage work. Then, when that doesn't work, it'll be the next world war. I can live at my parents' for a few months, and I intend to start getting comfortable there right away, but I've got to make ends meet, so I want enough time to get a bit more by me. I'm not going to drag things out, just figure out how to support myself."

The only sound for several moments was the faint whir of the pool jets.

"I've got money," Sandy said. "I've certainly got enough to keep you till you get on your feet."

Relieved, Emma went to hug Sandy but looked at the orange frosting and changed her mind. "Thank you, doll. But no thank you. This one I have to do on my own. And can you imagine what Carl would have to say about you supporting his partner's runaway wife?"

"Let's get practical," Frances said. She began applying her own gravity-defying elixir, not that Frances's lovely body needed any help. "Living at home is good. Your folks will like that. Next you need a job. You do need a job, don't you?"

"Oh, yes."

"What can you do?" Suky-Jo asked. "Apart from... Why are we having this conversation? Will someone explain that? You'll keep on at the shop."

Emma shook her head slowly and deliberately avoided looking at the growing number of slimy women by the pool. "The lease is in Orville's name. I didn't have the money to rent it myself."

"When's the lease up?" Angela asked.

"About a month."

"Fine, so you tell Orville you're giving up the shop, so he can cancel the lease, and then we'll rent it for you until you've got your feet under you."

"Why do I keep crying all the time?" Emma said, her voice squeaking. "It breaks my heart to give up the shop, but I have to make it on my own this time. I'm going to get a job, any old job to begin with. And when I can, I'm goin' back to school to study music again."

Frances stood still, her eyes wide in the middle of her mudded face. "I didn't know you studied music. You gonna teach?"

"I was a marketing major with a minor in music. How's

that for a combination? I've always wanted to finish my degree, only just in music now. But what I really think I want is to find someone to let me play jazz piano for a livin'."

"Jazz piano? Oh, my." Frances capered and was a sight to behold. "Do you know what this one-horse town ain't got? *Music,* that's what. Strangest thing I ever did see, and I never even knew I missed it till I went out of Pointe Judah."

"There's a jukebox at Buzz's," Lynnette reminded her. "And a band comes over for festival time."

"There's a piano at Buzz's, too," Frances said, grinning with enthusiasm. "And there's one at Ona's Out Back. I'll just bet my tunnel to paradise those folks would love to hire you."

The assembly groaned at Frances's choice of words.

"Well?" Frances balanced her slippery fists on her hips. "Don't y'all think so, too?"

"Sounds possible to me," Sandy said.

"Okay," Suky-Jo hollered. "Wash off. I forgot to warn you how it burns off your skin if it stays on a second too long." She winked at Emma, held her nose and cannon-balled into the middle of the pool.

Screeches followed. The women cavorted, scraping the stuff off one another until they dissolved into a tickling, giggling mess and the pool looked like someone had mixed orange sherbert punch in there.

"Orville knows everyone in Pointe Judah," Angela said to Emma suddenly. "You realize that, don't you?"

"Oh, yes, I do. What I don't know is how many people would listen to him if he told them not to hire me. They wouldn't have to tell me that's why they didn't want me, all they'd have to do is say the position's already filled, or they've decided not to hire after all."

"Folks here think your husband's a fine, upstanding man." Angela gazed at the women in the pool. "A lot of folks do, anyway. You've got friends here who believe every word you tell them, but how do you think someone like Lobelia Forestier would react if you talked negatively about the mayor?"

"That woman's an idiot." Emma gritted her teeth in frustration. "Why should I have to care what people think? It's not their business."

"You don't have to care if you intend to go somewhere else."

With her feet, Emma made circles in water splashed from the pool. "I've had it!" Inside, she seemed to break apart. "I like this 'one-horse town,' as Frances calls it. I was born here and grew up here. Eventually my parents will come back and settle down here. I don't know when or if I'll go somewhere else—or for how long—but I'm darned if Orville Lachance is driving me out. Let *him* go, if he wants to."

"That's the spirit." Angela held out a hand, and Emma went to hold it. She bent to hug the other woman, and they started to laugh.

Angela smelled faintly of camphor, and up close, she looked much older. Emma wondered how often the woman washed the white-blond hair that often didn't look as if she combed it to the roots. Emma looked away and didn't like herself for being so critical.

"D'you know, Mrs. Lachance, that man manages to make people think they have to do what he wants, but all a person's got to do is refuse," Angela said. "I would like to be there when you tell him you're leaving."

Holly climbed from the pool and went directly to the showers. Within minutes she was back, wrapped in a short terry robe and with a towel around her auburn hair. She pulled her chaise close to the two other women and stretched out. "I do believe we come here to behave like a bunch of children," she said. "I never did do anythin' like that when I was a child."

"Exactly," Angela said. "We're setting ourselves free. I'm

not the frolic in the pool type, but I'm glad for those of you who are. You're making your souls whole."

A whiff of the lilies reached Emma, and she said, "Did you order all those flowers, Angela?"

"Heavens, no. They've been sent by kind folks who know we'll be suffering over Denise. Patrick Damalis sent the biggest arrangement. Sadie and Sam. Buzz, of all people. And the folks at the Bayou Funeral Home. There's one from Rusty Barnes, although I think that poor, sad man could use his own bouquet. Sandy's husband, bless his kind heart, and John Sims. He must have ordered his right before he had to leave town. And I call that real nice of him to remember. I do think I'd rather they'd all waited for the funeral, though, if you know what I mean."

She got a chorus of agreement.

"John left?" Sandy said, smiling. "Isn't he the travelin' man?"

"Nice thing is, he's been at his job long enough he always has appointments, none of that nasty cold calling. I don't know what I'd do without that man." Angela sighed, raising her considerable bosom. "Between him and my Mrs. Merryfield, I usually don't have to worry about much. You know I have a little problem with going outside."

"I know how difficult it is for you," Emma said. "Thank you for makin' the effort to come to my house last night."

Angela's eyes turned hard. "I would do anything for you, no matter what it cost me. I don't think your husband was too pleased."

"I apologize for him," Emma said. A mounting tension climbed her muscles. "John is a good man. He's so sweet to get your groceries in and always check on you. I think he'd help anyone he could. Reminds me of Rusty Barnes. He's like that, too. Makes you wonder that two good men like that are all on their own. Rusty's never been married. I don't know about John."

"I think he may have been once." Angela gave a wry smile. "It's something I feel about him sometimes."

Suky-Jo came from the shower in time to hear the last part of the conversation. "Rusty loved Denise. I don't know if he'll ever get over it." She squeezed her eyes shut, and tears slithered down her cheeks.

Sandy hopped up and hugged her. "Shh. There, there. We're all going to be crying when we least expect it for weeks, I should think."

"I wanted to ask you somethin'," Holly said. The calm she'd shown so recently disappeared, to be replaced by the restless movement of her hands that they'd all come to recognize. Holly wanted to do something, and she didn't think her husband would approve. There wasn't much Harold Chandall approved of.

"We're all ears," Emma said. She returned to her chaise.

Holly turned very pink. "I want to thank you for hiring me to do your party."

"Who else would I hire?" Emma said lightly. "Who else can do the kind of job you do? I met Annie Duhon today—meant to say that. She's a sweet thing."

"She's going to help me branch out a bit," Holly said. "She went to cooking school, and she's accomplished. Anyway, I've got to expand my business, because I've made a decision, too. I'm going to divorce Harold."

Emma looked at Angela and saw a rare pucker on her forehead.

"You do think it's a good idea, don't you?" Holly said. "All he wants me for is to cook his meals and wash his clothes and service him in bed. He gets in there and climbs on top of me, does his thing and climbs off. I swear, ten seconds and he's snorin'. Never says a word. It's almost like he's ashamed of touchin' me."

"I think we'd better be careful how this is done," Angela

said. "If two of you—Secrets members, that is—up and divorce your husbands without warning and at the same time, it could give ammunition to those just looking for a way to prove we're a bad influence on women here."

"You're right," Holly said quickly. "I should have thought of that, but you know how I am. I just rush off in all directions. I'll wait a few months."

"Hold it right there," Emma said. "You're backing off much too fast, and that's because you're scared to follow through. I don't blame you. I'm scared, too."

"You don't think I've got a point, *cher?*" Angela said, sounding the faintest bit peeved, Emma thought.

"Maybe." Emma scooted to the bottom of her chaise and pulled one of Holly's feet onto her lap. She started a firm massage, hitting the reflexology points hard enough to make Holly jump. It wasn't news that Harold Chandall didn't have an imagination.

"Holly," Emma said, "what you do isn't tied to what I do. It'll be nice to hold each other up, though. I don't want you waiting for me before you deal with your life. If you're ready, do it. I'm hoping the party I've told Orville I'll host in about two weeks will be a help. If he gets a lot of positive attention and support he won't care... I'm not even foolin' myself here, am I? He'll go mad, but I'm doin' it anyway. The day after the party, I'm goin' job huntin'."

"Good for you," Angela said. "You don't think—no, he wouldn't do anything to *really* hurt you."

"He might try," Emma said. "He'll wipe mud all over my reputation, that's for sure." She wanted to say she didn't care, but she did.

Holly let out a loud breath. "I'd like to see him try. Everybody in this town knows your character, Emma, and it's beyond reproach."

"Thank you," Emma said.

"Hey," Holly said, animated again. "I'm workin' toward full service event plannin'. You could play at parties and weddings and so on. I could put together a trio or a quartet. There's some talented people in this town, and like Frances says, we don't hear enough music."

Emma stopped herself from scoffing. "You think it might work?"

"I surely do."

"Okay, then. If you ever need someone, call on me."

"This is great," Sandy said. "Only I'm not giving up on Poke Around, so it looks like you're goin' to have a busy life, Emma."

"Holly," Angela said, "do you think Harold would ever get violent?"

"No!" Holly shook her head. "He's not a bad man, he just doesn't know how to love someone, is all. He loves rice because it's made him rich. That's as close as he gets to emotion."

Emma chuckled before she could stop herself, and she and Holly laughed together.

"Bun buster!" Holly yelled. "C'mon. Anyone still in the shower, get out here."

"I'm too tired for exercisin'," Sandy said. "I feel like I got ironed with one of them old flat irons like my grandma used."

"Didn't get you very flat," Frances said.

At a run, Holly pulled back the chaises and sat herself on the pink stone.

"Ow," Frances said. "Isn't that cold?"

"Get behind me," was all she got out of Holly. "Close. A leg each side of me, so I can hold on to your ankles."

"I'm not doin' that," Frances complained. "I'll get my panties wet."

"Won't be the first time," Sandy said, and Frances pretended to take her by the neck.

"C'mon," Holly called. "I'm freezin' my south pole off here."

"You don't have a south pole," Suky-Jo pointed out, but she knew better than to push Holly too far. She sat behind her, stretched a leg on either side of Holly's and held her around the waist. The rest followed suit, including Emma, who switched her tunic for a robe.

Angela watched, laughing aloud at the picture they must have made.

"Now," Holly said, "everyone lean to the left. *Up* on that bun."

Sniggering exploded while they tried to keep their balance.

Holly said, "Oh, yeah, one, two, three, roll on that right bun. *Feel* that fat squeeze?"

Back and forth they rocked, until Sandy, who didn't have much meat on that part of her anatomy, moaned for mercy.

"Step two," Holly announced. "A circuit of the pool. Everyone move your right leg forward, now your left. Right and left and bang those buns every time. Keep it up. Not so far to go."

"We've hardly started," Frances squeaked, but they continued on like a crazy caterpillar. The towels from their hair hit the floor, and faces grew red.

"Now," Holly said, sounding breathless, "modified pushups, just to give the upper body a workout."

Two or three pushups and they all lay on their backs, panting, too out of breath to laugh.

"Miz Angela!"

The booming voice of tiny Mrs. Merryfield sounded from the door to the room, and Angela said, "What is it?" in the irritable tone she saved for the woman who ran her house.

"Yep," Mrs. Merryfield said. "They all as decent as they likely to be. You come on in, boy, and set that down over there. On the safe."

No one but Mrs. Merryfield mentioned the brass safe Angela kept against one wall of the chamber and in which they assumed she kept her worldly wealth, since she didn't hold with banks. Mrs. Merryfield, who might be five feet tall in the high-heeled shoes she wore with stockings rolled down to her ankles, mentioned whatever she pleased. Her heavily made-up face and her carrot-red hair styled in finger waves reminiscent of the 1920s never varied. She wore shirt-waist dresses with skirts that didn't reach her tiny knobby knees.

Angela had stood up to stare toward the door with narrowed eyes. The members wrapped their robes around themselves and remained supine, mostly with their eyes closed, as if not being able to see anyone would mean no one could see them.

"Don't be shy," Angela said. "We could use a bit of masculine blood around these parts."

Emma sat up and made sure she was decent. A boy of about fifteen entered, carrying the biggest floral arrangement of all. To lilies had been added long stalks of pink gladiolus, and a large, white satin bow trailed streamers almost to the floor. Fortunately this tribute came in a huge crystal vase.

"Oh, my," Angela whispered reverently. "Our Denise surely was loved."

The boy held Emma's attention. No kid should be that gorgeous. He kept his eyes averted, but that didn't stop her from seeing they were large and dark, his brows perfectly arched and his mouth a crying waste on one so young. He'd started to fill out and must already be close to six feet. He tied his very black hair at the nape.

"Whoo-hoo," Sandy muttered. "Now some experienced woman should take that boy in hand. He needs to be carefully taught."

"Don't let him hear you," Emma said, quietly but firmly. "He's just a kid doin' an after-school job."

"Deliverin' for Fabulous Flowers," Sandy said, her chin raised to get the whole picture. "Now that's a cryin' shame. I think I'll see abut givin' him a job at Casa Viator. I need someone to put on my suntan cream."

"Is there a Mrs. Lachance here?" the kid said, his voice already a mellow tenor.

"That's me," Emma said, bouncing to her feet with an unpleasant sensation that she wouldn't like what she was getting. When she got closer to the boy she stopped and said, "Aaron? Aaron Moggeridge?"

"Yes, ma'am," he said clearly. The corners of his mouth turned up sharply, and he had dimples in his cheeks. In fact, he looked a whole lot like his uncle Finn.

"You are just like your uncle Finn," she said.

Aaron's smile widened.

Emma went first to her purse and took out some money. She popped it into Aaron's pocket, producing a pink tinge over his cheekbones, and pointed him toward the safe.

He set the vase there and backed away. "We had to go buy the vase," he said. "It's pretty."

"It is," she said. "You've had a lot of deliveries today." She looked around the room.

"Yes," he said. "Fred said he's never done this much business in a day, even for a wedding. Just about everybody with an account sent flowers."

Emma blinked, noticing the comment about accounts. "Lots of telephone orders?" she said.

"Every one of them," he said. "And all the same except yours. That came in later than the others. Shall I tell Uncle Finn you said hello?"

She didn't dare glance at her friends. "You do that. I expect you're off up there now."

"No, ma'am. School in the mornin'. But I'll tell him when I see him."

The boy left, and Emma made herself go close to the flowers. Rather than a sympathy card, the butterfly cutout read, "To the most beautiful woman in the world, from the man who can't live without her."

She backed away, sickened at Orville's display of false affection. Going from one display easel of lilies to another, she found every other card bore the same "With sympathy on the death of Denise." There was even one there from Orville with the same inscription.

Emma bowed her head. An awful blackness crowded into her mind, an anger beyond understanding. "Damn him," she whispered. "I owe him nothing."

"What is it?" Sandy asked, sounding anxious. "Emma?"

"I said I don't owe him anything. Mrs. Merryfield, is there a Dumpster outside?"

"There's one behind my place," Lynnette said. "That darn Lobelia Forestier says all businesses have to have a Dumpster. Says it's a health regulation, and a hefty price we pay for 'em, too, even if they are empty most of the time."

Emma picked up the vase Aaron had just delivered. "Would you mind if I throw these in there?"

"Of course not," Lynnette said, sounding uncertain.

"I'll take 'em," Mrs. Merryfield said. "I'll keep the vase, if you don't mind. Very nice that'll look in my room."

Without a word, Emma gave the flowers to the woman and was, as usual, amazed by her apparent strength. With her back straight and her heels clipping on the pink stone tiles, Mrs. Merryfield marched from the chamber.

"Why did you do that?" Suky-Jo said. "Orville's a snake, but he was trying to make peace. You…well, I don't know."

"She could have been a more generous person?" Angela suggested. "Is that what you were trying to say? I think Emma's given enough and she's had it."

Emma hurried toward the dressing rooms. "You bet I've

had enough. I've got every reason to be mad, and I don't know why I'm trying to act sensibly, but it's over. Don't ask me what I'm going to do, because I don't know, and I wouldn't tell you if I did."

"Emma," Frances said, her big eyes baleful. "Don't—"

"I've had it," Emma said, disappearing behind a curtain to put on her clothes. "I'm so mad my brain feels swollen. I've been betrayed and walked on, and he's still trying to pull my strings. If I had that Orville here right now, I'd tell him why he's going to suffer for what he's done to me. Just as well he's not. I'm going to plan this. It's going to put him through hell."

"Don't do anything without thinking it through," Angela said.

"Oh, I've thought it through," Emma said, hurrying from the dressing room, her shoes in one hand, her honey-colored hair standing out in shiny curls and color in her cheeks from her own emotion. "It's all very simple, really. One good turn deserves another."

13

Would he be in better shape if he'd killed the guy himself?

The sheet wound around his naked body and legs. Sweat coated him, burned his eyes, plastered his hair to his head. At least he was luckier than some poor bastards. He'd been in one too many battles, and it had messed him up, but he'd learned to cope, and the monster didn't show up as often as it used to.

What the hell. It hadn't been battle that messed him up, but his *friend*. What kind of madness made a man try to kill the one person who would have given his life for him anyway?

Finn tossed. The sounds, the old visuals, began to play in his mind.

"Get down and stay down!"

Damn, he couldn't get any lower.

A flashlight beam blasted across discarded burlap draped between knots of vines. The rebels had been here before them, and not so long ago, judging from the garbage left behind.

"Go on, Finn," Bo whispered into the earpiece Finn wore. "Push under that stuff. They're gonna see us like a fuckin' shadow show in here. I'm right behind you."

"Gotcha," Finn whispered back. Funny, but he couldn't feel Bo behind him like usual. But he was there. They were a team, a crack sniper team, and Bo was always there.

Stretched as flat as his body would allow, his fifty-caliber rifle on his back, pushing his pack with his left hand and praying it wouldn't be the one thing that caught the rebels' eyes, Finn inched forward.

God, keep the fuckin' snakes away—just this once.

He clamped his teeth together. Just as if he'd summoned it up, a cold, soft, spineless body slithered under his outstretched arm, vibrating ever so gently. Finn couldn't see the thing. All he could do was stay still.

Oh, Christ, help me. *It was big and taking its time. Waiting for the strike, Finn closed his eyes and pressed his face into the mess of slime and fallen vegetation beneath him. The snake slithered across the back of his head, a heavy sonofagun. He dared not make contact with Bo, not while he didn't know if the reptile had reared up, ready to whip its poisonous fork into any flesh it could find.*

Across his neck, the creature flowed.

Finn held his breath. From the weight, he could be toting an anaconda. The head tucked around his neck, under his chin, nuzzling...deciding if it would wrap him up like the filling in a great, big bun and squeeze him until blood popped from every orifice on his body. At least he would be dead before he was dinner—probably.

A scream burst inside Finn's chest and grew. He didn't hear it yet, but it would erupt, and the prehistoric beast would snap him up.

Slowly, caressing the skin it touched, the snake whispered over Finn's ear, retreated, pressed under the collar of his fatigues, began a sensuous probing down, down between his shoulder blades.

The intimate touch withdrew, oh, so slowly.

The head left his shirt, started over his back again, on top of his clothes this time. Slowly, slowly, the great snake trav-

eled over his torso as far as his hips, then headed away, still without a sound, until the weight and the disgust, but not the horror, completely left Finn.

The beam of light had shifted away, and for that he gave thanks.

"Watch out for a snake," he said into his mic. "Big sucker."

"Fuckin' well move," Bo said. "What's keepin' you?"

Finn smiled a little and crawled forward, under the burlap, using the curled fingertips of his right hand to get purchase, and still pushing the pack. He glanced back, searching for the sheen of Bo's mud-and-cork-smeared face.

"What's with you?" Bo said. "A little snake make you shit your diaper or what? We don't have time, buddy. We get them or they get us. Now get going."

Finn frowned but propelled himself forward, crablike, until he paused to adjust his night goggles and reached for another handful of roots.

Burning pain, a rage of agony, flared up his arm. His fingers extended and stiffened. Squeezing his eyes to clear them, he got his left hand on a pistol. His breath clicked in his throat, tears and sweat mingled, and he fought to stay conscious. The slightest turn of his head and he saw the glitter of a metal spike, driven through his right wrist and into the ground. There should be blood, oceans of it spurting. The stake must be sealing the wound so the bleeding was internal.

He felt warm wetness fill the ground under his palm and saw the blood at last, forced up between his fingers. What he didn't see was the enemy. Pistol in his good hand, he rose onto his right hip as far as he could without tearing at the metal in his wrist.

Nothing, not a soul. "Bo, I'm down."

Bo didn't answer.

"*I'm down*," *Finn repeated. "Can't get up. Shit, I'm bleedin'.*"

"*Put your face down,*" *Bo said at last. "Keep still while I make sure the bastard's gone.*"

Finn rested the side of his helmet on his outstretched arm and kept his grip on the pistol.

Life moved into his sight. Big, green and menacing, a figure rushed at him, a figure dressed like he was and holding a machete in both hands.

He got one shot off. Wide.

The machete flashed through the night, and Finn knew where it was intended to strike and what it would sever. Another shot went wild.

"*Stop! Bo, for God's sake, stop, you freakin' idiot.*" *A battalion commander's familiar voice blasted in Finn's ear.*

A noise, half scream, half sob, broke over him. Another shot sounded. And Finn felt himself torn apart. A heavy thud moved the ground in front of him.

His buddy, his lifeline when everything else failed, fell like a tree, his face inches from Finn's. A hole between Bo's open, flat eyes showed where someone's bullet had felled him. Blood ran from his nose and mouth.

The lights went out.

Shaking, breathing through his open mouth, Finn dragged himself to sit up in the bed. He was all the way out of sleep, not that he'd rested well. He would have laughed if the old dead ache weren't back in his hand, and if the scars on his back and arms, the ones Bo made when he missed Finn's neck with the machete, didn't itch and throb and bunch together as if fingers were twisting the welts.

He blinked at the ceiling, where shadows of oak leaves outside the window swept to and fro hard in the wind that moaned and slashed at the house. Finn hadn't bothered to close the curtains, and he saw how rain came sideways at the glass. The clattering sounded like handfuls of ground grit.

Months had passed since the last time that night had come to him so clearly. Why now? Because he'd been around death again and expected—no, feared—there would be more?

Dammit, he was a big boy. He'd returned to Pointe Judah for a number of reasons, one of which he hadn't discussed with anyone. Sooner or later he would have to or he would never find out the truth about his father.

A shower sounded good, not that the relief would last long on this steaming night.

Something fell outside. He heard the sound, like a branch hitting the wall or a door. Tomorrow he would be cleaning up around here.

Tearing at the sheet, he freed himself and sat on the edge of the bed with his head in his hands. The monkey had climbed on his back again.

More debris smacked at an outside wall. Finn shook his head, went into the bathroom and stood with cold water sluicing down on him. It felt like heaven.

He still liked this house where his parents had been so happy, and had made their kids feel safe and carefree. How long Finn would stay depended on how things worked out. He'd made some moves on a real estate deal. Thinking about it, he grinned. His competition was Orville Lachance, but the owner had been an old friend of Tom Duhon's and didn't like Lachance much. If the deal went through…and if there was something else to hold him, he might stay for a long time, even for good.

A big white Egyptian cotton towel awaited him when he stepped out of the shower, and he punished his skin with it, enjoying every moment.

He thought of his sister, and his good mood sagged. Moggeridge hadn't been home or made contact since Finn arrived back, but Eileen said the man just showed up when he felt like it, stayed a few days, then ducked out to spend the rest of his time off in New Orleans or wherever he could do what he liked best: drink and spread himself around the whores, any whores.

Back in the bedroom, Finn thought about what he would do next. Definitely not get back into bed and wait for another rerun of his most hated movie.

He pulled on jeans, and went along the landing and downstairs. By the time he hit the kitchen, lightning had started slicing the sky again…like spikes heading down. Unconsciously, he held his wrist. Nobody had ever figured out why Bo tried to kill him. Their commanding officer, who'd pulled the trigger and saved Finn's life that night, reckoned it was because everyone knew Finn was the best Ranger they had, and Bo couldn't take being second best anymore.

Finn didn't believe that. Bo had snapped, nothing more sinister than that.

But sometimes, on nights like this one, when the memories were all so clear, Finn wondered again if the devils that hung around would be satisfied if he'd made that hole between the other man's eyes himself.

The rat-tat-tat he heard had to be the screen on the front door, banging in the wind. He turned back, and went to open the front door and stop the noise.

He only opened the door a crack and managed to snag the flapping screen. Pulling it shut was easy enough. Frowning, he peered at the catch, which he could see by the yellowing bulb outside. A darn good catch. Tom Duhon never did anything halfway or used cheap stuff. Finn remembered closing that screen tight and hearing the latch click home before he went to bed.

The wind was strong; it could have caught the thing and smacked it open.

He shut himself in again. The wind roared now.

Finn waited—in the dark, which was his habit. He'd learned that he had the advantage in the dark. The screen door didn't fly open again.

Slowly, he approached the kitchen. Sometimes he should remind himself that he was just a man; regardless of his training and experience, he was human and could get jumpy.

At the foot of the stairs, opposite what had been his mother's favorite room because of all the sun that came in, a passageway led to a side door. When they were kids, he and Eileen used that so they could go straight into the laundry room and get rid of any mud.

Finn started to walk across the passage to get to the kitchen. He changed his mind, without knowing why, and hung back. Crouching, the back of his head against the wall, he slowly rolled his face until he could just see the side door. Then he knew what had stopped him. Once again the screen was open, and it allowed a grayish pall to penetrate the window.

So the wind was knocking the old house around. It could take it even if he couldn't.

A face, pressed to the window, showed white and feature-less—some sort of cap pulled over the ears. He felt his muscles harden, felt the slight smile that came with the anticipation of danger.

"Bring it on," he murmured. "I was feelin' lonely. Come on in and entertain me."

The face moved away, to the right, toward the back of the house. He could go wait at the kitchen door or follow the creep from the side. The side approach appealed more.

On the balls of his bare feet, Finn slipped along the wall, reached the door and released the bolt with the silent care of a man who knew what he was doing. He turned the handle and opened it gently inward. This joker didn't believe in shutting screens after him. Finn thanked his own attention to detail for the oiled hinges and used two fingers to push himself just enough space to peer to the right.

His quarry had only gone a few feet and stood huddled to the wall, bent over and unmoving.

Finn took three steps and wrapped his arms around the man from behind. He clamped a big hand over the guy's face, ignored the kicking heels that connected with his shins, and made sure there wasn't a gun.

He spun the intruder around and slammed him against the wall so hard the closest window rattled. "You've got about ten seconds to tell me your name and what the hell you think you're doin.... Aw, hell. Emma." He continued to hold her against the wall, but only to make sure she didn't do what she was trying to do: collapse on the ground.

14

"It's my fault," she said. If she ever felt normal again, she would be amazed. "I was comin' to see you, then I lost my nerve and spent ages fussin' about it. Then I decided I *would* stop here on my way up the road."

"Inside," he said, half dragging her. "What the hell are you doin' walkin' around in a storm like this? Didn't anyone tell you not to be outside and under trees in electrical storms?" Some people didn't have the sense they'd been born with, and tonight he was in no mood for fools.

Unceremoniously propelled into a small, dark passageway, the one she'd tried to look into, Emma quelled an impulse to tell him to drop dead. It was his house, and she'd probably unnerved him by walking around the outside.

"What time is it?" he asked. He shoved his gun into the waist of his jeans, noting that Emma didn't seem surprised to see it this time.

"I don't know," she said. Rain sluiced from her coat onto the floor. "One in the mornin', maybe. I went to Orville's house and got a few things before comin' up here to go to Mom and Dad's. Then I knew I had to talk to you."

"I'm flattered." What was it with him tonight? He couldn't even manage to be civil.

She didn't know if she liked the way he'd said that. "I decided to do it much earlier, while I was at Secrets, but then I lost my nerve."

"So you already said. I must be pretty scary." Truth was, he wanted her to believe in him. "There hasn't been time for the locks to be fixed up there at your folks' place, and I surely haven't closed that pantry wall the way it needs to be."

"I'm not afraid to be there now I know to be real careful." And now she had her Bobcat in her bag. This was the first time she'd taken the weapon from its hiding place since she'd last fired it at a range.

It made her legs wobble just thinking about it.

Finn didn't answer, just stared at her, and for a sickening moment she feared he could see through her coat and bag to the gun.

"Look," she said with a conciliatory smile, "we're both still breathin', so how about givin' me a break, and I'll go get in my Lexus and not bother you again?"

"Where's the Lexus?" He hadn't seen it from the front door.

"Up by the road. Your driveway is steep, so I thought…oh, forget it. I didn't think a thing through. We're not all as together as you are, Finn Duhon."

He actually laughed, and that made her angry. "Glad to amuse you," she said. "Now, if you'll excuse me…"

Letting her go was the last thing he intended to do. "No way."

"I need to leave," she said, and all her carefully gathered courage turned to futile anger. "You've got to know I wouldn't come if I had anyone else to turn to."

Ouch. "I thought you had your friends at Secrets?"

"Damn, you're flip," she said. "But I've got the message. I need to do a lot more thinkin' before I act on anythin'. And I've got to learn how to judge character better. I'm mortified, and I hope that makes you happy. No, I don't. I hope you'll feel like a heel when I'm gone."

He already did.

They stood in that little passageway with her back against a wall—again—and him, half-naked and overpowering, glaring down at her from whatever ridiculous height he was. "Why don't you pick on someone your own size?" she said, and could have kicked herself for saying something so idiotic. "That sounded stupid. I'm not exactly feelin' cool-headed, but you've got no call to treat me like a criminal with designs on sneakin' in and jumpin' you."

He gave her enough time to consider what she'd just said.

"I'm not havin' a good night," he said, when he figured the innuendo had gone over her head. But he stepped away. Not much, but a little. "Why did you come, Emma? I shouldn't be givin' you a hard time just because I'm havin' one."

"Like lonely people sometimes do, I've read more into our brief relationship than I should have," she told him. "A couple of days' acquaintance and I'm here to drop my problems in your lap. So I'm the fool. Can we forget it?"

"How much more do you think you read into the relationship than there really is?" he said, and that tone was in his voice, the lower timbre that went with sexual suggestion. "Could be you've got the situation just right, couldn't it?"

She crossed her arms over the voluminous raincoat she wore, with her tote bag safely dry beneath. Typical. Was there a man anywhere who didn't find a sexy hint in almost anything a woman said? "I took you for someone I could call a friend. I thought I could maybe turn to you because I've got a big decision to make and you'd try to help me decide what to do without making me feel inadequate."

He found and disentangled one of her hands. "C'mon. I'm havin' a brandy, how about you?" He was glad when she allowed herself to be led.

"A little bit would be nice."

He took her into a room furnished with comfortable-looking chintz chairs and a couch, and furniture that would be highly polished if it got a good dusting. "Let me take your coat." She unbuttoned the navy trench coat and turned for him to lift it from her shoulders. He popped the woolen hat from her head and began to lift her heavy tote bag, but she stopped him and took it off herself.

Seeing her here in this house Finn still thought of as home felt good. Too bad he was such a jerk that he'd probably alienated her big-time. She'd caught him seriously tired and seriously off guard, and he hadn't recovered fast enough.

Emma smiled and envisioned herself in wrinkled jeans and a T-shirt, and with her hair in flattened-out waves. Lovely. "Everyone at Secrets will be very happy to see Eileen," she said. "I asked, and they were real enthusiastic."

"You were nice to do that for Eileen," he said. But she was *too* nice for him. "I hope she gets a kick out of bein' there with you."

"It is a lot of fun sometimes," Emma said, sucking in her bottom lip. "I'd be embarrassed for folks on the outside to see the way we cut up, but it's good for us. You should have seen Holly Chandall's group butt buster exercise—whooee, I'm still sore."

"Mmm." Finn grinned. "I'll bet that would be worth seein'. Invite me over next time you decide to practice."

"Dream on, you Peepin' Tom."

"Aw, honey, I don't intend to peep. I was thinkin' of walkin' right in and takin' a ringside seat."

They both laughed, and even a little silly banter felt good.

Emma remembered Aaron. "Your nephew delivered some flowers earlier," she said. "To Angela's place. He's a nice boy. He really looks like you."

"He looks like my father," Finn said. A little twist of the

stomach reminded him—again—how little he'd done toward getting at the truth about his father's death.

He set Emma's things aside and poured two brandies from one of several bottles on a brass inlaid trolley. "Sit down wherever looks good," he said, and when she did, he gave her a glass.

Just the smell of the brandy made her giddy, in a nice way. She noticed Finn had a way of turning his left side away some. It wouldn't be possible to miss seeing at least parts of a vicious scar across his back and shoulders, but he obviously didn't want to make anything of it.

Emma felt certain that if he wasn't hot—which he clearly was—he would cover up.

Finn kicked a big upholstered footstool close to her legs and sat down. "First, I *am* your friend. I know that strictly speaking we haven't done any talkin' until the last few days. But I'd like to point out that you and I have shared more in that time than a lot of people do in a lifetime. We've had a chance to see each other at our best and worst. More or less."

"I guess," she said, but she didn't sound convinced.

"You can come to me when you need someone to listen. Any old time, Emma. And I won't laugh and try to sway you when I shouldn't—not much, anyway." He chuckled. "This is kinda funny. I meant what I said when I talked about watching you in school. You were the blond, brainy princess who didn't seem to need anyone. I wanted you to need me, or at least to talk to me, but back then I didn't have the guts to approach you. I wanted to carry your books and all that dumb stuff."

"You're old-fashioned." She ducked her head. "I think kids had quit doing that even then, and I'd probably have run away if you'd tried. But I still wish you had."

All the time he talked, she watched his mouth, and when

he stopped, she looked at his eyes. At close quarters, his naked torso gleamed faintly. The black hair on his chest looked soft, sleek, and she needed willpower not to stare at his defined abs. Finn had shoulders that…he really had shoulders.

One thing a smart woman who had decided to divorce her husband didn't do was forget her vulnerability. And she didn't put herself in any positions where she would give her soon to be ex-spouse ammunition against her. She had to be careful not to misread signals from a man like Finn, who made it too easy to want him, or to go too far, too fast.

So far she was batting zero in the common sense department.

But Finn did more than attract her, he reached her in some intimate way, intimate like the slightest touch was a caress—and she liked him a lot, too. None of it should be happening so soon.

He smiled, and she had no doubt he had noticed how she looked at him. "Know something?" he said. "Since the first moment I set eyes on you that afternoon, I've had this funny feelin' we were meant to meet again." He bowed his head and looked up at her. "That's not something for a man to say to a married woman. Forget I did."

"There wasn't anyone else I wanted to see tonight," she said quietly. "I know it's dangerous, but I'm drawn to you, and it's not the way you think."

He turned the corners of his mouth down. "Well, darn it, and I was gettin' hopeful."

"No, no, I didn't mean that the way it sounded."

"Good." He raised his eyebrows. "And why is it so terrible to be drawn to me?"

"I'll get this right yet," she told him. "I don't think you'll turn me away because I've got troubles. And I do have troubles. Nothin' so terrible in some ways, but I've got to make a decision, and I'm afraid of rushin' into somethin' without thinkin' about it enough first." She shifted forward until their legs touched. "Is it okay for me to come to you like this? Not exactly like this, but to come to you because I feel comfortable with you?" If being aware of every breath he took was comfortable. *You're in over your head, Emma.*

"It's really okay," he said. He had always wished he expressed himself better. "Sharin' in a death binds people together. It feels like you were put on a special watch, maybe given a trust. Don't feel awkward. Drink some of your brandy."

She did, and it burned wonderfully all the way down. Emma drank some more, and then she finished her glass.

Finn drained his own drink and poured two more for them. Emma noted that hers was very small!

"I just thought of something," she said. "It could be that it's because we don't have a history that I thought of coming to you. There's nothing personal to get in the way."

He would like to change that. Finn saw the way she rolled the glass between her palms. A thoughtful woman, could be too thoughtful. He wanted a chance to know her better, which meant, since she wasn't available, he still hadn't learned to choose women wisely.

She was going to do it, Emma thought. She was going to tell him all about Orville and what she'd decided to do, and ask if he could help her decide what steps to take and when. All she had to do was start talking, then show him the envelope.

"Just a moment," she said, getting out her cell phone. She called Orville's cell. Oh, he really hated it if she called him when he was at one of his meetings. She gave a little laugh but choked it off when he picked up. "Hi there, handsome," she said, looking into Finn's face. "I just wanted to thank you for thinkin' of me and sendin' the beautiful flowers. You know how I love red roses." If he said he had not sent her roses— or the hateful funeral flowers—she would be glad.

She could be a little bit tipsy already.

Orville took long enough to answer, long enough to back up her theory that he knew nothing about those flowers. Someone else had sent them and wanted her to think they were from him.

"Well, *cher,* I'm glad you're enjoyin' them. You should have fresh roses all the time. I'll have to think of it more often. Aren't you in bed yet?"

You are such a liar. "I'll be in bed real soon," she said, infuriated by the tears that filled her eyes. Pride, that was what those were all about. "I'm not at home, though. I brought my red roses with me and came up to my folks' place." She didn't want him looking around his house for roses she'd invented. "I'll be meetin' Holly Chandall and her assistant in the mornin'. That was quite a list you gave me. I hope they all come."

"They'll come," he said. "This state is ready for a change. It's ready for someone who can make things happen for the right people."

"If anyone knows what they're doin', it's you. I'll come by your office tomorrow and see how you're doin'." That was something else he detested, being interrupted at his office. He need not worry too much. If she made it there at all, it wouldn't be until after she had visited her lawyer in Toussaint. "I'll try to pop in and give you a progress report."

He cleared his throat. "Call first, would you, sweetheart?"

"Sure I'll call first. Night, Orville." She hung up without waiting for him to respond.

Finn waited, but when she remained quiet, he said, "What's up, Emma? I gathered you and your husband might not always get along, but you don't sound real with him. It's like you're actin'." He cleared his throat. "It's none of my business, and I shouldn't have asked. I happen to think marriages are supposed to be forever is all."

"Yours wasn't." She drank some more.

"No," he said quietly. "Not my idea."

"You're still in love with your wife?"

"Ex-wife. No. Are you in love with your husband? And if things are just a bit shaky right now, do you think you could make them better if you put in the effort? If he's sending you roses, he must be tryin' to make a go of things."

She turned her face away from him. "You don't understand. He didn't send any roses—he just thinks one of his flunkies must have done it for him."

He had the feeling there was more but she'd decided not to tell him.

"I'm sorry, Emma. This isn't what you came here for, is it? Tell me what's goin' on and I promise I'll be a good listener."

"I don't love Orville anymore," she said, frowning at Finn. "That doesn't mean it's your problem. I'm going to divorce him once I can figure out the timing. End of story."

He didn't analyze the way her announcement made him feel. "Not the end of the story," he said. "There's a lot more, isn't there?"

Emma jutted her chin. "Okay. Yes, there is. Thanks to my bein' such an innocent fool when I married him, I've made sure I'll be left with nothin'. Not even the shop. My father begged me not to sign that prenuptial agreement, but I wouldn't listen. So I've got to have a job. I'm not afraid of that, Finn—I'm even kind of excited about it—but I've got the worst case of guilt you ever saw. Here's Orville, gettin' ready to run for statewide office, and I'm goin'…no. No, sir, *damn it all,* I don't owe that snake one thing. He's treated me like dirt, and I'm gettin' out before he convinces me I'm so worthless I get afraid to move at all. I already feel I'm paralyzed." Paralyzed but shaking.

Finn took her glass and set it aside with his own. "I'm listenin'."

"Finn," she said. "Everything in my life is upside down. Am I lookin' for attention from you because I haven't had much lately? Look at us here. We've hardly said a word about Denise. I'm afraid when I think about her, but she should be what's on my mind."

"She is on your mind. You have other things on your mind as well, is all. Sure you're afraid. So am I, and for the same reason. I want you safe. I want all the women in this town safe, and until they pick up the goon who did that to Denise, I'll be lookin' in all directions. Billy Meche's boys are all over town askin' questions. It isn't everyone who keeps hypodermics of Xanax and phenobarbital—and other stuff I can't remember—on hand."

"I can't understand why they're not getting any breaks," Emma said. "They haven't even found any of Denise's clothes."

"No," Finn said. "And a canvass of an area like the Willows is pretty useless. With no residents, no vehicles except mine, or none that they found, they keep comin' back to square one. I think the killer knew you'd be runnin' past that Honey Bucket—and I think he hoped the door would open the way it did. A lot of speculation on his part, but it worked."

Emma frowned at him. "It probably wouldn't have if that old Cadillac hadn't bumped it."

"Did you mention that to Billy?" Finn asked. "I did, but they haven't tracked it down."

"I did, too. Not having the license number didn't help, but why would either of us think to check that at the time? Do you think that could have been deliberate?"

Finn blew out a slow breath. He knew better than to ignore something set up to be invisible because it left no impression—like the Cadillac. "From the look of the driver, I would have doubted it. But it almost had to be. I'll bring it up with Billy again."

"What was the point of putting Denise there and wanting me to find her?"

"I think the idea was to suggest Secrets had something to do with it."

"Why?" Emma didn't even want to think such a thing.

"Don't you talk about food and diets and exercise and all that woman stuff?"

"I guess we do."

"It's a wild guess, but the syrup made me think of it. Could be some man who doesn't like the way he thinks the club has changed his wife or girlfriend."

She couldn't see that. "Denise wasn't married, and Rusty wouldn't crush a fly."

"You've got a point," Finn said. "Folks are gettin' even more nervous. And they're insulted that the cops would suggest…well, they think they're suspects, and they take it personally."

A question haunted her. "Did he rape her after she was dead?"

"I don't know."

"Do you think Billy went to Rusty and told him what they found at the autopsy?"

"Again, I don't know." He did know that Billy hadn't been as friendly as he used to be before Finn left Pointe Judah.

Another clap of lightning played hide-and-seek outside, and thunder followed almost immediately. "Rusty's always been a loner. Denise brought him out—socially. At least, he got to be less prickly. I want to get over to the paper and see how he's making out. There wasn't a chance to talk at Denise's house."

Finn rubbed at his chest with the flat of a hand. "That sounds like the decent thing to do. If it's okay, I'd like to come with you." He'd already intended to go alone and try to look around Denise's office, with or without Rusty's help.

She looked at him sharply.

"Okay," he said. "Caught. I'm concerned about you, okay?"

It is so *okay.* "You're very kind to me. Finn, do you think the police did a thorough job of searching Denise's place? They should look at the paper, too."

"From what Billy said, they took her house apart," Finn said. "I don't know about the paper. If Denise was workin' on a sensitive article, it could be in her office. But don't forget that she wouldn't be likely to leave it around for anyone to see, so it probably isn't there." He didn't want Emma to get more involved.

Emma nodded. She looked at her tote bag. The envelope contained photographs she'd been too horrified to look at closely. "It's getting late," she said. "We should give this a rest for tonight. I would appreciate your opinion on these, though."

The thudding in her chest would have been upsetting if she hadn't known the reason for it. Emma pulled out the manilla envelope and held it on her lap. She touched the still-sore spot beneath her eye.

This wasn't going to be something simple, Finn thought. She was struggling. He decided to wait quietly until she was ready to talk.

"This was thrown through my car window," she said. "It hit me here." She put a finger to her face again.

"Did you see who did it?"

"You always react like a cop," she said, and she wasn't smiling. "No. He parked a new black van so close to mine I had to get in through the passenger side. Then he reached out and opened my driver's door. I was so scared he would come after me. Then he threw this at me and drove away. I followed him as far as Circle Road, but knew I couldn't catch him."

Finn struggled with what he felt. *Get it together. Calm down.* "Damn it, Emma, what would you have done if you *had* caught him? Slapped his hand? Don't you have any sense? My God, you could have been kidnapped."

Her skin stung, and she turned cold. "That's why I stopped following, really. Once I calmed down, I knew I couldn't confront him."

"Well, get your reactions straight. You can't be impetuous when your life is involved."

"You're right." She was a wicked woman, but she kind of liked it that he got mad over what she'd done. "Look at these. Tell me if you think they'll help me."

Finn took the envelope and slid out the contents. Four photographs, all close-ups. Four angles on a man and a woman, mostly of the man. In one he sat in a chair wearing only a shirt while a dark-haired woman buried her face in his lap. In the second photo the man heaved upward from a bed, pushed himself inside a female while he fondled her breasts. The woman's head wasn't in the picture.

Damn. He wanted to shove the filth back in the envelope and throw it as far as it would go. Looking at Emma would take more courage than he could muster yet.

In picture number three, lover-boy kneeled behind a woman—Finn knew it was a woman from the rounded hips and partly visible breasts. With his hands on her hips the guy appeared to be having a bouncing good time.

The final shot froze Finn. This time Orville Lachance was masturbating while watching a partner use a vibrator.

He raised his face to see Emma. She stared back, her eyes glittering.

"You've got him," he said, surprised by his own rusty voice. "Or someone has. These are all posed so you can't see who the woman is."

15

This time she looked at them.

One by one, taking her time, Emma studied the photos.

"Do you know where they were taken?" Finn said.

"No."

"Are you doin' okay?" He could tell she wasn't.

"This is the man I'm goin' to divorce. Why do these pictures make me feel so bad?"

"Because he betrayed you." One day he would tell her his own story of betrayal and what it took to deal with it, to continue dealing with it, but not now. "I think the pictures are goin' to make things easier for you. I'm sure they will. Orville will do anything rather than have those spread around." He would like to know who had the originals and what they intended to do with them.

"I don't want his money, I just want him to let me go quietly." Emma stood up. "I'll take these to my lawyer tomorrow. I have an appointment with him." She lifted her tote, and crammed the photos and envelope inside separately. If she didn't want him anymore, he could go to his lady-friend permanently. Who cared? "I'll be on my way. Thanks for puttin' up with me. You've helped me. I couldn't seem to face the truth on my own, and I wouldn't show those to anyone who knows Orville well."

Loyal to the end. People like Emma were too rare.

"That's a lie," she said. "I'm too embarrassed to share them with folks I've known for years. Those...*things* feel like a slap in the face. And it's like being told you don't measure up."

Gently, Finn took the bag from her and put the photos back into the envelope. Then he set the bag back on the floor. "Sit down, Emma. You're shaken up, and I don't want you to drive right now."

What had she thought? That if she didn't want him, he shouldn't want anyone else? Their marriage had been over for a long time. If Orville hadn't changed so much, they would have been okay. He needed her for his image, but he'd fallen out of love with her....

"All I want is to forget everythin' for a few hours." She stared at Finn, remembered her hair and ruffled it with her fingers. "I'd better get goin'." If she cried, it wouldn't be here.

"Don't think I'm comin' on to you," he said in a voice that brought her closer to those tears. "But why don't you stay here? I've got plenty of bedrooms. I'll drive your car down here. It's not a good idea to leave it by the highway."

"Thanks, but I can't stay."

And he couldn't let her go back home alone. "Please, for me, stay here. You'll be safe, and I won't worry."

Her expression changed. Instead of lost in thought, she looked aware, speculative.

"Hey, you'll be safe from me, too."

She narrowed her eyes. "Of course I'd be safe from you." Orville had needed a woman who could excite him, who didn't shy away from experimenting. He found her dull, and Finn had to figure that, too.

"If you do go up there, I'll have to go, too," he said, doing his best to sound playful. "Even if I have to sleep in that truck."

"I want to lie down, that's all."

"I know, so quit arguin' with me and stay. I'll see to your car."

"I'll do it," she said at once and lifted her tote.

"No you won't do it."

"At least let me come with you. It's so dark out there."

He let the remark pass, didn't even roll his eyes. The lady was overwrought. "You won't come with me. You'll get soaked again. You can wait by the front door."

She did as he told her, watched him stride uphill to the highway with the gleam of rain on his dark windbreaker. He brought the car down and wasn't satisfied with parking it in front of the house, but drove it around the side and out of sight.

As if he didn't want anyone to know she was there. She stared into the rain. He was the smart one—she shouldn't want anyone to know, either.

"Done," he said, running through the door and taking off the wet jacket. He kicked aside the loafers he'd put on his feet.

"Okay," she whispered, still looking outside.

Finn closed the door and took her hand in his once more. "I'd give you the room I'm sleeping in at the moment. It's got the best view, but...I don't like changing sheets."

They both laughed.

"So you get one of the rooms at the back. The sheets are clean in there."

"I guess that makes up my mind, then." She sounded normal, didn't she? Emma's insides trembled. "I'll take the room at the back." An unnatural excitement made her feel giggly, and scared—as much of herself as of Finn.

She had her tote bag in hand, and at the bottom lay a clean outfit but nothing to sleep in. The T-shirt she had on would have to do.

Finn switched on the lights in a plain room with pale blue

walls and a white chenille bedspread. One blue-and-white rag
rug lay beside the white-painted metal bed, and another bigger one in the middle of the open floor. A chest of drawers
and a straight-backed cane chair stood against one wall, and
that was it. The door, like the others she'd seen upstairs, had
a small stained-glass fanlight above.

"The bathroom's in there." He pointed. "And believe it or
not, that bed is darn comfortable."

"You mentioned the room you're sleepin' in *at the moment*," she said. "Don't you always sleep in the same room?"

He looked at his bare feet, but she could see him smiling.
"Nope. I sleep in a bedroom till I need clean sheets, then I
move to the next. There are four rooms, so I can go about four
weeks without changin' sheets. Then I change all the beds and
start over."

"You... Look at me, Finn, not at your feet." He angled his
head and showed her a wry face. "You mean it! That wouldn't
work if you lived with someone else."

"No," he agreed, serious again. "It wouldn't work then."

She deserved the prize for stupid comments. She held her
tote in both hands. "Look, I honestly don't need to stay. I'm
imposin'."

"Try to leave and you'll be imposin'. Do you need anythin'?"

"No, thank you—but I'll mess up your sheet rotation."

He didn't miss a beat. "Toothbrush? Toothpaste? There's
soap in there, and shampoo. Clean towels. Would you like one
of my T-shirts to sleep in?"

She flushed. "I was going to wear this one. If you can spare
a clean one, it would be nice. I'll wash it for you and get it
back."

"Did you know that almost everything you say has a kind
of apology hangin' around in it?"

"No," she said. "You're just imaginin' things. I may be a

small-town person, but I've got plenty of confidence." *Sometimes she did.*

"I'll say good-night, then," Finn told her. "If you need me, just call."

He walked across the landing to his own room and left the door open a crack. After taking out a T-shirt, he retraced his steps and put it through her door. Back again with the bedside lamp on, he confronted his jumbled mess of a bed and scratched his head.

And paced. Took off his jeans again and paced some more.

With a single ripping tug, he yanked the top sheet off, balled it up and threw it in a corner with enough force to do a major league pitcher proud.

Any smug ideas that Emma Lachance had come here tonight because she wanted his body were likely to get him what he deserved: trouble.

But she surely hadn't come because she had designs on that sparse little room across the hall. For some reason she trusted him. She had taken him into her deepest confidence.

He put out the lights and stretched out on the bottom sheet. When he turned his head, the pillow felt damp.

She was divorcing Mr. Mayor.

If that didn't switch on every warning bell in his body, he needed an overhaul. The role of rebound boy didn't appeal.

With a revolution and a thump, he landed on his stomach, hooked his feet over the bottom of the mattress and gripped piping through the sheet with his fingernails.

Men and women were different.

Well, glory hallelujah, you are one enlightened fella.

A man wanted a woman. Pure and simple. Or impure and simple.

Sometimes, like now, sex wasn't all of it. He would admit that sex with Emma sounded like winning the Triple Crown, but the thought of holding her in the aftermath and feeling whole, as if he'd come home in the most real sense, opened up longings he hadn't expected to feel again.

You've been listening to too many silly love songs.

Finn revolved again, threw himself onto his back, tossed the damp pillows off the bed, and let his arms and feet trail from the mattress. This bed hadn't been long enough for him since he'd been about fifteen.

Through the crack in his door, a long, slim triangle of light reflected on the ceiling. The landing lights were out, so what he was seeing came from Emma's room.

He crossed his arms. Life could get pretty stupid. Here he was, driving himself nuts thinking about her, wanting to be close to her, and there she was, wide-awake a few yards away. Whether she was thinking about him was up for grabs, but he would put a dollar or two on him flitting into her mind now and then.

They could *talk* until she fell asleep. What was the harm in that? There was a lot going on. She'd already said she was divorcing Orville. He could be forgiven for smiling at the thought.

She'd come here because she needed to talk to someone, to show those photographs, and she didn't know who else to go to.

Finn put his feet on the floor, stood up and walked determinedly onto the landing. He made plenty of noise with every step.

"You still awake, Emma?" He didn't lower his voice.

"Yes."

"Want company." *Shee-it.* He let his head hang back. He could win prizes for saying the wrong thing. "I mean, do you want to talk? My room's too hot. It's cooler here on the landing."

"Oh, come on in here, Finn. It's ridiculous, you standin' out there and the two of us yellin' back and forth."

She made him smile like he didn't remember smilin' for too long. She had an odd mix of pragmatism and off-the-wall cockeyed optimism that he couldn't resist. "You're right," he said. "Ridiculous."

The bedside light was on, but not the others. Emma sat up in bed. The sheet and chenille bedspread were pulled up under her arms, and the neck of his T-shirt sagged off one shoulder

Nice shoulder.

Round, smooth, lightly tanned…soft.

He stood just inside the door. "The sooner you do what you have to with Orville, the better. I can see the whole thing eatin' you up. You could set things in motion tomorrow."

"I'm thinkin' about it," she said. He doubted if her almost painfully blue eyes could open any wider. Orville Lachance needed psychoanalysis.

Emma had fine bones. Although he knew she had full breasts, she was otherwise slender. Could be that Orville had gotten a taste for more substantial women. Damn the man. Or bless him.

"I can wait while you think," he said. "Or talk about somethin' else."

She separated a honey-blond curl and wound it around her a finger. "Sit by me."

He sat on the mattress, half facing her.

"If it wasn't for the party, I'd do it right away."

"Why consider him?"

Emma squinted. "I'm not anymore. But Holly Chandall is so excited to have the caterin' job. It'll probably get her more. She hired Annie on the strength of it, and I can't ruin it for either of them. Holly's already got her crew ready and Orville's stinkin' ice sculpture ordered. Friend of Annie's is doin' that. No, I've got to hang on just that long."

He considered what she said. "I guess I can see that." But

he didn't have to like it. And he surely didn't like the haunted look on her face. "You're bound to be shaken up. Those are things you don't expect to see in livin' color. Did it take you a while to decide you wanted a divorce?"

"In a way. It's only been weeks since it all came together."

"What made you decide?" He shouldn't push but couldn't seem to stop himself.

She appeared about to talk, but stopped. Emma shook her head. "I expect you'll move on once you've got a plan," she said, surprising him.

"I haven't decided. I told you, I'm checkin' things out to see if I can settle here."

Emma looked straight at him. "I'm a fool. I'm infatuated with you, Finn. That's all it is. You've shown me kindness. You've been attentive. You look at me as if you think I matter, and I've fallen for the whole package. You don't know how long it is since a man took real notice of me. I don't have to have a man in my life. No, sir, I need to stand on my own two feet, but I'm glad we met again." Her attempt at a smile wasn't so hot.

No woman had ever told him she was infatuated with him, and Emma wouldn't have said it if she was herself.

"Emma, it's not the way you think—"

"Drawn together by sex—lust? It *is* the way I think it is. How can it be anything else?"

"Hush," he said. "Listen to me."

"Please go. While I've got any pride left at all. And will you do something for me?"

"Anythin'." Finn Duhon, the man who had an answer for everything. Not tonight.

"It's not that I don't trust Billy, but they aren't used to dealin' with murder around here. Will you still do whatever you can to help figure out what's goin' on in this town—because somethin' truly is goin' on."

"You know I will."

"One other thing." She hunched her shoulders, and the T-shirt neck fell lower. He saw the soft rise of her breast.

"Just ask, Emma."

"Try to forget I came here tonight—and most of the things I've said to you. I'll be thinkin' straight again by mornin'. And I'll be out of your hair."

16

The bed creaked.

It didn't just creak, it gave that kind of *eeka-oog* noise, all tinny and in your face, getting louder the more you tried to stop it from happening. This bed moaned when you turned even an inch and howled if you had the nerve to keep on rolling over.

Emma shot to the floor, and stood with her toes together and her hands to her fiery cheeks. The sounds of Finn tossing had ceased at last, and she wanted out of here while she had a shred of pride left.

His T-shirt would have to be washed before she returned it, so she might as well leave it on. She jumped into her jeans, hopped from foot to foot to haul them up and close the zip. Shoes, shoes, what had she done with her shoes?

In the bathroom.

Emma went in there on the clammy tile floor without turning on a lamp, since it would glow through the fanlight over the door and Finn would see it. She couldn't see the shoes, so she would have to find them in the dark. She held still and narrowed her eyes, looking for a spot where shadows collected the way they did on something solid.

Down to her hands and knees she went and carefully covered the floor, sweeping her hands in arcs, patting here and patting there.

Light flooded the room.

Emma sat back on her heels, pushed her hair out of her face with the back of a forearm and sighed. She hunched her shoulders. No way would she look at him. "I was finding my shoes."

"That would explain it. Are you sure you lost them in here?"

"No." And now that there was light, she could see they were not in the bathroom.

"Up you come." He caught her by the elbows and lifted her to her feet. Then he shocked her to breathless silence by brushing his lips up the side of her neck and whispering in her ear, "You and I are going to spend some time together, *cher*. You're going to tell me what's on your mind, and I'll do my best to let you inside my messy head."

Emma closed her eyes.

"Okay?" he asked.

She couldn't be swept away by a pair of strong arms, a hard body at her back and firm lips on her neck. "Um…okay," she said, though she didn't intend to tell him more of the personal and humiliating details of her marriage.

"Good. Your bed or mine?"

"Finn!"

"Shall we sit on your bed or mine? Yours creaks."

"I noticed."

"But it's more comfortable than mine, and I've taken everything off mine now, anyway."

She broke from him, returned to the bedroom and got back into bed without removing the jeans. Once more she made sure the covers were tucked up to her armpits—and she switched on the bedside lamp. "Sit down, please," she said.

Finn wasn't wearing his jeans. Emma stared at his rumpled white shorts for too long, then looked away. He sat beside her, apparently perfectly comfortable with what he wasn't wearing.

And he sat facing the wall with his hands hanging between his knees and the lines of his face resigned. "Your shoes are sticking out of your tote bag," he said.

"Thanks." For the first time Emma saw the full extent of his scars up close. "That makes me mad," she said quietly.

"What does?"

"That mess on your back. Was it an accident?"

He looked at her over his shoulder and smiled slightly. "No, it wasn't."

"Whoever did that was really trying to hurt you."

His squint, the way his throat moved as he swallowed, unnerved Emma.

"The man who did that was trying to decapitate me," he said.

She couldn't catch her breath. The purplish red insult to his flesh made a jagged path. "He was an enemy, wasn't he? Where is he now?"

Finn rubbed his face hard. "He's dead. Drop it, please."

Crawling from between the covers, Emma put down her pillows and plumped them up. "Lie down," she said. "On your face."

"No."

"Please. You're never relaxed. That's bad for you. Do as I ask. Come on."

He shook his head, and Emma left the bed. She slid to the floor beside him and pushed his unyielding torso until he gave in and flopped sideways like a felled tree.

"You're being difficult," she told him, and managed to haul his legs, one by one, onto the mattress, although she wouldn't have been able to move any part of him if he didn't want it moved. She pulled his shoulder toward her. "On your stomach. Do as you're told for once."

So docile she expected him to bolt at any second, he arranged himself, prone, with his arms at his sides.

How many times has your mother told you to be careful what you wish for? Oh, lordy, lordy, he was one beautiful man. "Rest there. Keep your eyes closed."

When she found a tube of aloe in her purse, Emma gave silent thanks. She unscrewed the cap and squirted the pale green gel liberally over his back.

"Whoo!" He jumped and tried to turn his head.

"Aloe," she said. "Really good for softening up scars and relaxing them." Emma had no idea if aloe was good for anything but sunburn. "This should have been massaged regularly since it happened. You've got scar tissue all webbed and knotted up underneath here. I can feel it."

"So can I. Ah, ah! That stuff's cold."

"Tomorrow I'm goin' to get cocoa butter. That's the best."

His face rested straight down in the pillow, and she had to put her head next to his to hear what he said. "What was that, Finn?"

"Glad you're going to take over my massage routine," he mumbled. "Supposed to be done several times a day."

Emma had to smile. For all the trouble she was in, and he knew about it as well as she did, she could shut some of it out when she was with him.

A twist in the region of her gut reminded her that tomorrow she would set the ball rolling and have her lawyer start drawing up the divorce papers.

"That feels great." Finn almost moaned. "You've got fabulous fingers."

"Strong fingers from playing the piano. Keep your eyes shut and concentrate on relaxing your muscles."

"Oh, yes, I'll do that, ma'am. I'd like to hear you play."

"That could happen." She grinned, thinking of how he would react if he saw her playing at Buzz's Tavern—not that she ever would. Emma worked at the tight knots under the scar. She pulled at the stiff tissue along the tops of his shoulders, shook it gently, let it go, only to repeat the process.

"Have you ever had hot stones—a hot stone massage?"

"Uh-uh."

"It feels wonderful when you're all knotted up. I could do that for you."

"Mmm. Okay."

By the time she started thinking of getting him on his back, half the gel was gone. First, using her whole hands to grasp the heavy muscle, she kneaded his sides where the skin was smooth, never breaking contact with his body, always finishing each manoeuver with a series of long sweeps over the scars. She felt his body relaxing under her fingers.

He was tanned and toned, but she doubted he knew how to loosen up. Could be she had a mission there. "You feel softer," she said.

"Who thinks so?"

"I do. I can feel it."

"Ooh, not from my perspective. You've got your work cut out for you if that's what you're tryin' to accomplish."

He had a narrow waist for such a tall man. Gripping him there with her fingertips, she drove her thumbs along his spine, eventually dipping under his shorts to follow the vertebrae. The patch of coarse hair she encountered gave her pause, but she reminded herself she was no simpering virgin and kept on going.

"Um, Emma?"

"Now don't you go gettin' scared. This is therapy, and your honor is in no danger from me."

Without warning, he reached behind him to grasp one of her wrists. He turned to his side. "Lie with me."

She averted her face.

Finn noted she didn't try to wrest her arm from his grip. A

woman didn't do what she'd been doing to a man if she didn't want to get closer to him.

"You may not be playin' with fire," she told him. "But I am."

"I won't push you into anything."

"I want to get under the covers," Emma said. "Move over."

He did as she asked, and she took off her jeans again before climbing into the bed, intensely aware that he looked her legs over. There was no mystery about any of this. They were attracted to each other, and she didn't fool herself that she was more than a woman who turned him on, but she wasn't looking for more than a warm, hard body to help her through the worst time of her life, either.

Emma turned off the light and wriggled way down under the covers until only her eyes cleared the sheets.

"Good job it's a warm night," Finn said. "I'd definitely be on the wrong side of the bundlin' board if it was cold."

She laughed. "As long as you stay on your side of the bed, you can get under the covers, too. Only you won't want to, because it's too warm, right?"

His response was to bounce enough that she rolled toward the middle, directly into him.

"Hi," he said, wrapping his arms around her and clamping her face to his chest. "I'll sleep better holding you." *You, Duhon, are a liar, but who needs sleep?*

"We're going to empty our minds, remember?" Emma said. She would rather not do that, but promises, or excuses, needed to be kept. Besides, she wanted to see if he would tell her anything more about himself. She struggled to sit up and propped both of their pillows against the headboard. Emma patted his and said, "Sit up and let go of everything in that head of yours."

That would be a really bad idea, Finn thought, but he did sit up, reluctantly, and worked on slowing his galloping pulse. "You start," he said.

"I already told my story—and had illustrations to go along with it. I'll admit the last few years haven't been easy. I'm not takin' the steps I'm takin' lightly, but I have to be sensible."

He wondered if the last few years had been more than "not easy." Had they been like living in a satin cell with a mentally, even physically, abusive jailor?

"How about you, Finn? You had a terrible experience, and you don't want to talk about it, so you don't have to. But I'd like to know how it's affected you. You don't sleep so well, do you?"

"I don't," he told her. "They told me I have post-traumatic stress syndrome, but I think just livin' is enough to give you that. I'm copin' fine, thank you."

"You came back to Pointe Judah because you might want to settle down here. You've already got business feelers out." She tried to break off a thread from the sheet but only managed to unravel several inches of hem. She would have to fix that. "You haven't made up your mind if you really want to put down roots yet, though. I can tell."

"You might be wrong about that, but there's another reason I came home." He sounded as if he had dragged the words out. Finn turned his face toward her. "I intended to keep it to myself, but then I met you, and you've got a way of making me want to spill everything. Why not this, too?"

"We met when I needed someone strong," she said. "I don't know what your excuse is."

Finn struggled with wanting to comfort her and just plain wanting her. Parts of a man's body could be damned single-minded.

"I've got to find out what really happened to my dad," Finn said quickly. "It was classified as suicide, and his ashes were scattered over the bayou before I had a hope of getting home. Thing is, my dad wouldn't have taken that way out."

Emma felt sad, and sorry. She guessed it would be hard to accept that a parent thought they had nothing to live for and took their own life. Like *you* weren't worth anything. "You want to prove he didn't kill himself?" So many people had set out to do the same thing, and they usually failed.

"If Denise hadn't been murdered, I would have taken the case up with Billy by now. I know how busy he is, but I can't wait any longer. It's only about a year, but trails get old. And cold. I want to see the records. Then there will be other folks I need to talk to and things to follow up."

"I'll help you," Emma said.

Finn looked at her in the slight silvery wash through the window, his expression speculative. He slid the back of a forefinger along her jaw. "Now how did I know you were going to offer? You've got your own shit—you've got your own problems."

"I'm going to fix them." Almost unconsciously, she raised her chin to make it easier for him to stroke her. "Let me do what I can for you."

Sincerity rang in her voice. What the hell did he think he was doing, sitting here in bed with her, in the dark, baring his soul? "Thanks," he said.

"Your dad died of a gunshot wound to the head," she said. "Wouldn't they be able to tell if someone else pulled the trigger? Even if the gun was in his hand?"

"Yup."

"And they decided there wasn't anyone else around?"

Listening to logic shouldn't make him mad, but it did. He breathed through his mouth. "So I'm told. But it doesn't add up, not with what I know about him, and not with what Eileen says about the last time she saw him—hours before he died."

Enough questions, Emma decided. "You need to find the truth."

"He was good at what he did, and he loved it. He loved my mother more than anythin' and he loved his kids. Dad tried to be a father to Aaron, too. No, it doesn't sit right with me. It's my job to get at the truth."

"You worry me," Emma said. "Can you accept it if what you've been told turns out to be true?"

Finn shook his head no. "It's not."

"I was afraid you'd say that. You won't be happy until you find someone to blame."

"Blame isn't the point. Not now. You must have heard how my mother died of a stroke. She already had cancer, but she might have beaten it. That was only months after Dad went. Whoever shot him might as well have taken the gun to her, too, because she quit livin' when he did. I want whoever did it punished, is all."

"You want a closed case opened again. How likely are you to be able to force the cops to do that?"

"I don't give a damn if they open it or not. I want the records, a starting place," Finn said, and sounded so strange, so different. "The rest, I'll do myself."

Dread overwhelmed Emma. "It's not a good idea to take the law into your own hands."

"So the cliché goes," he said. "I'll do things my way. I know personally what it can do to you if you don't clean up your own messes. Allowing someone to do it for you doesn't cut it."

Emma turned toward him in the all but dead blackness. Wind hammered the window, whined in the trees outside, and rain clattered fitfully. She was grateful the thunder and lightning had quit. "You'll make sure this person—if there is one—you'll make sure they go to trial?" Her heart thudded harder.

"Of course," he said, much too softly. "The trial's about to begin. I even know what the verdict will be, and the sentence. All I need is the identity of the shooter."

17

"We're not goin' to discuss this anymore," Finn said, when the silence had stretched way too long. "Who knows what will happen? Can we leave it, at least for now?" He'd said more than he should have.

So chilled she had goose bumps, Emma turned to him. She felt him watching her. Resting her cheek on his chest, she slowly put an arm around his middle. She was reading too much into his words.

Finn held Emma and slid down in the bed, taking her with him. He'd been trained to kill but not to like it—or dislike it—when a subject had to be taken out. There would be no explaining how a man like him felt about such things, how he had learned to make peace with what he did and relegate each incident to a place in his memory where he hoped it would stay. He was one of the unlucky ones; he saw faces, and they were the ones who kept him awake, the faces and betrayal by a friend.

Tonight he needed this woman. He needed her because he'd wanted her for days, and because he didn't want to think about anything but the white heat of taking her body.

He pulled her over him and held her tight, too tight. She made a sound, and he eased up. Emma pleased him, because he admired her, too, and liked her, and enjoyed being with her.

Whatever he did, he must not forget that the needs weren't all on his side—or the dangers. Leaving victims in his wake wasn't his plan.

The struggle she waged turned her cold inside. She wanted to be here with this man. Her marriage was over in every way except the official one, but she still felt like an unfaithful wife.

Too bad Orville hadn't been able to keep it in his pants around other women. This probably wouldn't be happening tonight if he had.

Emma considered how she felt about that conclusion. She wanted to be right where she was, regardless.

Finn kissed her hair. He rubbed her back slowly, up and down, all the way under her hair, where he could settle his fingers on her neck. "Are you going to be okay with this?" he said. "With us bein' together? I don't want to be a reason for you to feel guilty."

"You won't." *I hope.*

"Are you leavin' early tomorrow?"

She swallowed. "Not until I check to see how many RSVPs came back. He'll want to know."

"I think I've talked Eileen into comin' to the party with me. It's time she had a special night out."

He made her throat tighten. "You are a nice man."

"That's true," he said. "Nice and trustworthy. Once the party's over, you're out of there, right? You'll leave him?"

"Yes." But she wouldn't be finished with Orville. "I'm goin' to find out what goes on inside that club he just about lives in. I'll take my time, but I wouldn't be surprised if those photographs were taken at Damalis's. Just once, I want to walk in on Orville at one of his *'meetings.'*"

His hand tightened in her hair. "You won't do that. Catchin' him might sound like some sort of payback, but it isn't worth the risk. Don't discuss it with me, just accept that you just suggested the most stupid move you could make and now you're goin to forget about it."

Emma stiffened, but she kept her mouth shut.

"Relax," he said. "You're mad. I can feel it. Okay, I'll go into greater detail about why you're not goin' to that club. Like you said, for all we know, those photos *were* taken there. That means it may be a...full service club. Booze, women, men losin' money and lookin' for someone to take it out on. *You* are a gentle woman, gently raised, and somehow you've stayed that way. You could get hurt in there, do you understand?"

"I wouldn't get hurt," she mumbled. "I'm not an idiot."

"A man who's wasted doesn't stop to ask permission. Promise me you won't do it. Orville's gonna get his. There are some people in this town who think they're entitled to whatever they want, but *no one* has any right to you unless you say so. Promise me."

She'd spent twelve years being told what to do.

"Emma?"

No promises. She didn't owe any.

"Okay, I didn't want to say this, but there's a murderer in this town, and we don't know who he is or where he is. Takin' risks in places like Damalis's wouldn't be smart."

She arched her neck and in the darkness saw the glitter of his eyes. "I won't do anythin' stupid," she said. "Quit worryin'."

She heard the start of a word from him and put her lips over his. The kiss she offered didn't part their lips. A soft kiss of comfort—and a kiss to shut him up and maybe make him forget his train of thought. Men weren't difficult to distract.

A man could be expected to react to a woman's kiss while they lay in one another's arms. Finn did, parting their lips a little, sweeping the tip of his tongue along the smooth, wet skin just inside her mouth.

Emma's nipples tingled, and the folds between her legs. They ached.

Finn slowly opened their mouths wider, and she was ready to give as good as she got. He rolled, pushing her to her back and using his fingers behind her neck to tip her face up to his. Clinging to him, Emma tried to keep up, but he was strong, and she didn't think he was long on control tonight. Elsewhere he was real long, hard, thick and heavy against her leg, and even while her excitement threatened to mash her mind, she feared, just a little, what she was doing.

He broke the kiss but repeatedly touched her mouth with his. "Emmy," he said, "has Orville ever been violent with you?"

She swallowed. "Why do you ask? Especially now?" Her laugh sounded false.

"Has he?"

"I don't want to tell you lies, so can we not discuss this? You've got things you don't want to talk about."

"I thought so," he said, resting his face on her shoulder and licking salt from her skin. "If I do anythin' that makes you feel uncomfortable or threatened, just smack me or yell at me. I'm not about to make you freeze up on me because you're waitin' to be hurt."

Her response? Emma shifted her arms to his neck and held him as fiercely as she could, and she urged him to look at her. She took his bottom lip gently between her teeth and sucked. His moan made her feel smug. She found his tongue with her own and went to war. They panted, and wound their bodies into positions that shouldn't be possible.

Emma slapped his chest.

"What?" He shot to sit up. Dammit, what had he done?

"Nothin'. *I* want to do somethin'. Lay down again." When he'd shifted lower, she sat on his belly, one knee on either side of his body.

"Ooh, Emmy," he whispered. "I don't know if you should do that."

"I do." Only her parents called her Emmy, but she liked the sound when Finn said it. She pulled the baggy T-shirt over her head and dropped it to the floor. "I should be dressed the way you are, and you can't see me in the dark, anyway, can you?"

"Yes," he said, and sounded breathless again.

"Mmm, as long as you can feel me, that's the main thing."

He closed his eyes and slid his hands up her back, eased her toward him, lifted his head and nuzzled his face into her cleavage. He opened his mouth on a full breast and shifted his head from side to side, wetting her skin and feeling how she got wet elsewhere. The idea of losing control had disgusted him as long as he could remember, and he couldn't let it happen now, but he was close. His penis pulsed inside the damn shorts he wanted to wish away. He could feel her through her panties, hot and damp against his belly.

The woman was as ready for sex as he was—or she seemed to be. He still wouldn't take anything for granted. He raised her right arm and nipped at the soft skin between her side and her breast. She wiggled and attempted to get him closer. He knew what she wanted him to do, but the more intense the need became, the bigger the charge she would get. And he would be the winner, because the more ready she would be for him.

Emma writhed, gripped the sides of his face and moved his mouth back to her breast, to her nipple. He closed his mouth, and flicked his tongue back and forth, slowly. She strained against him, begging for more.

Finn smiled, loving the faint rose scent of her skin, loving the power he had over her. He took her nipple in his teeth, then backed off and made circles on the swelling skin around it. Finally Finn sucked at her, harder and harder, moved to the other breast and sucked. Emma gasped and drove her finger-nails into him.

He slid his hands inside her panties and cupped her bottom, separated her cheeks, tipped her forward and smoothed a finger between her legs to find her sweet spot.

He found it, and she rocked on his hand, panted, kissed his shoulder, found his flat nipples and pulled at the tips until he jerked and said, "Ah, I can't take that. You're driving me mad."

"Good. Two crazy people in one bed."

Finn stroked her hot, damp body again and again, finding all the places guaranteed to drive her higher. He got rid of her panties and flipped their positions, disappeared under the sheet and sank his face into heated and moist hair between her legs.

Emma pushed on the top of his head, wriggled and tried to get away.

He held her hips and shot his tongue in and out, while her bottom rose and fell on the bed, moving faster and harder while he brought her closer to the edge.

She'd never experienced anything like this. Finn thrilled and embarrassed her. Her breasts swelled; her body burned.

Again he moved, twisting her to sit on the side of the bed, his hands holding her ankles in place on the mattress. He kept her knees wide apart and returned to making her writhe on the mattress.

Emma let out a moan. The sensation he made with his tongue, reaching it into her, withdrawing, reaching, withdrawing, making rapid, hard attacks on the most sensitive spot on her body, drove her wild. But she didn't try to stop him. She hovered, an instant from the brink, and he took his mouth from her. Already she throbbed. The beating in her flesh built, and she climaxed. Lying there, open to him while he watched, she tossed and forced a hand down to touch herself, to jerk with the ripples of pleasure.

Finn released her ankles, and Emma's feet slid from the bed. Her legs hung, as if useless. He pressed his penis hard but didn't relieve any of the demanding pressure.

Emma moved so fast, she caught him off guard. Laughing, springing to stand on the mattress and bounce, she taunted him.

"I would never have taken you for a tease," he said, with laughter in his voice. He flipped on the bedside lamp and enjoyed watching her breasts jounce, seeing how red and puffy her nipples had become, and the way her pubic hair glistened. She was a wet dream, and tonight she was his.

Finn got up and made a grab for her, but she was too fast. Off the bed on the other side, she ran to a corner of the room, but she'd stopped laughing. Emma knelt, knees tight together, and beckoned him near.

He didn't reach her before she stretched out an arm, took hold of his distended penis and pulled him gently toward her. Rising on her knees a little, she rubbed the pulsing end of him over her breasts. A glance up at him, and then he felt her take him into her mouth, draw him in deep, and move him in and out until his thighs shook.

Seeing her take him, turn her face to pass his bursting skin over her teeth, terrified him. He couldn't come, not like this. "Let's lie down, *cher,*" he said, and held the top of her head in both of his hands.

Emma let him slip from her mouth. Her lips wet and shiny, she stood, kept her body pressed to his while she dragged herself up.

He made a move to take her to the bed, but she grasped him in one clever hand and pumped. The last of his control snapped. She timed removing her hand to the second, and they clung together while his ejaculation pulsed.

"Emmy?"

She held him even tighter, and he knew what he felt on his chest was her tears. "Say somethin'."

Not a word.

Easing out of her arms, he ducked and picked her up. She didn't resist when he put her on the bed and got in beside her. She didn't resist when he held her against him again. "That was incredible," he told her. "Give me a few minutes and—"

"Hush," she said. "You're tired. Let yourself sleep." Where her abandon had come from, she didn't know. Orville was a fastidious lover—with her. Bitterness burned her throat at the thought of what she'd seen in the photos.

"I don't want to sleep," Finn said. The pliable quality of her body had faded. She lay stiff in his arms. He propped himself on one elbow and kissed her. Emma kissed him back, but only as a response, a sweet, undemanding response.

The sensation he got when he felt her hand on his back, smoothing its length, set him on a sexual edge all over again, but he held back. He flattened a hand against her stomach, and she moved a subtle distance from him.

Oh, God, she felt guilty, and they hadn't even done anything. Not really.

Very still, she remained exactly where she was. Finn tried to see her eyes. They were closed, and her breathing was regular. And he would lay odds that she was faking.

Finn got another erection. He rolled to his back, then carefully onto his other side, facing away from Emmy. She had been willing; she had wanted him. Then everything had changed.

He thought about the pictures. Could she have set out to get back at her husband, at least in her own mind, then lost her nerve? Finn clamped his teeth together. If he'd been used, he hoped she decided to use him again real soon.

* * *

Thunder had started again. Every few minutes quicksilver veins shattered the sky and a rolling boom cracked the night almost at once.

Finally Finn slept. Emma made several careful, experimental moves, to make sure he didn't wake or let her know he was pretending. She slid to the floor, gathered her jeans, his shirt and her tote bag, and glided out of the room.

In the bedroom Finn used, she stood in the intermittent flicker of light from the broken skies and pulled on her clothes. She stuck her feet into her shoes, stood by the door to listen a while, then moved like a wraith along the landing and down the stairs.

The raincoat hung in the passage where she'd entered the house. Emma put her bag strap across her body, pulled on the coat and let herself out into a night that took rain from the ground, boiled it and puffed steam into an opaque layer like a weightless feather blanket. The steam hovered feet above the grass and curled between trees.

Don't think.

The keys were at the bottom of the bag, and she wasted too much time scrabbling among her possessions to find them. The top of the Lexus, poking through the cover of steam, shone with moisture.

With the keys in her hand, she reached the car and got in. She would see Finn again. Perhaps they would be…close again. She hoped so. He was too special to let go, although that decision was probably out of her hands now. She wouldn't blame him for being wary around her.

His lovemaking had thrilled her, and she'd felt free as never before—until she froze again.

The engine sounded like a plane taking off. He would

wake up and discover she'd sneaked away. Emma bit into her bottom lip. If he still wanted her, she would be there for him...eventually.

Taking the time to snatch up his jeans panicked Finn. He heard the side door close and ran, naked, with his jeans in his hand, down the stairs. *Why do women have to be so complicated? Why do they think too much?* He struggled into the jeans, zipped them, but didn't bother to close the waist.

An engine hummed. The Lexus. Rather than follow through the passageway, Finn ran to throw open the front door in time to see Emma's vehicle steadily climb the steep driveway and turn right. She'd decided to head to the Balou house. At least she wasn't going where her husband might be. Finn couldn't have stood that. He still didn't like her being up there alone.

He turned, leaned against the side of the house to watch Emma's taillights head away. Soon she would be swallowed by trees on either side of the road.

With a hand over his face, he struggled to figure out what it meant. Had she wanted to use him to get back at Orville, then lost her nerve? In his mind, Finn saw the top of her blond hair while she took him in her mouth. He felt her touch all over him. Emma hadn't been using him, no more than he'd used her. But what they'd had wasn't nearly enough. He would go mad if she wouldn't let them finish what they'd started.

A hand descended on his shoulder.

A great, hot blast pummeled Finn's temples from within. He held his breath. Then, like a blind animal, he grasped whoever was behind him by the wrist and swung him around his own body. He bellowed, filled the air with his rage, and felt the shift when his tall assailant lost his footing. The man stumbled, arms flailing but still grabbing for any part of Finn he could find. The face went by in a blur, but Finn landed a punch he heard when it connected with bone.

Light-headedness agitated him. Sweat ran from every pore. The man struggled to get up, and Finn hit him, again and again, knocked him facedown, fell on him. Finn trapped both his attacker's hands and pulled his arms behind his back, pulled them upward until he screamed.

With both fists, Finn beat the man, landed body blows that hammered out gasps and sobs. *I can't stop. Don't stop. Never stop.* A white burlap curtain floated around them. The curtain should be brown, ragged. Finn saw flashes behind his eyes and yelled, "No!" No, he didn't need his commanding officer. He could do his own killing....

He squeezed his burning eyes shut, opened them and focused. His victim swayed on his hands and knees and made snuffling sounds. Blood ran from his nose.

"What the fuck do you think you're doin' here?" Finn said. "Get up. Get *up*." The man tried but fell, staggered onto one leg and fell again.

"Who told you to sneak up on me like that?" Finn hauled the other guy to his feet, and it took both hands and a lot of muscle to hold him up. "You could be dead for that. If you want to keep on breathing, say something, asshole."

"Denise—" A burst of coughing and spitting cut the man off.

Finn shook him and dragged him to the door. He reached inside and turned on a light—and looked down at Rusty Barnes's bruised, bleeding face.

18

"Have you lost your fuckin' mind, Barnes?" Finn barely stopped himself from giving the man a kick in the gut. "Get the fuck inside and pull your goddamn self together."

Shit, what had he done?

Clinging to the doorjamb, Rusty clawed his way to his feet. Finn got a good look at the man's face and rolled his eyes. No one would believe it if Rusty explained how he stood on the wrong side of a broom head and got whopped in the kisser by the handle.

Why did I do it? I never lashed out like that before.

Leaning on Finn, who held him around the waist, Rusty staggered into the house, and Finn kicked the door shut.

"Bloody hell," Rusty said. "I was going to say I wouldn't want to meet you on a dark night, but I just did. I'll have you for murder." Blood drizzled from his nose and split lip.

"I haven't killed you," Finn pointed out, steering for the kitchen.

"Bloody well have," Rusty mumbled. "On my way out. I can feel myself going."

Finn wouldn't have taken Rusty Barnes for a man with a sense of humor. He was probably delirious.

That was when Rusty's legs crumpled and Finn barely managed to keep him from collapsing to the floor. He half dragged, half carried him to the kitchen and dumped him on a chair.

"Came to tell you something," Rusty said, slurring each word. He put bloodstained hands on the table and rested his forehead on top. "Damned if I will now. I don't need a friend like you. What the fuck's your problem, anyway?" With his dark red hair looking as if he'd done it in a blender, he raised his head, turned his face from side to side trying to focus on Finn.

Sometimes you came clean because the alternative would land you in more of a mess. "PTSS. Haven't had much trouble lately, but it must have been the way you touched me." And the way he'd relived hell once already tonight. The stupid son-of-a-gun had landed his solid hand right on the spot where Finn's scars converged.

"Post-traumatic stress syndrome," Rusty muttered, opening his eyes wide and blinking—as if it would help his vision. "If I had to go fight, I'd go, but I'm buggered if I'd volunteer. Turns you into weird sods who attack innocent people in the dark. I suppose I should be glad you didn't have some damn great gun ready. Isn't that what you were, a shooter?"

"Yes," he said, but thought better than to produce the pistol from the back of his jeans. "Now shut up and let me clean this mess."

"I'm going to sue your ass," Rusty said. One eye had almost swollen shut.

"I'll sue your ass first," Finn said. "Trespass. Attack."

"Attack?" Rusty's voice broke.

"Your word against mine."

Rusty laughed and moaned as his split lip opened wider. "Look at you and look at me. Who are they going to believe?"

"Me. I'm the one with the special training."

It could have been anyone who came up behind him. Aaron…or Emma. He shuddered and went for clean washcloths and dressings. He didn't want to think about the possibility that he would have to get medical attention for Rusty.

He got a clean basin, filled it with hot water and dipped in a cloth. "They don't call me Nurse Finn for nothin'." Each time he removed blood from Rusty's face he was treated to a bellow, until the man gave a sick grin and cut it down to loud sounds of breath sucked through teeth. At least he didn't seem to be missing any of those.

"It's not as bad as it looked," Finn said.

"Damned well is."

This was the first conversation of any length that Finn recalled having with Rusty. He would probably be less truculent if he didn't have a broken nose.

"Aw, shit," Finn said with feeling. "Look, I don't know what to say to you. I've got a lot on my mind, so I'm uptight. I had something nasty happen to me once when someone came up behind me the way you did...." He sounded halfbaked. "I'm sorry it happened. It wasn't personal."

"Good. What would I look like if it had been?"

The guy was wry, funny in a way. He surprised Finn, who couldn't help smiling.

"It might not matter what you looked like anymore. Not to you."

Rusty tried to glare, but the effort clearly hurt.

"How did you get up here?" Finn said.

"Harley."

Finn gave him a suspicious look. "I didn't hear any Harley."

Rusty averted his eyes. "Prob'ly because of the other engine."

"Probably," Finn said without a pause. He had made a mess of Rusty's face, but it was true that with the blood removed, it didn't look quite so bad.

"Dangerous territory there, my friend," Rusty told him. "The mayor's lady."

"Thought you didn't need friends like me?" He didn't need the local news making something out of Emma being at his house late at night—neither did Emma. This was a small place, and they adhered to traditional ideas.

With one eye, Rusty regarded him steadily. "It's your business. And hers. And as far as I'm concerned, it stays that way."

"Thanks."

"I figured there was something with you two when you showed at Denise's to look around." Pain showed in that eye, and it wasn't because of the cuts on the man's face. "I don't suppose the two of you picked anything up while you were there?"

When he figured he hadn't misheard, Finn said, "Picked something up from Denise's house, you mean?" Now they were getting to the real reason for Rusty's visit, he decided.

Rusty got to his feet, waving the wet cloth aside, and walked stiffly around the kitchen. "If you didn't, I think someone did."

"You were there before us."

"Not long enough to do what had been done to her place. I wouldn't, anyway." He looked down. "She never did anything to deserve that."

"I'm sure she didn't. Whoever killed her is a pig, but we're goin' to find him."

"Denise was on to something."

Finn kept his face impassive and started a pot of coffee brewing.

"She was just back from a trip. I'm sure it had something to do with a case she was working on here, but she played a close hand, and I let her. I think she found out something that excited her."

"Is that a fact?" Practice had made Finn good at not showing emotion. "What makes you think that?"

Rusty raised a hand. "The way she was. Secretive. Her feet hardly on the floor. She said she had a scoop. Denise didn't talk like that if she wasn't sure of herself."

Finn couldn't imagine there were many scoops to be had around Pointe Judah, but he didn't say so. "Where did she go? Did she tell you?"

"Uh-uh. I think you've broken some of my ribs."

"Wouldn't be surprised."

"Cold bastard, aren't you?"

Finn considered. "Pretty much." Except where the people he cared about were concerned. He still kicked around his re-action to Rusty coming up behind him. Next chance he got, he would get to his laptop, take a look at Google and see if he could find more useful references to his condition—if there were any he hadn't already seen. "D'you think you broke anythin', apart from a rib, maybe?"

"You mean did *you* break anything else? No. Hey, I should have called out or something, but you were preoccupied watching your visitor leave."

"I thought you said that wasn't your business anymore?"

"It isn't. But I think that's why you didn't hear me get here."

Made sense. Finn went back to cleaning up Rusty's face. He greased a gash over one eyebrow and the lacerated lip. Only time would heal the rest, but there shouldn't be any need for stitches.

Finn put the bowl in the sink so he could clean it out later. He found a bottle of painkillers and slapped it down on the table beside Rusty, who didn't waste time before helping himself.

With mugs of coffee poured, Finn sat with Rusty, who looked, conservatively, like hell. "Now, how about you tell me why you came up here to creep around?"

"Goddamn it, I didn't—"

"No, of course not. Just felt that way to me."

"I wish Denise was here," Rusty said, very quietly. "For more reasons than I can tell you."

Finn didn't know what to say. He drank from his mug.

"She was something. Could have gone anywhere, but she liked it here."

"Close to you?" It was a risk if Denise hadn't returned any of Rusty's affection, but Finn took that risk. He needed Rusty as an ally.

Rusty sat back in his chair. He put his mug to his lips but said, "Ouch," when the heat met his skin. "I wanted to believe that. She was independent. I swear to you, I can't think of a reason why she was murdered. Unless she really was on to something with that case she wouldn't talk about."

Something about the oblique way Rusty referred to Denise's work clued Finn in that he was supposed to ask questions about it. "But you don't know what the case was?"

Rusty stared silently at Finn.

"You *do* know?"

"Very little." He broke contact with Finn's eyes. "Sometimes Denise got so charged up—usually if she'd made some progress—she threw me a bone." He smiled with one side of his mouth. "She loved to tease."

Finn knew when he was looking at a man in love. Rusty Barnes was still in love with Denise Steen. The idea made him feel empty.

"She'd opened up an old case," Rusty said. "Well, I guess you'd say she was interested in an old case and thought she could break it."

And Rusty felt he had to talk to Finn about it? He wasn't sure that made him comfortable. "What kind of bones did she throw you?" Finn breathed a little shallower.

Rusty shrugged.

Cat and mouse didn't turn Finn on. "How old is the case?"

"A year." Rusty smacked back the answer, and now he looked directly at Finn again.

Finn tapped his mug with a fingernail and waited.

"That's when your father died."

"Yes." He feared something might break the moment and stop Rusty from finishing.

"It's dangerous. Real dangerous. Things like that don't happen if the stakes aren't high."

"I'll bite," Finn said. "What things?"

"Are you satisfied with what they've told you about your father's death?"

"No."

"Denise wasn't, either."

"Why did she care?"

Rusty shook his head. "Chief Duhon was one of those respectful men."

"I knew him well."

"Of course you did. Sorry. He and your mother liked Denise. Maybe because she was good to Eileen. She had her do some work around the paper for her." Rusty colored. "She never let on to your folks, but I guess Eileen needed money."

"She did, and I wish she'd told Dad or me," Finn said. "It's hard to get her to take anything. I'd like to have thanked Denise."

"She wouldn't believe Chief Duhon killed himself."

Finn's head ached, but he'd never been more wide-awake. "She was right."

"You don't know that, and neither did she."

"I *do* know it. Which is something I don't feel like going into."

Rusty shifted in his chair and winced. "Do you intend to try doing something about it?"

"Maybe."

"Okay, you don't know me well enough to trust me. I'd like

to help. I think something went down here that's going to open up this town like a can of rotten sardines."

Finn wanted to wade in, believe the guy, ask him what he knew, but he knew better. "If you've got something you think I ought to know, I hope you'll tell me."

"You're going to have a hell of a time finding anything out about your dad," Rusty said. His nose began to bleed again, and he found a handkerchief to hold over the bridge. He changed his mind about that idea fast and dabbed at the blood instead. "I'm only here because of Denise. You understand that?"

Finn nodded.

"I don't have much, but you've got to say you won't tell anyone else."

"I won't," Finn said.

"Denise said most of the records aren't there."

"Shee-it." Finn let a fist fall to the table. "How did she know that?"

"She looked for them. What she found wasn't complete. Pages had been removed. That's what she thought, anyway."

"What *was* there?"

"She wouldn't tell me."

"Billy Meche has the file?"

"I don't know," Rusty said. "I kind of thought you might."

"Me?"

"If Denise had it at her place, it was gone after she died."

Finn pushed out his lips in a noiseless whistle. "I thought you didn't have anything to do with the mess her place was in? You said you didn't have time to look around."

"Like I said at the time, it was trashed when I got there. And I didn't have long before I heard you coming. Question on my mind is whether you'd been there before."

Finn studied him thoughtfully. "You think I'd tell you if I had?"

Rusty shook his head and winced.

"I wasn't there before you heard Emma and me arrive. But somebody was."

"Yeah, and if Denise had anything useful stashed—about your father's case—it walked." Rusty paused, thinking, rubbing a hand up and down his jaw. "I don't have proof, but I had the feeling she'd gotten her hands on some evidence. She said maybe she'd *show me something to prove she was right*. I kept playing devil's advocate. Figured that was my job."

"And then she died before she had a chance to prove anything to you."

"Thanks for reminding me," Rusty said.

Finn gritted his teeth. "Sorry. How did she get the file—or did Billy let her look?"

"Could be. Denise said Billy was a good guy, too. Maybe not as smart as Tom, though. Finn, your dad was in uniform when he died, but they never found his badge."

Finn studied his fist on the table. He raised his eyes. "You're sure?"

"Denise was. Said it was noted."

"So that's in the file?"

Rusty frowned. "Someone she talked to had noted it, I mean. I can't tell you what's in the file."

His father wouldn't have been on duty without his badge. He carried it, on duty or off. Finn gave a short laugh. "It's probably with his stuff in the attic."

"It won't be," Rusty said. "Denise knew it wasn't in the car or anywhere around the night your dad died."

"I'll look for it."

"I don't blame you. What if you're right and Tom Duhon was murdered? A killer could want the badge as a memento."

Finn had already thought of that. "Yeah. I'd better ask Billy to let me see the file."

"Does he have to show you?"

"He'll show me…if it's there."

Sharp rapping came from the front door. Finn jumped and saw Rusty do the same thing.

Emma could have come back.

But it was Billy Meche on the step, looking uncomfortable. Young Officer Clemens stood behind him. "Evenin'," Billy said. "How're you doin'?"

"Couple more hours and it'll be daybreak," Finn told him.

"Guess so," Billy agreed. He waved his hat to the right. "That's Rusty's Harley by the garage."

"Could be," Finn said.

"He here?"

"Yeah."

Billy walked past him, but Clemens hung back, looking apologetic. "Come on in," Finn said. "Might as well. Everyone else does."

"What happened to you?" Billy asked when he saw Rusty. He immediately looked at Finn.

"Fell off my damn bike," Rusty said without missing a beat.

Billy looked around the kitchen. He went to the sink and picked up the bowl Finn had used, which still contained used swabs. "You must have done it outside Finn's front door, huh?"

"Close."

"We'll get into that later." He looked at Finn's mashed knuckles and cleared his throat. "We'd like you to come down to the station with us, Rusty. Any problem with that?"

Rusty turned chalky. "Why would I do that?"

"Because we're asking nicely. It won't take long, unless your lawyer's not from around here. You got a lawyer?"

"No."

"You'll want one. We can get one for you."

Rusty shot to his feet, pushed back his leather bike jacket

and grasped his hips. "Whoa. Slow down here. Are you arresting me?"

"No. We just want to check somethin' out."

"What?" Rusty asked.

Billy spread his feet. "You'd probably rather we discussed this in private."

Rusty looked at Finn. "I don't give a shit if you talk in front of him."

Clemens wrote notes furiously, and Finn wondered what was being said that could possibly be worth preserving.

"Let's get this over with," Billy said. "We want to run a couple of tests on you is all."

19

Emma pushed open the door at Poke Around and called out, "Sandy? Where are you?" She and Holly Chandall had spent the morning with Emma's lawyer—now Holly's, too—in Toussaint, a town about thirty miles away. Emma had dropped Holly back at her place. When she finished at the shop she intended to hunt down Orville.

"Up here," Sandy said from beside a display of whimsical china set apart from the rest of the shop by bright paper screens. She was perched on a ladder, stacking boxes on top of an old wooden dresser with merchandise on its shelves.

"Nice fuchsia underwear," Emma said, and Sandy snickered, posing an exposed leg to greater benefit. "What there is of it. Come down. Sandy, I love you like a flower, but just in case the next person through the door isn't male, would you cover up the suspenders?"

Sandy climbed down, chuckling to herself. Her beige linen skirt, slit on one side to midthigh, wasn't made to accommodate ladder climbing.

Emma felt her own smile slip away. She turned abruptly, and looked outside at a hedge of red azaleas and a clump of banana trees washed to brilliant green by yesterday's storm. The colors gave her a focus. Holly planned to pack some bags and move out today, while Harold was at work. She'd rented a room over Ona's. Emma worried it was her fault Holly had decided to make her move so suddenly.

"We've had quite a few customers this mornin'," Sandy said. "Tapered off now, though. They don't seem to come back after lunch."

"This place could use a couple of restaurants," Emma said.

"Well, that's not goin' to happen now, is it?" Sandy said.

"What do you mean?"

"You know, with the owner thinkin' of sellin' out. Doesn't sound like restaurants and the like are in the works."

Emma swung around. "Where did you hear about that?" Her heart beat too fast.

"Carl." The sharp downturn of Sandy's mouth showed her concern. "Emma, you must know about it. Carl's been mentionin' it for days. Orville's in negotiations with the new owner."

It wouldn't have hurt Orville to tell her. Emma's palms became hot and sweaty; she felt her mouth tremble. "Oakdale's beautiful. Will they take everythin' that's old and turn it into one more piece of cheap shit?"

"Emma!"

"Don't give me that. I've heard you say a lot worse."

Sandy put an arm around Emma's shoulders. "How about some of my cappuccino? I am now an expert."

"Yes. A double."

She walked into the back room, put her purse in one of the cupboard drawers and returned to the front of the shop. "Why didn't you say somethin' about the estate being sold?" Orville would never have enough; he would always be grabbing more.

"I figured you knew and didn't want to talk about it. I wish I hadn't slipped just now."

The morning hadn't been easy. Holly had clicked with the lawyer, Joe Gable, and was ready to go ahead with a divorce. For herself, she felt as if her own personality, the way she hung on to memories of the good times and let them make her unsure of herself, was holding her back. Joe insisted she would be fine, that he would make sure she came through as easily as possible, but after seeing the photos, he'd been shocked that Emma didn't want to pursue a financial settlement. She'd told him she didn't even want to use the pictures unless they had to. A man might not understand that a woman could be embarrassed at the thought of people seeing pictures of her husband with another woman, so she hadn't tried to explain.

She would leave Orville within the next few days, but she'd decided she would find neutral ground to tell him what she planned. A sneak attack wasn't her style, not after so many years. Emma also had a proposition to make to Orville that could ease the way through the divorce for both of them.

"Come and sit down," Sandy said. "Did you eat lunch?"

"Didn't think about it."

"I anticipated that. Bought you a muffalleta at Ona's. It's still warm. Here. Eat."

Emma wasn't hungry, but she sat down and started on the bun. "Mmm," she said. "So good." And it was. The coffee was better.

"Secrets tonight," Sandy said. She sat on the opposite side of the metal table and laced her fingers together so tightly the knuckles turned white. "Eileen Moggeridge called and said she'd like to come if you still think it's okay. She was lookin' for you."

Another reminder of Finn—as if she needed any at all. "Did you get her number?" When Sandy nodded, Emma said, "I'll call her back after a bit. I should have talked to her about the group by now. How it works. If she still wants to come, she'll be the first new member since Frances. That's been years now—a couple, anyway. Maybe I can pick her up early and take her, so she won't feel funny goin' the first time. You feelin' okay, *cher?*"

"Great." Sandy gave her a sideways look. "You *would* be the one to think of things like lookin' after a newcomer. I'm a selfish bitch."

Emma poked her gently. "No such thing. It was just as well we decided you should stay and open the shop this mornin'. We don't need to miss more business than we have to. Or *I* don't." Even if it wouldn't be long before Orville would have a right to all the earnings from the shop he financed. "Holly did fine with Joe Gable."

"Emma," Sandy said, "don't think I'm goin' weird on you, and you know how I love the group, but I don't want to go tonight."

Emma cradled her cup in her hands and studied Sandy.

"You and I can say anythin' to each other, can't we?" Sandy went on.

"Uh-huh."

"It's Denise. It's her bein' gone and the police not havin' any leads. Mostly her bein' gone, though. Nothin's the same."

"Denise wasn't always there," Emma pointed out. "But I know what you mean. I keep expectin' to hear they've got someone in custody, or at least they're followin' a lead, but nothin'. Not a thing. Sandy, you're jumpin' out of your skin, and you're tremblin'."

Sandy flattened her hands on the tabletop and pressed, as if to prove they weren't shaking. They were. "The biscotti came in," she said, and Emma sensed the other woman wanted to steer the conversation away from herself.

"Good," Emma said. "I've got to talk to Orville." She couldn't ignore reality, even if Sandy would like to.

"Oh." Sandy crossed her arms and shivered. "What happened at the lawyer's?"

"It was just a bunch of formalities today."

"So why do you have to talk to Orville?"

Emma smiled a little and leaned to straighten copper poles in a big bucket. Each one had a crooked, wildly painted bird feeder on top. "Looks like we got rid of a couple of these."

"Yes," Sandy said. "Look at the flamingoes."

Emma turned in the direction of the pink metal flamingoes with necks like vacuum cleaner hoses, eyes that lit up and duck feet, only they weren't where she'd last seen them. "Where?" she said.

"Gone. A woman bought all three of them and would have taken more if we'd had them. Wants me to call if they come back in."

Emma pulled up her shoulders. "We'll get a couple." Every sale delighted her, and the shop had started to do quite well.

"So why do you want to talk to Orville?" Sandy said.

"You don't give up," Emma told her. "Don't worry about it. He isn't at home, and he isn't at the office. I really want to see him somewhere…" She let the sentence trail away.

"Mmm?" Sandy said.

"I'd rather it wasn't at home," Emma told her. "Let's leave it at that."

Sandy's eyes filled with tears. "Oh, Emma. Because you're afraid of what he'll do?"

"Not really," she lied. "I think it will be easier on both of us if we aren't in familiar surroundings, or not where…well, you know. Not in Orville's house."

"Well, you're goin' to get your wish, *cher*. The man himself is headin' this way with my own dear husband." Sandy coughed several times. "It'll be okay, won't it?"

"Sure it will." Emma smiled, but wouldn't let herself turn to look at the approaching men.

Sandy got up and opened the door, letting in a rush of hot breeze. "Hi, handsome and handsome. Come on in." She kissed Carl with enough relish to be heard from where Emma sat.

"Hello, Emma," Orville said. He sounded quiet. They hadn't seen one another for two days.

She wiggled the fingers of one hand in the air. Her throat didn't want to work.

Sandy and Carl, arms around one another, strolled to stand by the table. Orville remained behind Emma.

Average height, medium coloring and a pleasant face didn't distinguish Carl Viator, but he gave off energy in waves, and he was probably the most fit man Emma knew—with the exception of Finn. What he lacked in physical good looks, Carl made up for in charisma. Emma liked him. He had calmed a storm for her with Orville on more than one occasion, and she would always be grateful.

"How's my girl, Emma?" he said, grinning when Sandy stood on her toes to nip the lobe of his ear.

"I'm okay," she said. Chatter was beyond her today. "How's it going for you, Carl?"

"Good enough. The guy who owns Oakdale now is skittish. Inherited from old man Thompson—he's a distant relative of some kind—and he doesn't know a thing about running a place like this. What he really wants is to be certain he gets as much out of it as possible—and one or two other items. I think he'll sell—as long as he gets the special considerations he's looking for. That's a condition of sale. Not what we'd hoped for."

"It's not a problem," Orville said. "We shouldn't bore the ladies."

"I didn't know Mr. Thompson had died," Emma said. "Or that the property was for sale."

"It's all been on the hush-hush." Carl laughed. "It wasn't for sure until we got a great idea for the area and made the guy an offer he doesn't want to refuse."

Emma took a huge breath. "What's the idea?"

"Mixed use," Orville said, too fast for Emma. "Of course, we'll hang on to the ambiance. I know how much that means to you, Emma."

"And me," Sandy said.

Seeing the quizzical expression on Carl's face, Emma didn't believe Orville, but she couldn't say as much, and it was none of her business.

"What does the owner want in order to sell?" Emma didn't feel like being put off with a pat on the head.

Orville shrugged. "It's all in the family, so you might as well know. He wants the bundle I already mentioned, plus an invite into the golf club, and he'd like to be city manager."

Carl snorted. "He thinks it'll give him the inside track on land deals."

"He's the type who likes his fingers in all the pies," Orville said.

Like you. "We've already got a city manager," Emma said.

Orville gave her a pitying look. "That doesn't stop this guy from thinkin' I can make a change if I want to. I can, come to that."

"Will you?" She hated the maneuvering he took in stride.

Orville laughed. "Well, let's just say we couldn't have something like that written into the sales contract for this place. It would only be an understandin'. And there are things a person expects that don't happen, but you can't exactly step forward and complain. That's life. He'll just have more time to play golf, and it'll be no skin off any of our noses if he wants to spend his money at the club."

In other words, once Orville had what he wanted, there would be no new city manager. Emma was glad of that but detested Orville's underhanded methods.

"Will this old house stay?" Sandy asked.

"Do you want it to?" Orville said to her, and when she nodded, he added, "Then it stays. We like to keep the little ladies happy, don't we, Carl?"

"Real, real happy," Carl said.

"I want you to be thinkin' of any renovations you'd like made in the shop, Emma," Orville said. "There's bound to be construction goin' on around here, so why not use the opportunity?"

Emma got up and faced her husband. "I don't like to interrupt you in the middle of a workday, but could you spare me maybe an hour?" Even to herself, she sounded ridiculously formal. "Shouldn't take any longer."

Orville drew his mouth into a tight line, and she expected him to refuse. Instead he said, "Of course. Carl drove, so I'll have to ask you to take me back to the office afterward, Emma."

"I'll do that."

The four of them avoided looking at one another until Carl said, "I thought I could take you for a drink, darlin'."

Sandy didn't answer him.

"You go ahead," Emma said. "I'll manage just fine."

"Are you sure?"

"Sure," Emma told Sandy, and the other woman gathered her belongings and her husband and all but ran from the shop, a huge, false smile on her face.

"How are the RSVPs comin?" Orville said as soon as they were alone. "Less than a week to go."

"I think everyone wants to have a party with Mayor Lachance," she said, afraid her smile must be every bit as false as Sandy's had been. "The invitations could have gone out the same day as the event and they'd have accepted. So far, no regrets."

"I wish I didn't have regrets," Orville said, his hands deep in his pants pockets and his light hair falling boyishly over his brow. He jerked his head to move the hair back. "I went into Lafayette to see my doctor."

Her stomach rolled. "Are you ill?"

"Not the way you mean. I've always been able to talk to Roger. You know. Man-to-man. I was straight with him. Didn't pull any punches. I told him—well, I said things hadn't been so good between us for some months."

Roger French, M.D., old pal of Orville's and occasionally one of the gang at Pat Damalis's from what Orville said, always looked at Emma as if she was something he would like to study closely. She couldn't stand him, and he wasn't her physician, although he had been the one to examine her after she lost the baby, because he was at the house when it happened.

"Roger said it's natural for relationships to go through these patches. Disillusionment, he called it." Orville glanced toward the door. "Close up the shop. We'll go home for an hour or two."

Emma couldn't move or think of the next thing to say. Her legs seems weighted down. Orville couldn't be…yes, he was suggesting they have sex. Nothing between them could ever be love again.

He went swiftly to lock the door and turn over the sign to show the shop as closed. "We can get your things and go out the back way. If we make sure we don't bump into any customers, we don't have to make excuses for disappointin' them."

"Would you mind if we stayed here?" At least they were surrounded by windows, and Orville cared too much for his reputation to be seen losing his temper in public.

He approached her slowly, taking off his jacket as he came and draping it over a ceramic dog. "No," he said. "I don't mind, as long as you don't mind everyone watchin' me kiss you."

The way he moved, deliberately slowly, the drawling delivery of what he said, would be pitiful if they didn't unnerve her. Emma held her ground. "A lot has changed between us," she said.

He took her by the arms. "Roger thinks that's partly my

fault. You were young when we married, very young. Maybe I didn't make enough allowances for that."

He didn't make enough allowances? "I don't know what that means but it doesn't matter now. I intend to remember the good times."

Orville rolled back onto his heels and looked at her from beneath lowered eyelids. "You've gone back to the curls," he said, studying her with his head on one side. "Maybe I like it after all. It's in fashion now."

The kiss came without warning, a crushing, invasive kiss that unbalanced Emma. She grabbed on to him, and he took her touch as encouragement. He pulled the band from her hair and scraped his fingers across her scalp. She couldn't get her breath or turn her head. Orville pushed a hand inside her blouse and bra to squeeze her breast.

He gave her an instant while he caught his breath, and she jerked her head away. "Stop it. Anyone could walk by and see us."

"I wanted to go home, *cher,*" he said, his voice tight with a too familiar emotion. Aroused, Orville could be terrifying. He walked her into the back room and closed the door behind them. She heard him lock it. "Just in case Sandy decides she's forgotten somethin'," he said, pawing at her some more.

"Sandy has keys to all the doors," Emma said. She felt afraid, more afraid than she ever had even when he hit her in the past. "I don't want this, Orville. We need to be sensible, reasonable."

Several of her buttons had popped open, and he undid the front fastener on her bra. "You've got great tits," he said, staring at her breasts, pressing the nipples hard with his thumbs. "They were the first thing I noticed about you." His laugh wasn't pretty.

Her purse, and her little gun, were in a drawer in the dressing room. That she'd even thought about them shook her. "Get away from me," she said, dodging out of his way, fumbling to do up the bra. "I've got something to suggest to you. Something good for both of us, but I can't explain when you're like this."

"Roger's right," Orville said. "I put you on a pedestal and treated you like you were made of glass. You didn't really want that. You needed a man to take control."

She put a rack of clothes between them. "You've been in control from the moment we met. It was okay at the beginning, but it's not anymore. Not for me."

"Because you've changed?" He followed her slowly, and she retreated. "We'll talk about Secrets afterwards."

Afterwards?

"Women like you want to pretend they're pure. They want to be forced. Rough sex excites them. Baby, your wish is my command."

He could force her. "You haven't come near me in months. You don't want me anymore. I've seen a lawyer, Orville. I want a divorce."

Instantly his face turned purplish red. He didn't say a word, but he took hold of the rack of clothes and used it to trap her in a corner. Reaching across, he took her by the throat.

"You'll make marks," she said. Thinking was hard. "People will see what you did to me."

"You fuckin' slut. It's that soldier boy, isn't it? Your type always has to have a man to look after them. You wouldn't be talkin' divorce if you didn't have another bed to go to."

Quiet, quiet. Don't rile him more than he is.

"Answer me." He threw the rack aside and lunged at her, lifted her under the arms and threw her down on top of a table display. His hand clawed beneath her skirt to her panties.

Emma swivelled and kicked his midsection, hard, doubling him over, and threw herself off the opposite side of the table.

Orville clutched his gut and stared at her, his mouth hanging open, his eyes filled with loathing. "No divorce, y'hear me? I won't divorce you, not ever. I've watched you get more full of yourself with every hour you spend in the company of those dried-up, disgruntled females you call friends. If they had sex in their lives, men who could keep 'em where they belong, they'd be at home, not encouragin' weak-brains like you to disrespect their husbands."

The horrible question that plagued Emma was how she could ever have thought Orville wonderful, how she could have fallen in love with and married him.

He started coming around the table toward her, and she made a retreating move for his every advance.

What was wrong with her that she had allowed him to carry her away? He'd talked her down, worn her down, until she'd believed he was all she wanted.

"Stand still," he said. "You know you'll never get away from me."

"I will," she said, as clearly and steadily as she could. "As of today, we don't live together anymore. *Listen* to me, Orville. You stand still and listen to me. What matters most to you? Beating me down, or all the things you want to accomplish? What about your ambitions, Orville? This isn't the big city. People don't like it here when the people they're supposed to look up to have sordid lives."

"I swear," he said slowly, "that you will regret ever tryin' to mess with me."

"I already do. I'm going to offer you a deal. For me, Orville, not you, but you'll benefit. I don't want this whole town to know the fool you've made of me. Give me what I want quietly, and you'll get what you want, too."

"I've got what I want, and I'm gettin' a lot more. You'll be at my side until and unless I decide to get rid of you. You understand?"

They continued to circle the table, Emma holding the edge with both hands to steady herself. Orville sweated. Sweat stained the collar of his blue shirt dark, and rings from beneath his arms all but reached his waist. He drew in shallow breaths and never took his eyes from her face.

"If you will agree to separate right now, without any more of this, I'll stand by you in public, at least through the next few weeks. I'll be your hostess, whatever you need, but I can't keep on being your wife."

He slammed a fist on the table, and swept scarves and trinkets onto the floor. "I want *you.* I want you at my side. I want you in my bed. I want between your legs whenever and wherever I please, you uppity bitch."

Emma drove her fingertips into the table. Her legs shook so violently she feared she would trip. At the sound of her phone ringing in her purse, she panted, darted her attention toward the changing room.

"That's probably lover boy," Orville sneered. "No man gets what's mine. I'll see him dead first."

Emma didn't say anything, but the thought of Orville locked in combat with Finn brought her teeth together hard. Too bad her husband wasn't the type of man to use his fists, except on a woman.

The phone stopped ringing, and Emma's heart seemed to stop right with it.

"I loved you," she told Orville. "I really did. I wish it hadn't ended, but it did. It has—for both of us."

"It wasn't my fault you couldn't give birth to a live child." His saliva hit her face. "Any more than it was my fault you messed up your insides so bad gettin' rid of the thing you never got pregnant again."

Within her, Emma felt a cold, quiet space open up. Tears stood in her eyes, but even they felt cold, as if they had turned to ice. She couldn't feel her hands and feet. Her lips tingled.

Again her phone rang.

This time Orville backed toward the noise, located her purse and threw it at her. She let it land on the table but didn't touch it. For an instant she'd expected him to go for the phone himself and answer it. He could well have found the gun.

The phone kept on ringing.

"Answer the goddamn thing and watch what you say. We aren't finished, sweetheart. You and I are never goin' to be finished. The only question is how miserable your life's gonna be from now on."

You have no idea what I can do to you.

She pushed a hand into her purse, took out the phone and flipped it on. All the time she looked back at Orville. "Yes."

"Emma?" Why did it have to be Finn?

"Yes."

"Can we talk?"

"No." She wanted to break off the call. Even as she needed to cry out for help, she knew she would not involve Finn Duhon in this sordid skirmish.

"Something's wrong," he said. "Speak to me. Tell me."

"No."

"Things have happened since last night. I need to discuss them with you."

"No."

Orville leered at her and nodded slowly, as if whatever she was doing pleased him. As if he approved of the way she was handling the call.

"Okay, you can't talk to me. Can you tell me where you are?"

"No."

She was lucky he kept his voice low.

"You're with him?"

Emma didn't answer.

"Okay, I understand. Just tell me this, are you safe?"

She wanted to close her eyes but didn't dare. "Yes." The pistol was only inches from her fingers.

"Last night was the best night of my life." Finn paused. "You're an old-fashioned girl, and the guilt monster eats you up, but you're the greatest. Believe it. The greatest woman I ever met, and I won't give up on you, Emma, so get used to the idea. I'll hold you every time you let me, and it'll be enough. Almost enough. I'm a patient man."

Emma blinked rapidly. Tears didn't fall. Perhaps they *had* turned to ice.

"You need me, and I'm going to find you," Finn said and hung up.

Emma slid her phone shut and dropped it back into her bag. She kept her hand inside and closed it over the gun—and saw Orville look at the bag, the way she had her hand, and frown. He swallowed.

"I want you to go away," she said. "Walk out the door without looking back, then go somewhere and think about what I've offered you."

"You've got a gun."

She ignored the statement. "I don't want my parents to know what you really are or what you've done to me. I want to live in this town in peace, and I'll do what I have to, to make that happen."

"You wouldn't have the guts to pull the trigger," he said.

She ignored him again. "We are going to pretend this is amicable. Understand? And then there will be a peaceful withdrawal and you'll never bother me again."

"You'll be left with nothing," he said through his teeth.

"I've got nothing now. Things can only get better, and I'll make them on my own terms. Now get out."

"I'll spread rumors around Pointe Judah that'll make you want to go as far and as fast as you can," he said. "I can link you with Duhon, no sweat. You'll never make a life here. Adulteresses and whores are all the same to people in this town. I won't need your phoney *help*. I'll run my campaign as a brokenhearted husband betrayed by a round-heeled wife. You'll get me more votes this way than you would have simperin' in photographs."

Emma took the small, wooden-handled weapon from her purse. She didn't point it at Orville, simply held it. Next she removed a copy of one of the photographs, the one of Orville with a woman's head in his lap. Joe Gable had made it with his scanner and computer, and kept the original with the others. They were in his safe.

"I hate simperin' photographs, don't you?" she said to Orville. "What would you say you were doin' in this one?" She turned it so he could see. "I don't think you're simperin'."

20

Emma didn't know how Orville got back to his offices, and she didn't care. He had walked out the back door of the shop, his face rigid, his eyes darting toward and away from her. After she'd shown him the picture, he didn't say another word.

She sat in the back room for twenty minutes, just giving herself time to calm down. After that, she brushed her hair and left it down, took a new turquoise shirt off one of the racks and changed into it. The turquoise looked good with her white skirt. She splashed water on her face, and applied new lipstick and mascara—and felt human again. Shaken, but human, and filled with hope that her life was going to change, not that it would be easy, at least for the near future, but different. That was good.

Hammering at the shop door reached her loud and clear. Emma considered ignoring whatever impatient shoppers might be there, but, as she knew better than ever, whatever money she could make and stash away before Orville kicked her out would be essential.

She walked into the shop and stopped when she saw Finn, his hands cupped around his eyes, peering through a window. He saw her and waved. It was too late to retreat, even if she wanted to.

She didn't.

Running, Emma arrived at the door and let him in. He reached for her, but she stepped quickly back. "The windows," she said. "Where's your truck?" A more cautious woman would just send him away, but she was beyond some forms of caution—especially when it came to Finn Duhon.

He pointed. "I left it on the other side of the palms."

"I want to be with you," she said, in such a hurry she wondered if he would understand.

He did. "You have no idea how much I want to be with you, too. Were you here when I called?"

She filled her lungs and let the breath out slowly. "Yes, but I couldn't talk."

"Because Orville was here with you? You sounded frightened."

"He was here." If she hoped for a smooth exit from her marriage, giving Finn a reason to go after Orville wouldn't be smart. "Nothing major, but I didn't feel right having a conversation with you in front of him."

Finn gave a wicked smile. "I'm glad you think I'm too important to chat with around your husband."

Men had impossible egos. "Go to Ona's. Out Back. It's pretty quiet there. I'll give you a head start and join you. Don't park in the lots."

Finn saluted. He gave the surrounding area a once-over and kissed her quickly. "Drive carefully."

When Emma walked into Ona's Out Back she didn't immediately see him, and her heart performed a silly flip. Her sandals slapped against her heels as she walked. Then she saw him. He was at the table closest to the kitchen, out of sight of the restaurant door, but he had stood up and leaned around the corner to watch her approach. She wanted to rush to him, and that made her feel young and a bit foolish at the same time.

Finn saw the shine in her bright blue eyes from across the room. The lady was glad to see him, not that he had any reason to doubt it after seeing her at Oakdale. He wished there was no Orville and the two of them were free to just let this thing between them go wherever it might be headed. Where he hoped it was headed.

He smiled at her and pulled out a chair. "Note the sneaky positioning of this table," he said. "If an enemy approaches, one of us can hot foot it through the kitchens to Out Front. Perfect, huh?"

"I expect they teach you things like that in Sneaky Ranger School." Emma sat and watched him lower his loose-limbed body into his own chair. She liked looking at him too much. They ought to be careful, because she didn't want to give Orville any definite ammunition, not that he was likely to be so cocky about that or anything else in the near future.

Orville had cooked his own goose to a crisp.

Annie Duhon appeared as if she'd been waiting just inside the kitchen for Emma to arrive. "Tea?" she said.

"Uh-huh. Exactly the way I had it last time. Do I smell beignets?"

Annie nodded, a big smile on her pretty face. "Finn said you both needed them for strength."

When Annie returned to the kitchen, Emma raised her brows at Finn. "You are teachin' me so much. I never knew beignets gave you strength, but I do love them." She glanced toward the kitchen again.

"Don't worry about Annie," Finn said. "She knows we're friends, but that's all. Old school friends. And she wouldn't say anythin' to anyone."

"Because you've warned her not to."

Emma would never be fobbed off with facile explanations. "Somethin' like that."

"And you probably told Eileen, too—and Aaron."

He couldn't figure if she was annoyed. "We're family. We stick together."

She relaxed, and he breathed easier.

"Eileen's comin' to Secrets with me today. I'm going to pick her up early, so we can talk about what she can expect."

"I'm glad. Does it mean you all tell your secrets, or is it really that other thing you said?"

"Secrets of a Successful Life is our full name," she said, wanting to laugh. "We reinforce one another. And we share a few things we wouldn't tell anyone else."

"So you probably have rules about not repeating what you hear?" He sounded a bit disappointed.

Emma kept a straight face. "Absolutely. And if you don't share somethin' really awful, somethin' you'd go to prison for if it got out, we don't let you join. That's how we make sure each member stays loyal."

For a moment, Finn studied her, frowning. "Oh sure," he said, and shook his head.

"There aren't many of us," she told him.

"Quality, not quantity?" He raised a brow.

"Original," Emma said. "Most of us met in the same beauty salon. We talked about getting together, but we needed a place. That's when we got together with Angela. She'd rented the second house on John Sims's property on Mill Lane several years back. Just around the corner from the salon.

"She went to the beauty shop sometimes—to buy products or use the steam room." She didn't tell him about the burns on Angela's face that caused her to be shy in public. "One time Angela heard the owner, Lynnette, talking to me about not having any luck finding a place to meet. A couple of days later Mrs. Merryfield showed up to invite Lynnette and me to Angela's. That's how we got started, and we've been meetin' there ever since."

"Yeah?" Finn said, distracted. "Mrs. Merryfield?"

"She's one of Lobelia Forestier's buddies, and she looks after Angela. When we started Secrets, all a member needed was an invitation. We trusted our instincts that we would all be loyal." She thought for a moment. "Everyone joins in and shares the things that bother them—and the happy stuff, of course. We just bonded. Women can be like that."

He couldn't put off talking about Rusty any longer. "After you left last night, Rusty turned up. He wanted to know if we'd taken anythin' from Denise's house."

Emma screwed up her eyes. "Rusty heard us arrive. We were hardly there before Billy showed up. What chance did he think we had?"

"I don't know." He'd decided not to tell her anything about Rusty's comments regarding Tom Duhon's police records, or the badge. Hours of search in the attic of his parents' house hadn't turned up anything he wanted to find. Aaron would show up after school to spend the weekend, and Finn intended to ask him to start cleaning out up there. "Emma, after a bit, Billy showed at my place, too. He took Rusty in."

She stared.

Annie brought the tea, but Emma never took her eyes off Finn's. "Thanks, Annie," she said vaguely. "Why would Billy do that to Rusty?"

"Something to do with Denise's murder."

"That's ridiculous. Is Rusty still at the station?"

"Yeah. Or he was last I heard."

Why would they want Rusty? Gentle, sad Rusty, who wouldn't do anything to anyone? The beignets arrived. Emma picked one up without thinking and burned her fingers. She dropped it on her plate in a cloud of powdered sugar. "I don't get it," she said. "Even if Rusty had a way to get his hands on lethal drugs, he's not the type. They must be desperate to pin this on someone. Finn, we can't let them push Rusty around."

He leaned across the table toward her. "He's agreed to a DNA test."

"DNA? Oh."

"Right," Finn said. "They mentioned rape, remember?"

She looked at the teapot as if she wished it would pour itself, so Finn did it for her. He could see her connecting dots. "Milk, hmm?"

"Yes. Finn, I don't like talkin' about my friends' business, but Rusty really loved Denise, and she was fond of him."

"I figured that." He pushed the cup and saucer toward her. "Drink some of this."

"What I'm trying to say is that they were lovers."

"Which means the semen could be Rusty's anyway."

Emma turned slightly pink. "Mmm." She drank the tea almost to the bottom of the cup. "Rusty will tell Billy that, won't he?"

"I should think so. Unless he thinks…aw, hell, I don't know. It wasn't a secret, was it?"

"Kind of," she said, sounding miserable. "Denise wasn't into commitment, and she never actually said they made love, not in so many words."

"So maybe they didn't."

"They did." She realized she'd raised her voice and pressed her lips together. "I didn't mean to shout. I saw Rusty leaving Denise's place in the morning on more than one occasion. Denise and I used to meet for early coffee. Being me, I just waded in and asked about it. She smiled and didn't say no."

"But she didn't say yes?"

Emma's faint blush turned scarlet. "I saw something in the bathroom," she said. "Rusty wouldn't rape Denise or anyone else. It's a disgustin' suggestion, and I'm goin' to tell Billy so."

Finn figured it would be a waste of time to suggest Emma stay out of it. He also didn't think it was his place to say the lab doing the tests thought they had mixed DNA, male and male, as well as Denise's. They believed two men had sexual contact with Denise shortly before she died.

"Celebration!" Holly Chandall walked into the conversation room at Secrets with four pastry boxes, strung together in twos and carried by a loop, one set in each hand. She had already donned her tunic. "Mrs. Merryfield? Where are you, *cher?*"

Emma sat beside Eileen Moggeridge on one of several overstuffed tartan love seats. She looked at the other woman and smiled reassurance. "This is Holly," she said. "She's—"

"I've seen her," Eileen said, her dark eyes uncertain. "She doesn't live far from me. Her husband farms rice, I think."

"Holly," Emma said. "This is Eileen. She's our first novice in two years, and she's understandably nervous, so be nice."

Holly laughed aloud. Mrs. Merryfield arrived, and Holly gave her the boxes and told her to stay put before marching determinedly to shake Eileen's hand. "Hi, almost neighbor. I've seen you, too. Welcome. I should have made sure we met before now. Your husband works out on one of the rigs, doesn't he?"

"Yes," Eileen said, with little expression.

"We're an impossible bunch," Holly said. "And we'll only make you impossible, too, but it's a great way to be."

Eileen said, "Thanks, I'm lookin' forward to it." A tall, voluptuous woman with black hair that waved to the shoulder, her face was a feminine version of her brother's.

"Where is everyone?" Holly said. "I'm never early."

"You are tonight," Emma said, and grinned. "Maybe it was easier to leave home—your current home."

Holly put a finger to her lips. "Shh. I get to tell all about it."

The others straggled in, Frances with red-and-white beads in her cornrows tonight and looking beautiful in her pink tunic. Emma hadn't changed into hers yet, because she wanted Eileen to have a chance to get used to things first.

"How long am I supposed to stand here like this?" Mrs. Merryfield said. Tonight she wore a crushed black velvet hat on top of her red fingerwaves, and Emma figured she'd forgotten to take it off when she returned from shopping. As usual, a pair of rolled-down stockings rested on the tops of Mrs. Merryfield's black lace-up shoes.

"Mrs. M," Holly said, making everyone's eyes widen. They had never been invited to shorten that lady's name or to be familiar in any way. "Like I said, this is a celebration. A double celebration now we have a new member. Eileen Moggeridge, meet Mrs. Merryfield, who looks after Angela and the house. Mrs. M's a gem."

Lynnette, who had already waved at Eileen in welcome, snickered at Holly's newfound affection for Mrs. Merryfield and at Mrs. Merryfield's sour expression. Stretched out on a love seat, Lynnette wore pink bunny slippers to match her tunic. She bobbled her feet up and down. Her nails were inevitably an advertisement for her salon. Tonight they were painted in black and silver stripes, with rhinestones adhered along the tips.

Suky-Jo saw Eileen and opened her arms wide. "Eileen, we've met, and I've seen you with that handsome boy of yours. Time we got to know each other. This is for you." She swished across the room to give Eileen a rainbow sachet. "Put that under your pillow and dream sweet dreams," she said in a stage whisper.

Eileen held the sachet to her nose with soft pleasure in her expression.

"I've brought tasters of a lot of the desserts Annie and I will be serving for Emma's big party next week, Mrs. M," Holly said. "And I hope it was all right for me to put some bottles of champagne on ice in the kitchen." She didn't give Mrs. Merryfield a chance to respond. "If you'd rather not fuss with putting all these things on plates, I'll gladly do it. Just tell me which plates to use. Annie's the dessert maker. I'll explain some of how we're goin' to present it all at Emma's."

Angela, who usually arrived first, came into the room, her silk tunic swishing. She looked immediately at Eileen and nodded. "Welcome, Eileen," she said. Her hair was combed forward on one side to hide the worst scars, something she'd stopped doing a long time ago. "Emma has told us about you. I hope you understand our little rules."

Why make a big deal? Emma didn't often get annoyed with Angela, but she was now. Or maybe she'd been through too much for one day and it wouldn't take anything to set her off. "Eileen understands," she said.

"We're having a celebration," Mrs. Merryfield announced. "Holly's brought food and champagne." She raised her nose. "Is that something I smell cooking in my kitchen?"

"We-ell," Holly said. "I'm reheating the red-bean soup I made yesterday."

A long, "Oooh," went up from everyone present, even Angela.

"It's my mother's recipe, and red-bean soup doesn't come any richer than that. If we're goin' to drink champagne, even with desserts, we need a coat on our stomachs."

Angela sat in her upholstered rocking chair and stretched. If anything, she seemed even more pale than usual, but she gradually relaxed.

"If y'all had asked me what I wanted most in the world, I wouldn't have known," Wendy Saunders said, her green eyes bright with anticipation. "Now it's as obvious as the nose on my face. Holly Chandall's red-bean soup. I'll just bet you crushed plenty of those red pepper pods in there. And a mess of onion. And ham bones." She waggled her head as if in ecstasy.

"And big chunks of ham and a little more cayenne than most people use, on account of my mama says it makes all the difference." Holly beamed.

Emma suffered through another wave of misgivings about her friend's rapid decision to divorce her husband and move out into an apartment. The decision had been Holly's, but Emma just knew she'd spurred her on.

"I'll serve the soup," Mrs. Merryfield said, shocking all of them. "And I'll take the desserts to the kitchen and put them on plates. Will you have those at the same time as the champagne?"

"Why, yes," Holly said. "Thank you. I'll let you do the soup, then I'll help with the other a bit later."

"We share everything here," Angela said to Eileen the instant the door closed behind Mrs. Merryfield. "Our hopes and dreams, and our pain. We laugh a lot, but we cry some, too. Where's Sandy?"

Emma had noted her absence, though she'd hoped Sandy would change her mind. "She's really upset about Denise. I don't think she'll join us."

Something like annoyance tightened Angela's features. "She knows we need to help one another through this sadness. Does she think she's the only one who feels bad about it?"

The comment wasn't like Angela, and Emma wondered if she was unconsciously exerting her leadership in front of Eileen.

"Forgive me," Angela said. "I'm tired. It's been harder to sleep lately."

Mrs. Merryfield delivered soup bowls with handles on the sides, each one on a large saucer with a spoon. She set them on top of the large coffee table in the middle of the room and left again.

Seated on the floor around the table, they ate in silence for a few minutes before Holly said, "I've got so much to tell all of you."

"Did you put your name in the book?" Angela asked.

"Of course."

"If we have something we really want to discuss, we write our names in that book by Angela's chair," Emma told Eileen. "Don't you go thinkin' we're just about serious stuff, though. We're always lookin' for ideas to help us and just plain havin' fun, right, ladies?"

"Right," the chorus came back.

"I'm first in the book," Holly said. "So I get to go now."

"Uh-uh," Angela said, but she gave her whispery chuckle. "Not unless Eileen feels she can share something near and dear to her."

"She can share when she's ready," Holly said.

"Yes," Emma said quickly. "She understands how much we rely on the group not to repeat anything they hear."

Angela frowned.

"It's okay," Eileen said. "I know you came together at first because you needed to feel safe and be understood—and to help each other be stronger women. You've got a lot of history, but you hardly know me. This is the best soup, Holly."

Holly said, "Thank you."

Eileen set down her spoon. "If I don't share something really personal, you won't feel comfortable talkin' in front of me." She looked from one woman to the other. "There's someone I've been in love with for years. Not my husband. He doesn't know about it, of course. I still hope I'll get together with him one day—my dream lover, I mean."

Spoons paused or were set down with care.

Emma's skin turned clammy.

Laughter rang out. Eileen's laughter. She laughed until she got hiccups and subsided into gusts of chuckles. "You should see your faces," she said. "I was supposed to share a secret hope, wasn't I? I'm hopin' for a dream lover."

21

Emma toiled along the roads spreading around the golf club. She hadn't run since Denise died, but she couldn't suspend her routines forever.

A storm threatened. This was the time of year for bad weather, and hurricanes could hit at any time. Clammy, her tank top stuck to her skin, she glanced at a sky turned deep green and slashed with black. The wind at her back blew hot, but at least it eased the stillness that fell between gusts.

Tile roofs on the houses shimmered in the heat, and mica glittered on white sidewalks.

Last night she had slept on top of a sleeping bag on the floor of Holly Chandall's new, very small, apartment over Ona's. She intended to go there again tonight. It didn't make sense to isolate herself at her parents' home until she and Orville came to some sort of agreement.

Yesterday, leaving Sandy to deal with the shop, Emma had spent the day alone in Orville's house, waiting for him, staying until it was clear he wasn't coming back for the night. Today had been the same, except she'd left earlier, her car parked out front, to go for her run. She'd expected him to contact her earlier, almost as soon as he'd left her on Friday, but there had been no word from him.

Determination controlled any fear of confronting him

alone, but she had taken the precaution of telling Sandy her plans and the pistol stayed close at hand.

The clubhouse came into view on her right, set well back from the road and surrounded by lush grounds. The greens, still dotted with straggling players, stretched behind and in both directions from the club. Sand traps and stands of oaks stood out against the emerald-colored course.

Sunday evenings were busy at the club. She scanned the parking lot for Orville's Mercedes but didn't see it, although it wouldn't be hard to miss among so many similar vehicles.

The next move had to be his. She'd already decided that if she didn't hear from him today, then tomorrow she would send word to his office that she wouldn't be available for his party. She would move on and try not to look back. If he didn't try to complicate her life, she would stay out of his way and never bad-mouth him.

Finn had called yesterday, and she'd told him she needed to get through this on her own. He hadn't called back, and she wasn't sure she was glad. Finn had lived through woman trouble before and could have decided he didn't need more.

Humidity made the going hard. Emma ran around the wide curve that would bring her back to Orville's—and saw the Mercedes parked in the driveway, with Orville leaning on the trunk and looking up and down the street.

Emma stopped, grasped her knees and let her head hang down while she got her breath. And while she decided if she could face her soon to be ex-husband.

"Emma?"

His voice reached her, stunned her. Orville didn't shout in public. She looked up and raised a hand before running on, closing the space between them, her feet keeping pace with the drum of her heart, a deep sickness gripping her stomach.

Get it over with. The words sounded good inside her head, but putting them into action wouldn't be so easy.

As she drew closer, he separated himself from his car and walked to meet her. She wondered where he'd been staying. At Damalis's? They had rooms there, or so she'd been told.

"Emma," Orville said when she reached him, his voice soft and foreign. He took her unresisting hands in his and asked, "How are you? I was a pig, and I'm sorry, not that I expect you to care how I feel."

He must keep clothes elsewhere. The tan suit and cream shirt he wore were uncreased. Apart from the drawn expression on his face, he showed no sign of having suffered.

"I'll be leavin' shortly," she told him. That wasn't what she'd intended to say but rather what she wanted to do—as soon as possible. Emma wanted to get away from him.

"Aren't you here to talk to me?" he asked.

"I was here yesterday and today," she told him. "Now I'm almost out of time, but I can stay a little while."

The truth was that she didn't want to be alone with him anywhere without her gun, but most especially inside his house. She walked briskly to a gate in the fence around the grounds and let herself in.

She heard Orville close the gate behind him.

"I ran into Harold Chandall," Orville said. "He's lookin' for his wife. Any idea where she might be?"

Emma managed not to break her stride, but she felt suddenly very cold. "She's probably shoppin' or somethin'." At least it wasn't an outright lie. Harold had been in New Orleans for the past few days, and that had given Holly a chance to move into Ona's unimpeded.

Dragging a chair from a table by the pool, Emma sat in the shade of some clump bamboo. The sky seemed to get closer to the land while she watched.

Orville picked up another chair and placed it so he would face her rather than sit beside her. He took off his jacket and tie, and threw them over the back of the chair. Once he was settled, he regarded Emma steadily for long enough to make her uncomfortable.

Finally she said, "What's the stare for?"

"I want to remember the way you look now, while we're still man and wife. I've been a fool, and I wish I could change it."

She didn't respond, didn't help him in any way.

"Stay with me, *cher.*"

Emma had expected that. "It's too late. It was probably too late the day we married. Like you said the other day, I was pretty young. People change. I've changed a lot, and we don't work together anymore." They had never worked, not really.

"What will you do?"

"Live at my folks' place until I can afford to go away to school again. Work. I'll get a job."

"I don't want you to do that."

She inclined her head and gave him a look that said what she did wouldn't be his decision.

"You like the shop. Sandy likes it there, too, and she's your best friend. It's good for the two of you to be together."

How long would he try to wear her down? Emma wondered. "We'll miss workin' together and havin' fun with it, but Sandy and I will always be friends. She doesn't need what I pay her. It's peanuts, anyway."

"I'm givin' you the shop."

She thought she'd misheard him and squinted into his face.

"The whole property will belong to me. What I do with it is up to me. You get the shop. You've earned it."

What the shop made wouldn't keep her, but she wanted to accept, even while she feared accepting anything from him at all. "Thank you," she said. "I can't take it, but I'd like to manage it for you, and you can pay me a small salary. It doesn't make a lot, but it's gettin' better. Would that work?"

"However you want to do it. But whatever you take in is yours—you'll need it."

She smiled. He was right, and she didn't want to leave Poke Around. "I've packed clothes," she told him, and got a stupid lump in her throat. Leaving was what she'd dreamed of doing, but it was like her to get maudlin at the end. "I haven't taken anythin' else."

"You can have whatever you want," Orville said, leaning forward and resting his elbows on his knees. "Emma, we have to separate, I know that, but we don't have to rush into a divorce. Give it some time."

"I've given it time."

"Yes." He nodded. "I know you have, but I'm still askin' you to take more time over this. You don't know how much I need you. I'm such a fool, I couldn't tell you till you were leavin' me." He wiped the back of a hand across his eyes.

"At the shop I told you I wanted us to be friends," Emma said. "It won't happen overnight, but we could aim for that—if you want to."

"I want to," he said, nodding his head up and down but keeping his eyes shut. "I suppose everyone's gonna know. It isn't my reputation I'm worried about. I just don't want people tellin' me how sorry they are for me."

Emma swallowed. "It'll come out, but I'm not goin' to run around shoutin' about it. And I meant what I said about bein' your hostess, at least through the nomination."

"For now it helps that Rusty's lost it and the damn newspaper isn't comin' out," Orville said. "I shouldn't say that but I don't need grief from that direction. Thank you, darlin'. We'll be the best of friends, I truly believe that. But it's gonna hurt like hell to lose you."

"Only for a while," Emma said. He slumped like a broken man, and she hated to be responsible for that. "You'll marry again."

He looked at her, and tears shone in his eyes. "You're the only woman I ever wanted to marry. There won't be anyone after you."

She straightened her back and thought of the woman with her head in his lap. "There will in time." He might actually believe some of what he said, but it had taken real fear for his public image to help him find his conscience. She needed to remember that, to remind herself of it frequently.

"Is it safe at your folks' place?" he said. "When you're in town, I want you to stay here. It's your home, too. I promise I'll never bother you."

Over my dead body. "That's a nice thing to say. I'm very safe at—"

"You have credit cards. Use them. You don't need to go short of anythin', you understand?"

She had no intention of taking his charity. "We don't need to talk about this anymore now. I should go." Before he did a personality switch.

"Emma, you will be here for the party, won't you? It's just a few days away."

"Of course." She wanted to make sure Holly and Annie got the opportunity to showcase their skills and get more business.

"There'll be other parties," Orville said. "They don't have to be here, but I will rest easier if I know you'll be at my side."

"I said I would." But she already regretted it.

"You buy whatever you need. A whole new wardrobe. You'd be beautiful in jeans, but I want you to knock 'em dead. Just lookin' at you, I... Get whatever you want, honey."

"Thank you." She had more than enough already, including gowns she'd never worn. "Orville, the divorce will go ahead. It has to."

He shook his head slowly. "It's not havin' children, isn't it? And what I said to you, Emma, I should never have said that to you. I was angry, is all. We don't know you can't have more children. They said it shouldn't be too soon after, that's all. You've had time to mend now."

Ten years. She didn't trust herself to respond.

"I know," Orville said. "I shouldn't bring it up now, because it hurts you too much."

Emma stood up.

"Thank you for all you're doin', Emma," Orville said, getting hurriedly to his feet. "You won't regret it, but I'm not goin' to stop tryin' to change your mind."

"I'll be talkin' to you in the next couple of days," she said.

He followed her to the gate and let her out. When she sat behind the wheel of the Lexus, he said, "My dad will feel so bad about this."

"He doesn't know anymore," Emma said, but gently. "He might if he was himself."

Orville sighed. "Before you leave, could I ask you one question?"

She feared what it would be. "All right."

"Do you still have a private investigator followin' me?"

"No." She wouldn't tell him she never had.

"Did you have him give you the negatives of the photos?"

In his position, she would want to know, too, but he was making it easy to get in her car and drive away. "The photos are in a safe place. Goodbye, Orville." He couldn't be any more worried about those photos than she was, she thought. She still had to wonder who had taken the photos of him with his lover—and why?

22

"Most people think it's a good idea to leave me alone in the mornin' until I've had my first pot of coffee," Billy said, eyeing Finn with something close to disbelief. "Particularly on a Monday mornin'. Who let you into my office?"

"I did," Finn said. "I figured you had a long, busy day ahead, and I know I do, so why not start early? How's the Steen investigation comin'?"

"You asked me that yesterday, and I told you." Someone had already brewed Billy's coffee, and he poured the gurgling black liquid into a huge mug with a skull and crossbones on one side. "Coffee?"

"I'll pass," Finn said. "I expect you checked all the veterinary folks in the area. And the docs and pharmacies. Who all has drugs like that, anyway?"

"When I need you to suggest the obvious, I'll let you know. If someone wants to get their hands on drugs for purposes of euthanasia, they're gonna do it."

"Sick," Finn said. "You still got Rusty?"

Billy swallowed coffee, kept his eyes trained inside the mug. "He lawyered up. Out on bail."

"You know he didn't kill Denise."

"Do I?"

Billy in a truculent mood was no fun at all. He crossed the

office, his face a little pasty in the yellow overhead lights. Finn could smell aftershave. Billy's dark uniform had its creases in all the right places, and the caps of his shoes shone bright.

"He's only out because of the mixed DNA. Damn nuisance."

"So it would make you happier if all you'd found was Rusty's, and you could make him the murderer and wrap up your case?"

Billy smacked his mug down on his metal desk, and coffee spattered a nearby stack of papers. He ignored the mess. "I don't make murderers, Finn. Any more than your daddy did. I didn't realize Rusty Barnes was such a buddy of yours. He had sex with her."

"Accordin' to the lab, so did someone else. He was in love with her. They were lovers."

Billy narrowed his eyes. "How do you know that? He didn't even want to talk about it to save himself."

"Denise wasn't ready to have it all over town," Finn said.

"Denise is dead."

"Some of us don't stop lovin' after someone dies." Which was his segue into other things. "I'd like to take a look at my dad's records."

Billy looked at him sharply and frowned, turning his bristling brows into one straight line. "Why would you want to do that after all this time?"

"A year isn't long. I wasn't in a position to get here when it happened, and when I did come a few months back, it would have upset my mother for me to go pokin' around into Dad's death. She was upset enough." And hadn't made it past a few more weeks alive.

"Are you tryin' to tell me somethin'?" Billy flopped into his chair and put his feet on the desk. He jerked forward to tap his computer mouse and peered at the screen when it came to life. He swore and turned back to Finn.

Finn shook his head and hoped he looked innocent. "Wouldn't you want to take a look if you were in my position?"

Billy thought about that. "Maybe."

"I'd like to see the records."

"So you just said. Okay, why not? Sorry I don't have time to go through them with you. Just got a warrant to search Rusty Barnes's place and the paper. If they'd moved on it, we could have been in and out yesterday while the guy was out of the way."

Poor Rusty. Finn wondered what his dad would have done in Billy's position. The same things, he supposed, only Tom Duhon wouldn't have been wishing he could just pin a crime on the easiest possibility. "Records still in the same place?" he asked.

Billy nodded. "Someone back there will give you any help you need." He got up and left without a backward glance, but Finn heard him yelling in the reception area. Billy wasn't himself this morning.

The records room covered a sizable area. When Finn got there, he was relieved to see that except for the addition of more computers in the center of the space, everything looked pretty much as it had the last time he'd been there.

"Just talked to Billy," he told a woman working at an open cupboard packed inside with stationery supplies.

She looked at him and said, "Hey, Finn. Look at you, boy. You just get better."

"Hey, Mrs. Valenti, it's been too long. You're lookin' pretty good yourself."

He should have known better than to use flattery on this one. "For sixty-five goin' on ninety-five, you mean?" she said. "Uh-huh. Don't butter me, boy. Spit it out. What d'you need?"

"My dad's records?" he said, and couldn't keep on smiling. "Billy said it's okay if I take a look."

She sighed and turned away from the cupboard. "Back this way." File cabinets stood in rows, and she threaded her way through, then waited for him to catch up. When he joined her, she said, "I miss Tom. He was the best ever."

"You won't get any argument from me."

She bowed a head of curly white hair and crossed her arms. "Mmm," she said finally. "It's none of my business, but why make it all fresh again? You can't bring him back."

"I'm havin' trouble with it still," he told her. "I need to put it to bed."

Mrs. Valenti nodded. "I didn't expect to change your mind." She pulled out a cabinet drawer. "You'll find everything in there." She checked the letters on the front of the file drawer and said, "Yep. In there. Call me if you need me."

He stood alone, looking at tightly packed files. Nothing he did now would bring his father back. Reading the details of the death would only stir up more feelings of rage and disbelief.

Finn knew he would look anyway.

The damn files were so crammed in, he could hardly move them, and he couldn't find one for Tom Duhon. He started at the front again and went through one by one.

Thomas Duhon.

He'd missed it because it was thinner than the ones on either side. Flipping through the contents, he walked to one of the computer tables and sat down, pushing the keyboard aside.

Half an hour later, he looked up and turned his head toward the cupboard where Mrs. Valenti had returned to her stationery.

Finn closed the folder and returned it to its place in the drawer. When he turned to leave, Billy stood in the doorway to the records room, his eyes like black holes. He turned on his heel and walked in the direction of his office. Finn caught up before he could close the door.

"Leave it," Billy said, his back to Finn, who closed the door and stood just inside. "Sometimes it's better to let the truth go to the grave. Tom was a fine man who made one mistake. He was human. Forgive him."

"He didn't die at the scene," Finn said. "Nobody told me that."

"You were a long way away. The details didn't matter afterwards."

"They matter to me. What happened to the uniform he wore that night? And his badge."

Billy turned on him. "How the fuck should I know what happened to his uniform after all this time? Or his badge? I went with him to the hospital in Lafayette. All that stuff was taken off him and bagged. It would have gone into evidence."

"Where are the rest of his records? There's nothin' there but the notes from the hospital and the autopsy report."

Billy didn't recover quickly enough to hide either his shock or what Finn decided was the relief that followed.

"Everything's there," Billy said, and his voice broke. "You didn't look closely enough."

"I'll take you back and show you," Finn told him. "I need to anyway. You can't brush this under the rug any longer. I want the truth. All the crime scene notes are missin'."

"Don't you accuse me of mishandling a case," Billy snapped. "Go home. Get some sleep and settle down. I'll have you over to the house for one of Blanche's home-cooked dinners. Your folks would have liked that idea. We'll go through everythin' until you're satisfied. Okay?"

"Not okay," Finn said. He took a step toward Billy, who held his ground. "You're hiding somethin'. Why wouldn't you tell me he died in surgery? You don't have to answer that. We both know that if my father decided to do the job, he'd have done it right. He'd have stuck the barrel in his mouth and blown away his brain stem. No risk of livin' as a vegetable for Tom Duhon. The bullet went in through the top of his skull, and with a half inch of luck it would have missed his brain."

"What's your point?"

"My father was murdered."

23

She was going to play again.

For an audience.

On Wednesday evening.

Emma drove toward the center of town, trying to decide if she was totally thrilled or scared out of her mind. Holly and Annie had brought lunch to Poke Around and persuaded her to play at Ona's Out Back, for a benefit, on Wednesday. She hadn't touched a piano in months.

Mondays could be slow, but business had been good today. She and Sandy had kept the shop open an extra hour. As the customers dwindled, the timing had been good for Emma to explain what would probably happen with the shop after her divorce. Sandy reacted as expected, with a hug and a promise to fall in with whatever came along for Emma and Poke Around.

Emma had decided this was the night to settle in at her folks' place. Staying with Holly had been good for both of them, but the camping-out phase was over.

Rain fell again, hitting the windshield in splatters so big the wipers had trouble clearing them.

She should have refused the request to play.

But it was for a good cause, to raise funds to renovate and restock the children's library. How could she have said no?

Holly and Annie had ulterior motives—they'd admitted as much. They would serve hors d'oeuvres and drinks to anyone who came and hope to pick up interest in their catering service. And new people would find out about Ona's Out Back.

They also thought Emma should make herself available to play for more of their events.

No one would come, she told herself.

Emma leaned forward to see better. Her palms slipped on the wheel, and she held on more tightly. She was nervous about playing the piano among friends. Shop lights had been switched on along Main Street, and neon signs appeared to run together with the water on the windshield. If the rain didn't calm down, she would have to pull over.

On her right, a cyclist without rain gear rode with his head down. Water sluiced off his bare elbows, and flew from the handlebars and wheels of his bike. She slowed as she passed to see who it was and came to a stop yards in front of him.

She rolled down the passenger window and shouted, "Aaron!" as he toiled past. "Aaron!"

He wobbled and slammed his feet down on the gravel beside the road. Bending over, he looked at her and smiled. "Mrs. Lachance? Hi. You have a problem?" His black curls stuck to his head, and his eyelashes spiked together. The white polo shirt and dark jeans he wore were completely soaked.

"You're the one with a problem," Emma said. "Here, the back's open and the seats are already down. Put your bike in and I'll drive you home."

"I'll be fine, but thanks."

"Bike in the back," she said, grinning at him.

"I'm goin' all the way to Finn's place, not home."

She only missed half a heartbeat. "And I'm goin' to my folks' house, so I go right by. Hop in."

He didn't waste more time but lifted his bicycle easily beneath the hatch at the back of the Lexus and got in beside Emma. When he'd slammed the door, he said, "I'm gonna make this car a mess."

"Put on your seat belt," she told him. "If you insist, you can clean this jalopy for me one day."

"Deal," he said, holding out a palm.

Emma slapped it and said, "Deal," before checking her side mirror and pulling back onto the road.

"This isn't going to be a fast trip," Emma said. "It's hard to see."

"Stormfront goin' through," Aaron said. "I like it."

She nodded and smiled. "Me, too."

"I'm goin' to straighten out the attic for Finn," Aaron told her.

Emma nodded. "How long d'you think he'll stay at the house?" She shouldn't use the boy to get answers to questions that plagued her.

"He likes it here," Aaron said. "He's looking for property."

"To build a different house?"

"Nope. He's staying where he is. I think he wants something commercial, but I don't know what. He thinks Pointe Judah could have more housin' if there was more business, and everyone would do better. Sounds good to me—until I can go away to school, anyway. Finn's smart at business stuff— that's what my mom says a lot. I told him I want to come back from school and work for him, but he thinks I'll change my mind. I won't."

"I'm sure you'll do whatever you set out to do." All she really heard or cared about was that Finn wanted to stay in Pointe Judah.

"I don't think he wants to clean out the attic himself because of Grandma and Gramps's stuff bein' up there. Old stuff. Papers, photos and such. My mom wants the photos, but she'll probably never look at 'em."

"Your mom's special," Emma said. A rumble of thunder sounded in the distance, and as she left the town behind, trees beside the road bent before a strong wind. "I like to keep things, too, and I don't always have a good reason."

"Finn likes you."

Emma glanced sideways at Aaron. A splotch of red showed high on his cheek. "What makes you think so?" *Shame on me.*

"My mom talked to him about you. She said how she likes you, and he said he did, too."

Not quite what she'd hoped for, Emma thought, but she didn't deserve better after her fishing expedition.

"He hasn't had girlfriends since he got divorced."

None that he's brought home, anyway, she thought.

"I don't think he liked women much after he got out of the service—because of what happened when he was married—but he's different with you. You're married, of course, but it's good if you two can be friends."

This time Emma didn't pursue the subject.

"Rusty Barnes's back home," Aaron said. He put on the defroster. "It's foggin' up in here."

"How do you know about Rusty?" Emma had hoped the news of his being questioned by the police wouldn't get out. Too much to expect, she guessed.

"Finn told me," Aaron said. "I'm not to tell anyone else, but that doesn't mean you. I expect you know all about it."

"I do know. If we can keep it quiet, the case may get solved without Rusty being dragged in more than he already has been."

"Yeah. I don't repeat what Finn says except to my mom, and now you."

Emma knew when she'd received a compliment.

Aaron was quiet for a moment. Then he said, "My dad's due in from the rigs. I won't be comin' to Finn's much for a bit."

"You'll be helpin' your dad, I expect," Emma said judiciously. "I'm sure the chores pile up at home while he's gone."

"Dad doesn't do chores. When he comes home he relaxes. He likes Mom and me to stay close, though. But he isn't around long."

Aaron's attitude toward his father shocked Emma. The boy sounded as if he would be glad when his dad left again.

She remembered something that had nagged at her. "Aaron, remember all the flowers you delivered after Denise Steen died? The ones to Angela's house?"

He sighed hugely. "Oh boy, do I! I'm lucky Fred's a nice guy or I'd have been fired."

She let him go at his own pace.

"It was a joke, if you can believe that. Pretty mean. None of those people ordered any flowers." He cleared his throat. "Not even Mayor Lachance. Someone called in and had the numbers of the accounts, so I thought it was okay. Then the bills went out and the calls came in. Geesh, I thought I was toast. Some people paid for the orders anyway, but not all of them."

"Fred's a good man. I get all my flowers from Blossoms." Of course she did, on an account in Orville's name.

The so-called joke was more than mean, it was creepy, but she figured that was the idea. Creepier was the probability that the flowers sent to her had come from the same source.

"You didn't recognize who called? Maybe it was a—" She stopped herself from saying "kid."

"Maybe it was a kid?" Aaron gave her arm a mock punch. The boy didn't know his own strength. "It's okay. I'd have thought the same thing if it hadn't been a woman."

Emma was fresh out of snappy comebacks.

At Finn's place, she turned in and drove down the steep driveway. "I don't see the truck," she said.

"I've got a key," Aaron said. "He said he had business to

deal with today. Maybe he found that place he's looking for." He hopped out and retrieved his bicycle. "Thanks," he called, walking toward the house, wheeling the bike beside him.

Emma watched him unlock the front door and go in before she took off for the Balou house. She owed it to her parents to let them know what was going on. Tonight she would put in a call. If she didn't get through, she would leave a message asking them to get in touch with her.

The drive from Finn's house to the Balous took almost exactly ten minutes. Emma checked her watch as she turned in at the driveway.

Finn's black truck, complete with canopy and looking massive, stood outside the open garage.

Walking from the side of the house, wiping mud from his hands with a rag, he saw Emma arrive. "Hello, Emma," he murmured under his breath. "Finally." For most of the day he'd worked on putting on siding where the door to the pantry had been. The tiredness he felt was the good, well-worked kind, and it made him think about a long, lazy evening. Although he could wake up fast if there was a good reason.

He would leave without going into the house, he told himself. Even if she asked him to.

Struggling into her big raincoat, she got out of the Lexus and came toward him. His thighs jerked rigid, and his belly. He was in a bad way. "Hi," he said, so cheerfully he congratulated himself. "I still have to put a coat of paint on the sidin' I put on back there. Otherwise it's finished and as tight as it's ever goin' to be."

"You are so kind," she said seriously. "Finn, what can I do for you in exchange? I'm good at cleaning. I could clean your house for you."

"You could try not to insult me when I do a good turn," he told her, way more sharply than he'd intended. "Forget I said that. I wanted to do the job for you, okay? I'm not into pay-back." He didn't look into her face for fear she would see what he was really thinking. Finn knew exactly what she could do for him. Men were animals.

She opened the front door. "In with you," she said, winc-ing as lightning crackled. "A hot shower and a good meal will make a new man of you. I dropped Aaron at your place. He said he's goin' to work on the attic."

Finn grasped at the excuse. "I'd better get down there and give him a hand."+

"I think he wants to do it for you," she said. "The way you wanted to do somethin' for me. You're his hero."

Was he? Finn wondered. Then he'd better make sure he never did anything to disillusion the boy.

"Get warm and dry before you go, please," Emma said, walking into the house. He had to follow to hear what she was saying. "Use my shower. Throw out your clothes, and I'll pop them in the dryer."

Pop them in the dryer. Yes, ma'am, you do that. I know just where I'd like to pop you, sweet Emma: in the shower with me.

Mentally, he gave up the fight. Why not go with it and enjoy being around her? "Rusty's out on bail. He's got a law-yer, but I'm surely hopin' he won't need him."

"Me, too," Emma said. She hung up her raincoat and went directly upstairs. He followed and encountered the funny-looking, almost bald white cat on the landing. The critter opened her mouth wide and let out a weak high-pitched meow.

"Hi, Teddy, love," Emma said, scooping her up. The cat watched Finn over the boss's shoulder, and he had to admit the critter, sparse white curls, butterfly ears and all, was cute in an alien way, especially the different-colored eyes.

Emma went directly into her bedroom, plopped Teddy on the bed and went into the bathroom. Finn stood there feeling like a grubby boy about to be thrown in the bathtub—well, not really like a boy at all, now he thought about it.

A new, or at least a different, puffy duvet covered the bed. Tasteful sprigs of grass weren't his thing, but he guessed it looked okay.

He didn't feel okay. What the hell was she doing in there?

"Clean towels, soap, shampoo, toothbrush," she said, reappearing. "I'll get my dad's bathrobe for you."

"Don't bother. I'm not shy. I'll make do with a towel until my stuff's dry."

"Okay. Take your time."

Finn went into the bathroom and considered whether or not he should actually close the door all the way. That seemed kind of prissy or something, so he left it ajar and stripped. He pushed his clothes around the door and felt Emma take them. "Enjoy," she said. "Nothing like a hot shower when you're damp."

He didn't trust himself to answer. *Damp?* Being damp wasn't his problem.

For far longer than was polite, he stayed in the shower, loath to go out wrapped in a towel, warm, and in the mood to be welcomed by an equally warm woman—as long as her name was Emma.

She liked him.

He could still remember how she'd felt in his arms.

When he'd washed himself all over for the third time, he decided he had to quit. Slicking his hair back, he got out of the shower, toweled himself more or less dry and wrapped a huge bathsheet securely around his waist.

Emma wasn't in the bedroom.

Of course she wasn't, but a man could hope.

He combed his hair, cleaned his teeth and went softly downstairs in the darkened interior of the house. He heard nothing and walked through, saying Emma's name in hopes of not startling her.

From behind a door on the right side of the kitchen Finn heard a washer and dryer operating. He tapped the door and waited. Emma didn't respond, so he went in.

He had found a long, narrow laundry room. A deep sink faced him. Emma was over a clothes dryer at the far left end. Beside the dryer, hot water ran into the sink, sending steam surging into the low-ceilinged space.

"Emma?"

She still didn't hear him, not that he spoke loudly.

On bare feet, he went to her over tiles damp with moisture. "Emma?" he said. "Don't jump." He placed a hand on her bare back, where her red-and-white striped top rode up from the waist of a flippy red skirt made of a silky material.

She jumped and straightened to face him. "You scared me."

"Sorry," he said, but he wasn't.

He stood very close to her. Emma glanced at his broad naked shoulders and chest—and no lower than the white towel that rested below his navel. "Did the shower make you feel better?"

"I'm a new man." Steam on her skin gave it a moist, pink and faintly sparkling glow. "Steam suits you."

She inclined her head in question.

Finn brushed a thumb across her cheek. "You're all shiny." Blood pumped too hard through his veins. He slid the tip of his right forefinger over her bottom lip, her chin, beneath her jaw and slowly into her cleavage. Then he held the finger up. "See? Wet." He put the finger in his mouth.

Despite the heat, Emma shivered. She spread her hands over his collarbones, stroked his shoulders and down his arms. Finn kept still while she concentrated on his chest, where the rapid beat of his heart met her palm, and he didn't move even when her touch circled to the middle of his back and returned to stroke his belly. Her thumbs came to rest where the towel met his skin.

"Do I feel hot?" he asked. "I feel so hot. My skin burns."

"Yes," she said.

Finn caught her by the waist and sat her on top of the washer. He smiled. "How about you? Is anythin' too hot for you?"

She shook her head, and Finn kissed her, eased her lips apart with his tongue, nipping the sensitive skin, touching the sharp edges of her teeth, drawing her tongue into his mouth. He caught at the hem of her cotton top and pulled it up, bared her breasts, slowly parted his mouth from hers and pulled the tank over her head without opening his eyes.

Finn started at her waist and slid his hand upward until his extended thumbs and fingers rested beneath her breasts. "Lean against me," he whispered, and she moaned when her nipples met the hair on his chest. Slowly, breathing through her open mouth, she rubbed herself from side to side, exciting her flesh, driving near pain between her legs. Before Finn, she hadn't known that touching a man could bring such out-of-control passion.

His penis nudged her leg. Emma pulled the towel loose and took him in her hands. A big, strong man, but a gentle one, with enough control to do the almost inhuman, as he had the other night when he hadn't pressed her for more than she was ready to give.

Now she was more than ready to give everything.

The warm, moist air coated them. He felt slippery in her hands. A single scoot brought her hips to the edge of the washer, and she wrapped her legs around him.

His own drive warned Finn to slow down. He held Emma's shoulders and kissed her breasts, slowly, repeatedly, rubbed the flats of his hands up and down her sides, back and forth on her thighs.

He couldn't stop now. If she pushed him away...yeah, if she pushed him away, he would make himself stop, but he would die in the process.

Her breasts were beautiful, round, big on so slender a woman. He'd never thought he cared about size, but he was crazy about the way she looked and felt.

She crumpled against him, bit his shoulder, tore aside her flimsy panties and guided him inside. He set the rhythm. She took it up. They came together in a rush, a race. Emma slid from where she sat and clung to him with her legs. Finn held her in his arms, thrusting, thrusting, her hips meeting his.

Orgasm broke, stealing Emma's reason, throwing her body into spasms.

Finn let himself go, let the heat and power drain out of him, and locked Emma in his arms for fear he would drop her.

She sobbed against his neck, let her head fall back and her eyes close.

He had to lie down.

Stumbling, Finn carried Emma to the stairs, banged into the walls and the bannisters repeatedly on his way up the steps, and finally fell with her onto the bed.

"*Cher,*" he said, gathering her up, kissing her again.

She reached past him and switched off the bedside lamp.

24

Arm in arm with Mrs. Merryfield, Lobelia Forestier scurried across the parking lot toward Ona's Out Back. After suffering indignities at the hands of the likes of Billy Meche, this looked like it was turning into a satisfying day after all.

All she'd done was go to Billy earlier in the afternoon and ask for a progress report on the murder case. He'd told her it was none of her business, if you could believe that. This town wasn't taking the killing seriously enough, and before they knew it, another poor woman would be raped and murdered. Lobelia made sure her blouse was buttoned to the neck.

That was another thing. If these youngsters didn't flaunt themselves, they wouldn't inflame men's base instincts. Lobelia had kept herself well covered whenever Mr. Forestier was around, God rest his soul, and he had known he'd better keep it simple and quick.

"Can you believe it?" Lobelia said. "The mayor's wife playin' piano at Ona's? And Sandy Viator singin' along? I know what that Sandy said about me behind my back. She said I was a primped old fool. She said it to Rosa Valenti, and I made Rosa tell me so. But now we'll see who makes fools of themselves." She looked toward the heavens. "There is a God."

Mrs. Merryfield, who was a member of Lobelia's September Festival Committee, didn't say a word. Dull thing, Lobe-

lia thought. Didn't talk for the longest time, then came out
with a mean zinger like to cut someone to the bone. And the
way she looked! If Lobelia hadn't needed every pair of hands
she could find, she never would have let Mrs. Merryfield on
the committee.

"There's Rosa and Bob. Now how did she get him to come
with her?" They arrived at the restaurant door before Lobelia
ran out of her monologue, and Rosa and Bob Valenti caught
up with them. You couldn't count on Rosa to discuss the truth
of what went on around here, either. If you said you heard they
practiced snake handling at one of those churches out of town,
she would likely tell you she'd heard snakes make good pets.
Workin' at the police station made her feel too important, and
she went on as if it was a trust not to share what she saw and
heard there.

"Afternoon, Lobelia," Rosa said. "You, too, Mrs. Merryfield. I guess we're all here to face the music." She giggled at
her own small joke.

Mrs. Merryfield opened the door and walked in ahead of
the others. Already a crowd had gathered, and Lobelia saw
with disgust that some of the lower types who frequented Out
Front—and maybe even Buzz's—were there.

Extra tables and chairs had been set up. Lobelia pulled two
tables together and crammed as many chairs as possible
around them. She left four down and insisted the Valentis sit
with her and Mrs. Merryfield, then tipped the other chairs forward, rested their backs on the tables. "This way we don't
have to sit with people we don't like," she said, craning her
neck to see the old black piano.

"Just a few more minutes," she said, looking at her watch.
"Will you look at all these people comin'? Must be expectin'
that Vanderburn fella on the piano and maybe—who's the big
soprano? If someone asks to sit here, say the chairs are saved."

"Don't know about the soprano," Bob Valenti said quickly, too quickly for Lobelia's liking. He was another one above himself, because he had a bit put away.

"Who's that?" Lobelia asked. A fair girl pushed out a long trolley heaped with plates of food, mostly on heating trays. The smell of a good fry started the taste buds watering. "I haven't seen her before."

"That's Eileen Moggeridge's cousin," Rosa said. "Seems a nice little thing. Quiet."

Lobelia crossed her arms. "More than you can say about Eileen," she said. "Well, enough said about that. If you can't say somethin' nice, don't say anythin' at all, that's what I was taught."

The door opened again, and Lynnette from the nail salon came in with one of the hairdressers, Frances something. They looked around and came toward Lobelia's table. She straightened her shoulders and said, "Come on, you two. We saved you chairs." As long as she kept certain people away, she would be able to uphold her office as president of the chamber of commerce. In her position, she had to be careful she didn't seem to ignore the little people. This pair would help.

Mrs. Merryfield stood up suddenly. "Eileen! Over here," she called out with more enthusiasm than Lobelia had heard from the woman, ever. "You and Aaron, and your other friend."

Lobelia hunched her shoulders. Mrs. Merryfield liked to stir things up. She knew Lobelia didn't approve of Eileen Moggeridge.

"That's Finn Duhon," Rosa Valenti said. "Eileen's brother. Isn't he a hunk?"

Lobelia stared at her. "A *hunk?* Where would you get a word like that from, Rosa Valenti? Too much of that awful reality TV, I expect." Lobelia's favorite show was *Desperate Housewives* but that was different altogether.

"He's such a nice boy," Rosa said. "He came by the other day, and he reminds me of his father—"

"God rest his soul," Lobelia interrupted.

"Yes," Rosa said. "Finn's still not at peace with Tom's death. He'll accept what happened in time, but he's not ready yet."

"Why would he come by to see you?" Lobelia asked. Of course she knew why. "He's nosing around, I suppose. Could be he'd be better off leavin' that alone."

"Shh," Rosa said.

Eileen sat next to Mrs. Merryfield and gave her a shy smile. Finn and the boy said something about wanting to be nearer the door for more air and took themselves off. "I don't suppose we're interestin' enough for them," Lobelia said, but she forced herself to smile. "It's nice for you to have your brother home, Eileen."

The noise level rose abruptly. Emma and Sandy emerged from the kitchen, both of them overdressed if anyone ever had been, and helped the new girl and Holly Chandall fill plates with softshell crabs, crawfish, shrimp and little puff pastries—deep-fried like the shellfish, Lobelia hoped. She could smell fresh hot biscuits and hotter honey.

The women gave up trying to push the trolley between the tables and stationed it in front of the piano instead. They plopped overflowing plates on each table, passed out napkins and plastic glasses, and stood back for Ona to pour beer. Lobelia liked a little beer in the evenings. Made her sleep better.

Finn studied the room, checking to see who was there. He thanked Annie when she brought food for him and Aaron, and Ona for the beer she poured. Aaron got a glass, too, and looked sheepishly at Finn, who pretended not to notice. He and Emma had exchanged glances when he arrived, and he'd decided it would be easier on both of them if he didn't sit too close.

"Everyone in town's here," Aaron said. "I'd be scared if I had to play the piano in front of them."

"You don't play the piano," Finn said.

"If I did."

John Sims came in looking harried. He saw Finn and slid into a chair beside him. "Wouldn't want to miss this," he said. "Big deal in a town where nothing happens." He put a whole softshell crab into his mouth and crunched. When he could speak he said, "Best thing I ever tasted—since the last best thing I ever tasted. I just got back in town. Haven't even been home."

Finn had met John a couple of times since he came back and remembered him from childhood summers John had spent with his grandparents in Pointe Judah.

"How's the cleanup coming?" John said.

"Mmm?" Finn raised his brows.

John demolished another crab and drank some of his beer. "I know what it's like to clean out after old folks. Took me forever, what with all my traveling. The grandparents kept everything. You getting ready to sell?"

In this town there were few secrets. "I haven't made up my mind," he said.

"I didn't think I'd stay," John said. "But I got a territory out here—I'm a pharmaceutical rep—and I like it here, so—" he spread his hands "—here I am. You can live cheaper here, and I figure I can always make do with the money from the rental if I have to."

Finn was getting more information than he needed, but folks around here talked freely, something Finn had gotten away from. "Sounds like a good deal."

"You know who's next door?" he said, elbowing Finn. "In the house I rent out? You remember my grandparents had the two lots they made into one, and two places on it?"

Finn shook his head.

"My great-grandmother used to live in the second one. That Secrets group uses it now." He shook the fingers of one hand. "Some of them are *hot*. I don't know what goes on in there, but you should hear the screaming. The woman who rents the place is wacko—never goes out."

The idea of John Sims watching Emma come and go from Secrets made Finn's scalp prickle.

Emma wore a cream lace top over a camisole and drapy cream silk pants. Finn did his best not to watch her every move and failed. He'd caught a glimpse of her feet in high sandals for the first time, and the sight had given him a sexy jolt. So he'd developed a foot fetish—he could get to like it. Her slender feet and deep pink toenails turned him on. Everything about her turned him on. Lying in her bed, holding her, making love, sleeping, talking, sharing what mattered to him most, had brought him close to a woman in a way he didn't remember.

Holly Chandall rang a fork against a glass and kept on ringing until the crowd quieted down. "I hope you're enjoying the food," she said, smiling and spreading her arms. "You'll find my cards on the table by the door. Annie and I will be glad to cater your events. Now, what you've been waiting for, Emma and Sandy are going to entertain us. You didn't have to buy a ticket, but we know you'll be generous with your donations for the children's library. We'll pass out envelopes."

When Emma sat at the piano, Finn's pulse speeded up. *Nervous?* He had to be nuts. It wasn't as if *he* was about to play for a bunch of people.

Annie ran to turn out some of the lights.

A murmur of male voices came from outside, and Orville Lachance walked in with Carl Viator. Rather than sit down, they went around the edge of the room until they could stand in the lights that shone on Emma and the piano, and on Sandy in lowcut coral chiffon.

"Look at that," John Sims said, leaning closer than Finn cared for. "How about them apples?"

He did not, Finn decided with a glance at Aaron, like John after all. Aaron was too engrossed in the front of the room to have noticed what the man said.

Emma ran her fingers across the keys and gave a thousand kilowatt smile. She'd told him she would be terrified, but it surely didn't show. She played, "I Wish I Could Shimmy Like My Sister Kate," with Sandy singing in a full, husky voice, and the place erupted. A contingent of refugees from Buzz's stamped their feet and hollered until they were loudly shushed.

Finn couldn't keep himself from looking at Orville Lachance, who smiled as if the woman at the piano was his adored wife and they had a perfect marriage. *It's all over for you, buddy. You had your chance.* A man shouldn't feel the way Finn did about Lachance. Emma had shared every word that passed between her and her soon to be ex-husband on Sunday. Why would he come here tonight?

"She's got a great voice," John whispered as Sandy quit "shimmying" and belted out, "Didn't She Ramble" with enough volume and body language to start a chorus of whistles. Emma played flawlessly, effortlessly, that big smile never faltering.

When the piece finished and Orville could quiet the applause enough, he yelled, "I give you Mrs. Viator and Mrs. Lachance. Who says Pointe Judah can't compete with N'awlins?"

More applause.

Finn made fists and fantasized about wiping the smile off Orville's face.

"Now Emma's going to play somethin' I can't sing," Sandy said. "Take it away, Emma."

Emma bent over the keyboard for a moment, settled her fingers and played a medley of Strauss waltzes that had the mostly older audience swaying to the music.

"I'm outta here for a smoke," John said. "I'll be back for the brunette." He slipped outside.

"Emma's real good," Aaron said in Finn's ear. "People your age like this, don't they?"

Finn punched the kid in the side, just hard enough to tickle, and Aaron poked him back. "She can really play," Finn said. Emma could play Strauss for him anytime. She could play anything for him. "I think she likes jazz best." He'd better not sound too knowledgeable about the lady. "This is probably because she thinks this audience is mostly older."

As if to make a liar of him, Emma switched to "Soul Sister," slipped easily to "Steppin' Fast," and raised hoots with "Such a Night." She played one Cajun song after another, and the folks sang along—including Finn. It wasn't Emma's fault if Lachance didn't know when to quit.

Sandy drank a long glass of water and opened a door from the kitchen to the side of the building with a Dumpster view. She'd seen John leave when she stopped singing. Her stash was getting low, but she couldn't be sure he would have anything on him. But John didn't hand out if she didn't put out. She would have to get back inside in minutes, so she'd better make the best of the goodies she had left. She reached between her breasts and hooked out two pills, which she popped with some of the water. A girl with active fat cells had to do something to look after what she had. The highs were a side benefit, a side benefit she had to have.

"Smart girl," John said in her ear.

She hadn't seen him coming.

"Get back there. Over there behind the Dumpster." He held

her tightly around the waist and hurried her where he wanted her to go. "Don't make a sound."

In the black, rancid-smelling space where he spun her to face him, he whispered, "You don't have to be here. Give the word and you can go back. I just thought you might be glad to see me."

He needed to be put in his place. Her time would come. Tonight she wanted what he wanted. "I'm very glad to see you," she told him, and he curled her fingers around a fat little envelope.

"Thank you," she said. "What's mine is yours, but make it fast."

The arrival of Harold Chandall galvanized Finn. The man, big and blond, his eyes searching the room, smelled like trouble. Emma had told Finn about Holly's decision to get a divorce, and from the look of Chandall, someone had told him, too.

"Stay put," Finn told Aaron. "Everything's okay." He stood up, moved around his chair and leaned against the windowsill at the back of the room. From there he could move quickly to intervene if necessary.

Emma had played to the room in every way, and they gave it up for the good time she'd shown them. She stood and gave a quick bow, then sat again when Sandy ran back to her place by the piano. Before they could start again, Orville called for silence.

Chandall saw Holly, and his chest rose and fell visibly. He opened and closed his hands at his sides. He took a couple of steps, then stopped while he looked for the best way through the crowd.

"I hadn't planned to make a public announcement at this point," Orville boomed, "but I'm too pumped being here with all of my friends to keep it to myself any longer. I'm runnin' for state governor, and it's people like you who give me the strength to go ahead. I want to be your man at the state capitol."

Finn shook his head. The guy was unbelievable. With every shout of "Orville Lachance, Orville Lachance," he glowed.

"To celebrate this wonderful evenin'—" He jogged to Emma's side and snatched up her hand. "I'm announcin' I'll match whatever gets collected for the kids' library tonight. And double it!"

Don't let him use you like that, Emma.

But she kept a smile on her face, and she didn't take her hand away.

Chandall took advantage of everyone's attention being elsewhere and made a lunge, but Finn was faster. He stepped in front of the man and said, "Evenin', Harold. I need you to step outside."

"Get out of my way." Harold's face worked. He struggled with his rage.

"Get hold of yourself. You won't help anythin' this way. Come on, let's talk."

"Who the fuck are you?"

Noise in the room swallowed the epithet. "You used to know me. Finn Duhon."

Chandall blinked. He seemed to hover between rushing Holly and doing what Finn asked.

He turned on his heel and hurried from the room. Finn followed and caught up with him beside a dark SUV. "Get the fuck out of my way," Harold said, climbing in and slamming the door. He floored the gas and shot backward before screeching out of the parking lot.

Finn looked through the windows of Out Back. He could hear laughter and raised voices from inside. Looking at Emma with Lachance tonight, he would defy anyone to think they were other than a couple. Emma wouldn't be the first woman to change her mind about something major.

If she did, what did that make Finn—a convenient lay?

25

Taking the first step didn't make you weak.

Emma waited for Finn to answer his phone and sat down. "Duhon," he said, and there was nothing welcoming there.

"It's Emma."

"Hi."

She rested her elbows on the kitchen table. "All day I've been tellin' myself I shouldn't be the one to make this call, but I'm makin' it anyway."

"Sounds as if you're not good at takin' your own instructions."

What did that mean? "I guess not. Was I wrong to call you?"

"Why would you think you might be?"

Teddy jumped on the table, and rather than shoo her off, Emma gathered the cat onto her lap. She needed something warm and alive to hold on to. "I saw you at Ona's last night."

"Wouldn't have missed it. I told you I'd be there. You were really good, and so was Sandy. You could take that show on the road."

You're staying away from the subject we should talk about: us. "Thank you very much. I think Sandy had fun, and I know I did. I'd forgotten what a charge it is to get lost in the music and only come out when people clap. Heady stuff."

"You should play a lot, Emma. You've got too much talent to waste."

She bit her lip.

"Emma?"

"I'm here. Thanks again. One minute you were there at the back of the room, the next you were gone. What happened? Did somethin' important come up?"

"You don't have any idea why I left?" he said.

"No." But from the question and the way he asked it, she could tell that something had happened.

"We've made love. We've shared things I've never shared with anyone."

Her heart thudded. "We both did. You didn't have to remind me about what's happened between us. I'm not goin' to forget. Ever."

She heard him expel a breath, a long, long breath. "I thought… It seemed right, but maybe it wasn't. Maybe you aren't in a place where you can know what you want yet," he said.

Teddy screeched, and Emma released her. She'd been clutching the cat to her. "How can you say that?"

"I'm thinkin' out loud. It's not what I want to believe, but how did you think I'd feel, watchin' you hold Orville's hand and smile around while he was talkin' as if you were the happiest couple in town?"

She thought she'd explained how she intended to get through her divorce, how she hoped to do it without anger. "You wanted me to make a scene when Orville got near me?"

"Look, if you'd changed places with me, you might have understood. You might understand now. You should be able to figure out what I'm feelin', but you can't. I'm not blamin' you, just tellin' you the way I see it. Let's give it some time."

Emma held her breath, bracing for him to hang up. He didn't. "I'm at home," she said. "My folks' place. Would you like to come up for an early dinner? I could fire up the barbeque."

"I'm not at home."

Where are you? "I see." She couldn't ask him where he was. "Maybe when you get back?"

"It'll be too late, but thanks for the offer."

"Finn, did I hurt you last night?"

He snorted. "What makes you think that? I'm a grown-up, a man. Men don't hurt."

Sarcasm didn't suit him. "I thought we understood each other," she said. "I still think we do, but we haven't had enough practice together to deal with a scene like last night," she said.

"Emma… Emma, we never could have enough practice at scenes like that. Or I couldn't. I wouldn't want to."

She was out of things to say. If she told him she would cry as soon as he went away, it would sound like emotional blackmail. "So you think we shouldn't…" If she said it, he might say yes, and she didn't want that. "What do you want to do?"

He thought about it for so long. "I'm out of brilliant things to say, if I ever had any." She heard him swallow. "I think we should both take a step back, then just wait and see."

Suehanna Lake sat on the surface of the land, or so it seemed from Finn's viewpoint. Stretched out on the ground, he propped his elbows on a fallen tree too old to recognize as anything in particular.

He and his dad used to come here to fish, and they'd invariably stayed late. That was why Finn had decided to hang around tonight after driving the twenty miles or so from Pointe Judah and having lunch at the only place to eat on the lake. A scatter of houses, some of them boarded-up for years, hugged the lake on one side. A couple who lived in a lodge where he doubted anyone stayed anymore served some of the best gumbo he'd tasted in a long time.

He should have been the one to call. The basic differences between men and women were no secret to him, and he'd known she would be waiting to hear from him. If he had known what to say, he might have done it.

A red and mauve sky turned the lake to rose and purple. The reflections of cypress trees wavered on the flashy water, and the trees themselves were inky outlines against the sky.

The day had been hot, just like yesterday, just like most days. Finn liked it hot, but a short temper fed on stillness and stickiness, and turned his mind to dark thoughts. He had knocked around the idea of seeing if they could scrounge up a room for him at the lodge and might still do that.

Damn it all. He punched in Emma's preprogrammed cell number, and the phone rang four times before she answered. "Hello, Finn."

"I didn't handle your call worth a damn. I'm not tellin' you I've changed my mind about what's botherin' me, but I don't have to be a boor."

"Last night, when I had to put on that act with Orville, I felt so bad," Emma said. "But I thought you'd understand."

He squinted into the brilliant colors on the lake. "I don't see why you had to put on *that* much of an act. Let's drop it. You did what you thought you had to, but I wasn't ready to see it. I've been thinkin' about somethin' else. I don't suppose you mentioned the pictures of Orville to Billy."

She breathed sharply. "Why would I do that?"

"Because we need to know who took them and pushed them at you. And why."

"I think it was that creature who came here. The cowboy clown. He's still out there, Finn, and we don't know what he wants."

He didn't want to frighten her, but she needed to be careful. "He wanted you. He's obsessed with you—enough so he's prepared to buy you. But he didn't have to be the one who took the photos."

"What if it isn't me that freak wants? What if he wants to use me to bring Orville down? People make enemies, and Orville's probably got more than his share."

Finn had already thought the same thing. "If that's the way it is, we're stuck waiting for someone to make another move. You still don't think Billy needs to know everything?"

She muttered something.

"What?"

"You don't understand. I may not owe Orville much, but letting those pictures get out would make a laughingstock of him with some and curl the toes of some others. Either way, this isn't the time. He's got a lot going on."

"You're going to have to clear something up for me," he said. "I didn't think you gave a shit about him anymore. I thought you were divorcing him because he's a pig."

"Okay, I don't want to say this, because I'm ashamed of it, but I don't want to be the spurned wife." She gave a short laugh. "I already *am* spurned, I know, but don't expect me to get excited about someone looking at evidence of how my husband betrayed me."

"Pride," Finn said, and wished he could grab the word back. He couldn't.

"You don't have any pride?" She sounded as angry as she had a right to be. "I've gone through enough embarrassment at Orville's hands. Do you blame me for wanting to slip out of this marriage without any fuss?"

"No." This conversation was going nowhere. "You've decided to support Orville for the foreseeable future?"

"I explained all that to you."

"Perhaps you did. Evidently I didn't completely understand. I didn't think an amicable divorce meant you had to protect a man who had mentally abused you—and physically, too, if I had to guess. Are you one of those women who will keep going back to a violent husband?"

"No! How can you ask me that? You're right, we moved too fast—we need distance."

"You've got it."

She beat him to the "end" button.

26

Every door in the house stood open. The first guests had arrived only an hour earlier, and already the throng had grown to fill the rooms on the main floor and spill out around the pool.

Emma, balancing on four-inch pavé heels she hoped wouldn't land her on her tush, circulated among Orville's guests. She stayed away from him as much as possible but couldn't avoid him when he sought her out, catching her firmly by the waist, or boyishly by the hand, and introducing her to people. There were a number she hadn't met before.

The confident smile on his face meant things were going well. Frequently she saw him move apart from the crowd with a man or group of men, sometimes with a woman, and have a conversation that left him nodding, smiling, gesturing.

Orville looked the part of the gubernatorial candidate. He looked like a winner.

"Everything is spectacular, Emma," Sandy said, popping a glass of champagne into Emma's hand. She emptied a glass herself and waved it in the air, signaling to a server for a re-fill. "Who decorated the house?"

Emma smiled. "I did. Fred at Blossoms outdid himself with the flowers. He made the rest easy."

"Gorgeous," Sandy said of massed blue delphiniums and

orange tiger lilies. Sprays of white stocks turned the other colors luminous and filled the place with their heady night scent.

She stood still while her glass was filled.

Orville had been careful to include useful locals. John Sims, his hands clasped behind his back, strolled around, taking in his surroundings. He arrived beside Emma and smiled. "Beautiful home and a great party," he said. "Only one complaint."

She raised one eyebrow.

"Where's the parade of gorgeous single women?" He elbowed her, and she laughed. "We need a few more females who look like you and Sandy but who aren't attached."

"You should get out more, John, and I don't mean for your work," Sandy said.

John shrugged and gave her a critical appraisal. "Are you getting too thin, babe? Not the boobs, the boobs are great, but in other places?"

Rather than be angry, Sandy broke into almost hysterical laughter. Tears squeezed from the corners of her eyes, and she patted John's cheek. "You are a naughty boy," she said, rubbing his neck. "You aren't supposed to be looking at another man's wife like that. If you do, don't talk about it."

He looked at her seriously. "Are you okay? I didn't think what I said was that funny."

She laughed louder, put a hand over her mouth and quieted to bursts of giggles.

The episode made Emma uncomfortable. Why would John try to make Sandy look foolish in front of her? And that was the only reason she could think of for what he had said.

"Hello, Emma," a deep, charmingly accented voice said from behind her. Patrick Damalis, his mane of dark curly hair drawn back into a tail at his nape, moved forward to join her, Sandy and John. "I don't see you often enough. That husband of yours must keep you locked away. I don't blame him, but you are too lovely to waste." He nodded at Sandy.

"We allow ourselves to be too busy," Emma said politely. "It's good to see you, too, Patrick."

He had bright blue eyes and a manner that suggested he considered a lot of attention his due. "Orville will be a great governor."

Emma inclined her head and hoped she looked pleased.

Damalis watched her closely enough to heat her cheeks. "I'll make him bring you to see me at the club. You'd enjoy yourself."

"Thank you," Emma said, with no intention of going near the place. "Have you met John Sims? John has a couple of houses in the middle of town. He's also a pharmaceutical rep."

Damalis shot out a hand, and John took it. "I've been meaning to talk to you about membership at your club," John said. "I travel, but from what I hear, it would be fun when I'm in town."

"Carl thinks a great deal of John," Sandy said. "I'm sure he would speak for him."

"I'll speak for him, too," Emma said, smiling. "Not that I suppose that counts for anything."

"What you say counts a great deal, Emma." Damalis's nostrils flared while he looked John over. John carried himself like the comfortably positioned man he was, and Damalis's type responded to confident people. He took a card from his inside breast pocket and gave it to John. "Show this to the receptionist at the club."

John took the card and gave Damalis one of his own. "I'll drop by sometime and take advantage of you." He was the only one who chuckled at his small joke.

Damalis excused himself.

"What do you think of him?" John asked, his voice pitched low.

"I don't know him, really," Emma said. "Orville seems to like him a lot."

Sandy rubbed the long stem of her glass between her palms. "He's done very well. It's a good idea to be one of his group."

"I need a drink," John said. He gave a sloppy salute and drifted away.

In the center of a spectacular buffet table stood the ice sculpture Orville had requested, a reproduction of the tall capitol building in Lafayette. Emma gave it frequent, nervous glances as it showed signs of blurring around the edges. She had no idea at what point the sight of the building in melt-down would become embarrassing.

"How long do I dare let the capital melt on that table?" Emma whispered to Sandy. "It could get ugly."

Sandy tipped back her head and laughed, showing her perfect teeth and pulling attention from every direction. "I could say what I really think and tell you to let the thing turn into a puddle, but you wouldn't do that, even for me. It's got another hour, doesn't it?" She wore red, a perfectly wrinkle-free gown encrusted with small disks that turned her into a vision reminiscent of a spectacularly shaped scarlet fish. Few men in the room didn't look in her direction often, and more than one woman cast admiring, or envious, glances at her.

"Maybe. When Holly comes back in, I'll ask her to keep an eye on it, too. What do you think of the food?"

"This town never saw anything like it before," Sandy said. "Just look at the way people are eating—that should tell you how the food is."

"True," Emma said.

Sandy tucked a curl behind her ear. "Annie's the genius with food, I gather. Apparently she's got some notion of having a dance hall, of all things. A dance hall with great food."

Emma inclined her head. "She seems so quiet." She laughed. "Just proves how you never know what someone else dreams about."

"I thought Finn was coming and bringing Eileen," Sandy said, craning her neck to search the crowd.

"This house wouldn't take many more people," Emma said, avoiding Sandy's comment. Keeping her eyes away from the door and not watching for him took almost more restraint than she had.

He wouldn't come, not after their last exchange.

"Ladies?" Carl bore down on them with an older man of many chins in tow. "Rupert Douglas insists on meeting you. And what Rupert wants, Rupert gets." Carl's laugh was too loud.

"Good evening, Mr. Douglas," Emma said, offering her hand. "I'm Emma Lachance."

"And this is my gorgeous wife, Sandy," Carl added.

Douglas draped an arm around Emma and brought his face close to hers. "Rupe to you, sweetheart. Hi there, Sandy." He swayed and gestured with the glass in his spare hand. "Some guys get all the luck. Not that Cissy's so bad." He winked and blew a kiss to a redhead practically too young even to be his daughter.

"Tell me about yourself," Emma said dutifully.

Carl snapped his fingers and pointed to Rupe. A waiter materialized with a decanter on a tray and filled his glass with pale gold liquor.

No ice, Emma noted.

"Rupe's the CEO of Bolin International."

"Are you in plastics?" Sandy asked, and giggled.

Rupe chucked her under the chin and took a good look down the front of her dress. "We do a lot of things, sweetie. What we aren't in would take less time to tell you."

"Isn't Bolin somethin' to do with munitions?" Emma asked, remembering something she'd read.

Rupert Douglas gave her his full attention. "Like I said, we do a lot of things. I like that husband of yours. Governor can be just one step to bigger things, much bigger things." He put his fleshy mouth close to her ear. "Try to make sure he keeps his nose publicly clean. That boy of yours likes to play. If you need someone to talk to, I'm here for you, Emma. Or even if you don't need to talk. Okay?"

"You're very kind," Emma said through her teeth. She could smell garlic and scotch on his breath.

Carl slapped the man on the back. "It means a great deal to us to have you on our side," he said, his face absolutely serious, his eyes filled with sincerity.

Douglas studied him. "You're a comer," he said. "I hope Lachance knows what he's got in you. You've got a bright future."

Emma wished she could disappear and find herself somewhere quiet, where there were no phonies.

She saw Billy Meche and Blanche, and grinned as she excused herself.

"You look dapper," she told Billy when she reached him. "And you should make this man take you out in pretty dresses more often, Blanche."

"I'm only here to keep an eye on the silver," Billy said, straight-faced.

Blanche, a surprisingly ethereal-looking little woman beside her solid husband, leaned on him and said, "You're just awful, Billy Meche. I can't take him anywhere, Emma."

They chatted, and Emma relaxed—until she glanced across the room and ceased to hear a word.

A very tall man in black, his shirt bright white against his tanned skin, stood in the vestibule, his jacket pushed back and his hands sunk in his pockets. He planted his feet apart, and the muscles in his legs flexed visibly.

Finn Duhon and his lovely, shy sister made an arresting pair.

"More guests," Emma managed to say. "Excuse me for a minute." She left the Meches, and walked toward Finn and Eileen.

Eileen in a black sheath could steal most shows. She glowed the way a woman glowed when she felt her best and knew it was good enough. Finn stood a little apart, watching her while she talked to Orville's doctor, Roger French, and his date. Finn's smile suggested he enjoyed seeing Eileen attract attention.

Emma pressed a hand to her breast. She struggled with her jumpy reaction to Finn. When he saw her, he turned completely in her direction, and his hands came slowly out of his pockets. With each step she took, his eyes appeared darker, more unreadable. His lips came together, and the laugh lines on his face seemed deeper, harder.

"Hi, Emma," Finn said. *Agony and ecstasy. Oh yeah.* He had a whole new use for the phrase. It described this moment, standing feet from Emma in her white satin gown. He thought they called the way it was made bias, or on the bias, and it caused the dress to cling everywhere a dress ought to cling on a figure like that. She wore diamond studs in her ears but no other jewelry, and her hair was loose and crazy-curled.

His resolution wasn't going to happen. He would not be able to stay away from her, and from the expression she showed him, if he didn't go to her, it was only a matter of time before she came knocking on his door.

"Finn," she said.

Not a ghost of a smile on her face.

"We're late," he said. "Forgive us."

Eileen turned around. "It was my fault," she said, and

hunched her shoulders. "I got cold feet, and Finn had to drag me out in the end."

"With Aaron pushin'," Finn added, smiling at his sister. He loved seeing her dressed up and being appreciated.

"You look lovely, Eileen," Emma said, and kissed her cheek. Turning to Finn, she put out a hand, and he shook it. She smiled now, straight into his eyes. "I'm glad you both came." She dropped her voice. "Very glad."

"So am I. Some things are too good to miss."

French tapped Eileen's shoulder and asked if he could get her a drink. She turned back to him.

"We'd better not do this," Emma murmured.

Finn put his hands carefully back into his pockets. "We're goin' to have to do somethin', and soon, *cher.*"

"Be patient with me."

He looked at his feet and said, "I doubt if I have any choice, not anymore."

"I never intended to put you in a position like this," Emma said.

Finn stuck his thumbs in his belt. "I want to hold you, Emma."

There was no way others would overhear, but she glanced around anyway.

"Look at me," he told her.

She did so slowly. "People are goin' to notice us," she said, and her eyes crinkled. "I ought to care more."

A bell rang.

Finn made himself look in the direction of the sound. From the direction of the kitchen, a server pushed a huge trolley ahead of him. Blue ribbons floated from a point atop orange chiffon draped over the trolley like a sheik's tent.

Annie walked forward. In chefs' whites, with her hair pinned tightly back, she looked all business. In the center of the living room, she stood beside the cart and waited while the lights were lowered.

Candlelight flickered over expectant faces.

"You know how to put on a party, Mrs. Lachance," Finn said softly. "Look at that cousin of mine. You'd think she did this stuff every day."

"Somethin' tells me the time could come when she does," Emma said.

Annie glanced over her shoulder, then at the other server, who nodded. Between them, they took hold of the chiffon where it came together in blue ribbon streamers and whipped it off like a flock of colorful birds in flight.

Clapping guests crowded forward, and Finn risked moving at Emma's shoulder to look with the rest. Sighs and exclamations whispered through the group.

A dessert extravaganza rose in layers on top of floor-length white organza cloth. Finn said, "Wow," then drew his lips back from his teeth. "Cover it again," he said loudly, and reached for the chiffon drape.

Too late. A woman screamed. He saw someone collapse at the same moment as Billy Meche strode forward, taking a radio from his hip.

A few people fell back. More held poses like statues. Soft crying wrenched at him.

On one side, protruding from beneath the layers of desserts, whipped cream and fruit decorated a woman's head and neck. Slices of kiwi hid her eyes. Her hands, arranged palms up, supported bunches of sugared grapes, and more grapes draped her ankles and feet.

Tiers of pastries hid the rest of Holly Chandall's body.

27

"I hope I never have to deal with another crime scene like that one," Billy said to Finn. Hours had passed since the two of them had moved people back from what would always come to Finn's mind as an elaborately decorated funeral pyre.

"A nightmare," Finn said. "In a lot of ways." Billy had given him orders as if Finn had been on the force, and Finn followed them until reinforcements arrived, both from the Pointe Judah police department and the East Arcadia Parish sheriff's department.

Now Billy sat in Orville Lachance's study, behind Orville's desk, while Finn lounged in a leather chair. "The best thing we've got on our side," Billy said, "is that most likely she'd only been dead a few minutes when she was wheeled in. They said her temperature hadn't gone down that much, considerin' she was lyin' on a refrigerated trolley. I still can't get over it. We were all millin' around, fillin' our faces and drinkin', and she was dyin' under our noses."

Billy had been interviewing in a separate sitting room. A lot of his "chats" had gone quickly, given that the interviewees acted as alibis for one another. Most people had left the house by one in the morning.

With the corpse and the crime lab crew in the living room, and the driveway mostly cordoned off, officers had filed folks out to the cabana by the pool, where seats were set up in rows. Guests had been interviewed one by one and dismissed as soon as Billy finished with them.

"Rusty's still not back at home?" Finn asked. He'd come to bring Billy more coffee and stayed when asked.

"Nope," Billy said. He sighed and laced his hands behind his neck. "He'd better not be gone too far for too long, or he'll find himself in the lockup regardless of whether or not I think he's involved with this one."

"You know he's not," Finn said. "Any more than he was with Denise."

"I don't know any such thing, do I?" Billy said. "I don't know one goddamn thing for sure except that woman out there was murdered inside a catering van backed up to the garage on this property."

"That's what you've decided?"

Billy gave him a bleary-eyed scowl. "You got a better idea?"

"That's what happened."

"Anybody but Sandy need the medics?" Billy asked.

"Nobody seriously but Sandy." Sandy had passed out in the cabana and needed assistance. "She seems tougher than that."

Billy shifted a laptop computer inches closer. "She is. Combination of alcohol and some medication, they thought— and shock. She managed to get a lot of attention she's probably going to regret. Carl must know she's over the edge with somethin' or other. He wouldn't let them take her to the hospital. He surely didn't like the way John Sims hung over her, or was I imaginin' things?"

"I noticed," Finn said. "She's doing okay at home. Emma checked on her."

"Where's Emma now?"

"With her husband," Finn said. "Emma's too quiet. She tried to hold Holly."

"I saw it," Billy reminded him. "You know she's blaming herself?"

"Mmm. Because she gave Holly and Annie the job. And she keeps mentionin' Harold Chandall. I shouldn't have told her how he behaved at Ona's that night."

"If Harold had been on the premises tonight, someone would have seen him. There were people everywhere, and from what I've been hearin', he hasn't stopped drinkin' or rantin' for days."

Finn thought about the way Harold had left the parking lot at Ona's. "I don't think he's got it in him to pull off anythin' that takes plannin' or subtlety, not at the moment." He visualized Harold's face. "All he wanted was his wife back. Do we know where he is?"

"At the station," Billy said, pounding keys again. "He's a suspect, Finn."

"I suppose he is." From where he sat, Finn could see through a window to the brightly lit front walkway. "Looks like they're gettin' ready to take Holly away."

Billy stopped typing and scrubbed at his face. "They'll expedite the autopsy. Damn, I hate this."

"Death goes with some jobs," Finn said, thinking of his own experiences.

"This is a small town," Billy said. "We don't expect serial murders. In New Orleans, or any big city, there's a good to great chance the cops don't know the victims. We're losin' friends here. I'm gonna need safeguards for the rest of the women who belong to Secrets. Manpower's the problem. There'll have to be outside help brought in."

Finn had heard Secrets being whispered about among the guests waiting for interviews, but this was the first mention Billy had made. "I don't envy you," he said. The potential link between the group of women and the murderer couldn't be ignored. For himself, he would be watching Emma whether she wanted him to or not.

"This entire property's a crime scene," Billy said. "The Lachances will have to get some things and move out until it's clear. Who knows when that'll be."

Finn didn't say what he believed, that Emma, at least, would never want to live here again.

"Your cousin was probably the last person to see Holly alive," Billy said, eyes on the screen. "She thinks so."

"She said that? Without a lawyer?"

"She volunteered the comment, Finn. I didn't suggest. The guy who pushed the trolley into the house said he opened the back door of the van, put down the ramp and got behind the thing. The fancy drapes were already in place and ready to go."

"You've only got his word for that."

"True. But he was seen climbin' into the van and doin' exactly what he said he did."

The catering van had been impounded, of course.

Finn stood up to see the gurney lifted down two front steps and wheeled toward the medical examiner's vehicle. He looked at the body bag, and pure hate hit him. He opened his mouth and snapped his jaw.

Billy joined him at the window.

A cop stopped Emma and Annie from approaching the body.

"God," Finn muttered under his breath. "Senseless."

"This is part of someone's plan," Billy said. "Emma said somethin' interestin' when I talked to her. She wondered if these deaths are a smokescreen to cover somethin' else."

Finn nodded slowly. The doors at the back of the medical examiner's van closed the body bag from sight. "She's lookin' for somethin' with meanin' to explain senseless killin's. Sometimes there isn't anythin'. But I suppose she could have a point."

"I keep goin' over what I saw with my own eyes, and what Annie Duhon filled me in with," Billy said. "I saw Holly checkin' on the buffet table and takin' a walk around to make sure the glasses were gettin' filled."

"So did I," Finn told him. He hated it that Annie was embroiled in this.

"But I didn't see Holly leave the room, or the house. I don't know if she came back and went out again." He shook his head. "I want a cigarette."

"You don't smoke."

"That's right." Billy found his tin of mints and shoveled a handful into his mouth. He crunched loudly.

"Think how many versions of that scene we'll read about or hear conjectured about." Finn didn't even know why he'd thought about the media.

Billy looked grim. "You can't stop people from talkin'."

"Can I have Annie taken home now?" Aaron had come for Eileen earlier, but Annie had still been needed for more questioning.

"I want to go over the sequence with her one more time," Billy said.

Finn looked at his watch. "Wouldn't it be better if everyone got some sleep and started again in the mornin'?"

"Annie will be here any minute," Billy said, checking his own watch. "Just a formality. And to see if anythin' she says changes this early in the game."

"You'll want me to leave," Finn said.

A tap, and the door opened to admit Annie with a female officer. They both came in and shut the door. Annie smiled at Finn, but her mouth gradually turned down. "I can't believe it," she whispered.

He put an arm around her. "Neither can I."

"She was so excited. Everythin' went perfectly…until it

happened." Annie cried without making a sound. Tears flooded her cheeks faster than she could wipe them away.

"You can stay, Finn," Billy said quickly. "This is pretty informal. Annie, come and sit down." He went around the desk, waved her to a love seat and sat beside her.

"I'm sorry," she said. "It's not fair. What happened to Holly's not fair. People work hard to make their way, and just when it looks as if they're gonna get a break, it all gets messed up."

Finn blinked. "It isn't fair," he said. "And I hate it when people say, 'Life's not fair,' as if that makes misery okay."

"Do you think her husband did it?" Annie said.

"We don't know who did it," Billy said with a meaningful glance at Finn.

The female officer kept a careful eye on Annie.

"I don't like askin', but I have to," Billy said. "Please run through what happened before you came back into the house to wait for the dessert cart to arrive."

Annie slid deeper into the seat and swallowed. She wiped her face again and sniffed. "We were runnin'," she said. Her voice broke. "We were so happy because we did it, didn't we?" She looked at Billy. "We pulled it off. Everythin' was beautiful."

"It surely was," he told her. "Blanche, she's my wife, is a good cook, but she was talkin' about gettin' some of the recipes."

Annie smiled. "The ice sculpture was about to be history, so we decided to get the desserts in, then get rid of the sculpture while folks were distracted by the sweets."

"I'd never have thought of somethin' like that," Finn said. "Sorry to interrupt."

"I wouldn't have, either," Billy said.

"The desserts were ready in cold boxes inside the van. They were arranged on platters in separated layers. Everythin' just had to be put together, and we'd talked it through and practiced several times. Servin' dishes went down on the trolley, then the second tier went on top. The upper tiers each had four legs, see, so there could be plates underneath to pull forward when the outside ones got empty. Three tiers on top of the trolley, and they all bolted together so they wouldn't move. It was beautiful…wasn't it?" She choked on the words.

"Yes," Billy said.

To hell with keeping his mouth shut, Finn thought. "It was great," he said. "Emma told me how you'd talked about it, and I didn't think you'd pull it off. Shows what I know."

Annie nodded. "Holly told me to go back inside and send Walter out in twenty minutes. Walter's the server who brought the trolley. Then she was supposed to join me to pull off the tent, only she didn't, and I knew I shouldn't wait, because of the ice meltin'."

Finn met Billy's eyes, and Billy nodded. The killer must have already been hiding inside the van, waiting to get Holly alone. "But the door to the van stayed open," Finn said, mostly to himself.

"No," Annie said. "I closed it, because we wanted things cool, and we didn't want anyone to see the display ahead of time."

Billy patted her hand. "Thank you, Annie. Officer Murray here will drive you home to Eileen now. Do you think you'll be able to sleep?"

"When I can't stay awake anymore," she said, and got up.

Once they were alone, Billy said, "I know some people can do a lot in twenty minutes, but he moved fast."

"Don't forget, he would have had a little time after Walter left to finish with any final cleanup he had to do."

"Then get away," Billy said. "Shit, you'd have to be driven to go do it. Sounds like a war plan."

"Yeah," Finn said.

The door opened again, and Orville came in. He hadn't bothered to knock. "There are TV cameras outside," he said. "Nice way to kick off a campaign."

Finn stared at him.

Orville shook his head. "That didn't sound the way it was meant to. We've got huge trouble on our hands. I'm just a bit bemused it started here tonight."

"It didn't," Billy said. "Denise, remember?"

Orville frowned into the distance. "The opposition will go to any lengths to destroy the competition. I'll make sure this backfires."

Finn saw Billy make the decision to hang on to his temper and did likewise.

"I heard all about Barnes," Orville said. "You need to look into everything about that man. Do you have him back in custody yet?"

"Who told you about Rusty?" Finn said.

Orville's distaste for Finn showed. "It doesn't matter. I know. That's good enough."

"You don't have to worry, Mr. Mayor," Billy said. "We're on top of our job."

"If you were on top of your job this wouldn't have happened," Orville said. "You'd never have let Barnes out of custody."

"Rusty didn't kill Holly," Finn said. "Or Denise."

Orville turned to him. "You're not here in any official capacity. I don't know why you're here at all."

"Because he's had experience in difficult situations," Billy said. "And because I asked for his help before my people got here. There was a lot goin' on."

Billy didn't mention that Orville had been useless, that he'd walked to and fro wringing his hands while others tried to calm the situation.

"Make yourself at home," Orville said in a sneering tone, looking at the laptop on his desk.

"Thank you," Billy said.

"I'll be at my club," Orville said.

"The golf club?" Billy said, all innocence.

Orville pressed his lips together. "Of course not. Damalis's. I have my own rooms. Feel free to call for me there if you need anythin' else tonight."

"You may not be able to get back inside this house for some time," Billy told him.

"Fine," Orville said.

"So Emma will stay with you, then?"

Orville's pinched face pointed at Finn. "She prefers to go up to that damn place of her parents'. Says she feels at home up there." He took a calming breath. "I want her to be comfortable. You live fairly close to the Balous, don't you, Duhon?"

"A few miles closer to town."

"This is an imposition," Orville said, watching Finn closely, "but if there should be a need, you could be there—"

"Sure," Finn said. He made sure he showed no emotion but wondered at Orville's angle. He couldn't imagine the man doing anything without his own benefit in mind.

"I told her to get started, Billy," Orville said. "I hope that's okay."

It isn't okay, asshole. Finn kept his expression impassive, but he hated that Emma had already left for an empty house.

"Didn't I hear the locks were all changed up there and deadbolts added?" Billy said. "That was a good move."

Orville wasn't quite quick enough to cover his surprise. "Yes, my wife is good at takin' care of those things."

You didn't know about the new locks. Finn felt no remorse at his satisfaction.

"No more questions for me, then, Billy?" Orville said.

"None that I can think of now," Billy told him. "I know where to find you. Make sure you get anythin' you're gonna need from here before you leave."

Orville nodded shortly. He passed Officer Clemens in the doorway.

"You aren't gonna like this, Chief," the man said. He shuffled his feet. "Couple foolin' around off the road found somethin' south of town, not far from that abandoned dairy plant."

Billy stood with his fists on his hips, crunching more mints and looking like he wanted to spit them at Clemens. "Speed it up, will ya?"

"Pretty close to the Nespique," Clemens said. "Undergrowth is so dense there, it's a wonder they could see anythin'."

"Where is this couple?" Billy said, his jaw tightening.

"We took 'em home. Their vehicle wouldn't start. They're reliable, sir. They were the ones who called us in. They didn't have to do that."

"Good, Clemens, good. I'm always impressed by public-spirited citizens. Now, are you goin' to share the nature of this find they made?"

"Sure. A Harley. Rusty Barnes's Harley. Don't worry, I've already got a search party out lookin' for him. Sergeant Boudreaux gave the okay for that. Greyhound bus stops pretty damn close to the old dairy. You don't suppose he skipped town, do you?"

28

"Will you come right now, Emma?" Rusty asked.

She'd pulled off the road near the mobile home park and sat in the darkness, listening to Rusty Barnes on her cell begging her to do things that terrified her.

"How do you know I won't hang up and call the police?" she asked him. "That's what I ought to do."

He was only quiet for a moment. "You won't. Denise trusted you, and so do I. Don't do this for me, do it for her. She's the one who got the bum rap."

"And what happened to Holly was fun?"

"Don't lecture, Emma. I'm on overload. Just say you can't do it and I'll act accordingly."

She grimaced. "That sounds like blackmail, Rusty. I'm not jumpin' at comin' to your place at this time of night with a killer runnin' around."

He laughed. Not a pleasant sound. "What do you mean, running around. I'm right here."

Even if she did know he was clean, she wasn't in the mood for black humor. "For all I know it *is* you. How did you find out about Holly?"

"By killing her, of course."

"Stop it!"

"It's all over the news," he said. "Emma, there's someone

else who knows what's going on, someone who knows everything. I can't tell you who, because I promised not to."

"I'm callin' Billy."

Rusty didn't answer.

"Did you hear me?"

He still didn't say anything.

"*Rusty,* don't hang up."

"I haven't."

"Tell me who you've been talkin' to."

"If I did, I wouldn't get any more information. What we
have may be enough, but in case…"

"This person's life is in danger, too?"

"Unless I'm being lied to, and set up."

Emma gave the Lexus some gas, swung around and headed
back the way she'd come. "You'll be there?" she said. "Stand
in the front window with the light on so I can see you."

"I can't do that."

"Then I'm not comin'."

"They've already been to my place to look for me," Rusty
said. "If they come back, I've got to be somewhere else."

Emma drove through the middle of town. A ghost town by
this time, except for the usual crowd at Buzz's.

"I can't do this," she said, and almost put her foot on the
brake. "What do you want from me? Rusty? You're not goin'
to be there, so what do you want from me?"

"Take the papers you'll find inside the back of the TV. The
back slides up and off. Give them to Finn—he'll figure out
what to do."

"Tell me what has to be done."

"I don't know what they say. I haven't seen them, either.
That was the deal."

As soon as you got away from town, in any direction, there
were no streetlights. An occasional gas station or illuminated

billboard sometimes cut the darkness, but not for long. On a moonless night, car headlights on worn street markings were all that kept a vehicle from going off the road.

Emma had set her gun on the seat beside her. She wouldn't be going anywhere without it for the present, if ever.

She'd only been to Rusty's home once, and that had been with Denise driving.

Necessity could give you, if not courage, then bravado. Rusty deserved to be trusted. "I don't believe you had anythin' to do with what's happened," she told him. Only the truth would do now. "You're your own worst enemy. You're so awkward with people, and the cops need a suspect. Rusty, you look like a suspect. You could go through a lot of pain before the authorities give up tryin' to pin these crimes on you."

"Thanks, I think. Are you sure you're not being followed?"

She looked in the rearview mirror. "I almost wish I was, but I'm all alone out here."

"You know how to get there, though?"

"I went with Denise once. I'll manage. It's on the right fork where this road divides. At the end? Close to the bayou?"

"You've got it."

Her headlights picked up the fork, and she made a right. "I'm to give these papers to Finn?"

"He'll know what to do with them."

"Can't you wait till I get there? It won't be long now."

"Emma, I'm not there now." He paused. "Denise said you were the best, and she was right. Denise was a great judge of character—too bad she didn't think more of me."

"She wasn't ready to settle down," Emma said with a lump in her throat. "But there wasn't anyone else but you."

"No. I know that. Get away from my place as quickly as you can, okay?"

Tiny hairs rose along her spine. "What should I be afraid

of?" The road became unimproved, and the vehicle dipped into ruts.

"Nothing," he said. "Just get in and get out, and get rid of the papers. And, Emma?"

"Yes?"

"Will you promise me you won't say where you got them, or what we've talked about? Someone else has risked everything to do this. Don't ask more questions, just say you promise."

She thought about it. "Finn will ask. I've got to say somethin'."

"Okay, tell him I'm the only one involved, that I asked you. He doesn't need to know there was anyone else involved. Deal?"

"Billy's gonna find out, and I'll be grilled."

"I hope that doesn't happen, but I can't do anything else. Do we have a deal?"

"Deal," she said, and regretted it immediately. "When will I see you?"

The phone went dead.

A deep lot separated Rusty's house from the bayou. Lights burning at the entrance to the driveway lifted Emma's spirits a little. The dark A-frame structure, built on tall stilts, cast her down again. She parked at the bottom of steps leading to a screened gallery and switched off the engine.

Before she'd left Orville's house, she'd changed into cotton sweats and running shoes. Moving quickly, she ran up the front steps and opened the screen door. It creaked, and she slapped a hand over her heart—then realized it was the hand that held the gun and smiled to herself.

Once inside the unlocked front door, Emma stood and listened to the sounds every house made. Her heart slammed against her ribs. The noises of silence almost deafened her. By the faint reflection of the driveway lights, she could see the television screen.

At each step she expected to be grabbed.

A clock chimed twice, and Emma let out a cry. All she wanted to do was turn and run, only someone might run after her.

Emma crossed the room on her toes, grateful for the way her eyes gradually adjusted so she could make out furniture and avoid bumping into things.

The TV sat on a table placed in front of a window on one side of the wraparound gallery. A scatter of pinprick lights showed in the distance outside, and she figured she was seeing buildings on the other side of Bayou Nespique.

She didn't like the uncovered window at her back but went behind the TV and ran her left hand over its back. Keeping the gun in her right hand, she tucked her fingernails into a crack where the panel rested against the set and managed to get a grip. Slowly, dropping the panel back twice and having to start over, Emma eased it up, took it away and set it against the wall.

She found what she was looking for immediately. A large envelope, not unlike the one that had contained the photos, but much thicker.

The temptation to leave the back of the TV where it was and make a run for it didn't last. Carefully, she replaced the panel...and heard someone on the gallery. With the envelope clutched to her chest, she dropped to the floor where she was. The sounds came from right behind her.

On her hands and knees, Emma crawled rapidly to the front windows and peered out from a corner near the sill.

Her breath caught. A small person, short, thin, crouched over, trod rapidly along the gallery. Emma tensed and got down. She trained her gun on the front door.

But it didn't open.

Once more she dared to peer outside, just in time to see the little figure hurry past the pale-colored Lexus and duck into the undergrowth before reaching the driveway lights.

Only then did Emma realize how badly she was shaking, how soaked with sweat her tank and jacket were.

An explosion of noise jarred her, and she heard a powerful engine rumble to life, roar, saw headlights swing across dense trees on the opposite side of the dirt road and turn away. The vehicle noise took a long time to recede.

Bent almost double, running at the same time, Emma made it to her vehicle and got in. She double checked the door locks and backed out of the driveway so fast the Lexus swayed.

Her phone rang, and she screamed. Hardly able to breathe, she found the cell phone and switched it on. "Yes?" she all but shouted.

"Where the hell are you?" Finn said.

29

If he could have made himself go home, he would have done it, but he had to see her. Finn made himself remain in his truck outside the Balou house while Emma got out of the Lexus and came toward him.

He wanted to shout at her, to shake her and tell her she'd scared him to death. Finally he knew how a parent felt when a child ran across the road and narrowly missed being hit by a car.

She tapped on his window. Her wan, upturned face almost made him relent, but not quite.

Taking his time when he wanted to hurry, he got out and stood on the gravel beside her. "Are you out of your mind?" he said through his teeth. "You choose tonight to take some sort of detour on the way home? You've taken ten years off my life." He hadn't intended to sound so worried, but he couldn't help himself. "It's almost three in the morning."

"I didn't want to be gone," she said in so pathetic a little voice that he finally softened. "Finn, this has been so scary, but I don't think I had a choice."

He took the door key from her hand and let them into the house—and stood there watching her turn on every light she could find. "There," she said from the middle of the living room. "That's better." She held her hands, palms in, against her hips. Her eyes glowed huge and questioning.

"What is it?" he asked, approaching but taking it easy. "What's the matter with you?"

"I haven't done anything wrong," she said. "I'm really edgy, Finn. I'm... Ooh," she moaned, and her face crumpled.

"Emma?" He reached her and held her by the shoulders. "*Cher,* tell me what's happened?"

She bowed her head and cried quietly. Finn took her in his arms and rubbed her back, noticing that she had something crackly and stiff inside her sweat jacket. He could feel it.

"I've seen Rusty," she said.

Finn stopped rubbing. "Where?"

"Well, I haven't actually seen him. But I talked to him, and I went to his house."

The angry fear returned. "You went to Rusty Barnes's house? It's by the bayou south of town, right? In some deserted place, right? Billy told me. They're lookin' for him all over. Where is he? We've got to let the cops know."

"If I knew where he was, I wouldn't tell them. But I don't know."

"Emma, the police are looking for Rusty Barnes in connection with a murder investigation. You can't play games."

She shrugged away from him. "I'll have to unpack the SUV in the mornin'. I don't feel like it now."

"Emma!"

"I've got things to tell you and somethin' to give you. But I don't know where Rusty is, and I've got nothin' useful to say to Billy." Into the kitchen she went. She found two water glasses and half filled them with red wine. She gave him one glass and slumped into a chair by the table. "Sit down." The first swallow she took sounded like water running down a drain.

"Slow up with that," he said.

"Don't tell me what to do. Sit down and drink your wine." At least he could tell when a woman was punchy and not herself. He sat down and eyed the front of her jacket, where a flat oblong spoiled the customary view.

"I wasn't goin'," she said between gulps. "If I didn't know Rusty's a good guy, I wouldn't have. It was so scary. It's dark down there. His house is all on its own, and I couldn't turn any lights on inside."

He would go along with this quietly. "Where was Rusty?"

"He had to leave. And while I was in there, someone ran along the gallery. I thought I was goin' to die on the spot, but he went through the trees, and I heard him drive off."

"You're sure it wasn't Rusty?"

"Not unless he shrank to a third of his size. The clock chimed while I was there. It was awful. When you first go into the dark, you can't see a thing, so I thought I'd fall over and—"

"You're gabblin'. Calm down."

"Yes." Her hair still shone, and even if she looked frightened, she was beautiful.

"You need rest, Emma. You've been through some bad stuff."

She blinked and looked away. "We both have. Why did I hire Holly for the caterin'?"

"Because she was good. Damn good."

"If I hadn't, she wouldn't have died like that."

He tried to hold her hand, but she pulled it away. "Whoever killed Holly would have found a way," he said. "It had nothin' to do with you."

"If it was Harold, it did. She got the idea for the divorce from me." Emma scooted her bottom forward on the chair and tipped her face up to the ceiling. "But I didn't expect her to move out the way she did."

"No. Emma," he said gently, "you said you had somethin' for me."

"Yes. Rusty said you'd know what to do with these." She

fumbled to unzip her jacket. "Don't ask me questions about them, because I don't know any answers. Rusty didn't know, either. He never saw them."

"I don't get it," he said while she wrestled a big envelope to the table.

"There wasn't time to find out why the guy went to Rusty with this. Maybe because Rusty's bein' hounded and this person feels hounded, too."

"Who is this guy, Emma?"

"Sheesh, I said I wouldn't say there was a guy. Now I have."

Finn flexed his tight back. "Rusty asked for too much from you. He should have reached me. I would have gone. Who's the man?"

"I don't know." She stared at him. "Honestly, Finn, I don't. Rusty told me it was important for us not to know, because it would be dangerous. Don't blame Rusty for not callin' you. He doesn't really know you."

"That's for me?" He nodded at the envelope.

"Mmm. At least you don't have to expect pictures of your wife with another man." She heard what she'd said and quieted inside. "I shouldn't mention your wife like that. Flippantly."

"It's okay," he said, and didn't appear concerned, but he didn't take his eyes off the envelope when she pushed it toward him.

"Rusty seemed to think you'd really want these and know what to do with them."

She admired his steady hands when he squeezed the metal clip together at the back of the envelope and slid it through its hole. First he looked inside, then slid a stack of forms onto the table. They were official looking, with printed headers, but handwritten.

"Rusty told me to tell you we talked, but he doesn't want Billy to know," Emma said, suddenly desperate to protect Rusty.

Finn stared at the papers. He fingered the top right corners repeatedly.

Emma pushed the wine away and folded her hands in her lap. She wasn't sure what she saw in Finn's face, but it was something entirely new to her. He was, she realized, reading and rereading the first couple of paragraphs in front of him.

He picked up his glass but set it down again untouched and began reading in earnest, resting one forearm along the edge of the table and narrowing his eyes. He turned the pages faster and faster, got to the end and sat with his face in his hands before starting from the beginning again.

Once more he reached the last page, and this time he looked at Emma as if he'd forgotten she was there. She let him set the pace, decide when he was ready to speak.

"Do you know what this is?" he asked. His voice sounded unused.

Emma said, "No."

He'd run his fingers through his hair so many times it stood on end in front. "I don't know for sure what it means," he said. "But I intend to find out."

She waited again.

"These are the police notes taken at the time of my father's death. They'd been removed from his file. Billy didn't know where they were or how they'd disappeared. Or so he said."

"Finn," she said, wishing she knew how to comfort him, "I'm sorry. I had no idea what they were or I'd have made sure they didn't show up in front of you like that."

"No, no." He cupped her cheek with his palm and stroked his thumb back and forth. "I needed to see them. I just don't understand how or why they came to be at Rusty's."

"He didn't know what they were, either."

"I know. That's what you said. I've got to think how to talk to Billy about this." He tapped the top page. "He couldn't bring himself not to write his real findings in the record, but he lied to everyone else, includin' my mother and me. Then he took his chances no one would look at the file again."

He wasn't making any sense to Emma.

"I knew my dad didn't kill himself. He never would." He rolled the sheaf of papers. "But there's somethin' wrong with Billy's conclusions, or what I think his conclusions probably were."

Anything she considered saying sounded wrong to her. "How can I help you, Finn?"

"Emma, I can't talk to anyone else about this."

"I understand." Of course he didn't feel he could share really personal things with her. She looked at her hands in her lap.

"Only you," he said. "Dad wasn't dead when they found him. I already knew that. He died on the operating table. But accordin' to this, he'd struggled with someone in the car and the gun went off. He may not have fired the shot."

"But…Billy wouldn't cover up somethin' like that."

"To save my mother's feelings when she was so ill he might. Dad was with a woman when he was shot. They'd… They'd been together."

30

Where else but in a little town like Pointe Judah could you walk into a police station after four in the morning without anyone stopping you? The reception desk was deserted and the chairs in the lobby empty.

"We should have waited for mornin'," Emma said. "There won't be anyone to help you."

Finn held her elbow. "You're always supposed to be able to get at the evidence room. Crime isn't nine to five."

"Aren't you supposed to call or somethin'?"

"Who knows? The front door of this place should be locked at night, and you should have to identify yourself over an intercom to get in. Time for some shake-ups around here." He knew he needed to strike out at something, and he was picking whatever was handy. "Let's go."

This building had been like a second home to him since he was a kid. Finn moved confidently through the corridors. Located in the same area as Records, the evidence room door was shut. He tapped, and after some scraping sounds, the top half of the door swung inward, revealing a counter attached to the lower part and an elderly officer standing on the other side.

"I'm sorry it's so late," Finn said. "I'm—"

"You're Finn Duhon!" The man's white hair had diminished to a fringe around the base of his scull and his pudgy, pink face could belong to anyone's sweet old grandpa. "Son of a gun. I heard you was in town. Why didn't you come to see me before now?" He landed a sideways punch on Finn's arm. If the blow was friendly, an unfriendly one would be nothing to laugh at.

"Hey, Colin," Finn said, awkward at not having recognized the man at once. "I should have come." And he would have, if he'd realized Colin was still there. "Things have been busy since I got back."

Colin tutted. "Whole damn town's gone to the dogs." He jutted his chin to look more closely at Emma. "Mrs. Mayor? What you doin' here? Specially at this hour of the mornin'?"

"Hi," she said, shooting out a hand, which he shook enthusiastically. "You know what happened at my house last night, I'm sure."

He nodded but looked blank.

"It's put all our schedules off," Finn told him. Billy must have decided to keep Colin on as the night man in the evidence room despite his being past old enough to retire. Now it was time to lie. "Billy's been helpin' me take a closer look at what happened to my dad."

The smile dropped from Colin's face. He sniffed and raised his chin. Finn saw his Adam's apple jerk. "Best police officer this place ever saw or will see. Could have held his own in any department anywhere, too."

Finn agreed, but he had things to accomplish. "Thanks, Colin. I thought he was pretty special, too."

Colin glanced at Emma again. The man might be old, but he wasn't senile. Finn prayed there wouldn't be more questions about her. She should have remained in the truck, but he didn't like her being alone—and she wasn't keen on the idea, either.

"What can I do for you?" Colin asked. "I just do the night

work, so I'm not as familiar as the day shift, but I'm sure we can work out what you need."

"I'm looking for Dad's uniform and the rest of his personal effects. Mom was too sick, and they didn't get picked up."

"So you thought you'd get 'em now?" Colin looked at his watch. "And you're the second one tonight. Askin' for Tom's stuff, that is. The other one called, though."

Finn realized he was digging his fingers into Emma's arm and released her. "That's strange," he said. *More than strange.*

"That's what I think," Colin said. "The other one was rude. Sure I didn't know what I was talkin' about, that sort of thing. Reckoned the stuff had to be there, I just hadn't looked hard enough. I told him, there's entries for Tom Duhon's effects, but they must have been checked out, because they're gone. There. Simple as that. And you know I'd help you if I could."

Finn kept a smile on his face. He felt as if he'd been punched in the gut. "Who was it who called?"

"How should I know? He didn't say. Wouldn't say, more like it. I told him if there was anythin' here, he wouldn't get it without a court order, anyway. Only there's nothin'."

Finn knew what he had to do next. "Thanks, Colin. Sorry to interrupt you."

"It's nothin'. You sure someone else in the family didn't take Tom's things? That's what usually happens in a case like that." He rubbed his ample belly. "Awful sorry, boy. Never would have thought it of Tom, but you never know what's happenin' in another man's head, do you?"

Emma kept quiet until they'd driven away from the police station. She wasn't sure what to say. Finn had behaved like a man possessed since he read the records she'd brought to him.

"Before you ask," Finn said, "we're goin' to Billy's. It's time he gave me some honest answers."

"He was tryin' to protect you," Emma said. "And the rest of your family."

Finn pounded the steering wheel. "I don't need protectin'. What he should have done was dig deeper, not accept what it seemed he was seein' and make up some lies."

There was nothing she could do or say to lessen his anguish. "Billy may be exactly what you need right now," she told him. "Once he knows you've seen the truth, he'll be straight with you."

Finn glanced at her. "Only because he doesn't have a choice anymore. Will you be okay if I leave you in the truck this time, *cher?* I don't want to deal with Billy askin' questions about us yet."

Yet? He talked as if he thought a time would come when they would be open about their relationship. Emma looked at his profile. She had struggled with thinking she was no better than Orville, another unfaithful spouse, but what she felt for Finn wasn't all about sex. That didn't make her right, but it did mean she could be gentler with herself—or choose to be.

"What are you thinkin'?" Finn said.

"I agree I should stay in the truck," she said, and turned her suddenly flushed face away.

"Good. But that isn't what I asked, is it?"

She shook her head.

"So let it out. Tell me."

"I'm a married woman," she said. "I've made excuses for myself, made it all right that… I've told myself it's all right. But am I any better than Orville?"

Finn slammed on the brakes.

Emma's seat belt crushed her chest, and she cried out.

Spinning the wheel, Finn steered onto the verge, spewing troughs of soft gravel. The vehicle stopped under the low branches of a stand of trees.

"Finn!"

She expected him to shout. Didn't men always shout when they were angry? From the vibes she felt, Finn was real angry.

He didn't shout. In slow motion, he switched off the engine, crossed his forearms on the wheel and rested his face on top.

Emma didn't move, didn't dare to.

Branches scratched gently on the windows.

She breathed with care, very shallow breaths. He had taken another blow to the treasured memory of his father. His personal sands were shifting beneath him.

"Did you sleep with me to get back at your husband?" he said.

Shocked, she stared at him.

"Did you, Emma?"

"No. I wanted you. I still want you. My marriage was over a long time ago, but I'm dealin' with notions I believed in. I'd still believe it them—one man and one woman—if I hadn't married the wrong man."

"Okay," he said. "Okay, I get that. Did you do something to make your husband behave like a cock in a henhouse?"

"No," she said. "He didn't want me. I don't know if he ever did—not the way a man's supposed to want a woman. He treated me like his special doll to be taken out and admired, but there wasn't any... We weren't passionate together, not really."

"Passion is different with different people."

"We were passionate, Finn. You and I. I know the difference now."

Faint light penetrated the trees, a pewter light. Morning on its way.

"I want you now," she said under her breath.

Not enough under her breath. He jerked around in his seat. "And I want you. I can't look at you without wantin' you. I can't sleep for wakin' up and wantin' to be inside of you. If that makes me a bad man, so be it. You're special, too special for the life you've been livin'."

Emma had undone her seat belt and rubbed her chest absently. She looked at his face, and he was watching what she did. He took her hand away, unzipped her jacket and used both hands to pull the tank over her head.

"I bruised you," he said, touching red marks on her skin. "I've got a temper, Emma. I nearly killed Rusty Barnes when he came up behind me."

"So you've told me several times," she said. "You've got some issues left over. You'll deal with them."

Finn leaned slowly closer and touched his mouth to hers, nudged her lips apart, and she met his tongue. There was no hurry. They sat by a road just out of town, barely hidden by a few branches, and kissed. Emma undid the buttons on Finn's shirt and pushed it from his shoulders. He took it all the way off.

"I want to feel you against me," she said, starting to unhook the front of her bra.

He stopped her and did it himself, his eyes hot as he freed her breasts and bent to lick her skin with the tip of his tongue. Every languid move he made set Emma's nipples tingling. She grew wet and contracted her muscles to hold in the sensations.

"Wait!" Emma pushed him away, knelt on her seat and stripped.

"Emma, Emma," Finn whispered, following the dips and curves of her body with his hands—and his eyes. "Oh, God. I don't want to take another risk. I need something."

"No, you don't." She didn't stop tugging at his clothes until she'd freed him and sat in his lap, legs astride, taking him deep inside her. Any light went out except the lights behind her eyelids. He gripped her hips and moved her. Emma helped. She used her own strong thighs to jounce on him.

Finn arched his back, pressed her bouncing breasts to the hair on his chest, and she moaned through her teeth. Madness, the most desirable madness, had taken her. And it had snatched Finn, too.

She felt him come in her, hot, wild, a flood of the man himself.

"Emma," he said again, and finally grew still.

They huddled together, Emma naked, Finn all but naked, in the driver's seat of his truck. The pewter light turned silver.

"I didn't plan that," he said.

"I know, but maybe I did. At least, it came real naturally and real fast when the opportunity presented itself. Thank you, Finn."

He laughed. "Thank *you*. We're gettin' real good at makin' love."

"Real good," she echoed.

"If we don't want some highway patrol car screechin' off the road with its lights flashin', we'd better do somethin'," he said.

"Yeah," she sighed, and climbed off him.

Between kisses, they dressed quietly.

"Can you stand it if I still go to Billy's?" Finn said.

She could stand anything that would help him. "Of course." What she feared was that talking to Billy would take away Finn's last hopes of proving that his father was the man he'd believed him to be.

"Emma?" Finn said, covering one of her hands. "You said I didn't need to do anything before we made love. Are you doin' somethin'?"

What he was asking, Emma thought, was whether she used birth control with Orville. She didn't tell him she and Orville and sex were over too long ago for that.

"I was pregnant once," she said. "I lost the child. There was never another sign of a baby. I was told they didn't think there ever would be."

31

Billy opened the front door of the Meches' picture-perfect little white house wearing a plaid broadcloth bathrobe. Barefooted, his hair looking the way it always looked, like a gray bristle brush with red roots, he didn't appear nearly as surprised as Finn thought he should.

"I hope I didn't wake Blanche," Finn said.

"You woke me, didn't you?" Billy said. "You think she's deaf? Don't worry, Blanche knows when to stay out of the way."

"May I come in?"

"Sure." Billy turned away and left Finn to pull open the screen and go into the house. He closed out the cool air from the night and followed Billy into the kitchen.

"Coffee?" Billy said, pulling forward the coffeemaker.

"I just want to talk," Finn told him. "I went to the station. Did you call Colin earlier tonight and pretend to be someone else?"

Billy stared at him. "Why would I do that?"

"You told me Dad's stuff must be in evidence. Someone called to check up on it. I thought it might have been you."

"No, but I'd like to know who did."

"So would I, but it didn't do them any good, did it? Any more than it did me any good to ask to see it."

"You did that?" He put a filter in the pot and scooped in coffee.

"Why wouldn't I?"

"Because there's nothing to be gained. You're just torturin' yourself."

"You think it didn't torture my mother to be told her husband killed himself? She was only weeks from passing away herself. Didn't she deserve the truth?"

Billy flipped the switch on the pot. "Her husband was dead. What did you want me to tell her?"

"I already told you. The truth, if you knew it. Only you didn't."

Slowly, Billy set down the mugs he'd taken from a cupboard. "What does that mean?"

Finn had carried in the envelope of forms. He took the papers out and tossed them on the table, on top of a snowy cloth printed with cherries and leaves. The paperwork lay there for a long time before Billy approached and looked down at it.

"You couldn't quite bring yourself to lie on record," Finn said. "Only you got it wrong anyway. When did guesswork take the place of good police work?"

"You've said enough." Billy picked up the sheaf of papers and started reading. "I've forgotten more about police work than most people will ever learn. Where did you get these?"

Finn shook his head slowly. "I can't tell you that."

"Yes, you can. It's easy. Just answer the question."

"No. And given what it could do to you, you won't push."

Billy breathed heavily through his nose.

"He didn't shoot himself," Finn said.

"Maybe."

"That's something, anyway—comin' from you," Finn said. "You wrote there was a struggle."

"There was."

"But you thought he was with a woman."

"He'd had a woman in the car."

"And she overcame him, got his gun and shot him."

Billy glanced toward the rest of the house, and Finn saw him listening for Blanche. There was no movement. "Let it go," Billy said. "This is a cold case now."

"Not for me. A year is nothin'. Was the woman still there when you arrived?"

Billy snorted. "What d'you think? Of course she wasn't."

"But you knew a woman had been there."

Billy threw the papers down again and hooked a thumb toward the back door. "Come see my garden."

Walking between rows of potato mounds, greens past their prime and unlikely sunflowers that could only be Blanche's idea, Finn listened while Billy gave him the "facts" in a monotone.

"Tom's clothes were in disarray. His pants were round his ankles. There was lipstick on his face and various other parts."

Shaking, Finn said, "I didn't see anything about lipstick in the autopsy report."

"I cleaned it off. I cleaned semen off the car seats, too."

Finn covered his ears.

"You asked," Billy said. "I put your father's clothes back ‚n—wrestled them on. That's when I figured a zombie would notice what was in his pants and on his pants. So I got the clothes off again. That's how they thought he was found in the first place. They thought—after I suggested it—that he took his uniform off before shooting himself. To keep the blood off. People do strange things before they kill themselves."

"You…" Tom Duhon was a good man who loved his wife and children, he wasn't a bad cop who picked up women in his patrol car. "There had to be blood on the uniform anyway."

"His mind was unbalanced," Billy said, like a recording. "Blood went everywhere, but he wasn't thinkin' about that when he took his clothes off."

Finn bowed his head. He dropped to sit on his heels. "I

think you did what you thought was right for your friend. But I also think you got it wrong."

Billy put a hand on his shoulder. "I'm fine with you thinkin' that, Finn. I don't know why what happened, happened, but the man who died that night was the best. So he was human, too, and stress got to him. Hell, I don't know what he was thinkin', but I didn't want your mother to die thinkin' about him with another woman and wonderin' if it was because she'd been so sick. Better the other than that. I'm beggin', Finn, leave it now. You pushed, and I told you. I never wanted to."

Finn thought over what he knew. "Location?" he said. "Where did you find him? It says an unimproved lot. Where? What does that mean?"

"You don't miss a thing," Billy said. He watched pigeons land on his fence. "Does it matter where it was?"

"Just answer the question."

"I liked you better when you were a kid," Billy said. "Okay. North about thirty-five miles, in the middle of nowhere. He'd driven way off the road."

"Thirty-five miles? It was real late, wasn't it?"

"Uh-huh. He must have tried to put distance between himself and Pointe Judah. Nearest town is Wells. Couldn't find anyone who saw him there."

"He probably didn't get that far," Finn said. "Did you burn his clothes? Everything? Did you even take off his wedding ring?"

"The coroner does that. It was given to your mother. This isn't goin' to make anythin' easier, but it's what you want." He took a key from the pocket of his bathrobe and went to a shed behind a trellis heavy with roses. "In here," he told Finn.

"No," Finn said, suddenly sickened. "I believe you. Let it go."

Billy unlocked the door and stepped inside. Shelves lined

each wall, and each shelf held a row of tidy boxes. Billy took a ladder and climbed to pull a box from the top shelf, a box smaller than the others. And returned to the ground.

"The last uniform Tom wore," Billy said.

"You couldn't bring yourself to get rid of it," Finn said. "You're a good cop."

"I wish I had. That was my first instinct." He pushed the box into Finn's hands. "Take my advice. *You* burn it. Do it for your father."

32

Patrick Damalis's restaurant and club resembled a Tudor house. The story went that Patrick had attended Oxford in England and fallen in love with the architecture there. Emma found the stone around large windows and the archway over outsized front doors elegant but misplaced, and Patrick had become carried away with topiary in front of the building.

She had driven by a few times but usually avoided the street altogether. A call from Carl Viator had brought her here today, when she would have preferred to remain curled up in her bed, thinking about Finn and trying not to wonder what his silence had meant when she mentioned her infertility. He had said he was sorry she lost her baby, but nothing more.

After the visit to Billy's, Finn had withdrawn completely, given her distant smiles—his eyes worried—but he'd taken her straight to her folks' house and made sure she was safely inside before leaving for his own place.

A smaller door cut through one of two large ones stood open. Emma thought it almost ridiculously reminiscent of something out of a gothic movie. The great doors were fortresslike, painted black, with iron studs.

Through that door came Carl, walking toward the Lexus with a disconcertingly grim expression on his usually pleasant face. As always, he was impeccably dressed, in a white suit today, and walked with the confidence of a man very sure of his place in the world and pleased with his fate.

Emma got out before he could reach her and make a fuss over opening her door. She hit the lock button on her keychain and met him a few feet away.

"Thank you for comin'," he said in the same earnest but troubled voice she'd heard on the phone earlier. "Let's make this look natural." He glanced all around.

"No problem," Emma said, less secure than ever. He'd invited her for lunch and been insistent when she tried to get out of it. Carl had also made a point of mentioning that Orville would not be at the club.

He took her by the hand, which she disliked, and led her inside the building. Instantly the scent of well-polished wood took over. Dark paneling covered the walls of the entry hall, and wide stairs rose from one side.

Carl nodded in the direction of a man in a green uniform who stood behind the reception desk. Overall, subdued lighting and a hushed atmosphere added to the impression that she'd just entered a gentlemen's club from another era.

"I've got us set up in my rooms," he said. "More private that way. You've eaten at Patrick's, haven't you?"

"Yes. But you go directly into the restaurant through a separate entrance. I've never been in here before."

Carl gave a discreet cough. "I doubt there's a club to duplicate this outside New Orleans. It does very, very well."

She couldn't imagine there were enough wealthy men in Pointe Judah to account for its success. "Some of the clientele must come a distance," she said.

"You have no idea," Carl said with a confidential little grin. "Let's walk up. The place is worth seeing."

But Orville had never thought to take her there. "I didn't know anyone had rooms here until last night," she said, and narrowed her eyes, facing an instant picture of Holly dead and defiled. "When Orville said he had a place here, I was shocked." Or she would have been if other things hadn't been so much more shocking.

"Horrible experience last night," Carl said, jogging up the curving staircase beside her. Deep-piled green carpet swallowed any sound of feet. "Poor Holly Chandall. I didn't know her, but she was good at what she did, and no one deserves that."

"No." This morning she'd eventually taken the phone off the hook rather than take more calls from people wanting to go over what had happened because they needed to talk about it, not to mention those who were merely fishing for salacious details.

"One more flight," Carl said, when they reached an expansive landing where two corridors forked away. Emma could see doors along the walls. "I would have preferred this floor, but there wasn't anythin' available," he said.

She wanted to ask where Orville's rooms were but contained herself.

Carl's home away from home reeked of cigar smoke. Emma didn't mind an occasional whiff, but the smell in the enclosed space stifled her.

In front of a window overlooking more topiary, this at the back of the house, a table had been set with linen, crystal and silver.

"I told the waiter I'd take care of us myself," Carl said. "I hope you don't mind, but that way we won't be interrupted."

"What's this all about?" she asked him. The secrecy had gotten to her. "We could just have talked on the phone."

"No!" He shook his head. "No, that's not safe. Sit down here." He held a chair for her and leaned over to kiss her cheek when she was settled. "Relax. I'm goin' to make sure everything's okay. You are never goin' to have a thing to worry about."

Except whatever you're hinting at.

"There's potted shrimp," he said, producing little white crocks from storage beneath the table.

Emma looked at the shrimp and toast points with complete disinterest.

Carl took a bottle from a silver bucket and poured white wine into their glasses. He had set quite a scene for this "essential" meeting he'd insisted on.

He sat and dug into the shrimp.

Emma sipped wine.

"Eat," he said, pointing to her plate with the tip of his knife. "You're too thin."

The Viators had heard Orville tell her she was too heavy on a number of occasions. Carl calling her thin now sounded forced and ingratiating.

"It's comfortable in here," she said. Overstuffed furniture upholstered in red-and-gold stripes, an Asian rug that all but covered the shining oak floor and Audubon prints on more paneled walls were almost too self-consciously tasteful.

Emma itched. Her teeth itched. The skin between her fingers itched. She had to get out of there.

Carl looked up at her and set down his knife. He shifted back in his chair. "Aren't you hungry?"

"No," she said. "I'm sorry to have put you to unnecessary trouble."

He raised his eyebrows. "Don't worry about it. Okay, we might as well get to it. I'm not lookin' forward to this."

"I don't know what *'this'* is, but I'm dreadin' it."

He tipped his lips up at her. "Whatever happens, I'll make sure you're okay."

"You already said somethin' like that."

He cleared his throat. "I'm doing the best I can. Emma, this mornin' I got somethin' that destroyed me. A delivery addressed to me and left on my doorstep at the house."

She'd spoken to Sandy at the shop, and she hadn't mentioned any delivery that upset Carl.

"I'm not sure why this was sent to me, but better me than someone else."

Emma fiddled with a fork beside her plate. She gave him a quizzical glance and found herself skewered by his watchfulness. Her tummy flipped. Carl was easy to feel comfortable with, but not when he behaved as if he expected his companion to shed her skin at any moment.

"Did you get anythin' delivered to you recently?" he asked. "I wouldn't be surprised if you didn't want to talk about it—or if you tried to forget it—but did you?"

"I don't know what you're talking about, Carl. Give me a break, huh, and tell me quickly. You're scarin' me."

"Oh, baby girl." He leaped up and went to Emma's side, where he knelt and put an arm around her shoulders. Gently, he turned her toward him and pressed her face onto his shoulder. "You are never to be afraid. Understand me? Look up, look me right in the eye, and promise you're going to relax, because you've got *me*, and I won't let you get hurt."

When Emma was able to raise her head, Carl's face was closer than she found comfortable. *He* was closer than she cared for.

"Promise," he repeated.

She nodded, but she straightened her back. "Stop this, Carl. You aren't yourself. Why would I promise you somethin' when I don't know why?"

He stood up and looked down at her, suddenly disarmingly uncertain of himself. "I've never had to do anythin' like this before, and I hope I never do again. I got some pictures. Photographs. They're of Orville with a woman." Distaste crossed his features.

Emma composed her face into neutral. He would be expecting her to cry out or faint or something. She couldn't pull either of those off, but she could buy time by pretending she didn't understand.

Carl went back to his seat. "I've admired him for so long. I still believe he's a good man, but somethin's gone wrong. He's on a power trip or somethin'."

As if Orville hadn't been on a power trip for years, Emma thought. "I don't know why someone would bring pictures like that to you, either," she said.

"They're incriminatin'," he said. "I think they're a threat."

"What kind of threat?"

"I'm not sure. You don't seem shaken up. If I didn't know better, I'd think you don't care."

"I care," she said.

From a briefcase beside his chair, he pulled out photos, and she didn't have to see them any closer to know they were the same ones she already had.

"This isn't the kind of stuff we can have floatin' around when Orville's about to throw his hat in the ring for governor. Men, a lot of men, will laugh and talk about how boys will be boys. Women don't like it—unless they're the ones havin' the good time." He turned pink. "Forgive me. I spend a lot more time talkin' to men than women. Sometimes I forget myself."

"What should we do about it?"

"Don't you want to see them?"

"I already have." Emma wished she could avoid it, but she had to come clean. "Please put them away. I was disgusted enough already."

"You didn't say anythin'."

"I'm dealing with this my way," Emma said. "And I'm not talkin' about it."

"If you've got copies and I've got copies, they came from somewhere."

"True."

"What's to stop whoever took these from usin' them elsewhere?"

"Perhaps they're going to blackmail us, although I'd think it would be Orville they'd go to." She hadn't thought of any of this. That was what happened when you got tunnel vision. All she'd been thinking about was what the photos meant to her marriage.

Carl considered. "You're right. I was caught so off guard, I'm not sure I've been thinkin' straight at all." He paused and frowned at her. "You must be devastated."

"I'm disappointed in Orville."

"*Disappointed?* You're not really upset? I don't understand you. He stands to throw away everythin' we've worked for, and all you can manage is disappointed?"

He had, she realized again, expected her to cry, to be destroyed by her husband's betrayal. "There's somethin' you need to know. We had decided to keep it quiet, hopefully until the election process is further along, but you deserve to know. Orville and I are gettin' a divorce. It's already bein' processed. That shouldn't be a big surprise to you."

"Divorced?" He dropped back in his chair. "You were already gettin' a divorce?"

"The photos cinched it."

"Orville never said a word to me." Anger didn't suit him. "I'm his right hand, and he didn't let me know the kind of obstacle we'd be facin'."

So much for his concern about her marital bliss. "We've talked," she told him. "We haven't been happy together for a long time. I suggest you get rid of those photos and pretend you never saw them. They don't make a difference to you."

"That's where you're wrong," he said, pushing back his jacket and hooking his thumbs under his belt. "He's a liability. Mud sticks. If those photos got to you and me, someone intends to get somethin' out of them."

"Like money," Emma said.

"Or political advantage. He can't run when somethin' like this is bound to come out."

"If necessary, he can tell people he made a mistake. Isn't that what happens? As long as the candidate throws himself on the mercy of the constituents, or would-be constituents, everyone forgets what he did?"

"That might happen if he was already in office. He's not. Opponents will take this to the bank."

Emma got up. She was too tired and too sad to hash this out now—if ever. "I don't intend to make those photos public," she said. "I'm sure you don't, either. Why don't we hold on and see if this goes away? If we've got a blackmailer out there, we'll know soon enough."

He snorted. "I'll be damned. You're a lot stronger than I thought you were, and a lot more savvy. He never was good enough for you."

"I thought he was your best friend?"

"That doesn't mean I can't be objective. You're special, too special for him. Okay, let's see what happens." He got up. "You haven't eaten a thing."

She shrugged and said, "Somehow I'm not very hungry. I think it's seein' a dear friend laid out like a fruit flan that may have taken my appetite away."

He looked stricken. "You must think I'm callous. I'm not. And I'm sure you're scared, just like the rest of the women in town. I suppose your group will quit meetin'."

Emma blinked. "Why would we do that? Right when we need each other most?"

"*Emma.* Stay away, I tell you. I won't let Sandy go there. Two members murdered. It's obvious there's a connection to the club. You girls need guidance. You need your eyes opened. What do you do at that place?"

"What...? We give each other support. We laugh. We cry. We share."

"And you talk about the one thing women always talk about, losin' weight. Food. What you should and shouldn't eat. The diet of the week."

"We do some of that. It's kind of funny."

"A woman who looks the way you do might think so. I doubt if Suky-Jo thinks it's a big laugh."

This was an extraordinary conversation. "You don't know her. She doesn't take these things seriously."

"Whatever. Some husband or boyfriend isn't amused by all this shared support. It makes you woman too independent. So these deaths have been a warnin' to stop. You and Sandy don't need to be told again."

He sounded more like Orville by the moment. "I appreciate your concern. Really I do. I'm just going to let all this play out—with Orville, I mean. I intend to make a new life."

"You sound cool about this. Maybe you already have plans."

Let him think whatever he wanted to. "School, for one thing. Just as soon as I can get established."

He joined her near the door. "I know about the money situation," he said.

"I thought Orville would have told you. He's pretty proud of it, I think."

"He should be ashamed," Carl said. "Just let me know when you need my help, and I'll work on him to change things."

"I don't think he'd do that for anyone."

"He'll do it for me if I threaten to make the story public. Not that I think he can hide it for long anyway."

She raised her chin and looked directly into his face. "So you think if these photos get out it'll be the end of his political career? You'll pack up your tents and go home? Concentrate on business?"

"It's Orville who pissed in his chili, not me. My party's going to need me more than ever."

Emma had no doubt she could be losing her objectivity, but Carl didn't sound sorry about a thing. He sounded as if he thought he might get handed an opportunity—like stepping into Orville's political shoes.

"I'd better get back to the shop," she said. "Business is quite good these days."

He chuckled. "The more guys who find out you're there, the more business you'll get, gorgeous. Just keep 'em in their places."

Carl stepped into her, framed her face with his hands and brought his mouth down on hers. She stood there, her lips pressed tightly shut, until he made a frustrated sound and stepped back, holding her shoulders as he did so.

"It's sweet of you to care," she said, just as if she'd received a brotherly peck. "You can count on me to do the right thing."

33

"The big bass drum led the big parade," Finn sang under his breath while he beat out the rhythm with the tips of his fingers, "All on a Mardi Gras day. Oh, yeah, the big bass—"

"D'you mind?" Billy said, glaring over his coffee mug.

"Just singin' along with the music."

Billy peered around his office. "What music?"

"In my head," Finn said, completely honest. "We gonna start whatever you got me here for? It's late." And after not seeing Emma since early the day before, he intended to drag his sorry butt up there and apologize to her for being a boor.

"I'm waitin' till everyone's here," Billy said. "You doin' okay with…you know?"

Finn slid to the front of his chair and stretched out his legs. "Just great, Billy. Instant recovery, that's me."

"You gotta let it go."

"Maybe I will one day—when I find out the truth."

"Shee-it." Billy slammed down the mug, spraying the usual drops everywhere. "You are just like your old man. Instincts of a bulldog."

Finn showed his teeth.

"I've got some interestin' stuff here," Billy said, tapping a couple of folders in front of him. "I probably shouldn't share any of it with you. Maybe I won't."

"Suit yourself." Finn shrugged.

"On the other hand, you might be useful to me, on account of I think you've been pokin' your nose in where it doesn't belong."

"Me?" Finn opened his eyes wide.

"You and the mayor's lady get along real well, don't you?" Billy said.

Scrambling, Finn collected his wits. "Well now, that was a swift change of subject."

"You like her, and she likes you."

"What's not to like?"

Billy's grin was too satisfied. "I may not be Sherlock Holmes, but I notice things. Somethin's been sparkin' between the two of you since that first day you sat in here together. You want to be a home breaker? Your daddy wouldn't have approved."

"No, he wouldn't," Finn said. "My father believed in the sanctity of marriage, just like I do. Only sometimes a marriage is in name only and there's nothin' to keep sacred. I had one of those myself, remember?"

"Yeah. And I'm sorry about that. What about Mrs. Lachance? Is she in an unholy alliance?"

Finn laughed shortly. "So to speak. And that's all I'm sayin' on the subject. It's already a whole lot more than I should say. I'll be more careful in future—I don't want rumors, and neither would she." If they ever crossed paths again. Ah, hell, he was dramatizing. Of course they would cross paths—and more, if he had his way. He lowered his eyelids and relived a little of the previous early-morning drive. Emma had been mighty enthusiastic herself.

A patrolman let the lady in, and Finn sat upright. "Emma? Is somethin' wrong?"

In a red dress with a deep vee neck and narrow skirt, she

looked good enough to eat, and Finn had become very hungry after almost two days of starvation.

"Billy said he wanted to see me," she said. "So here I am."

"Sandy Viator landed in the emergency room around an hour ago," Billy said. "Looks like an overdose. Carl was out, so she called 911 when she decided she was slippin'. Just as well. Maybe she can get a handle on her problem."

"What problem?" Emma said. Her breasts rose and fell rapidly.

Billy met Finn's eyes. "Prescription drugs, they think. She had some of the stuff in her bag."

"I'd better get over there," Emma said. "Why didn't you tell me on the phone? You'd have saved me some time."

"No need to go. Her husband's on his way, and she's about out of it already. Nothin' like a good stomach pumpin' to bring a person around—and make 'em think twice the next time."

"Sandy?" Emma scrunched up her face. "There's been a mistake."

"No mistake," Billy said. "We'll wait for the lab to figure out what she ingested. They're thinkin she's into cocktails. And I don't mean the kind that come in a glass."

Finn felt ticked off. He didn't like the way Billy had dropped information on Emma, as if he hoped to surprise facts out of her. What reason Billy could have for bringing the two of them in here together, he couldn't imagine.

He got up and pulled out a second chair for Emma. "Looks like we're stayin' where we are for a bit. Make yourself comfortable." He smiled at her. She smiled back. He didn't touch her, but he felt her.

A call came in, and Billy took it. Some grunts and scribbles later, he hung up again. "Sandy's doctor says he's never given her diet pills or sleepin' pills or uppers. Other stuff was mentioned. And he makes it a rule not to give out samples."

Emma looked more confused.

"Would you two tell me if Rusty Barnes contacted you?" Billy asked.

"Movin' right along," Finn muttered, and dropped back into his own chair. "What brought that up?"

"So far, we haven't had any luck turnin' him up. But I'll come back to that. Holly was killed the same way as Denise. Injection. She wasn't raped."

Emma squeezed her eyes shut.

"I'm not surprised that there was no rape," Billy said. "No time. Plus he wouldn't be likely to give us another DNA match. Now we're supposed to think he didn't have anything to do with it. Holly could have died just to get Rusty off the hook."

Finn didn't take his eyes off Billy, who was too cool to be real. "So Rusty murdered Holly but didn't rape her so you'd think someone else did it?"

"Somethin' like that."

"You don't believe that." *Not even close.* "The DNA they found on Denise was mixed. Two men."

"Didn't find the other one on Holly, either," Billy said. The can of mints was open, and he scrabbled for a handful.

"So how do you decide which one had the great plan to divert suspicion?"

"Divert it?" Billy crunched for several seconds. "We don't know who the second man is. We don't have a match."

"So it's Rusty—Denise's boyfriend—by default?" Emma said. "I don't think so."

"Have you talked to Rusty?" Billy said.

She did exactly what Finn had feared she would. Emma blushed and shook her head.

"That's good," Billy said, as if he hadn't really noted her reaction.

Finn wished he were close enough to hold her hand, then felt grateful he wasn't.

"They're still workin' on the van," Billy said. "They got a bunch of trace evidence."

"Careless boy," Finn said.

"Some trace evidence," Billy amended. "Maybe one thing. Or two. A hair."

"A dark red hair, I suppose," Emma said. "Ooh, and Rusty has dark red hair. Don't you have to check that against his mother or somethin'? I wonder if Rusty has a mother."

Finn hid a smile.

Billy didn't look amused. "I don't have that information yet," he said. "What I do have is this." He opened the top file on his desk. "Seven years ago an actress died from a lethal injection. They never caught the perp."

Finn revolved his thumbs, one around the other.

"One of those low-budget films. Hot sex, no plot, minimal wardrobe and single location."

"Back up," Emma said. "You mean a movie actress workin' on some B movie got killed?"

"You're quick."

"I don't know how many people get knocked off by lethal injection," Finn said. "But even if there have only been three...ever...I hope there's a connection."

"The film was made around an hour north of here."

"No shit—kidding," Finn said. "What do you have there?"

"I can't just hand over stuff like this to civilians."

"Of course not," Finn said. "Just like you can't call civilians into your office and discuss cases with them."

"Unless it's possible they have information they're not sharin' and they need a little push."

Emma gave Finn an anguished glance.

"I need to find Rusty Barmes," Billy said. "Frankly, I'm

amazed he's managed to drop out of sight. I wouldn't have thought the guy had it in him."

"But you think he has it in him to kill people," Emma said, her back stiff again.

"What I think is that Denise got her hands on somethin' she shouldn't have and gave it to Rusty for safekeepin'—just in case."

Finn didn't play games well. "Just in case what? He decided to rape and kill her?"

"Your father liked Denise," Billy said. "She pretty much got the run of this place."

"The chief had good taste, then," Emma said. "Denise was a good woman."

More mints found their way into Billy's mouth. "You were on your way to the Balou place after the party—night before last. You pulled over by the mobile home park to talk on the phone. Then you turned around and drove the other way. Patrolman had to stay well back to avoid you seein' him. He stayed too far back and lost you, but you were well south of town. Same patrolman saw you drivin' back later. Who did you go see?"

Emma's lips parted slightly, and she wet them. "Why would a patrolman take an interest in me?"

"Because we wanted to make sure you got home safely."

"Thanks. But where I go is my business."

"You won't tell me if you went to see Rusty?"

She didn't answer him.

"Good enough." Billy flipped pages in the file. "Nice of Rusty to pass the information on to you, Finn."

Billy Meche wasn't just a pretty face. "You've got quite an imagination," Finn said.

"You got the stuff on your dad from someone, and you're not talkin' about who. The possibilities are limited. Meanwhile, this town's in an uproar. They want a murderer caught. I intend to give them one."

"We want you to," Emma said. "Billy, we didn't have anythin' to do with those killings, and neither did Rusty." She closed her mouth fast, but it was too late. "How are you comin' with questionin' Harold Chandall."

"We're not. He's got an alibi. The lady he turned to for solace the same night he found out Holly left him."

"Pig," Emma said with feeling.

Billy sucked one of his mints and stared at her. "You may be right about Rusty bein' innocent, but I'm not wrong about you bein' tight with him. Obstructin' justice is a crime."

"Are you going to charge us with that?" Emma asked, her voice not quite so steady.

"Uh-uh, not today. Got other fish to fry today. But I want you two to be careful, and I want you to start includin' me in anythin' you think might help this case. If I've got you figured as involved somehow, could be I'm not the only one. I'll be back in a few." He got up and left, closing the door behind him.

"We're supposed to look at that file," Emma said.

Finn nodded. "Billy's real subtle." He got up, but Emma beat him to the desk. They turned the manilla file around and read quietly. At one point Emma gripped his arm. She must be reading the description of how the dead actress was found. In a bathroom stall, naked and propped on top of the toilet. No edible decorations on this one, but she'd been raped.

"DNA," Emma said.

"If they kept samples properly, they'll be checking it against the ones from Denise by now," Finn told her.

They carried on reading. The film had been made in a rural area.

"Near Wells," Finn said, frowning.

"That's right," Billy said, coming in again. He carried a single piece of paper. "Thought this might have arrived. The movie was made near Wells. You can get there in forty minutes. Maybe thirty, if a speed trap doesn't get you."

"Dad died near Wells," Finn said.

Billy shook his head. "Don't go makin' this more complicated than it already is. What happened to your dad a year ago had nothin' to do with a killin' on a set *seven* years ago."

He was probably right, Finn decided.

Billy sat behind his desk again and looked at the paper in his hands. He got a wide-awake expression on his face. "It's a match," he said. "They've got samples from the actress, and they match what we found on Denise."

"Are you talkin about semen—DNA?" Finn asked.

"Yup."

Emma's exhaled breath came out in bursts. "Rusty's?" she whispered.

"The other one," Billy said.

34

Driving his mother's old Thunderbird, the one he kept in pristine condition in a back barn, Finn headed north through the darkness with Emma at his side.

"If Billy finds out we've gone on our own fact-finding mission, we're history," Emma said. "We should have told him."

"He didn't want us to tell him."

She took a moment to figure out what he meant. "You think?"

"I surely do."

"He can't get us officially involved, but he knows us well enough to figure our next move? I'm not sure I like that idea. I'd kind of prefer to be mysterious."

"You are," Finn said, with laughter in his voice. "Take it from me."

"Uh-huh." She rested her head back. "I think you read me real well."

His chuckle was the only response she got.

They drove without speaking for several minutes. The narrow road wound through a tunnel of trees. The car headlights slid along peeling cypress trunks on one side, the side closest to the bayou.

"What if there's no room at the inn?" Emma said. "Or no inn, period? I don't remember being in Wells."

"Maybe I have," Finn said. "I'm not sure. We may not get to sleep at all, but if necessary, you're in the backseat, and I get the front with the console. That's the kind of nice guy I am. We agreed that every moment counts and we'd better beat any competition to the newspaper archives. If they even have archives in Wells. And you're the one who said you had to be back in Pointe Judah by the middle of the day tomorrow, remember?"

"True." At Finn's suggestion, she'd called on Eileen and Annie to go in and open up Poke Around in the morning. Emma expected them to do just fine, and they needed a way to get their minds off Holly's death, but Emma worried that Orville could show up at the shop and ask questions.

"I wish we had Rusty along," Finn said suddenly. "He'd be better at approaching people at the paper than we will be."

"We'll do fine," she said, not sure she would be of any use at all if someone was rude to her or got angry. "Rusty would have been good to have along at the paper, though. This could be a really bad idea. It could be a dead end."

"If folks didn't do things they thought could be dead ends, they wouldn't do anythin'," Finn said. "We're lookin' for somethin' that was only a blip in the major media at the time. B-movie actress killed while we were all watchin' hurricanes tear into Florida and look like they were comin' for us next. The actress got lost. Now we've got to hope there's still somethin' to turn up locally. We're primed for failure, so what do we have to lose?"

"Nothin'," Emma said. "If only we could find out somethin' that'll help us in Pointe Judah."

"I'm hangin' on to that hope."

"You really think Billy hoped we'd come up here?" Emma said.

"I know he'd rather not risk mixin' it up with the sheriff in

Wells. Not on this topic. Billy mentioned it when you were in the ladies' room. He'd found out the sheriff didn't do so well at the time of the investigation and a lot of reinforcements went in. I guess the guy's still touchy about it."

"So Billy came right out and asked you to look around in Wells? I didn't think—"

"No. He was just fillin' the time till you got back, and he mentioned what he'd heard, is all. Five more miles and we're there."

Emma nodded. "It's really not far." She watched the head-lights make a hole through the darkness. "I've had a bad thought about Sandy. I don't even know if I should repeat it."

"Now you want me to beg you to tell me about it?"

She crossed her arms and smiled. "You never let me get away with anythin'."

He glanced at her, and the dashboard lights put a glitter in his hazel eyes.

"What if Sandy got the pills from John Sims?"

Finn took his foot off the gas and coasted. "John wouldn't give her drugs. He'd lose his job if someone found out."

"I was thinkin' she could have taken them—stolen them. John's a friend. He comes in the store every couple of weeks just to say he's in town. He always has his bag with him."

He shrugged. "It's a thought. She's getting them from somewhere she shouldn't."

"Unless she's going from one doctor to another getting prescriptions," Emma said. "I suppose some doctors might give her samples to try."

"From Billy's description," Finn said, "she got her hands on a lot of samples."

The sign for Wells popped into the headlights. The local citizenry had planted flowers around the base of the signpost, and a green elf held a plastic welcome banner.

"It's not that late," Emma said, peering at her watch. "There could be somethin' open."

The town, one central street five blocks long and a scatter of houses spreading behind on either side, had a gas station and a feed store that appeared to carry everything from groceries to machine parts. Emma knew about the store stock from an illuminated list of merchandise spread the length of an outside wall.

A gray two-story building at the other end of the main street, designated A Street, advertised Eats, Beds, Barter and Beauty in a painted black arch over the open door. Light shone inside, and several men sat on the front steps with glasses in hand.

Finn and Emma returned greetings on their way to a minuscule indoor mall. The beauty shop had closed for the day, but Buy or Barter was open for business, as was Jambalaya Jim's, where a swamp pop band played foot-tapping music and what appeared to be everyone for miles around had gathered. A number of them, including children, danced between tables.

"So where are the beds?" Finn said, raising his voice to be heard.

"The back seat of the car is lookin' good to me," Emma said. "After some jambalaya."

A thin senior citizen, with white curly hair and skin he'd treated to plenty of sun, saw them and hurried from behind a counter where every stool was filled. He took Finn's elbow and led him from the café back into the hallway.

"Strangers." The man looked them over with bright eyes. "You stayin'?" he asked.

"We're hopin' to," Finn said. "Just the one night."

"I'm Jim," the man said, and opened another door. "Come on in. We got two rooms upstairs, but one of them's taken.

Could you manage with one?" He didn't crack a smile, although Emma thought he might be making some sort of joke.

"One's fine," she said. "How much?"

"Pay in the mornin' after you have breakfast. You may see a doo-dad you fancy before you go, and I can just add it on to the bill. I'll have you sign the book. You havin' dinner?"

They said they wouldn't miss it when the food smelled so good and got a wide smile for their efforts. Jim showed them to a small, comfortable room in an upstairs corridor. The bathroom also opened off the corridor, with the second guest room on its other side.

Jim didn't mention their lack of luggage, though they each had a small bag in the car, and left them with the promise that he would cook them up the best mess they ever had.

Finn looked at the undersized double bed and said, "Maybe one of us should sleep in the car after all."

"We aren't going to be in the bed long enough to get insomnia," Emma said, too on edge to be embarrassed. "Let's eat." She hadn't been hungry until she walked through the fragrant, deep-fried smells below.

Seated side by side in the end two chairs at a table that could seat ten, they put their heads close together. The immediate arrival of two bowls filled with unidentifiable chunks of something in deep gold batter put off the conversation. They used their fingers to eat oysters, crawfish, shrimp and some of the best catfish Emma had ever tasted. Hush puppies fell apart in the mouth, and big glasses of beer tasted unbelievably good.

"This could be pay dirt," Finn said in Emma's ear. "If anyone knows anything in this town, this is the place to find out."

Emma got pulled into a two-step and circumnavigated the room with an enthusiastic if sweaty young man in dungarees and a baseball cap.

"You're not from around here," he roared.

"No," she said, but didn't say where she was from. "This is a nice place."

"The best, I'd say," he told her. "Lived in Wells all my life. Wouldn't live anywheres else." He smiled down at her from a considerable height, and his honest face made her feel comfortable.

"What's the name of the local newspaper?" Emma asked, expecting to be told that Wells didn't have one.

"Wells," the young man said. "It's just called 'Wells.' Comes out once a week." He hooked a thumb over his shoulder. "It's right here, next door. They like to welcome folks who stop on their way through town. If you stop by the office, they'll take your photo and put it on the front page."

Emma doubted if anyone outside Wells ever saw the paper, but she would make sure she and Finn missed the mug shot.

Back at the table, she told Finn what she'd found out.

Jim returned to remove their bowls, then brought larger steaming ones. "Black-eyed peas, pigs' tails and rice tonight," he said. "Reckon my wife makes the best jambalaya around."

Already full from the first course, they still ate the jambalaya as if they'd been starved.

"Reckon you got a taste for that," a man sitting across from Finn said.

"It's the best," Finn said.

The man nodded his bald head. "Anythin' you're lookin' for in the area? Richie at the end there does the real estate around here. Knows most everythin' that goes on, too. He likes any chance to talk. O'course, I'll help wherever I can." He put a beefy hand across the table and shook Finn's hand. "Just call me Bull."

Finn introduced himself and Emma—without last names—and felt better about the prospect of getting information around here.

As soon as he finished his food, Finn whispered his intentions to Emma and excused himself to go locate the newspaper.

At the paper, small windows onto the hallway showed an empty front room with a counter stretching from end to end, and he could see through glass behind the counter into a room beyond. Several people were working there.

Finn pushed through a stiff door into the anteroom and waited, sniffing at the comforting scents of ink and paper dust. In the other room, a woman looked up and waved before bustling out to help him. "Good evenin'," she said. "I'm Marge. How may I help you?"

After he explained, she said, "I thought someone else might turn up askin' about the movie death. The other one was supposed to come back, but it's been weeks now."

"I wonder if the other person was someone I know." The chances that he'd get a name out of her were slim, but he had to try.

Marge rubbed her nose. "Good-lookin' young woman. Now you ask, I'm not sure I got her name—not one I remember. I told her there's unlikely to be much of anythin' to find in the archives, but she got real excited and said I'd never know how much I'd helped her. She talked like someone in the business. Journalism, that is."

Finn wished he had a picture of Denise Steen with him. He would be surprised if Marge didn't identify her as the previous visitor with an interest in the old crime.

Within half an hour, he and Emma were in the dusty attic, where naked lightbulbs hung from wires and turned the place yellow. They were shown rows of oversized binders filed according to date. Marge helped them go through until they found those for the approximate date of the movie-set death.

The attic was stifling. Without as much as a fan to move air about, the place reeked of old paper and older dust. Marge sneezed several times and said, "If there's somethin' you need to clarify, come on down and get me," she said. "It's too bad Belinda couldn't have died at a slow news time, but you know how seriously we take weather around here."

Finn knew. "Thanks for your help, Marge."

"You'll find it easier to put the binders on the table over there," Marge said. "Please feel free to make copies down in the office." She all but ran from the attic, coughing as she went.

Emma staggered under the weight of a stack of binders, and he took it from her.

They went through each volume page by page. Finally Emma found a write-up on the death, with a slightly fuzzy picture of Belinda Page in one corner. The article stated what had been found, by whom, and that an investigation was under way.

Finn removed the page from the binder to get a copy. Most pages were in duplicate, but he didn't want to take originals.

Two hours passed, and they'd collected very little on the case, and nothing to make them as excited as the woman Marge had described. Footsteps scraped heavily up the stairs, and a man appeared. He wore a pale, sweat-stained fedora and suspenders to hold up his jeans. He raised a hand and gave a big, tired smile. "Marge told me you were here. Thought you might like to paw through these. Doubt there's anything here, but you never know." He put a file box between Emma and Finn, and took the top off. The inside was crammed with photographs.

"Took 'em around the set of that movie," the man said. "It was interestin', and we published a few of 'em. But then that pretty thing was murdered and it didn't seem right to keep on using 'em. Maybe there's somethin' in there that'll mean somethin' to you."

Finn thanked the photographer.

"Sorry to hear you've had some of the same trouble down your way. We'd sure like to hear it was the same jackass and you caught him."

Emma looked up at Finn, and that was when he realized these good people assumed the two of them were there in an official capacity.

When the man had gone away again, Emma said, "The sheriff may not like outsiders, but the locals surely do. We'll get copies of everything relevant and take a look at the photos in the room—if that's okay with you. I can hardly breathe up here."

"Okay with me," Finn said. There weren't any chairs in the room, so they would have to sit on the bed. He would take any opportunity to get close to her.

As soon as they had made copies on the ancient machine in the newspaper offices, they left to go upstairs to their room.

"Hold up." The photographer caught up and gave Emma a card. "I shoulda said I'm Jackson, not that you'll remember, with there bein' so many of us around here." He chuckled. "I wanted to tell you to take any of the photos you want. Just put a note in the box to let me know which ones so I can replace 'em. They're numbered."

The instant they closed the bedroom door, Emma remembered their few toiletries. She wanted to go down and get them, but he wouldn't let her. "Put your feet up. I'll be right back."

Still wearing her scarlet dress, she flopped flat on her back atop the bed. "I'm glad I'm a woman. Always havin' to be the strong one would get real old."

"I'm glad you're a woman, too," he said, studying her and holding his breath at the sight of her. The most single-minded part of him stirred. But what else could he expect?

She met his eyes, and he left in a hurry.

The men still sat on the front steps. Finn took it they'd demolished a number of glasses of whatever they were drinking by now, but he noted the only extra animation was the thumping of their feet in time to the music that still came from Jambalaya Jim's.

"How late do they play?" Finn asked on his way down to the car.

"Never any later'n you want 'em to," he was told. "Should be done around noon."

Finn left the subject there. He got the bags and went back into the building.

Walking along the corridor toward the room, he contemplated spending the next few hours alone with Emma. He didn't just want her, he needed her. Before too long she would be divorced and a free woman. What would that mean? What would each of them want it to mean?

He passed the second guestroom and the bathroom, and put one bag under his arm so he could use his key.

The fan in the bathroom clanked as if screws were rolling around inside. Then the fan went off and the door opened.

Rusty Barnes stuck his head out to look in both directions.

35

Squished into the one small room, sitting cross-legged on top of the bed with their knees all but touching, Finn, Rusty and Emma talked their way through what they knew and what they didn't. To Emma, it felt as if there was a lot they didn't know.

Rusty had seen the tear sheets from the newspaper before. Denise had them. "That's why I came here," he said. "I hoped I could find something to help out with the Pointe Judah cases. And help get Billy Meche off my back. Denise told me months ago that she had a story folks would read all over the country. With every day she got more excited and more sure of herself. Then she was dead." He bowed his head.

Emma and Finn looked at each other. They gave him all the time he needed to get himself together.

"It was something to do with your dad," he said, looking at Finn. "You'll never know how much I wanted to read those papers I left for Emma. But I couldn't risk it."

"Why not come straight to me, then?" Finn asked.

"I didn't know you. Still don't, but if you're good enough for Emma, you're good enough for me. Denise loved her. He's out there. Whoever's done all the killing doesn't stray too far. He could stop now, but he'll be back. I want him."

Emma arched her neck. "We all do, Rusty."

"No. You don't understand. *I want him.*"

"I do understand," Finn said. "But you and I should stick together—and hang in with Billy and the police, because they've got access to things we can't get at."

Rusty didn't say he agreed, but neither did he protest. "The papers were about your father, weren't they?"

"Yes. Denise must have taken them out of the record."

"She didn't," Rusty said. "Like I told you before, only you weren't listening, she told me there were and still are things missing. Like your father's badge—and those records."

"So how did you get them?" Emma said.

"Anonymous call from a woman," Rusty said. "She was scared, but she was angry, too. She said it was wrong for Denise to die and he ought to pay for it. *He.* That's as close as I got to an identification. She said she had papers that needed looking into and Finn Duhon was the one to do it. All the rules were hers, including telling me she'd find out if I broke 'em and read the stuff myself. She made it clear if I messed up, it was all off, so I didn't mess up. What did the papers say?"

Finn got off the bed and stood with his back to them.

Emma looked at Rusty and shook her head for him to leave Finn alone.

Nevertheless, Rusty said, "Denise and your folks got along, Finn. Your dad liked the way she went after things, I think." He cleared his throat. "She told me once that Chief Duhon said she reminded him of his son."

Finn didn't move or say a word.

"She didn't believe he killed himself," Rusty said, making patterns on the quilt with a forefinger. "There wasn't too much she shared. She was a reporter to her soul and kept things to herself. But she told me bits and pieces, as if she wanted to be sure someone knew at least some of it. This last year since Tom Duhon died, she was possessed with the case. She hardly slept. In the middle of one night she said there were times when she wished Tom could have let the movie actress's murder go, but he never would."

"Chief Duhon was really involved with it?" Emma said, ever conscious of Finn's back, his crossed arms.

"Oh, yeah. He hated the way it was done and how Belinda Page never got any real breaks in her life. Her father left when she was a little kid. Her mother managed to keep things together, then died of cancer only months before Belinda died herself."

"And my mother was dying of cancer," Finn said. "He would have identified with that."

"Denise said, just once, that she thought the chief was on to something."

"How long before he died?" Finn asked.

Rusty looked up sharply. "Not long, I don't think. Denise liked your mom, Finn. She went up there and helped out. Eileen's husband made it hard on her, because she wanted to be with your mother all the time, but Denise talked to Eileen and convinced her to ignore him."

"I'm glad," Finn said.

"I knew when things started to break for her," Rusty said. "She got so excited, and she let it slip that she thought she had the case cracked.... Then the bastard killed her."

"Because she knew too much," Finn said. He sat on the floor, his back against the wall and his knees drawn up. "You sure she didn't say anythin' else, Rusty? Any little thing?"

Rusty shook his head slowly. "She lost her free run of the cop shop once your dad died. Billy Meche took over and... Y'know, she said the funniest damn thing once. She said she sometimes thought Billy blamed her for Duhon's death. Now why would she think a thing like that?"

Emma heard the back of Finn's head hit the wall. "He was off base, but Billy had his reasons," he said. "I'm goin' to tell you what I've got for the same reason Denise shared some of her information. In case somethin' happens to me, I don't want what I know to die with me. Too bad Denise held things back."

"Don't say that," Emma said. She couldn't bear it. "You're goin' to leave this investigation to the police now."

He smiled into her eyes and blew her a kiss. "Why did it take so long for me to find you?"

She couldn't look at Rusty.

"Emma and the mayor are history," Finn said to Rusty. "They were before Emma met me. I owe you that much information about us."

Rusty didn't comment.

In a steady voice that showed little emotion, Finn told them what the papers contained. In one place he stopped, and she wondered if he would continue, but then he went on. She didn't think he missed a thing, and she felt the hurt it cost him, even though he didn't believe the conclusions that had been drawn about his father.

At last it was finished, and Finn turned to Rusty. "I want you to hole up here," Finn told him. "In your own room, if you don't mind. Just until we let you know Billy's moved his attention elsewhere. What are they callin' you here?"

"Sam Smith."

"Original," Finn said. "If it's okay with you, we'll say good-night. Don't use your cell phone in case they trace it. I'll get to you another way."

"I already chucked the phone," Rusty said. "Way back. I've been using phone cards and public phones—and cash."

He got off the bed and left.

Finn got up and stretched out on the mattress.

Emma lay down beside him, slid an arm under his neck, held him, her face in his hair, kissed him softly and watched him fall asleep.

Until the first light fingered through the blinds, she sat beside Finn and went through Jackson's box of photos. The man had wanted to share them, and she knew why. They were good, full of fun—full of life. Those photos were a small-town photographer's view into a world of making movies, of a flirtation with make-believe, and he'd reveled in every moment.

Most of the photos were in black-and-white, and Jackson had an eye. Dozens of shots took in the set, brought one frank moment after another to life. There had been lots of laughter. He caught his moments for all the right reasons. Belinda Page flinching as a stream of soap bubbles headed for her pretty face, the way she pursed up her lips when she looked at herself in makeup room mirrors—the admiration on a man's face, the awe on that of a teenage girl.

Emma looked at every shot, some of them several times. One or two scraps of paper marked a missing photograph Jackson hadn't gotten around to replacing, but there were plenty to take their places.

She closed the box and put it on the floor. The light had never been turned off, but Finn continued to sleep. Soon they would head back to Pointe Judah and the race would start again, but for the moment they were set free, just the two of them.

Leaning over him, Emma touched her lips to Finn's. He smiled, and his eyes moved beneath the lids, shifted his lashes, before he looked at her and gathered her into his arms.

36

"Are we glad to see you!" Eileen said the instant Emma entered the shop.

"What's wrong?" Emma said. "Oh, I'm sorry, I should have known better than to expect you to deal with this place—not without even knowin' where anythin' is."

"It wasn't the shop," Annie said, doing a poor job of smothering a grin. "Your husband's called about every fifteen minutes since we opened up. Although we haven't heard from him for a bit."

Emma felt her stomach land somewhere very low. "That's too bad," she said. Darn the man. He had an uncanny way of knowing when she wasn't where he thought he could control her. "I'll give him a call. How have things been?"

"Great," Annie said. She'd cried too many tears for her eyes to be anything but puffy, but she still smiled. "I can understand why things sell so well. I want everythin' I look at."

"Me, too," Eileen said. "The man who owns the place was in, too. He said he hopes he'll have a chance to stop by again soon."

Emma dropped her purse on the floor, aware that her red dress must look as if she'd slept in it, which she had, when she hadn't been sleeping without it. "Is that all he said? He just wanted to drop by? Funny, he never did that before."

"He was very nice," Eileen said.

"Good." Emma couldn't worry about the owner now. If Orville had changed his mind about letting her keep the shop, she would cope. She'd coped with a good deal more and survived. "How are you two doin'?" They'd know what she meant.

"We've decided we've got to talk about Denise and Holly," Annie said. "If we don't, it's like they weren't here except as somethin' to be sad about. It is a frightenin' time."

"Annie's wise," Eileen said. "She's the one who makes sure I don't do my usual silent number and go inside myself. Emma…"

"Yes," Emma said. "Eileen, are you tryin' to tell me somethin' big?"

"In a way. Chuck's not comin' back."

Emma frowned. "I thought he was due back any day? Aaron said so."

"Chuck changed his mind. He says he never got a chance to do any of the things he wanted to do. Being tied down with a family—you know the routine. He's moving on."

"I'm sorry—"

"I'm not," Eileen said fiercely. "For Aaron, I've stuck with it, but the man hasn't been a real husband to me."

"Does Finn know?"

Eileen smiled. "I'll let him know as soon as I see him. It's not going to make a big difference, except financially. Chuck has less than a year to pay anythin' toward Aaron. But I can work—I want to."

"We'll talk much more about it," Emma said. She might have a little advice for Eileen. "I'd better give Orville a call now."

She went into the back room and shut the door before dialing his office number, only to be told by his assistant that he'd gone out for a few hours.

Emma didn't really want to, but she phoned Carl, who came on the line immediately. "Hi, Emma. I'm so glad you called. I didn't handle things well the other day. I'm—"

"Forget it. We've all been going through extraordinary times. Any idea why Orville's been tryin' to get me all mornin'?"

After only the slightest pause, Carl said, "Weren't you in?"

Nosy bastard. "No, I wasn't. But I'm at the shop now so I was hopin' to talk to him." No way would she explain her movements to Carl Viator. "How's Sandy? I want to see her as soon as possible."

This time the silence was longer. "She's doing just fine. She's embarrassed and won't go out. If you want to find her, she's at home. You'll probably have to go over there. She doesn't answer the phone."

Emma sighed. "I should have noticed somethin' was wrong, shouldn't I?"

"If anyone should, it was me," Carl said. "I didn't because she hid it well. Go see her now, Emma. She needs you."

Sandy came before the shop. "Okay. I'll do it. Any idea what Orville wants?"

Carl laughed, and the sound wasn't nice. "Afraid so, *cher.* We lost Oakdale to another buyer, and he's fuming."

If she could feel sorry, she would. She couldn't. "I see. You'll find other property, you always do. And I guess I'll probably be saying goodbye to the shop. Ah, well."

"Did you tell anyone about the little *lagniappe* the owner was going to get? Or thought he would. You know, the value-added deal we mentioned? It got leaked to the current city manager, and he threatened to sue, so that got squelched in a hurry. Orville has to keep it clean right now." He laughed too hard.

"I didn't say anythin' to anyone. I wouldn't have thought about it."

"You're gonna have trouble convincin' Orville of that."

"Why?"

"He'll get around to tellin' you himself. For myself, I'm glad it's happened. I didn't like the arrangement."

Emma caught sight of herself in a mirror and looked at the ceiling. "I'm goin' to see Sandy now."

The Viators also lived close to the golf course, but on a different street from Orville. Emma didn't even like driving in the area anymore. Eileen and Annie had been thrilled to stay at Poke Around, so there was no excuse not to leave again.

She thought of Finn and swallowed. He'd refused to promise he wouldn't get involved in the murder case today, not without letting her know what was going on. He'd also refused to let her stay with him, pointing out that she'd made a fuss about all the work she needed to do. And he had business, too, he'd told her.

Tonight, when he expected her to be available, it would be her turn. Angela had called a gathering, and although Emma didn't feel like going, she knew how much healing they all had to do—together. She would rather be with Finn, but she wasn't going to be.

The Viators' three-story, antebellum-style mansion could be the largest house in the parish. Orville sneered at the place and suggested the Viators were in over their heads financially. Emma only knew that Sandy took huge pride in her home.

Emma pulled into the circular driveway and parked beneath the *porte cochere* to give the Lexus some shade on the relentlessly hot day.

She wasn't surprised when no one answered her ring at the front door, but her spirits sank lower. How could you help a dear friend when you didn't really understand the problem? All she could hope was that Sandy would confide in her, let Emma inside whatever had pushed her to damage herself.

Just as Sandy had a key to a side door at Orville's house, Emma carried one to let herself in through the Viators' kitchen.

She didn't need the key; the door wasn't locked. Inside, the sight and fragrance of freshly baked cake layers cooling on racks and a bowl of yellow frosting lifted Emma's spirits. Sandy considered baking one of her major talents but only did any when she was in a good mood.

"Sandy?" Emma called, swiping a smear of lemon frosting and licking it from her finger.

She wandered through etched glass doors into the breakfast room, where the breakfast dishes remained on the table. The housekeeper dealt with those things and must be late.

Room after room showed no sign of life. "This house is too big, Sandy," Emma muttered. "You shouldn't be able to get lost at home."

She looked up the grand staircase in time to see Sandy's miniature dachshund negotiating a downward path, her tummy sliding over Persian carpet as she came. Bijou arrived and patted at Emma's shins with pointed little paws. Emma picked her up, and the velvety creature settled at once into the crook of an arm.

How like Sandy to forget the cake she'd been making and wander off. Probably luxuriating in the bath with a novel if she'd followed one of her regular patterns.

Nuzzling Bijou's snout into her neck, Emma went upstairs and walked into the Viators' open master suite before she heard the noise. She stood, toe-deep, in peach-colored carpet, before she saw the couple sweating together against a gilded French writing table that stood in one of the room's two bow windows.

The filmy drapes at the twelve-foot-high window were drawn back, and, framed against a hot blue sky, Orville had planted his naked butt on the edge of the table. With his head thrown back, he gripped the gilded edge, probably to help anchor him against Sandy's onslaught.

Sandy by sunlight was an acknowledged sight to be seen. Beside a swimming pool, she could create enough diversion to cover for a murder in progress in the rose garden. Kneeling in the sun streaming through her own bedroom window, her black hair beamed faintly blue, her perfectly even, perfectly all-over tan glowed, and her coral-colored lipstick outshone Orville's now you see it, now you don't, pride-and-joy.

Bijou howled.

37

"Are you drinkin' champagne?" Finn ran up the steps to the gallery behind the Balou house and looked down at Emma. "I've been lookin' for you. You haven't been answerin' your phone."

Using the big toe on her right foot to keep gently rocking, she sat in the old glider and cradled a champagne flute against her chest.

She gave him a vague smile. A navy-blue halter top and shorts didn't help him keep his attention on her face.

"How long have you been here?" he said. "Eileen and Annie are having a great day at the shop. They love it. But you told me you'd be there for the afternoon."

"It's still afternoon."

He ducked out of a patch of sun and sat down beside her. "But you're here, not at the shop. Don't shut me out. Somethin's eatin' you."

"Carl Viator set me up." She raised her glass and looked at him through the pale champagne. "Don't worry—I've had two sips, and I'm not enjoyin' it. I'm too mad, mostly at myself for being such an idiot."

"Set you up how?"

"I went straight to see him afterward, and he didn't try to deny it." She stared straight out at the trees that edged the property. The white cat jumped onto her lap, and she gathered it up, kissed its head until it squalled and leaped away. He would be glad to take the cat's place.

Sometimes it paid to keep your mouth shut. Finn figured this was one of those times. He considered holding Emma's hand but decided against trying.

"I don't know why I didn't pick up on it a long time ago, but Carl Viator hates Orville. I don't blame him, but I don't know how long he's hated him. I think he wants to destroy him. I'd lay odds he just made sure a real estate deal Orville wanted fell through."

"Do you care?" A man had to ask what a man had to ask.

"Care? You've got to be jokin'. I guess I'm just disappointed Carl's such a dud, too. He made sure I caught Orville with his obligin' female friend. The one in the photos."

Finn held his breath.

"I accused Carl of taking those photos. He didn't admit it, but he didn't deny it, either. The other day he pretended a set had been delivered to him. That was because he wanted to see my reaction to the ones he threw at me. I just know it was him. Now I'm thinking he must have been the cowboy, too. Creep."

Shit. "Why would he do things like that? Emmy, maybe you're wrong on this."

She took her third sip of the champagne and wrinkled her nose. "This couldn't have been a good year," she said. "Carl did it because he was hurt, and he wanted me to hurt just as much. He wanted me to feel as betrayed as he does."

Finn tried to take her glass and set it down. Emma slapped his hand.

"You told me you had a busy day planned," she said. "All business."

"I'm through with it." And he was pleased, at least with parts of the day. "I bought Oakdale."

Color rose in her face, and her smile was secretive. Not exactly the reaction he'd hoped for.

"I've only been workin' on it for a few days, and I didn't think I had a chance. The owner said he had an offer I couldn't improve on. Then we had an appointment today, and he said the place was mine. Just like that. His people have to meet with my people and deal with papers."

He didn't know what to make of the narrow way Emma studied him. "I didn't know you had *'people,'*" she said.

"It's just a figure of speech, Emmy. I'd made up my mind I want to put down roots here, so… Emma, don't look at me like that."

She kept right on looking. "I'm glad for you."

"I'm sorry, I didn't mean to change the subject, but you asked. You've had a horrible shock, and I'm not doin' a good job of helpin' you deal with it." He was doing a lousy job. "Just let it all out, *cher*." All he'd dreamed of doing throughout the drive up here was telling her about Oakdale.

"With Carl's help, I walked in on Orville and Sandy—*in flagrante delicto*. Buck naked and buckin' in the sunshine."

"They were outside?"

"No. The sun was shinin' into Sandy's bedroom. Sandy and Carl's bedroom."

What could he say? Finn very cautiously put an arm around her shoulders. Her body felt stiff, and without warning she threw the glass of champagne over the gallery railing.

They sat quietly.

"You're hurt," Finn said. "It's one thing to know your spouse is unfaithful. It's another to catch him in the act. And with a friend."

"I'm glad I did," she said. "They know I saw them, and they had nowhere to hide. I loved it."

He smiled a little. "Remind me never to get on your wrong side."

His cell phone rang, and he considered not answering but saw it was Billy. "Yes, Billy?"

"What did you find out?"

Finn smiled some more. "Nothin' new, or nothin' we didn't already guess. The shootin' of that movie was obviously a big deal around Wells."

Emma looked up at him with laughter in her eyes. Now she knew he had been right about Billy wanting them to go where he would rather not go himself.

"News," Billy said. "John Sims ducked out. Seems to be an epidemic of men dodgin' out of Pointe Judah at the moment. I wanted to talk to him about Sandy, just to see if he was missing drugs he couldn't account for. He's gone."

"John travels a lot," Finn said.

"Not for a pharmaceutical firm, he doesn't. I had that followed up, and he hasn't worked for them in more than a year."

Finn rubbed hard at the skin between his brows. "So what's that all about? The guy was lyin' through his teeth. He let everyone think he was still a rep."

"He could have been embarrassed to say he'd gotten the boot," Billy said. "I'm gonna be here late this evenin'. If you feel like stoppin' by, bring booze."

Finn switched off without committing and gave Emma a précis of what Billy had said about John.

"Did Billy make sure John's not working for a different outfit?"

"I don't know." But if someone was going to come right back with that question, it would be Emma.

She hopped out of the glider and stretched.

Finn was grateful.

"Stick around, if you like," she said. "There's plenty to eat if you want to make something."

He blinked. "Aren't you hungry?"

"I'm goin' out for the evenin'. A few of us need to get together." She sighed. "If we get much fewer, there won't be anyone left."

Finn shot to his feet. "Don't you ever talk like that. Whoa, you take my breath away, and it's not a good feelin'. Where are you goin'? Who else is goin'?"

"Excuse me?" The indignation didn't ring a hundred percent true. "I have an engagement this evenin'."

"And it's none of my business?" he said. Inside, he fumed. Why didn't she get it that he had good reason to worry about where she was all the time?

"Secrets," she said, planting her hands on her hips. "Where else would I be goin' to meet with friends?"

He was a tough guy, a warrior. Warriors didn't suffer from nervous stomachs, so why did he feel like his gut had been punched? "I don't think that's a good idea," he said. "Don't get the wrong idea. I know I can't tell you what to do, but…"

"You're right."

"Emmy, two members of that group have… You know what's happened. Could it hurt to be careful?"

She bounced to her toes and kissed him. Before he could catch her and do something about the opportunity, Emma had slipped out of reach. "Don't worry about me," she said. "I'll be with friends."

38

Emma hurried into Angela's house. "I'm sorry I'm late," she said, avoiding the other woman's eyes, not wanting to see the reproach she expected. "I've had some busy days."

"You're not late," Angela said, her voice even more husky than usual. "You're the first one. Thank you for coming, Emma." She held out her arms, and Emma returned a long hug.

"What are you doin' openin' your own door?" Emma said. She studied Angela. "You always have Mrs. Merryfield do it. Does this mean you're feelin' better? I haven't forgotten how you forced yourself to come to me when Denise died. It had to be so hard."

"Sometimes we do hard things when they're for the best. Come on in and get changed."

Still breathless from hurrying and being nervous, Emma said, "Let's sit down first. I think anythin' I had to do would be too much right now."

"We always wear our robes," Angela said. "They're part of what makes us a group. A dear, very close group."

"Do I see tears in those eyes?" Emma said, looking more closely.

Angela pulled hair farther forward over the scarred side of her face. She lowered her gaze. "It seems to me as if everything we've had is fading away. The closeness, the under-standing…the deep love that has allowed us to share things we wouldn't share with anyone else."

"Get *on*," Emma said, slipping past. "We need to talk. Two of our friends have died. It's terrible. I can't imagine… I would never have imagined anythin' so horrible happenin'."

She went directly to the sitting room, kicked off her san-dals and curled up on a love seat.

Angela followed slowly. She repeatedly tugged at the hair falling over the damaged part of her face.

Emma frowned. "I didn't think you did that anymore."

"What?" Angela looked at her sideways.

"Worry about a few marks on your face. I thought one of the first things we did as a group was work on that."

"Do you think I should have carried on with the surgeries?" Angela asked. "I still could, I suppose."

They had visited this place before, a long time before. Emma had believed the other woman had made peace with the disfigurement. She had been adamant about not having more surgery.

"What do you think?" Angela said. "Would I be more lov-able if my face wasn't ruined?"

Emma hated this. "You're the only one who can make a decision about somethin' as serious as plastic surgery. If you do it, it has to be for yourself, not because you think it'll make a difference to someone else."

"Do you put on makeup for yourself? Do you wear a sexy little halter and shorts for yourself?"

"This isn't like you," Emma said. She wasn't sorry to sound sharp. "You know the things that matter most to me, and they're all about people and relationships."

"Don't you sound holy?" Angela looked away. "I'm sorry. I'm really sorry. I'm not myself. We've hardly gotten together in the past few weeks. I call, and all of you have excuses not to come."

"You called me once to come," Emma said. "And I'm here. I'm sure the others will be, too. These haven't been normal times. We're all trying to make sense of senseless things."

"Look at me," Angela said. "Look into my eyes and tell me your feelings toward me haven't changed."

Emma knew it was silly, but she got a creepy feeling. "Nothing has changed," she said. "Except that Denise and Holly are dead, Angela. They're dead, and we're grievin'. Grief takes time. I think about them every day, many times a day, and wonder what I could have done to stop what happened."

Angela snorted. "You couldn't have done anything. Don't be silly."

"No, I suppose not." Emma dropped her bag on the floor. "But I still wish I could. When everyone's here, we'll get into this. There hasn't been an opportunity until now, so stop tellin' yourself you're bein' ignored." She smiled. "How could any of us ignore you? Without you, we'd never have come together, and look what we'd have missed."

At last Angela smiled. "My, what we would have missed," she said.

Emma snapped her fingers. "I know what I wanted to ask you about. John. When's the last time you saw him?"

"Why?"

"Billy thinks he may have left town, because he lost his job some time back and now he's embarrassed in case we find out. I think that's more or less what Billy was suggestin'."

Muttering under her breath, Angela got up and paced. She tossed the skirts of her robe behind her and confronted Emma.

"John wouldn't do a thing like that," she said. "It's not that I see much of him, but he's a gentleman, and he's honest. In all the years I've rented this place from him, there's never been a thing he's said I couldn't do. How many landlords would let a person add on to a house and put in a pool—an *indoor* pool? He's caring."

"You've added a lot of value to this place," Emma said. "You paid for those things, not John, and he still owns this house."

Angela pinched her mouth shut and breathed loudly through her nose. "I thought you were different—not judgmental. I thought you could see when people were something other folks didn't understand."

Taken aback, Emma crossed her arms over her bare middle. She felt chilly and uncomfortable.

Angela walked to the other side of the coffee table. She bent and took matches out of a drawer. She lit candles on a table behind a couch and in an ornate floor-standing branch. "I'm worried," she said, shaking out a match before it would have burned her fingers. "What if John's sick over there and not answering his phone? What if he's *dead?*"

"Don't say that." Emma put a hand over her mouth. "Please, don't say things like that, not with what we've been through."

Angela threw down the box of matches. "I haven't seen him. When did I see him?" She turned one way, then the other, the skirts of her robe flying. "Emma, I don't remember."

"He was at Orville's party," Emma said. She thought about it. "He was there all that horrible evening. He was great, just like he always is."

Angela stopped twisting. "I wasn't there, of course."

"You wouldn't have liked it," Emma said, not thinking. "I mean, you wouldn't have enjoyed all the noise and fuss."

"You think a lot of John, don't you?" Angela said. "I've seen how well the two of you get along."

"We do," Emma agreed. She looked at the door. "The others are really late. Are you sure you told us all the same time?"

"Lynnette said she and Frances would be late because they've got late appointments. Suky-Jo's one of the appointments. You told Sandy, didn't you? I couldn't reach her."

Emma set her teeth. "Sandy's indisposed."

Angela frowned. "But you did talk to Eileen?"

"No," Emma said. "I just assumed... I didn't think about it. She might not have wanted to come tonight, though, and maybe that's a good thing. She doesn't share the memories we do, or the long relationships. This should probably be a night for the old crew."

"What's left of it," Angela said.

Emma stood up. "This is starting to feel bad, Angela. I...it feels as if you're trying to hurt me. We shouldn't be doing that to each other."

"You were always too touchy," Angela said. "You spend too much time thinking about yourself."

"I see." Emma closed her eyes and exhaled. "You're making this too hard. I'm going to leave now. We'll meet when we've both done some healing."

"I'm sorry," Angela said. "Really sorry. I can't get it together, Emma. I'm brokenhearted."

"Of course you are."

Angela smoothed her pink gloves repeatedly, then pulled at her hair. "Do you forgive me?"

Emma sighed. "Forgive and forget. It's over."

"You must be looking forward to your divorce so you can get on with your new life."

Emma twisted her wedding ring. "Yes. It's almost a shock how quickly a marriage can be over."

"But that's what you want. You've said you do, and I know you do. You don't have to pretend you're sorry with me. I'll still think you're a good girl."

"I'm not sorry," Emma said. "Let's drop it." The ring

needed to come off her finger. She would see to it when she left Angela's.

"Will you come with me and check on John?"

"I told you he's not here," Emma said.

"Billy doesn't know that for sure, and neither do you. I've got his key in case he needs something checked in there while he's away."

"We can't... *No,* I'm not going into John's house without being invited."

Angela nodded. "Of course not. You're right not to get involved. I'm the one to do it. You go on. I'll be fine."

"You're funny," Emma said, without meaning to voice her thoughts. "I mean, you're a bit like a mom tryin' to guilt a kid into doin' what they don't want to do."

"I—"

"Hush," Emma said, grinning. "If you think it's right to make sure John's not lyin' in there with two broken legs, that's good enough for me. I wish some of the others were here by now, though. I like the idea of safety in numbers."

Angela opened the drawer in the coffee table again and got on her knees to peer inside. She located a key and held it up. "Thank you, Emma, dear. We'll take a look around, that's all. And I'll leave a note for John to say we did it." She shrugged. "If he gets mad, he gets mad. He should be grateful we care."

"And we do," Emma said. "Let's get it over with. This is bad for my nerves. I'd never make it as a cat burglar."

He must be hard up, Finn thought, to take a crusty cop up on an offer of company because there was nowhere else to go. Or nowhere he wanted to go that was available.

"This is good scotch," he said. "Thanks." He'd forgotten to bring anything with him, but Billy had produced an unopened bottle of single malt.

"Now and again a man should have the best—if he can," Billy said. "My dad said that to me a long time ago, even though he rarely got mediocre anything, let alone the best."

Finn appreciated the pale gold fire slowly. "Glad I dropped by. I was expectin' that mud you call coffee."

Billy smacked his lips. "Damn good coffee, boy. You don't know quality when you get it. But this is somethin' else." He settled back in his chair behind the old metal desk and rested his glass on his solid but flat belly. "Tried John Sims again. No luck. I had a car stop by, no response."

"If you're really worried, get a search warrant," Finn said.

"I would if I could get Sandy Viator to tell me he was givin' her drugs. She denies it. Way she tells it, she never did O.D. She's just been upset about the murders, accordin' to her, and oversensitive to whatever she eats."

"And the samples?"

"Someone must have dropped them in her purse. Either by accident or because they don't like her. I didn't realize before, but the woman's pathetic in a way. Appearances are everything to her. I got in touch with Carl, and he said she's doin' fine, as far as he knows—whatever that means."

Finn figured he owed it to Billy to come clean about something. "I appreciate the way you gave me Dad's uniform. It's being looked at for DNA. If they find what I hope they will, they'll check it against mine. I think it'll prove what I want it to."

Billy pulled his lips into a straight line, and his mustache bristled. "Wish you hadn't done that to yourself," he said. "Or to me. I want to put it behind me, and so should you."

"I'll be the only one who knows the results," Finn said. "And you, if you want to. There won't be any talk about it, but I had to give Dad a chance to tell his side."

"You've got a strange way of puttin' things."

"You know what I mean. What if whatever you found on

the seat of the car was there before he got in? There are ways
it could happen."

"You're graspin', but I guess I don't blame you."

"Billy—" Finn shifted to the front of his chair "—I believe
you want the truth as much as I do."

"Why not?" Billy's expression suggested he wasn't a
happy man. "Your mother can't be hurt now. The FBI will be
in my pockets by mornin' anyway. I'll have to get used to havin' my decisions questioned."

Finn turned up a palm. "Are you goin' to be okay with that?"

"As okay as a local cop ever is. A word to the wise—just in
case you happen to know where he is. If Rusty Barnes doesn't
get his butt back into this town, he'll be on more suspect lists
than mine. Ah, shit, now what?" He answered the intercom.

"Can we give out an address?" came a voice from reception. "There's a man here looking for a local address. He's got
the name of the person."

Billy, who looked more tired than could be healthy,
scrunched up his face. "Does this guy have ID—and a reason
for wanting the address? And is he prepared for us to check
him out before we give it to him?"

A short cough, and the female officer said, "He says he is."
Then, with emphasis, she said, "He's looking for *Finn Duhon.*
This guy's name is Jackson."

"Give me a minute," Billy said before turning off the
speaker. He turned to Finn. "Know anyone called Jackson?"

"Mmm, nope." There could have been someone in the service. "I don't think so."

"Okay, no address for Jackson, whoever he is."

Finn got up. "Let me take a stroll-by, just to make sure."

Billy shrugged and returned his attention to the papers in
front of him and to his scotch.

The man at reception wore a light-colored fedora with a

line of sweat around the band and suspenders to hold up his jeans. He grinned when he saw Finn. "Bingo," he said. "And I didn't even know you were a jailbird."

"Good to see you, Jackson," Finn said, remembering the photographer from Wells immediately. "Come and meet a friend of mine."

Back inside Billy's office, Finn introduced the two men and said that Jackson had known Belinda Page.

"I didn't really know her," Jackson said, flushing. "I just took pictures on the set for the paper."

Hundreds of pictures, Finn thought. Jackson had been taken by the lovely Belinda Page.

"That's why I came," Jackson said. "I'm goin' to Toussaint, but I thought I'd stop in on the way. Emma enjoyed the photos. When I got them back, I took a look through to see if she'd marked any she wanted. Wouldn't you know, there were several I hadn't replaced from the last time they were looked at— by Denise."

Billy's welcoming smile slipped. "Denise Steen?"

"Yes." Jackson shook his head. "I know what happened. Terrible. Just like Belinda. Anyway, I thought I'd drop these off for Emma, since she said she liked lookin' so much."

Finn took the envelope of pictures. He wondered if Jackson really had to go to Toussaint at this time of night, but he wasn't about to question the man.

"I'll make sure she gets them," he said. "Mind if I look, too?"

"Be my guest."

"They are so great," Finn said. "I looked at some Emma picked out for me. I like the one of someone blowing bubbles at Belinda Page."

"So do I," Jackson said. "I'd better get on." He walked out, and Finn was left feeling there was something else he should have said to the man, but he didn't know what.

"These were taken on the set of the movie up by Wells," he told Billy. "I expect you've seen plenty of photos of Belinda Page."

"Not really. I had almost nothing to do with the case."

Finn gave Billy the photographs and went behind him to look at them. "That's the main street of Wells. I didn't know they'd filmed there. Looks different. They put other names on the businesses."

Billy grunted and came to a photo of Belinda clowning in front of a makeup mirror. She'd blown up her cheeks and made her eyes huge.

"Looks like she didn't take herself too seriously," Billy said. "I appreciate that in a person."

"Me, too." Finn looked at the woman, and at the makeup artist reflected in the mirror from behind her. "She made other people laugh, too."

The next shot was similar.

Finn reached over Billy's shoulder to stop him from turning it over. "Let me see that." He took it, and the one before, the one after, and looked from one to the other. His skin shrank, tightened. Sweat broke out on his forehead. "Shit, look at that."

"What?" Billy studied the photos, but not for long. He pushed to his feet, pointing at the people in the picture. "That woman, there, the small one. You couldn't miss the red waves. It's that Mrs. Merryfield who works for Angela. Looks like she was working with hair."

Finn hadn't even noticed her. "Yes," he confirmed. "And the guy doing the makeup, the one with the beard, is John Sims."

John's house and the one Angela rented were closer together than Emma had realized. Bamboo many feet high separated the two, but the pathway through the canes took only moments to cover.

"The houses are really close," Emma said, while Angela bent over to unlock a door at John's. "I'm surprised they got planning permission to do this."

Angela said, "Spoken like the mayor's wife," and tiptoed into a kitchen that didn't look as if it was ever used.

"A neat freak," Emma said, closing the door behind her.

"Just neat," Angela said. "He's like that with everything. Careful."

"John, you here?" Emma shouted. She wanted to leave the moment she could.

"*Don't* shout like that," Angela said, spinning toward Emma. She put a hand to her chest. "You frightened me."

"Why?" Emma said. "We're lookin' for John. I don't want to poke around his house if I don't have to."

Angela pulled on her hair repeatedly. She turned away. "I'm pushing you too far. You'll stop loving me. This is why I never tried to make friends before—I was afraid my troubles would get in the way."

She needs professional help. Emma spoke softly. "You're reacting to leaving your house again. Relax. We'll do this and get you home. I really don't think John is here."

"I'm not sick," Angela said. "Don't think I am. You do, don't you? I can see it in your eyes."

Emma glanced toward the door to the outside. John wasn't here. "Let's go back," she said. "You're getting upset."

"*I'm not getting upset.* I'm not." Angela breathed slowly. "Yes, I am, and I'm useless when I panic. You're right. We'll be quick here. You go first, if you don't mind."

"Surely." Emma did mind, but whatever she had to do to deal with the situation successfully, she would do.

Throughout the ground floor of the house, each room contained old-fashioned furniture, clean and tidy, but dated. What looked like black-and-white family pictures stood on tables.

Crocheted cloths draped the backs of originally inexpensive, old but well-cared-for chairs and a couch.

Angela shook her head. "He's never changed the furniture," she said, her voice very low. "All of this was here when he inherited the place. He said he wants to keep it the way it is so he'll remember."

"Remember what?" Emma whispered.

"I don't know. There's the upstairs, and a storeroom off the back. Which should we try first?"

Neither. "I'm sure John's away."

"So am I, but I'd never forgive myself if I went this far and just missed him. People have strokes."

"People have a lot of things," Emma said, injecting a sensible note into her voice.

"Stay here," Angela said. "I expect I'll be right back."

She took off upstairs, and Emma heard her footsteps overhead and the banging of doors as she searched.

Angela returned, smiling.

"Everything's okay?" Emma said. "You look better."

"I went up there alone," Angela said. "I am better. I have been for a long time. I don't know what came over me just now. I've never been in the storage room, but it's probably filled with tools and suitcases and all that stuff."

Just inside the kitchen, Angela paused again. "The storeroom's off here," she said, indicating one of two side-by-side doors. She shuddered. "There are probably mice in there. I don't think John uses it."

Emma thought, but didn't say, that if he didn't use it, there was no need to go in there.

Angela turned the handle. She pushed and pulled but it didn't open. "Locked."

"Good." Emma breathed again. "He wouldn't lock himself in there."

Angela smiled faintly. "No." But she looked thoughtful and took the door key from her robe pocket. It fitted the lock in the handle, and the door opened. "I thought I remembered him saying the key fitted both doors," she said, and reached inside to switch on a light.

"Okay now?" Emma said.

"I guess." Angela walked into a short entry and turned left.

She would not be coming back to Secrets alone, Emma decided. Angela had done so much in bringing them together as a group, but they'd been good for her, too. Experiences like this, however, were not fun or supportive.

A scream reached Emma as if it came through thick folds of cloth. As if it were muffled. As if someone had grabbed Angela and covered her mouth.

Emma's heart bumped. She remembered the gun in her purse. At least she'd picked it up before coming to John's. "Angela?" she said, slipping a hand inside the bag she carried over her shoulder and feeling the gun at once. She drew it out and entered the space beyond the door.

At the corner, she hung back against the wall, watching for movement in the shadows on the walls. The light Angela had turned on was immediately overhead. It was impossible to tell if there was another one to the left.

Emma edged forward until she could lean out a little to see.

A bag was slammed over her head and yanked tight around her neck. The attacker jerked her.

She stumbled.

Emma got off a shot and heard a man say, "Bitch, bitch," before a blow to her wrist took the feeling—and the gun—from her hand.

39

"Evening." Rusty Barnes walked into Billy's office with his wrists together and his hands extended in front of him. "You can cuff me now."

"Nobody stopped you on the way in?" Finn said. He pocketed the keys he'd left on Billy's desk and looked around to make sure he hadn't dropped anything else while his mind had been frozen. "That probably means they aren't lookin' for you."

"You think?" Rusty said. "Where's Billy?"

"All hell's breakin' loose," Finn said. "You're off the hook, John Sims is on it. Billy can confirm that. I can't stop to explain."

"John?"

Exasperated, Finn looked at him. "I have to round up a lady," he said. "She won't like it, and Billy will be pissed, because he'll say I interfered with police business, but I'll handle it."

"Where's Billy?" Rusty repeated.

"Gettin' a search warrant," Finn told him. "For John's house. There's a full-scale hunt on for him. *Rusty,* I can't talk, I gotta *do.* I came back for my keys. Go out to the desk and ask someone to let Billy know you came in. Then wait."

Rusty actually grinned.

"What?" Finn said.

"I don't know how I'd get through life without you telling me what to do."

Finn gave him a mock punch to the belly. "I need to get Emma." Given a chance, he planned to hide her until Sims was found and locked up.

Over and over again.

Over and over again he stroked her neck where the bag met her skin. Back and forth, thumbs anchored in the dip between her collar bones, two shaky fingertips skimming to her spine, to the slender cervical vertebrae.

Shaky fingers.

Not as shaky as Emma's legs. Her body trembled in waves that forced her teeth tightly together.

He hummed.

Emma would not speak, would not react…and she would not cry out. Anything she said, any sign of fear she showed, could incite him.

He hadn't spoken to her, but she felt how his mass displaced air.

Where was John? Had this man killed him?

She heard stifled moans. He had done something to Angela, and Emma couldn't help her. What felt like sharp plastic bag closures bound her wrists together. She had tried to kick him and lost a sandal. And for her efforts he had stood on her bare foot while he pressed his wet mouth into the cleavage between her breasts.

"I love you," he said.

A buzz grew to a roar in Emma's ears. She shook so violently her knees jerked, and she locked them to stay on her feet.

"I've loved you since the first time I saw you. Why have you made it so hard?"

Emma willed herself to be quiet inside.

"I wanted to help you get rid of *him*. I brought you money, but you took it to the police. You told the police about me when I only wanted to love you."

The cowboy mime. That had been John, not Carl.

Angela coughed, and Emma felt her blood stand still. The other woman's mouth was obviously covered; if she choked she could die. "Let her go," Emma said, as firmly as she could.

The man laughed. "That's one of the things that make you so special. You care about other people. I never met anyone like you before. Everyone wants something for themselves, and they want it so much there's no space in them for anything else."

A deep cold struck at Emma. She knew the voice.

"There's still time for us," he said. "They don't know about me. We can get away, far away. I got your passport from your house, your parents' house. You didn't miss it, but I've had it for days. And your marriage certificate. I burned that. See? You aren't married to him anymore."

Should she call him by name? Would he be angered that she knew him now? "John," she said. "It's you, isn't it?" She had no option but to hope she did the right things.

"Yes," he said. "I wanted a way to get you out of Pointe Judah without having to do something like this to you, but Finn Duhon showed up, and you were infatuated with him. You ignored me and welcomed him."

"I've never ignored you, John. You're my friend." In her mind, hopelessness sounded in every phony word, and she was sure he heard it.

"Just one of your friends?" he said. "I wanted to be your only friend, and I will be—when we leave this place forever."

As long as he thought they were going away together, she had a chance to free herself and Angela. And if this went on long enough, someone would look for them. Would the other members of Secrets try John's house when they didn't find Angela at home?

She cast back, looking for the signs she must have missed. There had never been a time when she gave John the impression she was interested in him.

Angela coughed again.

"She could choke," Emma said.

"Forget her. I already have."

His hands passed from her neck to her shoulders. He stroked her arms and pulled her close, licked and bit her shoulder, and the soft rise of her breast.

He wasn't wearing a shirt.

"John," she said, shaken. "Where will we go?"

"It's a surprise," he said. He rubbed her back and shoulders, spread his hand over her bare midriff.

If only she'd changed before going to Angela's, but the day had remained humid, and clothes only added to the stickiness.

Inexplicably, her eyes filled with tears. She wanted to put her hand in Finn's. They wouldn't have to speak, only stand quietly, the skin of their hands warm.

She detested being in the arms of this man for whom she felt nothing but pity and disgust. He touched her hip with his palm and curled his fingers down to knead her bottom.

Beyond the storeroom, a door slammed. Rapid footsteps ran through the kitchen.

"Keep quiet," John said. "Not a sound."

They heard the footsteps run this way and that in the house, then pound on the stairs.

John gripped her tightly, and she felt suddenly sick to her stomach and light-headed. A shirt wasn't the only thing he'd decided not to wear. John was naked. She felt his private parts, aroused, digging into her. Hot, smooth, probing flesh brushing her forearm.

"John?"

The voice came from a distance, but Emma knew it was a woman's. One of his friends? Why didn't someone else come, someone who could help them?

The steps came back downstairs. "John, are you here?" *Sandy.*

With a hand over Emma's mouth, he pushed her backward. She grasped for him with her bound hands, trying not to fall. Still he walked her backward, quickly, brought her to rest where she felt a wall at each shoulder. He'd put her in a corner somewhere.

"You will stay where you are," he said, and as if to underscore what he said, he hooked a heel behind her knees and caught her when she fell, guided her to sit on the floor. His hand remained pressed to her face until he yanked the bag up as far as her nose and shoved cloth in her mouth. Rapidly he snapped a handcuff on one ankle, caught the punishing plastic between her wrists in the second cuff and closed it on the other ankle. "I don't want to do this. I have to. I'll be quick."

She thought she would vomit. The cloth in her mouth pushed her tongue back and her throat tightened. He slapped a piece of tape over her lips.

Fighting against panic, Emma quieted her mind. Fighting wouldn't release her. She let her body go limp, as limp as she could with her knees trapped against her chest, driving the air from her lungs.

"On your side," John whispered, rolling her sideways. "Keep still. You'll be okay."

He sounded…*reasonable.*

Angela had stopped making any sounds.

Emma's heart bumped. She hurt all over.

"John?" This time Sandy was in the kitchen.

"Sandy?" he called back. "Coming."

Emma felt a current of air and knew the storeroom door was open.

"What are you doing in there?" Sandy said. "I can't see a thing. Put on the light."

He didn't answer her.

"Thank God I found you," Sandy said. "If the outside door had been locked, I don't know what I'd have done. I need to get away quickly. Come *on,* John. Come out of there. Emma's Lexus is parked at Angela's. If she sees me, I'm dead."

He didn't answer her.

"John, don't play games. I came to help you. The police are suspicious about the drugs. They asked if I got the samples from you."

Emma closed her eyes tightly to listen and heard John's heavy breathing.

"Get in here, fool," he said.

Sandy yelped. "What's the matter with you? Let me go— you're hurting me. John, you're naked! What are you doing?"

"I'm hot," he said, as if speaking through his teeth. "What did you tell them about me? They called. I heard them on the answering machine. They called again and again, and came to the door. This is your fault. I made my plans. They were perfect. You're ruining them."

"I didn't tell them anything. *Let me go.*"

"You like it when I hurt you. You've always liked it."

"No," Sandy said, openly crying. "I never have. Please don't hurt me again. We can do it here. You can do whatever you want, just like always, but don't hurt me."

With each breath, the bag sucked against Emma's nostrils.

"What's the matter?" John said, and he sounded hateful. "Do you need more goodies, bitch? Did you finish everything I gave you already?"

"They took them away," Sandy whined. "I had to say I

didn't know where they came from and insist they weren't mine. So they took them away. They said they knew you lost your job because you stole drugs. All kinds of drugs, they said. They came back today and talked about you being dangerous. I didn't tell them a thing. Honestly, I didn't. John, I need something. Thank goodness you stockpiled so much."

The conversation stopped.

A pulse in Emma's throat twitched. Sweat ran into the corner of her eye. She counted in her mind. Seconds, many seconds. Five minutes passed at least, then more. And more.

Not a sound—until the storeroom door closed very softly.

John and Sandy had left. All she had to do, Emma told herself, was wait. Eventually she would be found. Wouldn't she?

At both ends of the alley, but out of sight of John's property, police cars were parked at angles. Unmarked cars had arrived, and men in plainclothes conferred with the local police. Billy pointed from time to time. The set faces on the men, the purpose with which they moved, closed out anyone who wasn't one of their own.

Finn tried Emma's cell again. He'd tried it every few minutes. She wasn't answering. But she wasn't answering at the Balou house, either. He'd even tried Orville's and gotten no reply.

Calls to the other members of the group had found some of them at home. They hadn't planned on a meeting this evening.

He would try one more time to get Billy to let him check Angela's.

His approach and request earned him a wall of those serious, impatient faces.

"I told you not to concern yourself with Angela's at this point," Billy said. "Leave it, will you, Finn? We know what we're doin' here."

"Yeah, thanks."

He was certain they did know what they were doing, but so did he, and he'd spent too long responding to threats to stand back and hope they would pull off a safe resolution if necessary. John's car was missing, and Finn knew the authorities believed John was also missing. Mostly, they were going through the motions, and their main concern was securing the area and searching his house. But if Emma was somewhere around—and he had no proof she was, but if she was—he wanted her out.

A young cop ran up and said, "We came at the second house from the other side. We couldn't get any closer to Sims's without riskin' bein' seen if he's there."

"No sign of anyone at Angela's?" Billy said with one eye on Finn.

"Cars," the patrolman said. "They're parked beside the house. You can't see 'em if you don't go close, because of the hedges."

"How many cars?" Billy said, while Finn wiped any reaction from his features.

"Three. A van, a Mercedes and a Lexus SUV."

Finn took the last announcement in the gut. Where was his famous control?

"Angela has a van," he told Billy. "I don't know about the Mercedes, but we both know who drives a Lexus SUV. What color?" he asked the patrolman.

"Beige."

"Relax," Billy said to Finn. "We've got everythin' under control. From what I've heard about the antics they get up to at those women's meetings, they're probably maintainin' phone silence while they wax their backsides."

Finn forced his already balled fists into his pockets. "Yeah. I'll be in my truck if you need me." *Liar.*

His cell phone rang, and he answered before the end of the

first ring. "Duhon. Yes." He breathed a little shallower, but part of him grew calmer while he listened. "Thanks. I know, but this is…I can't thank you enough."

He pocketed the phone. Billy watched him, and he looked back at him. "I sent off my father's uniform after you gave it to me," Finn said. "I've got one or two very useful contacts. That was a preliminary report, but it's pretty certain. There's a match between samples from Belinda Page, Denise Steen and what you found on that car seat that got on the uniform. They've already looked at swabs from me and from Eileen, and there's no way my father was involved, other than being one more victim of a serial killer. Billy, I think Dad confronted him and somethin' went wrong. He died, but I'll always believe he cracked the case."

John took the cuffs off Emma's ankles. "I'm sorry, darling," he said. "Be patient. I have to hurry now."

He withdrew from her, and she could hear him dressing.

He intended to take her away with him.

"Let's go," he said, pulling her to her feet. He took the hood from her head, and she blinked in bright white light. Halogen bulbs lined the top of mirrored walls. A single high stool beside a counter littered with tubes and brushes, and a small refrigerator, were the only furniture in the uncarpeted, windowless room. A row of drawers ran the width of the wall beneath the counter. John's hair lay flat to his head, slicked with some sort of oil. His clothes consisted of loose, white cotton pants and a shirt.

On the floor beneath one end of the counter something shadowy moved, rolled out. Duct tape wound around a blanket-covered bundle made it mummy-shaped.

John laughed. "She moves," he said, sneering.

Angela had to be in there. Emma inclined her head and made noises in her throat.

John looked at the writhing body. "I know," he said. "Your soft heart hurts for her. But she betrayed me. She went over to the other side. She wanted to make me look bad to you. Did she give you Tom Duhon's records? She says she didn't, but I don't believe her."

Emma shook her head from side to side.

"She took them while Mrs. Valenti wasn't looking, like I told her to. But then she got angry with me and gave them to someone else. You're sure it wasn't you?"

Once more Emma shook her head.

"Too bad. I need them back."

From one of the drawers under the counter, he carefully removed a black leather box. To Emma, it looked as if it could contain drafting tools. John opened two latches and lifted the lid. With reverence, he showed Emma the contents. A hypodermic rested on white satin. The satin showed several small blood stains.

She stared at the needle. More drugs? Did he use, and would he become even more crazed when he shot up again?

"It took them a long time to suspect I was stealing from them," John said, stroking a finger along the barrel of the hypodermic. "My employers, that is. But they never found out about this. Not at all. And it was never missed—none of it except the pills. I only took those to exchange for other things I needed. Don't you think they were unreasonable to complain?"

She nodded. Her eyes stung as if she hadn't blinked in too long.

He gave her a brilliant smile, set the box aside and lifted her to sit on the counter. "I want to take the gag away, but you mustn't make a sound. You won't, will you?"

Emma shook her head no.

He ripped the tape from her mouth, and she winced at the pain. Next he took the cloth from inside her mouth. "We'll take the van," he said. "It's already packed. We're going to be so happy. But the police are out there. We must be careful. They won't know about the path through the bamboo." His face contorted. "I hate the sound when they bang on my door. *My door.*"

She would wait until they got outside, then risk shouting for help.

John stared at her. He brought his face closer, and she felt his breath on her face. "A kiss for the road," he said. "Please, my love." His mouth touched hers; he parted her lips. She must not vomit, but if he put his tongue in her mouth, she would bite it.

He caught sight of Angela rolling over again and stepped back. He kicked her, and she made a gurgling sound.

"Stay where you are," he told Emma.

For several moments he disappeared into the passageway leading from the room to the kitchen. When he returned, he wore a tunic made of heavy pink silk, and pink crocheted gloves without fingers. Beside her, he dropped a wig, a blond wig.

He caught her expression and smiled widely. "Enjoy watching a true artist, Emma. I am the best in the world."

From beneath the wig he took some pale, thin rubbery stuff. A mask...

In only seconds, he pulled on the burn-webbed skin of Angela, set eye sockets, nostrils, mouth, ears, neck, applied lipstick and mascara, and placed the wig. Next came his hands. With amazing expertise, he applied long pink nails that adhered over his own.

He turned his head from her a little and tugged a lock of white-blond hair forward. Then he laughed and stood back, spreading his arms. "Well?"

She couldn't speak. This was brilliant. John Sims and Angela were the same person. Emma looked at the human bundle on the floor. So who...?

"Don't worry about that," John said. He went to the refrigerator and took out two vials. He filled the hypodermic, held the needle up and depressed the plunger the smallest amount, expelling a bead of fluid.

Emma couldn't move, couldn't utter a sound.

Lethal injection. He'd decided to kill her like the others.

"Where's Sandy?" she asked before she could stop herself.

"You should mind your own business," he said, the corners of his mouth turning down sharply. "If you knew what Sandy Viator's been doing to help me, you wouldn't care what happened to her. I'll make sure she doesn't trouble us again."

Sweat in her eyes blurred Emma's vision. "Who is that? Please, I've got to know."

"Then you shall, sweet," John said. He knelt, ripped duct tape from the person's neck and freed the head.

Emma pressed her cuffed hands together. Mrs. Merryfield blinked into the glaring light.

"Get the tape off her mouth," Emma said when she could speak. "What has she ever done to you?"

"She wanted me to get caught. She couldn't turn me in herself, but after all these years, she wanted to watch me suffer."

Mrs. Merryfield closed her eyes. John took her by the hair and pushed her head back and forth. "I should have killed you a long time ago."

"Why shouldn't you know everything?" he said to Emma. "I want you to share my treasures, and my triumphs. Let me show you what your Mrs. Merryfield showed Denise, and then I had to kill her, too so she wouldn't turn me in or write about it in the paper." He took another drawer all the way out, reached behind and pulled out a brown paper sack.

Emma realized Mrs. Merryfield was crying without sound, the tears running across the bridge of her nose, slipping to the floor.

Still holding the needle aloft, John got on his knees in front of the woman and emptied the bag with one hand. A second, chamois bag fell out, and he unsnapped a closure. From this he slid a little assortment that choked Emma.

He held up a ring. "Remember seeing this? It's not fancy, but when Harold put it on Holly, she must have thought he would make her happy. See the three little rubies? Most men don't get anything different, but Harold got this. Once he cared, but she emasculated him, didn't she? We know that."

Memories crowded in, all the times they'd gathered by Angela's pool, naked, playing with lotions and potions, swimming, laughing. Only Angela had been John, and he'd watched them in their most vulnerable states, watched their bodies, lusted after them.

She shivered and couldn't stop shivering.

He held up a bracelet made of rose quartz. "For peace," he said. "She asked me not to throw it away because it brought her peace. I told her she would have all the peace she needed."

"That's Denise's," Emma whispered.

He tucked it back into the chamois bag and worked out something larger. "This was the hardest one. And the best." He showed her a police badge, and she didn't have to ask whose it had been. "He was on to me. That night it was him or me. If he hadn't slipped, it would have been me. It was his fault Denise knew too much."

Please, God, let this stop. He seemed to have forgotten the police. His voice, full but dreamy, wasn't the husky, grating whisper of Angela, who had "burned her vocal chords in the evil fire." John's voice sounded wrong coming from Angela's mouth, the mouth that looked like Angela's. What she'd thought was Angela.

"Look at this," John said. "This was the second one. Belinda, beautiful, stupid Belinda. All she had to do was look at me and see me and let me have her. But she looked elsewhere. She made moon eyes at some nothing, hayseed photographer." On a silver chain hung a finely engraved silver bottle. "If you unscrew the cap, you see a little bubble blower attached underneath, so she could carry bubbles in the bottle around her neck and blow them. The hayseed gave it to her. I took it away. And I had her."

Hiding in plain sight wasn't a new concept to Finn, though his size made it harder than it might have been for a smaller man. Dressed in white coveralls, with a crime team hood he'd casually lifted from the back of a van obscuring everything but his face, he had walked past three patrolmen at the opposite end of the alley from the place where Billy and his buddies were.

He'd heard the cops say that hammering on John's door hadn't produced an answer.

John Sims was considered armed and dangerous, and if he was in his home—which the cops and FBI seemed to doubt—he couldn't be confronted without precautions.

Finn entered Angela's house with ease. Some skills never failed a man. He felt the emptiness before he confirmed there was no one there.

But Emma's vehicle was in the drive.

He went outside again. Skirting the house, his face trained on the ground as if searching for evidence, he worked his way along the back until a wall of bamboo stopped him. Beating his way through would draw the attention he didn't want.

He turned the next corner of the house and went slowly along the side closest to John Sims's house.

A narrow path opened through the bamboo. Finn paused to gauge if the density of the vegetation would be enough to hide him from the alley. He walked quickly, reached John's house and couldn't believe he was looking at an open door.

He brought his Beretta into the daylight and, with a single finger on his other hand, pushed the door. It swung wide on a kitchen where a woman lay on the floor, fresh blood trickling across her face from a wound to the side of her head.

He felt for a pulse and found one. Sandy Viator was down and deeply unconscious, but not dead. He recalled that she drove a Mercedes.

"Stop it." Faintly, he heard Emma's voice and moved silently toward it.

"John, no more, please. Let her go," Emma said. She screamed.

Skimming across the floor on the soles of his shoes, Finn reached two more doors. Emma's voice had come from one of these. One handle had no keyhole but the other did. Using intuition, he chose the door that could be locked and turned the handle with exquisite care. The hinges were well oiled and didn't make a sound.

A short passageway turned to the left, and from that direction bright light shone.

"They're trying to get in here," a man said. John Sims. "You heard them at the door. They'll break in shortly. We're going out the way you came in. Then through the other house and into the van. If I have to use you as a hostage, I will. Trust me."

"You won't get away," Emma said, and Finn willed her to keep her mouth shut and avoid antagonizing her captor.

"I told you to trust me. Quiet, or the gag goes back. I have to do this. She knows too much, and she doesn't care what it costs her to hurt me now."

Finn had his center. He had pushed back the emotion, and all was calm and very quiet inside. He felt nothing.

A single fluid step took him into the passageway, a second to the corner, a third put him in the wash of light from the left.

He didn't see anyone, but the movement he heard came from his right, the right side of the room he looked into.

"John," Emma said. "What happened isn't her fault."

"Everything's her fault. She loved Connie best. She said she didn't, but I knew, and so did Connie."

Emma didn't answer him.

"That woman down there," he said. "You don't know who she is, do you? I let her live this long because she's my *mother*, but she loved my sister best."

"I'm sure you only thought that," Emma said, and the way she made herself sound consoling impressed Finn. He knew every muscle he moved had to be with total control if he was to avoid triggering whatever John Sims planned.

"Don't do this. Just walk out and leave her."

"I want her to see it coming," John Sims said. "I warned her. See this."

Finn wished he could see, wished there was less light, wished a lot of things, mostly that he didn't have two civilians in the way of hitting his mark.

"A dreamcatcher," Emma said. "It's pretty. I used to have one."

"Would you like this one, sweetheart? You can have as many as you like. You'll hang them above our bed to catch our dreams. This one was Connie's."

A beat passed, and another, before Emma said, her voice strangled, "You killed your sister?"

"She slipped," John said at once. He sounded petulant now. "Into the bayou she went, and she couldn't get out. She kept trying, but she fell back again every time. It was tragic. She couldn't swim, you see, so she drowned. And she was only fifteen. Then I had to be son and daughter to mama, you see, and I was. Only she kept on crying for Connie. That's because she loved Connie best."

Finn swung around the final corner, took in the area fast.

He frowned and raised his gun a fraction—but only for a moment.

"I don't need her anymore." John's voice came from Angela, Angela in pink, her blond hair awry. No, not Angela. *John.*

John saw him, John on his knees over the woman he said was his mother. Swathed in a blanket, she kept her eyes closed. In the loving son's right hand, poised to plunge into the woman, a syringe caught the light.

"Finn," Emma said.

He didn't let himself look at her.

John's hand descended—and dissolved into a bloody mass. His unearthly howl bounced from mirrored walls. The single bullet Finn fired destroyed the drug-filled hypodermic and the hand that had held it.

Drops of fluid glittered. A piece of the shattered syringe stuck from the stump of a finger.

Finn held out an arm, and Emma stumbled from the counter, her hands cuffed together, to come to him.

His face contorted, saliva running from his mouth, John held his wrist, his mangled hand aloft, and staggered toward Finn and Emma. They stepped out of his way.

Voices came from the kitchen. The cops were in, and they'd found Sandy.

Billy barked orders. They were ready to fan out and search for John.

Only John fell through the door into the kitchen and sprawled on his face with his hand cradled.

"Finn," Emma said, as they followed John, "the stuff, the poison, it must have gone in his hand."

"Not so much that they won't be able to save him, unfortunately," Finn said. To Billy, he added, "He needs treatment and fast—unless you want to save a whole lot of public money and let him die right there."

40

When they had finally been allowed to go home, he and Emma left the police station side by side but about a mile apart.

They walked as if they were either afraid to get too close or were acquaintances leaving the same party, late at night, and going their separate ways.

And they had gone separate ways, in separate vehicles to separate houses.

An hour had passed, and Finn sat on the gallery out back of his place and lifted his face to a warm wind. Stars loaded the skies. He had taken long enough starting the truck to let Emma leave the parking lot well ahead of him. That way they didn't have to look at each other's lights all the way back.

She'd hesitated when they walked out of the building, cleared her throat as if she would say something. And she had. "Good night, Finn. Thanks for everythin'."

Shee-it.

Well, of course they'd both felt a bit like they'd just survived a hurricane by hanging on to the same tree and now they could stand alone—without the tree—and walk on their own two feet. Separate pairs of feet. But…*thanks for everything?* It wasn't as if he'd just helped her change a flat tire, for hell's sake.

And what did I say? How did I help get us past feeling awk-

*ward once the pressure was off? I said, You're welcome. Good
night, Emma.*

He swung his legs off the swing lounger and pulled his shirt
over his head. The air felt good on his skin. All the final
pieces had fallen into place. Mrs. Merryfield had admitted to
putting the documents in Rusty's TV for Emma to find. The
woman wanted to purge herself of what she knew about her
son, but she had tried to make sure there was no way John
would ever connect the betrayal to her.

Mrs. Merryfield apologized again and again, and, mad as
he had been, Finn felt sorry for her. The details John had
thought of continued to amaze him, even such things as having all the flowers delivered to Secrets. Everything had been
intended to unnerve Emma, and it had worked.

Something, or someone, moved. Rustled. There were
things other than humans that crept through the night out
here. Still, he situated his hand where it would find the butt
of his gun real easy and turned in the direction of the subtle
whispering through brush at the side of the house.

Emma walked into view, only her head and shoulders
showing above the level of the gallery floor. She glanced
sideways as she came, and he figured she saw him just fine
by the light of the moon—and a bug candle burning in a
bucket.

"It's awful dark back here," she said. "I almost went away
when you didn't answer the door."

Finn got to his feet. "I've warned you not to come creep-
in' up on me." He couldn't stop himself from smiling.

"That's why I'm makin' all this noise, Finn. I'm stampin'
my feet, but you can't hear them on account of the grass is
growin' out of everywhere. Did you ever consider usin' a
lawn mower and pullin' a few weeds?"

"You wouldn't be naggin', would you?"

"Me? No way. This isn't my place. Grow the ugly grass and weeds till you can't see the house for all I care." She made it to the steps. "There's somethin' I just can't get over, Finn. That old Cadillac that hit the Honey Bucket right before we found Denise."

"I know. We said somethin' about bein' too obvious, and it was. John made his own mother help him. Did you hear the way he carried on at me for 'ruining' his plans because I didn't belong there? Nothin' was supposed to get in the way of his expectations."

"Sicko."

"*Cher,* I think he's more than sicko. You were supposed to be there alone. He was goin' to scare you out of your mind when you didn't have a soul to turn to. I wonder how he intended to be the shoulder you cried on? I'm sure he had that worked out."

"I'm glad he isn't going to get off by dyin' before he can stand trial." Emma shivered. "I don't want to think about it, not now."

"Then we won't. Suits me."

He heard her sigh before she said, "Would you rather I stay down here and keep shoutin' at you, or am I allowed to come up?"

He walked down to meet her, stood so close their feet all but touched. "How come you're so much smarter than me?" he said.

"That would be because I'm a woman."

Finn thought about it. "You're only smarter now because you knew we blew it when we left town today and you were the first to figure out what to do next. You weren't smarter in town. You didn't do any better than I did."

"Maybe I thought you should make the first move," Emma said. She wasn't sure what she thought, except that she couldn't stay away from him unless he made her.

"I feel terrible," Finn said.

She tilted her head to the side and looked up at him. Moonlight suited his face. "So do I," she told him.

"No, you don't."

"Huh?" Sometimes he said the darnedest things. "How do you know how I feel?"

"You're grinnin'."

"So are you." She had barely enough room between them to rub her sore wrists.

"Son of a bitch," Finn muttered. He took her wrists in his hands, and, as light as a butterfly, kissed the inside of each one.

Emma's legs turned to water. "We should be decorous," she said.

"We… What?"

"Decorous."

"I know the word. I'm tryin' to figure out how it fits here, is all."

Emma worked at straightening her face. "It's a good thing to set an example. I'm a married woman, and it's time I mended my ways."

"Who are we setting an example for?"

She pushed out her lips and looked around, then up. "The stars."

"If you say so." He lifted her into his arms and carried her up the steps to the gallery. She landed sideways on the big old swing harder than she would have chosen. "I was just goin' to come up there for you, y'know," he said.

"Sure you were." They were doing a good job of being flip. What did it mean? That this was all there was for them, a fun-loving, sexy interlude? "That's why you were sittin' out here stargazin'?"

"Stargazin' and kickin' myself for bein' all kinds of a fool when we were headin' home."

"I felt awkward," she said honestly.

"Mmm-hmm, me, too." He sat beside her knees. "Know what? I understand what that was about. How about that?"

"I'm impressed."

"It's over, Emmy, the hard times. That's what felt so strange." He felt lighter inside, euphoric. "The load is off. No more weird stuff, and you know what?"

"You'll tell me."

"You're on your way to gettin' a divorce."

She was quiet.

"Did I say something wrong?" he asked.

"No. I didn't expect to be where I am tonight, is all. Almost single. And I surely didn't expect to be with you."

"I'm grateful you are. *Darn*, why didn't I get up the road before you could come down? Now you can feel superior."

She felt a lot of things, but superior wasn't among them. "I'm glad I'm here, too."

"What are you wearin'?"

"My mother's old chenille bathrobe."

He looked closer. "Not sexy. Were you cold?"

"Nope. And now I'm hot. Didn't want to come down in my nightie with nothin' on top, is all."

Finn put a hand behind one of her calves, and she jumped. "Good," he said. "Nighties are good. They save time."

She sat straighter and crossed her arms. "I was talkin' about bein' decorous."

He stroked the back of her leg, let his fingertips hover on the tender skin behind her knee. "It's too late for that, and I'm grateful, ma'am. I am grateful." He settled his head on her shoulder and wrapped his arms around her. She didn't have a chance to react before he kissed her neck again and again.

Being with him made her happy, made her complete—

almost. "I am seriously hot and getting hotter. I've got to get this bathrobe off." With his help, she struggled out of it.

"I've got to say this, Emmy. I'm sorry about Sandy. It decks you when a so-called friend turns on you."

"Mmm."

"I guess she won't be working with you anymore." His teeth showed in a broad smile, and Emma tapped his naked chest.

"What?" he said. "You tryin' to get my attention?"

"That wasn't funny," she told him. "Mrs. Valenti said she heard rumors Carl will run for mayor once Orville moves on. You do know he'll move on, don't you? He'll find a way to come out of this smellin' like roses."

"No, he won't. He can end up as president and he'll still have lost you. Orville isn't very smart in some ways." Finn meant it. "His loss is my gain."

He lifted her again, sat down and put her on his lap, where she sat up straight, her arms wrapped over his, her feet swinging.

The nightie looked white. And she looked a darker shade inside it. Very nice. Yes, that was a view he could look at just about forever. "I love you, Emmy."

The next breath Emma took stuck halfway. She let it go and drew in air again. "Thank you. Oh, Finn..."

"What?"

"Have you ever been afraid to be happy?"

"Not tonight."

Emma curled up against him. "You already know I love you."

"Now you tell me, I do." He laughed, and his chest rumbled beneath her ear. "I was pretty sure the feelin' was mutual. Some would say I'm rushin' things, but I'd like us to be married, if that's okay with you. I thought we'd set a date right away. The day after you're free?"

It was Emma's turn to laugh. "Let me think about it. Okay.

Yes, I'd like that, thank you very much." But there was one issue they couldn't try to ignore. "You said you regretted not having children. I don't want you—"

He placed a finger on her lips, turned her face up to his and kissed her long and soft. Emma caught him around the neck, and the nightie hardly interfered with what he felt at all. Her nipples hardened.

"Emmy, listen to me." He collected his thoughts. "Either we'll have babies you give birth to or we won't. If you don't, it won't be for lack of tryin'. There's more than one way to bring children into a home."

"I do love you," she said. "I think I'm going to get boring real soon, but I love you so much."

"Not as much as I love you."

"Enough." She cleared her throat. "I don't want you to think I'm too practical, or that I only think about what matters to me, but what are you going to do with Oakdale?"

"I don't know." He tried not to chuckle but failed. "I'll think of somethin'. A man's got to work. At least, this one does."

Emma raised her head to look into his face. "Why would you buy an expensive piece of property like that without knowing what you intend to do with it?"

"Ah, you're runnin' my life already, makin' me accountable for my actions. It's simple, *cher.* I wanted to buy Poke Around for you, but the guy wouldn't sell it without the rest of the place."

STELLA CAMERON

32219 NOW YOU SEE HIM	___ $7.50 U.S.	___ $8.99 CAN.
32083 KISS THEM GOODBYE	___ $6.99 U.S.	___ $8.50 CAN.
66942 MAD ABOUT THE MAN	___ $5.99 U.S.	___ $6.99 CAN.
66795 7B	___ $6.99 U.S.	___ $8.50 CAN.
66734 SOME DIE TELLING	___ $5.99 U.S.	___ $6.99 CAN.
66666 ABOUT ADAM	___ $6.99 U.S.	___ $8.50 CAN.
66615 ALL SMILES	___ $5.99 U.S.	___ $6.99 CAN.

(limited quantities available)

TOTAL AMOUNT	$_____
POSTAGE & HANDLING	$_____
($1.00 FOR 1 BOOK, 50¢ for each additional)	
APPLICABLE TAXES*	$_____
TOTAL PAYABLE	$_____

(check or money order—please do not send cash)

To order, complete this form and send it, along with a check or money order for the total above, payable to MIRA Books, to: **In the U.S.:** 3010 Walden Avenue, P.O. Box 9077, Buffalo, NY 14269-9077; **In Canada:** P.O. Box 636, Fort Erie, Ontario, L2A 5X3.

Name: _____
Address: _____ City: _____
State/Prov.: _____ Zip/Postal Code: _____
Account Number (if applicable): _____

075 CSAS

*New York residents remit applicable sales taxes.
*Canadian residents remit applicable GST and provincial taxes.

MIRA®

www.MIRABooks.com

MSC0306BL